WATCH

A NOVEL

Daniel Barton

WATCH

© Daniel Barton 2017
All Rights Reserved

All rights reserved. This book or any portion thereof may not be reproduced or used in any manner whatsoever without the express written permission of the publisher except for the use of brief quotations in a book review.

WATCH is a work of fiction. Any reference to, or association with actual names, places, things or events—past or present—are solely intended as fictional story-telling.

Cover by Brandi Doane McCann, www.ebook-coverdesigns.com
Interior by Colleen Sheehan of Write Dream Repeat Book Design
Cover image—Jerusalem Old City Wall detail by iStock

First Edition. First printed in the United States of America

ISBN: 978-1-7751275-0-5

10 9 8 7 6 5 4 3 2 1

ACKNOWLEDGEMENTS

I would like to comment on a possible misconception. As per tradition, 'Daniel Barton' is the only name following the title. This may induce the reader to think that I am solely responsible for the creation of *WATCH*. This would be an erroneous assumption, as many people have assisted. These people need to be acknowledged, and I wish that I had a more deserving platform by which to credit them.

My wife, Carolyn, has provided me with invaluable inspiration and support through the years. She typed the full manuscript, corrected countless errors, proof-read, and saved money to fund this project. My daughter, Sarah Michelle, has been a co-creator from the early days of the outline to the final printed word. Her intellect and creativity have substantially enhanced the final work and my authorial skills.

The early beta readers who suffered through the first draft: Vera Beriault, Ron Hurak, Carla Rankin, Chris Sommer, Gloria Pearson-Vasey and Lisa Winter—these readers gave me the opportunity to view my writing in a more objective manner, resulting in, what I believe, is a more plausible storyline.

There have been advisors, who guided me through detailed aspects of the research: Amnon and Charlene Amit (Hebrew language and customs), and Debbie Merrill (medications and prescription drugs).

Other contributors provided invaluable critique and inspiration: Sarah Luttrell (outline content) and Melissa Wright (early chapters review), Francis Guenette and Kelly Elizabeth Martin (proof-reads).

Each and every page of this novel has been graced with the loving read of a person with a deep respect for English literature and the written word. This is how I would like to say, 'thank you' to my editor, Christine Penhale.

The list could continue, but tradition asks that you begin an adventure, made possible by the efforts of many.

— Daniel Barton

'He who would uphold honour shall forever be at court with himself.'
— *Anonymous*

YEAR: 1940
GLASSÜTTE GERMANY

PREFACE (TRANSLATED)

Young Herbert Osterhagen sat behind his very own chest high workbench. Before him lay many scattered internal pocket watch parts, and off to his right lay his neatly organized watchmaker tool set. He inspected each tool: a small holding vice, two pairs of slender pliers, a set of small screwdrivers, a light leather mallet, long thin tweezers, a peg wood holding implement, an assortment of small files, fine horsehair brushes, and finally his most prized possession: a watchmakers' loupe—a gift from his grandfather for his seventh birthday. As he centered the leather strap over his head and lowered the small cylindrical magnifier over his eye, he recalled his grandfather's advice upon receiving this most excellent gift, *Remember Herbert, always keep both eyes open. At your age now, the brain will quickly adjust.* He was right. Already Herbert could focus effortlessly. For a young boy of only seven years old, wearing his own loupe made him want to pretend he was a super-hero. He could enter another world, a place where only he could go, where great discoveries were made in the smallest of things.

Often, he would come here to his grandfather's watch repair shop after school. Occasionally, Grandfather would be having a nap. On those days, Herbert would quietly enter from the back entrance, make his way into the repair room and retrieve his loupe from the bench. Then, he would go back outside scouring the surrounding yard for small insects. When possible, he would place the willing specimen in his hand, and thoroughly examine it, head to tail. What a wondrous world indeed.

On just such a day, Herbert intently focused on a small, interesting spider when he felt a hand on his shoulder. This startled him. The spider scurried off, sensing danger.

"Herbert!" He looked up to the stern face of his grandfather, a tall, slender man, with slightly stooped shoulders, close-cut white hair, and a short square-cut white beard, which highlighted his crystal blue eyes. Herbert knew he was about to be scolded for taking his loupe outdoors. But there remained a twinkle in Grandfather's eyes.

"What have we said about taking our watchmaking tools outside?"

"That they could get all wet and dirty … maybe ruined."

"Indeed. And what form of punishment will be required to ensure that this does not happen again?"

Herbert cast his gaze downward, "My tools shall be taken away for a time."

"Do you believe this is a wise and just punishment, Herbert?"

He removed the loupe from his eye. Herbert stared into Grandfather's sparkling blue eyes, reached out with the loupe in his hand, and offered it, "Yes, sir."

As Grandfather gazed down at his young grandson, he could not conceal a soft smile that crept upon his face. He waved off Herbert's gesture and placed his arm around the young boy's shoulders. "I think, for the rest of this afternoon I would like to tell you a story. It's a story from a long time ago, about a special watch, a unique man, and your great-great grandfather, Hans Wilhelm Osterhagen."

Together grandfather and grandson, hand in hand, made their way back inside the watch repair shop. Herbert eagerly sat behind his workbench and watched as his grandfather strode over to a large cabinet located against the wall. He retrieved a set of keys from his pocket, selected one, unlocked the door and withdrew a silver pocket watch. Herbert could not help but notice a rather sad look come over him as he sat on his stool facing him. Saying not a word for many moments, grandfather gazed at the watch, "This is a copy of the original." His warm smile had returned, "It is a replica of the watch I referred to, a particular timepiece, created with the assistance of my grandfather—your great-great grandfather—Hans Osterhagen. The year was 1783."

"A gentleman, a man of great repute, commissioned him for some mechanical parts and an encasement. This person returned with the assembled watch to have the final engraving done. He paid quite handsomely in advance and insisted on paying a great deal more than the quoted price. Before he departed, he explained to my grandfather, 'This is a watch of significance, greater than the finest watches of our time. You are a young watchmaker with much skill Hans Osterhagen, but I am also going to call upon your honor. I ask you, no matter what may befall, to take great care of this timepiece.' He then left, never to return for the completed watch."

Herbert was breathless. He could feel his blood pulsing. He knew about his bloodline and loved his grandfather's stories, but this one was so very exciting. Who was this gentleman—a prince, a famous inventor? Grandfather reached over to Herbert, offering him the watch. The young boy held his breath as he accepted the watch in both his hands. He looked to his grandfather, who smiled at the boy's excitement, then gestured for him to open the encasement. As Herbert did so, Grandfather continued.

"The watch was a unique timepiece, as you can see by examining the replica; only one hand and the numerals on the dial are quite unusual, like some ancient calligraphy, and there is no winding or time setting crown—most strange. The watch was put away in a cabinet, awaiting the day when its owner might return. My grandfather checked on it often, but this became less frequent as time went by."

"Several years passed, and then one day he thought he noticed, upon inspection of the watch, that the single hand had moved from its original position. To address his curiosity, my grandfather decided to dismantle the timepiece partially. He removed the four slotted screws that secured the dial. Removing the single hand, he then lifted the plate away, revealing the internal mechanism. What he saw astounded him. The watch had motion! It had never been wound in any way, yet indeed parts were moving! He witnessed a movement he had never seen before. After much observation, and with limited understanding, he expounded that this mechanism was driven by a type of perpetual motion." 'Impossible,' he later proclaimed, 'dual or split magnetic fields are causing a slow rotation, geared to maintain an almost microscopic movement. But why?'"

Grandfather paused. Herbert no longer examined the replica. He sat fixated, hardly wanting to breathe, lest he miss one word.

"My grandfather, Hans Osterhagen, instructed, 'This timepiece is never to be harmed or dismantled for fear it will cease to perpetuate.' He also insisted, 'Due to magnetic suspension, this watch does not require lubrication, thus scheduled maintenance will never be required.'"

"He cared for and studied the watch intensely and documented all he could, making drawings, sketches and blueprints, with precise measurements. All information, he recorded in this handbook." Grandfather had risen and walked over to the cabinet. In his hand, he held a leather-bound book. "Finally, he would solder over the slotted screw heads that fixed the dial, making it quite difficult for anyone to ever dismantle the pocket-watch."

Herbert's gaze shifted back to the replica in his hands. He observed the small screws that held the dial in place and readily discerned the screw heads on the watch had not been altered. Grandfather returned to his stool. Once seated, he addressed his young grandson with a thoughtful smile, "I can answer the question you must be thinking Herbert. Although the watch you hold in your hands was made with great precision and precise detail, sadly it has no replicated movement. My grandfather, Hans Wilhelm Osterhagen was to become known as one of the world's greatest watchmakers of his time, both admired and respected by his peers. Ultimately though, the mystery of the unique watch eluded him."

"The care of the timepiece was taken over by my father when my grandfather died. After many years, we became quite occupied, preparing to relocate and establish the Osterhagen Watch Company, turning the business into a much larger manufacturing platform. My father became extremely busy, and he eventually entrusted the care of the watch to me."

With deep sadness, Grandfather declared, "I'm afraid I lost the watch." Herbert was startled, he squeezed and held tightly to the watch in his hands as Grandfather resumed. "You see, I had been doing my best to help out. Much had to be done; our tools, equipment, cabinetry, etcetera needed to be relocated, a most unsettled time."

"My father had taken on a new apprentice to help out with the many new tasks confronting us. It so happened that exactly at this time a man came to our shop to pick up a pocket-watch he had commissioned for us to build, several months prior. I do not recall his name. He was an oil rigger from a small Canadian town in the province of Ontario, apparently the first location for oil production in the world. It was 1881, and by that time the value of crude oil as an energy resource was widely understood; experienced men were required to locate and set-up drilling wells for oil in many parts of the world. Just such a group of these workers from

Ontario were working then in Germany—at Oelheim—just south of here, near Hanover. They were unsuccessful in their attempts to locate substantial oil reserves, so a decision prevailed to move their team of drillers out of Germany to a location farther east in Galicia, known to be within the borders of Ukraine and Poland."

"As fate would have it, this man—the oil rigger—arrived at the shop to pick up his timepiece at a most unfortunate time. Only the new apprentice was there to accommodate him. In great haste, he arrived, and in great haste, he departed. Many days later we learned an error had occurred. The oil rigger from Canada had been given the special watch by mistake!"

"Our many subsequent attempts to learn the location of the timepiece, alas, were in vain. Only this book and the replica remain with us." Grandfather held the book to his heart.

"Of the Osterhagen family, it is you Herbert, who I believe shall eventually have possession of this book, and the replica watch. You show a keen interest in watchmaking. I would be proud, when the time comes, to bequeath them to you." Herbert felt a single teardrop fall from his cheek, and splatter on the face of the watch he held in his hands. Grandfather smiled a somber smile, but the twinkle in his blue eyes? It was always there.

And so as young Herbert Osterhagen adjusted his loupe, selected a pair of tweezers, and began to assemble the gear train his grandfather had instructed upon for today's lesson, he allowed himself a quick diversion. He must get a beautiful glass jar, one with holes in the lid, to be used for bringing in his willing specimens from the outdoors into the shop, for inspection.

He hoped Grandfather would approve.

ONE

SATURDAY, APRIL 26, 2014. 9:00 A.M.
PETROLIA, ONTARIO, CANADA

THE BRIGHT MORNING sun streamed through the front bay window of an attractive, well-kept, east-facing home, on a usually quiet cul-de-sac in Petrolia. But on this particular Saturday morning, Sanway Court had an almost steady stream of traffic both pedestrian and vehicle.

Edward James sat in his recliner-rocker near the window. It was turned allowing him to look out to the street and observe the activity. This day was the town-wide garage sale, an annual tradition. Every year on the last Saturday of April, many of the local 5500 residents would participate, buying and selling mostly used items. Residents displayed their wares from their property and were almost guaranteed a high volume of shoppers—bargain hunters. From surrounding areas, they would come in droves, descending on the small town, looking for deals. *Traffic, congestion, mayhem,* Edward smiled as he looked on. *But yes, we all enjoy it. Kind of a coming out from winter,* he mused, an opportunity to get out and chat with neighbours and catch up on local gossip.

Edward laughed quietly. His wife Marie would be missing out this year. She had been called to do an extra shift at the hospital.

Registered nurses always seemed to be modifying their schedules. Oh well, Edward found comfort in knowing from experience that missing the annual garage sale would never keep Marie in the dark concerning local current events for long. There were always backup resources available. Edward grimaced. Thankfully he was not one of them. Married to Marie for over 24 years, Edward knew himself to be the quieter, more introverted side of their relationship. They had differences for sure, and that could be a good thing. It was working for Carmen. As their only child, it was becoming evident to Edward she adopted the most positive attributes from each parent.

He thought for a moment, this must be the first time in 23 years she would be absent from the town-wide garage sale. Throughout her four-year Honours Specialization degree from Western University, she made a point of being home during this annual weekend, if for no other reason than to purchase a hot dog from one of her former dance instructors, who sold them for charity every year. Brad lived close by on Ernest Street. He would not be seeing her this year, however. *Let's see ...* Edward glanced at his watch with its bright orange GMT 24-hour hand that he kept set to Carmen's local time in Tel Aviv, Israel. *Ok, so 1700 hrs or 5:00 p.m., 8 hours ahead, she will be just now getting ready for supper. Hmm ... I wonder if they serve hot dogs at Carmen's residence in TelAviv?*

Edward felt a familiar pang of discontent. He knew what it was, loneliness, although it was becoming less frequent now. Perhaps he was not sufficiently prepared for the recent life changes that confronted him. Carmen had chosen to continue her post-graduate education in a foreign land, and then 3 months later the commencement of his official retirement began, after 42 years of working in the construction trade as a certified high-pressure welder. It was a vocation not known for its good health environment. However, he did feel happy with himself for his personal commitment to physical well-being. Throughout his career, focused attention on safe work habits resulted in long-term health benefits. With an almost addictive passion for physical exercise, including mountain biking and road cycling, Edward also embraced a passionate interest in subjects like psychology and the sciences. He could easily see himself following up now on prior academic studies from the many college night courses he had taken in years gone past. So yes, confidence was realised for him going forward, embracing this new stage of his life. The trouble was, though, he could not share it with Marie. She was 12 years younger. He often wondered, given their age difference, if he was subconsciously seeking his own 'fountain of youth' and trying to be a better fit for her.

Edward glanced down again at the watch on his wrist—a retirement gift to himself—a white dial Rolex Explorer II. Saving for it by working many extra hours of overtime, he waited patiently for many years. When the time came to wear it proudly on his wrist, he became aware that the watch also generated a feeling, a kind of solace. But moreover, for him, the stature of a fine timepiece was the result of craftsmanship. Many of the skills required to make a quality timepiece could be related to the vocation of welding: precision, attention to detail, the art of creating or building something with your hands, the use of many different metals, and the understanding of their properties. Edward thought he was able relate. *Hmm … maybe I might learn watchmaking; I have more time now. Time—what time is it?* He had *just* looked at his watch, but he hadn't noticed, too busy making analytical comparisons. *Ah, Marie would understand.* Edward inwardly smiled, recalling her advice concerning his watch.

"Yes Edward, you worked hard for many years, you have saved, and you deserve a beautiful gift to commemorate your retirement. So, go to a jewellery store and find a timepiece that matches your eyes." He could still picture her playful smile. "Then let's move on with life shall we? You can't though, can you? Can you understand Edward, your future watch and my Wal-Mart special will both read the same time! When mine says 4 o'clock, yours will say 4 o'clock! Same thing!"

"But, I realise you cannot understand this. You have been, and will continue, to do research for months, years even, until you know every model number. You will need to learn all about the gears, springs, hands, nuts, bolts, I'm not sure, but 4 o'clock—still 4 o'clock! Do enjoy your new watch, Edward. I believe you will be happy." And off she went with that sly smile of assumed victory, reigning supreme, with things as they should be.

Yes Marie, enjoy your brief, assumed moment in the sun. But be warned: Carmen, our daughter who minored in Psychology, and I, are working on a new theory regarding watches and their ability to invoke passions and desires forming intellectual stimuli, both conscious and sub-conscious. When completed, perhaps I will title the theory in your honour, Marie. How about: 4 o'clock can be much more than 4 o'clock?

Edward smiled, knowing all too well how his relentless commitment to reason and understanding influenced his daughter's choice in her academic attainments. Her dream was to work within the realm of environmental sciences and bring into the vocation a solid understanding of psychology. Edward thought it an excellent match, and there was no greater pastime for him than to sit and talk at length with Carmen about her studies.

The loneliness returned, so he got up from the chair and started towards the front hall closet to get a jacket. While entering the garage and walking over to his mountain bike, a funny thought popped into his head. *Introverts don't talk much to people, for sure. However, do most talk to themselves constantly? I think yes, because they know they're the only ones who will listen?*

With a smile, helmet on, and passing through the garage side door, Edward went out into the crisp, bright spring morning, pedaling his way through the mayhem of treasure seekers, enjoying the town-wide garage sale of Petrolia.

TWO

THE GREEN BOOK was part of him and had been for many years. He was a young man when he found it, almost 40 years ago. *Wow! Could it be that long ago?*

Edward turned onto Discovery Line heading east. It was much quieter here. The road bordered the town, with a part of it flanking the Discovery Museum property, a tribute to oil exploration and production from the early 1800s. As he peddled on, he surveyed the ever-common sight of the old working oil wells in the fields. A faint smell of crude oil permeated the air. He wasn't particularly fond of the odour, but you sort of got used to it. The source of that smell spanned great industry. His former career in welding was directly related: the manufacturing and installation of high-pressure piping systems for the massive oil refineries located 20 km west of Petrolia in the neighbouring city of Sarnia. And it was there, while he lived and worked in the city, where he found the book.

Edward picked up his pedal cadence and switched to a higher gear. There was about 2 km before he would be in the east end and mainstream town congestion again. *A brief escape into the zone? Hardly worth it.* But he wanted to: deep breathing, heart rate climbing, all the way into the red if he wished. The red zone that is, where his cardiovascular limits would be pushed to the maximum. His body responded automatically, muscles warming, stored glucose triggered for immediate use, accompanied by natural chemicals being administered by neurons in the brainstem: dopamine, serotonin. A high, yes, and Edward knew the addiction. He settled his pace to a moderately high aerobic level; the zone he could count on for longer distances. It seemed to put him into meditative thought patterns as well, which in turn often brought him to the place of his own conscious presence; the place of 'I Am.'

*The "I Am" Discourses * Ascended Master Saint Germain* by Godfré Ray King, published in 1936, or simply 'the green book' as he referred to it now, was perhaps the real beginning of his own personal 'I Am' awareness. A similar setting to a garage sale was where he found the book.

That time was a defining moment in his life, a new beginning, a new path; a path that he traveled to this day, and the cost—mere pocket change. As the landscape rushed past, forming a kind of natural blurred abstract, Edward recalled the moment, the setting 40 years ago, still sharp and clear, when he saw the book for the first time.

He could see himself walking down a quiet, tree-lined street, close to the center of the city. Passing a small church, he read a brightly coloured temporary sign that advertised a sale of used items, set up for the weekend in the church basement. It was late Sunday afternoon. The sale would be winding down, with possibly not much left to choose from, but something on the sign prompted him to take a quick look: '*old and rare books.' Interesting*.

As Edward entered the building, located the stairs and began to descend, he could hear the sounds of activity beyond. He found the entrance to a large old reception hall. People scurried about packing up boxes, loading items on carts and cleaning up. The sale was basically over. Of the many stackable tables that had been set out, most were cleared off. Scanning the room with its many sign-boards still present, Edward spotted a big table made up of three regular sized ones, at the back of the hall, posted with its sign: *old and rare books*. The people packing things away had not yet made their way to the back of the room. However, what remained now were no more than half a dozen books. He was disappointed. *Oh well, you're here now, check it out anyway.* As he approached the long table, the few remaining books lay scattered in proximity to one another. At the far-right end, seemingly segregated from the others, lay one overturned green hardcover volume.

Many years later as he would play this scene over and over in his mind, the symbolism became striking. He was a shy young man and alone.

Purchased for a small amount of change, this book became a foundation of learning for Edward, helping him form his own personal, spiritual and intellectual growth. It stayed with him in spirit always. From this volume, he realized strength in positive thinking, which began in earnest that afternoon and continued to grow to this day.

The stop sign at the end of the road was fast approaching. A quick succession of downshifts, and a right turn onto Oil Heritage Road, brought him back into mainstream garage sale traffic.

Garage sales, you never know what you might find. Scanning an overflowing table set up at the side of the road, Edward thought of Carmen and Marie. He missed having them here, on this day. *Hey, cheer up! You had your best find ever, 'the green book' when it was just you! Alone.*

He had been out for almost an hour, circling the east end, and was now making his way back to the center of town. Pedaling along slowly and taking in the sights of this lovely old Victorian town, Edward recalled reading a few years back that Petrolia was rated number three amongst the most Historic Towns or Cities in Canada. He always sensed an underlying feeling of pride and dignity in this friendly place. Many times, he, Carmen and Marie went on self-guided tours through old Historic homes and buildings during scheduled open-house events hosted by the Town of Petrolia. There were many beautiful restored homes, mansions, and commercial buildings to be appreciated.

Arriving at Victoria Park, located in the center of town on the main street, Edward got off his bike and walked it across the road. The park was small, with many old trees shading the grass. Benches were positioned throughout, and surrounding the cenotaph, a tribute to the war veterans, making for a serene setting to view local downtown activity. Edward began walking with his bike around the perimeter. The three nearest sides were bordered by sidewalks, the fourth by Victoria Hall. Edward gazed at the magnificent building, 20 metres to the south, set back from the street: the crowning jewel of Petrolia. As a late 19th-century masterpiece, built in a Queen Anne style, with its old brickwork, stain-glass windows, and overseeing clock tower, this beautiful building stood a proud testament to Petrolia's heritage. The structure served as the town's municipal offices and council chambers, as well as housing an excellent theatre: the Victoria Playhouse Petrolia. Marie shared Edward's passion for live theatre, and together they attended dozens of live productions.

More importantly, the playhouse was for Carmen like a second home. She took acting classes there, at an early age, which led to her enjoying hundreds of hours of volunteer work for the theatre. Next for her came casual part-time help as an usher, then finally full-time employment during the summer, while enrolled in university. The stage, with its many expressions of fine arts, showed her a world full of classic, timeless wonder. Carmen revelled in it. Her own passion was dance and she performed in ballet productions at the theatre herself.

Edward was still looking at the building, but no longer seeing it; he was seeing Carmen on stage, performing en pointe, classical ballet. She was mesmerizing: tall, slender, toned, poised, elegant, and confident. Every movement, right down to the slightest of facial expressions, was precise. He could not look away for an instant, lest he miss even one second of her performance. Marie sat beside him squeezing his hand. She would be crying. All too soon the performance would be over. Then Carmen would smile and curtsey to the audience; she would search with those beautiful green eyes until she found them. They connected. His thought at that moment was always the same: How could he, Edward James, have ever in part, created such an exquisite creature?

As he turned away and began to mount his bike, any one of the many people passing by on the crowded street might have heard him say, "Life does indeed have its rewards."

"Where did all these cool old things come from?" Edward turned to the young couple monitoring this sale on Maple Street.

"We're not really sure about any of this stuff that's up for sale here," the girl offered, as she leaned over the table next to Edward. He guessed the boy and girl to be in their late teens.

"It was the old cane sticking out with the top hat swivelling about in the breeze that caught my eye," Edward smiled. He glanced over towards the boy, "You two don't live here?"

"Ah, no sir," the boy shyly replied as he stuffed his hands into the pockets of his jeans. "We live in Mississauga. Our mom got us this job for the weekend."

"Ah yes ... bring in the slick, suave, polished, high-profile sales reps from the big city to swoop down and prey on us small town folk!" Edward shifted his gaze from one to the other, holding a straight face. They looked at each other, then back to Edward, nervous smiles forming. *Having some fun with teenage awkwardness.*

"Welcome to Petrolia," a grin spreading across Edward's face as he went back to rummaging through the box. "Hey, you guys might want to check out the hot dogs two blocks north on Ernest Street. Brad uses a secret sauce, revealed to none, but loved by all who have tried them; they're rated by my daughter as five stars, with an 'awesome!' added on."

"K, thanks!" Both teenagers grinned now as they stepped a bit closer to Edward. The young girl continued, "This is our first time here. Our mom has a friend who is a niece of the man and woman who used to live here. The woman passed away recently, and the man has been gone for many years. Our mom's friend is responsible for selling the house and its contents."

"I see. Where do you suppose this box of stuff came from?" Edward held up an old pair of wing-tipped shoes tangled with a bright red pair of suspenders.

The boy offered, "A lady who was here earlier this morning said she knew the couple that lived here. When she looked at that box of stuff, she told us the man, hmm … she mentioned his name …"

"Lloyd," interjected the girl.

"Yea, that's right, she said Lloyd did lots of volunteer work for the local theatre here and that this would be an old box of props for sure."

"Makes sense." Edward examined a jewel-studded tiara. "You know these diamonds, rubies, and emeralds could use a cleaning. They have a film of black smudges on them. Actually, most of these items do." He looked up at the teenagers. "Never gonna get the millions this stuff is worth without a bit of polishing. Need to dazzle 'em a bit," Edward laughed.

"I wish we had more time," the young girl complained. "We didn't even get all the prices marked yet. But yes, the black smudges … when the lady noticed the black on most of those things she said that Lloyd would have gotten the box of stuff after a fire at the theatre where lots of things got thrown out. The fire was terrible she said!"

"Yes, 'terrible' would be an accurate description of that catastrophe." Edward ceased rummaging for a moment. "It happened over 25 years ago, four years before my wife and I moved to Petrolia, and was thought to be an electrical fire that spread quickly. The whole building was pretty much decimated. It burned for days, apparently."

"Thankfully, no serious injuries resulted, however, the town almost lost its most beautiful possession. But, with pride and determination, the citizens of this small town rallied together and fought to restore her, at a cost in the millions of dollars, which came mostly from the generosity of donors. It was a spectacular fundraising campaign, considering the population. These people brought a new beginning to Victoria Hall."

"If you guys get a chance, go check it out. Very impressive. Hey, you have part of the history right here!" Edward reached way down through a vast assortment of costume jewellery, brooches, tangled necklaces, bangles, and earrings, until his hand felt something round and flat that was not tangled up in any of the mess. He brought the object to the surface and held it up, for gesture purposes. *Have the props, might as well use 'em!* He held their interest.

"Yea sounds cool!" The kids nodded to each other.

"I'll start to work on the stuff in that box. Thing are slowing down a bit," the girl piped up.

"Okay, I'll go get some rags. There's some cleaner in a bottle on a shelf in the garage. Be right back." The young boy sprinted off into the garage.

Edward stepped back as the girl lifted the box up and carried it over closer to the open garage door. He examined what he was holding in his hand, and with his thumb began wiping dust and black smudges off a metal casing. *Hmm ... interesting, looks like engraving … feels solid.* He turned it over. *An old watch? Pocket watch? But no winding crown.* He ran his fingers around a seam that split the case horizontally. He located a small pusher that protruded slightly. Pressing with his thumbnail, it snapped open almost startling Edward. It felt like precision. Now he was genuinely interested. But what he saw confused him. *Damn!* He had forgotten his reading glasses. He now had to observe at arm's length. *Yes, well maybe … yes, a kind of pocket watch,* he thought. There was a dial, a circular pattern of markers and an intricate scale of close increments with no numbers—either Arabic or Roman numerals—but some form of symbols, perhaps copied from ancient Egypt or Pythagoras. *Strange for sure.* It had only one dauphin-styled hand. What was this supposed to indicate? *Not a clue.*

Edward closed the case again. He revolved it in his hand, looking for inscriptions. He could not see any, although there was a considerable amount of intricate engraving done by machine or hand. He thought the latter.

He glanced up at the sound of voices. Several people started up the driveway to peruse the displayed items. He walked over to the front of the garage entrance. The two teenagers were busy wiping down all the assorted items from the box of props which they had scattered all about.

"So, guys, how much for this? I think it's an old pocket watch, but I'm not sure." They both looked up from their task, then at each other. They shrugged.

The girl said, "We don't know either. Would you like to make us an offer?"

Edward smiled and then reached into his pocket for his money clip. Leafing through a few bills, he paused, "Let's see, you're going to need a bit extra for hot dogs, and more of your time will be required to check out Victoria Hall hopefully." He counted out all he had with him. "$50.00 okay?"

"Really?" they both responded together. The young girl stood.

"That's more than we've made all morning! Yea, thank you sir."

"Then we have a deal." He handed her the money. "You're welcome."

With his new purchase safely stowed in his pocket, Edward pedaled in the direction of home and his reading glasses. He turned back towards the young man and the young lady. They waved goodbye to him. He called out, "Again, welcome to Petrolia!" Lasting smiles that only diminished with the increasing distance was his parting vision.

◆─●─▶

With reading glasses adorned, and a small, high-intensity floor lamp pulled over close to his chair, Edward sat again in his recliner in front of the bay window at his home. With a magnifying glass in his hand, he focused intently on the newest addition to his modest watch collection. He reached over to set the magnifying glass on a coffee table to his left. Looking back to the pocket watch, a*t least I think it's a pocket watch, but I'm not sure!* He realized then that he didn't know much about antique pocket watches.

He glanced at the coffee table and his open laptop. The last page was still up: *History of Watchmaking.* He had learned the earliest watches made had only one hand. That was interesting, but did that apply to this watch? *No idea. But no winding or setting crown?* That appeared strange. *A child's toy?* That didn't make sense either. He was not completely sure, but the engraving on the encasement, to him at least, gave an indication of excellent craftsmanship. And then the single hand: dauphin-styled, brass or gold—he couldn't be sure—and very precise, finely made. Not something stamped from a press. Opening and closing the case, the hidden hinges, the clasp and its release mechanism all showed excellent build quality. The dial was simple yet elegant. It appeared to be a brushed steel alloy, or maybe silver, with engraved black markers. The graduations were intricate; the magnifying glass showed them to be exact. *But this scale? A mystery for sure.* There were seven dominant markers, in brass or gold, with some symbols over each, engraved with precision. Nowhere was any indication of a 60-minute, 24-hour scale, only graduations of seven, subdivided differently, sometimes by ten, sometimes by seven. *Quite confusing.*

And finally, to 'seal up the mystery', Edward focused on what appeared to be four tiny screws that fixed the dial. The removal of them would allow access to the internal movement of the timepiece. However, and this seemed the most confusing of all, the slots in the screw heads had been soldered over, making their removal most difficult indeed. The tell-tale signs of slight blueing or discolouring of the surrounding metal at the screw heads indicated to Edward a high silver content in the solder used, and a high temperature needed to melt it, approximately 1,000 degrees Fahrenheit. *But why? Why would someone do that?*

Edward swivelled his chair around towards the coffee table. He left the watch open and set it on the table. Reaching back, he turned off the light. Gazing at it, lost in thought, the minutes passed. *What is your story?* He turned away towards the laptop. The screen was dark, into power saving mode. "No help here," he said aloud as he reached over to shut it down. *Let's see ... time in 24 hr that is; 1100hrs 55 minutes, the only scale I know. I wonder if anyone else has heard of a different time scale?* Edward looked at the watch on his wrist. *I wonder... how about Colin?*

Colin was the proprietor of Nash Jewellers in London, Ontario, where Edward purchased his Rolex watch. Located right downtown, the store was a beautiful old historic building. 2018 would mark the 100th anniversary of the business: three generations. Colin's grandfather founded Nash Jewelers in 1918. Edward recalled getting a tour of the upstairs level of the building, where he saw many old photos and display cases set up, showcasing an excellent collection of antique watches and jewellery. He remembered seeing several old pocket watches on display. *Yes, that might be a place to start. Alright, let's do it.*

Edward got up, folded the laptop, and closed the watch case. Putting it in his pocket, he grabbed his coat from the couch and headed for the door. It would take a little over a one-hour drive to get to the store. He should be okay to stop by Brad's and get a couple of hot dogs for the road. Allowing 4 hours total, he could be home just before Marie got back from work. She would want to hear all about his garage sale adventures, and any local gossip he might have picked up along the way.

As he settled into the driver's seat of his Volkswagen and pushed the garage door opener button clipped to the visor, he had to grin. He thought of, and tried out a suave opening line to greet his wife, when she came through the front door later that afternoon: "Hi Marie, hope you had a wonderful day at work. Listen … I went out to the garage sales today, and, well, I bought another watch." A pause would be required here. "It's a pocket watch I found at the bottom of a box of theatre stuff. And well … strange, there's no 4 o'clock. Like … I'm sure it's a watch. However, like I said, *no 4 o'clock displayed anywhere! Wanna have a look?"*

Edward turned the car onto Ernest Street and parked along the side of the road, roughly 50 metres from Brad's place. Smoke was wafting up from the barbecue, with many people milling about waiting for their hot dog, or chatting with the master chef. *Okay, must keep this short. However, an excellent place, nonetheless, to obtain a few brief tidbits of local gossip.* This would be good hard currency to encourage Marie's acceptance of the new addition to his watch collection.

THREE

"You want to go *where?*"

"New York City. Ah ... Brooklyn, New York, to be more specific."

Marie had returned from her job at the hospital 20 minutes ago, and now was not looking overly impressed. They were sitting at the kitchen table, on which directly in front of her lay the opened, newly acquired timepiece. She was looking at it, with her head cocked to one side. Her expression seemed to be one of amused concern. Combined with her short blonde bob that framed her pure, unaltered facial features, Marie at times had a schoolgirl quality, *but opponent beware*. Edward thought his presentation had not been exceptionally convincing. Truthfully, a more loving and caring person than Marie, Edward had never met. Intelligence was included as well. If she were to be fooled, it would not be for long. He was giving her his best hopeful look. Acquisition of any local gossip he could present as an offering to her had not gone well. So, tact and diplomacy would now be in order.

"So, let's see if I've got this right." Marie's blue eyes held him captive. "You find an old pocket watch today at a garage sale. No, wait ... you *think* it's an old pocket watch. Although, it appears to be broken, as one of the hands have fallen off. You would really like to see if it might actually tick, but the device doesn't have the knob on top to wind it up. Well … maybe you could take it apart to find out why it doesn't tick. But no, someone welded it shut. Hmm, most perplexing, what to do … How about a drive to London to talk to someone more knowledgeable than yourself about watches, and get his advice? Good, but turns out he's as confused as you are. However, not to be defeated, he knows the answer! Go to the top, seek an audience with the 'Master,' the 'Sage,' the 'Guru.' A simple flight to New York and all will be answered!" There was a pause. Edward held her gaze. The pause was for effect. He admired her eloquence, a formidable opponent indeed.

"So, Edward, I must ask you, what esoteric wisdom is to be gained by this? I understand retirement can be a challenge. An adjustment period is required. But you're not alone. Many others just like you are in this situation. They like to support each other, meeting for coffee every day at the local coffee shop. They love to chat. Chat about … well you know, various things: the weather, politics, you like talking about the weather, don't you Edward? What do you think? Give it a try?" With a loving smile, a gleam in her eye, and an ever so slight bow of her head, Marie leaned back. She understood her role and played her part with the utmost of confidence. A brief interlude of accolades was permissible now.

"Thank you, Marie. You're in fine form today; that is evident, and I sincerely do appreciate your concern and insight pertaining to the many challenges I face with each passing day."

"However, I can believe now, perhaps we have a slight misunderstanding regarding my recently acquired timepiece. Yes, I would admit, confusion does seem to prevail at present, but both Colin and I are of the same opinion, that there are merits here which need to be acknowledged. I can assure you Marie, one of the hands did *not* fall off. The watch was designed and built this way. Welded shut? Definitely not. You may recall I said *soldered*. The screw heads were soldered—*big* difference. Seems like someone wanted to make disassembly quite difficult, but not impossible. I can assure you, Colin would not recommend I go to New York if he didn't think it worthwhile. He believes the timepiece shows much precision and hand craftsmanship."

"Ok Edward, apparently, you've come across something here that has piqued your interest. Please tell me again: Why all the way to New York to visit one particular watchmaker; Herbert Os …?"

"Osterhagen, Herbert Osterhagen." Edward recognized the slightest glimmer of interest in Marie's eyes. "Colin's father knew him personally. They had met several times at different venues of horology in the Greater Toronto Area. Herbert would be in his early 80s now. He owns a small watch repair shop in Brooklyn, no Internet access, doesn't even talk on the phone: in person only. He does have an answering machine in service, though. According to Colin's father, there is almost nothing about horology—watchmaking in particular—this man does not know. He is descended from a long line of family watchmakers, dating back well into the 18th century. To quote Colin's father, 'Herbert Osterhagen is a genius of watchmaking.' So, Marie," Edward leaned forward, picked up the pocket watch and held it out, "given the most unusual circumstances surrounding this creation, would you not agree it behooves me to further investigate?"

Marie smiled at his word choice. She could tell he was trying to impress her. "What I *would* agree upon Edward, is that we need to decide on what we're having for supper tonight. Are any of your investigative powers being allotted to this mystery?" Marie thought to herself: *Two can play this game!*

Closing the watch and setting it back down upon the table, Edward reached forward and softly held Marie's hands in his. "I was hoping to take you out, in celebration, to one of Petrolia's fine dining establishments this evening."

"Celebration?"

"You and me." Their eyes were locked. Marie cocked her head slightly, and said nothing. A quizzical look came into her eyes. Edward responded gently, "Just you and me. That's enough."

A soft, subtle smile radiated from her face, a smile from a special place deep inside her, for him and him alone. She had given Edward his answer. Marie released her hands from his, and then stood from the table. "I'm going to draw a perfumed bath. I want to enjoy a nice relaxing soak in the tub, and then I'm going to pick out a pretty dress. You've got a date!"

As he watched her walking down the hallway, he detected a slight spring in her step. The thought that came to mind: *Life should be about passion, and right now I'm not complaining.*

FOUR

"Mmm," Marie opened her eyes. She stretched within the comfort of the soft, warm bedclothes that cradled her. The bedroom had only dim morning light filtering through the drawn window curtains. The bed was empty beside her. A quick glance at the alarm clock on the bedside table showed 9:06 a.m. She took another stretch and rolled over. Edward sat at a desk positioned in front of the window, his laptop computer open in front of him. His index finger poised, he glanced over at her and smiled. He swiftly executed a final strike on the enter key, closed the lid and pushed his chair back.

"Well, good morning sleepy head." He walked towards her, leaned down and placed a warm lingering kiss on her mouth. Gently breaking off their morning greeting, he stood back upright and headed for the door. "Be right back!"

The warmth on her lips contrasted with the feeling of cool morning air on her bare shoulders. Sitting up and gathering the comforter around her, Marie shifted back until she was upright against the headboard. The noise of Edward descending the stairs two at a time and a blender starting up in the kitchen sounded.

No way that guy is 60 years old! After last night! I think he's been lying to me all these years. Leaning her head back, she closed her eyes, not to sleep again but to be in the moment. The blender stopped. With a faint sound of birds chirping outside the bedroom window and her rhythmic breathing, she could feel the ever so slight warmth still lingering on her lips. She searched for a word. Another sound presented itself as she slowly opened her eyes to the sight of his tall, slim figure in the doorway. As he started to move forward, the word came to her: *contentment*.

"To start your day," Edward held up two tall frosty glasses. "Bananas, fresh strawberries, and blueberries, with a slice of mango." He sat on the edge of the bed offering her a glass.

"You do know the way to a girl's heart." Marie took a sip.

"Yes, nailed it … the mango, right?"

"I wasn't talking about the smoothie. Although …" She took another sip. "Yes, it's wonderful too."

A big grin radiated from Edward's face. Marie thought a slight crimson colour too, but the light was still quite dim. "Edward, I would like to ask you… why do you think an exceptional bottle of champagne, when opened shortly after returning home from a wonderfully romantic dinner for two, seems to quite literally evaporate into thin air?"

"Hmm, I too have pondered this question, Marie, and using last evening as an example, I do readily agree that this unusual phenomenon does exist. I'm thinking … something to do with the bubbles."

"I'm thinking … something to do with *whom* you are sharing those bubbles." They sat on the bed, sipping their fruit smoothies in a contented silence, neither spoke.

Sometimes silence can portray that, which words cannot fully express.

Marie joined Edward in the kitchen just as he was serving up two omelettes he had prepared. Her hair was still damp from her shower. Both were dressed in their usual Sunday morning attire: jeans and orange sweatshirts. Place settings had been set on the centre island. From there, they could enjoy their meal and look out to the tree-lined backyard through the sliding glass patio doors. The beginning of the day was looking to be clear and sunny. "Have you heard the forecast for today?" Marie pulled out one of three tall high-back chairs and settled in at the island.

"Sounds real nice—15 degrees Celsius and sunny, with modest north-northwest winds. The open road is calling for sure. How about you, any plans?" Edward set the last plate on the table, slices of whole-wheat toast. Then he looked around; a quick check to make sure everything was in place. He pulled out a chair and joined Marie.

"I'd like to go for a run later, but right now I'm very hungry. This smells *so* delicious! I bet you could hear my stomach growling all the way from the bedroom."

"That's what the sound was! I thought the furnace was acting up again!" Edward raised his glass of orange juice. "Then, I am sure you will enjoy our Sunday special entrée: a spinach, mushroom, cheddar cheese omelette garnished with green onions, red pepper and parsley, served with bacon, whole-wheat toast and preserves on the side … accompanied with your choice of juice—as long as it's orange—and coffee. Please, enjoy!"

"Mmm, excellent." Marie tried her first bite of the omelette. "Edward, you do spoil me at times."

"I will concur on that point Marie, but I must warn you: dishwasher personnel will yet again be absent. I think it's union issues we're having again."

"Those issues, would they be money, benefits, or working conditions?"

"Well, seeing as how I've never actually seen any of them here, I think we can rule out the latter."

"Okay, we need to be firm Edward. I'm here for you. I say we go it alone. If we can't make do, we've always got Carmen for moral support."

"Now there's a saving grace if ever there was one! As I've come to understand our educated child, she doesn't major in, minor in, or even participate in household chores. She has her sights set much further upon the horizon." They both started laughing.

The joking around was fun, and they thought themselves humorous, but they knew it was a cover, used at times to help them adjust. They missed her so much. For 23 years Carmen, their only child, had been the main focal point of their lives. They wanted to believe she still was, but the 'letting go' thing, the 'leaving the nest' protocol, hurt. The laughter subsided, but smiles remained.

"Remember Edward, we're Skyping Carmen at noon today."

"Right, I've already sent her a Facebook message. I attached pictures of the pocket watch. In the description, I included most of the details." Edward grinned. "She's getting excited."

"Oh, I'm sure she is. You two will become an investigative team concerning this watch. Carmen would never pass up an opportunity to solve a mystery like this. I bet she's scouring the Internet seeking information." Marie had finished her omelette and was now spreading her own homemade strawberry-rhubarb preserve on a slice of toast. "Listen, Edward, I hope you know that it's not my intent to keep you from anything you enjoy or wish to do. I will always support you, no matter what. The passion you generate for things that interest you, is, at times astonishing, and maybe it's what I love about you the most. I believe Carmen shares in this trait with you, and we both know who she gets it from. And I think maybe, well … that sometimes I'm holding you guys back, but don't you think things balance out most of the time?" Marie set the uneaten slice of toast down and reached for her napkin. She looked at her husband for reassurance.

Edward could see that her eyes were starting to well up. He gazed deeply into those eyes. "I think I have been fortunate and our lives *do* seem to balance out, most of the time." He took his napkin, reached over and dabbed a single tear from her cheek.

"Carmen sent a message back, while you were in the shower. We both agree that your idea is best: to post some photos of the pocket watch online and request information. Makes a lot of sense, better to try that first, rather than me jumping on the first flight I can get to New York."

"I now have posted on three major watch blog sites. Hey, I bet being a Sunday, probably thousands of watch aficionados are now studying the photos. Good call Marie. Wisdom prevails. Thanks for holding me back!" Edward gave her a warm smile.

Marie set her napkin back down and retrieved her slice of toast to resume eating her delicious breakfast. In a couple of hours, they would be Skyping with Carmen. It would be a challenge to get a word in. The two of them would be all over this new pocket watch mystery. But they would be together again, a family. Well, at least electronically. There was that word again, *contentment*, appearing in her mind out of nowhere. She smiled at Edward. No, it did not come from nowhere; it came from happiness. Marie took a bite of toast. She loved strawberry-rhubarb jam. Marie was happy.

FIVE

SUNDAY APRIL 27, 2014. 3:15 P.M.
OWEN ROBERTS INTERNATIONAL AIRPORT, GRAND
CAYMAN ISLAND

A TALL YOUNG MAN stood in front of the flight information screen located near the entrance of the departure terminal at Owen Roberts International Airport. It was another beautiful day on Grand Cayman Island. He glanced around the airport. He did not want to leave. He never wanted to leave, especially this time under these circumstances. With a sigh, he glanced back up to the information screen and found his flight: *Air Canada Flight #587, departing for Toronto 4:35 pm, gate #7B, on time.*

The man reached into the front pocket of his collared short sleeve shirt and retrieved his boarding pass. He briefly read the printout to confirm his flight: *seat 3B—business class.* His boss had handed him this document no more than 2 hours ago, along with $3,000.00 cash in Canadian currency, a new Blackberry Z10 cell phone, including ten extra SIM cards, a key fob for a BMW 330I, and finally a road map of Ontario Canada. There could be no mistaking the seriousness of this trip. He brushed off his uneasiness.

Looking down at the carry-on luggage that accompanied him, he wondered how cold it would be. He only had a light coat packed. No checked baggage. Not allowed. He did not even know how long this trip would last. *Not long I hope. In ... out ... done. Short and sweet.*

He approached the security checkpoint that leads to the boarding gates and handed the guard his passport. "Aaron Dekr." The guard looked up at him, narrowed her eyes, and gave him the once-over. She then gazed back into his eyes and blushed. Aaron felt the heat rising in the back of his neck and nervously rubbed it with his hand, knowing the eyes of the impatient travellers in line were upon him. *Stay cool.* She looked him up and down once more, slowly handing back his passport. *Stop staring at me!* He quickly took back his passport and hurried toward the nearest scanner. He would need to stay in control of the situation. He had confidence in himself. Where lacking in experience, he would rely on his natural talents and abilities.

He thought of his parents; Aaron's father was Caucasian, a successfully educated man from California and his mother a stunningly beautiful native of the Cayman Islands. Their three children were now adults and on their own. Aaron, the youngest, and most difficult—according to his mother—grew to be a handsome young man. He stood 6'1" tall, weighed 190 lbs, and had a very athletic build. With a golden dark complexion, fine symmetrical features, and large, intelligent brown eyes, many thought him to be a professional model, or an actor maybe. If ever asked about this directly, his usual response, in a subtle Caribbean accent, was: "I prefer to be in my own space—not somebody else's—so I don't think that would work."

Aaron was around people now, lots of them. He pushed his carry-on bag onto the moving conveyor belt and began taking off his shoes and belt, placing them in a bin. This was a crowded place, and yes, he would draw attention. His choice of dress style really did not help. Quality, casual had always been his preference, an affordable quality that is.

He stood amongst the other travellers waiting to enter the body scan. *Okay ... look straight ahead and avoid eye contact that might be misunderstood as invitational.* Aaron Dekr never learned to use his good looks to his advantage. Often, he felt alone. He made it through security, no problem. Although, he was beginning to form a dislike for the newly implemented body scan machines now in service at most international airports. It just meant more attention, more stares.

Aaron found his boarding gate. He selected a seat on the perimeter of the clustered rows, which were centered near the gate entrance door. From here he had a view of most of the incoming passengers. The area was starting to fill up. A casual inspection revealed most travelers on this pending flight appeared to be vacationers, with lots of smiles and laughter coming from tanned faces. An ending of a fun-filled vacation no doubt. Then there were others, more placid, patiently waiting, business personnel possibly, in some way connected perhaps to the tax-free international banking enterprise of Grand Cayman. Either way, Aaron was sure of one thing: *They've all been to paradise. But now it's off to the frozen north for us.*

He had never been to Canada. Reaching into the front zippered pocket of his carry-on, he retrieved the road map, which had been given to him along with a small pocket-sized black notebook. He opened the book to the first page. Aaron observed the written name: *Edward James.* Underneath was listed an email address, home address, home telephone number, and cell phone number. Then, a brief outline: *60 years old, married to Marie (48 years old), one child—Carmen (23 years old).* The profile read on, he appeared to be an average guy: *retired welder, his wife is a practicing R.N., and daughter is away at university.*

An email had been sent, with a meeting set up for—he scanned further down the page—*Monday, April 28th, 10:00 a.m. Coffee Lodge, 4119 Petrolia Line, Petrolia, Ontario.* All this had been profiled in a matter of hours. From the Internet search engine to the acquisition of personal information, Aaron knew his boss had some powerful resources at his disposal. Knowing this did not overly reassure him now. He was starting to feel the pressure.

Closing the book, he tucked it back into the front opening of the case and began unfolding the map. He would need to focus and concentrate. He mentally outlined his route: *Highway 401 West to Highway 402. West to Highway 21 South ... Okay relatively straightforward.* Of course, driving would be on the right side of the road, which was wrong for him. *Probably lots of traffic too, much like California I'd expect, and with its more northern latitude, hopefully no snow.* He had never really experienced snow. *Someday I'll try alpine skiing. I have confidence; I could do well at it. Confidence: that's the key.* Much of what he had accomplished, he knew, came from his parents. He should be thankful. In the coming days, he would do what he needed to do.

Aaron looked up as he finished zipping up his carry-on to see more activity around him now. They would be boarding shortly. *Yes, I will do what I need to do. I just hope I'm warm enough!*

SIX

MONDAY APRIL 28, 2014. 10:45 A.M.
PETROLIA, ONTARIO, CANADA

E DWARD SAT IN A BOOTH third in from the entrance, inside Coffee Lodge located on the main street in downtown Petrolia. He arrived early and selected a bench seat facing the door, beside an entirely glass-paned wall. From here, he could keep an eye on his mountain bike, which was now locked to the fence bordering the parking lot. Edward also had an unobstructed view of the man he was here to meet, upon his arrival.

Unzipping a side pocket in his mid-weight cycling jacket, he removed the pocket watch and set it on the table in front of him beside a steaming mug of black coffee he had purchased. Edward felt warm and comfortable now. Taking off his jacket, he laid it on the bench seat beside him, along with his helmet and riding gloves. The morning was bright and clear. A high-pressure system was settled in over southern Ontario. It brought cool early temperatures and sunshine with northwest winds.

Taking a warming sip of coffee, he turned his attention to the watch. It had been interesting before, now it was intriguing. There were many responses to his online posts. He posted several close-up photos of the watch along with his request for information, but none were conclusive. It appeared all the watch enthusiasts were as baffled as him. No one could offer a solid theory as to the providence of this strange timepiece.

And now, well this just seems quite unusual. A man named Aaron was driving all the way from Toronto to talk with him about the watch. Edward received an email shortly after he and Marie finished Skyping with Carmen. He recalled the message: *Sir, I have an interest in this timepiece. I request from you an audience with my representative at the earliest possible convenience. S.C.*

Then Edward sent back a reply with a proposed time and place. He received an immediate confirmation listing the representative's name:

> *Aaron. 28 years old, tall with a dark complexion. He will arrive from Toronto at requested time and location. Thanks. S.C.*

The correspondence seemed to Edward rather formal and quite impersonal. He was not sure what to make of it. He was still puzzling over the situation when he noticed a shiny, late model, white 3 series BMW pull into an empty spot directly in front of the coffee shop. *So … is this the guy?* The clock on the wall said 11:33 a.m. The car was in plain view through the glass partition, although a glaring reflection on the front windshield prohibited any view of the vehicle's occupants. The engine shut down, evident by the daytime running lights turning off.

A few moments passed. The driver's door opened and the first thing that caught Edward's eye was the shoulder of a graphite coloured down jacket with the ever-familiar, conspicuous red, white and blue circular patch of 'Canada Goose.' *Nice.* A tall young man, dark in complexion, exited the car.

Must be the guy. He walked towards the entrance. Edward made a quick assessment: *There's no dismissing the quality sunglasses? I'm* thinking Gucci. Collared dark pink-orange buttoned cotton shirt, creased fine-textured black wool pants, and the brown shoes—maybe Mephistos. Physical shape—hmm ... doesn't get much better. Wow! This guy has just crawled out from the pages of some men's fashion magazine!

Edward had, for many years, fostered an interest in men's fashion. An interest not so much to keep up with the latest trends but rather to observe the quality and craftsmanship exhibited by the higher-priced brand names. He admired and sought to learn more about them. He firmly believed that value for dollars spent often required 'a study in detail', as he liked to call it, and presently he saw an attention to that kind of detail.

The man walked through the entrance door, removed his sunglasses, and scanned the room. Edward made eye contact and nodded to him while holding up the pocket watch. This brought a hand gesture of acknowledgment, and he came over to the table, smiled, and offered his right hand in greeting. Edward stood and accepted a firm handshake.

"Hi, I am Aaron, you must be Edward."

"Yes, pleased to meet you, Aaron. If you'd like something, it's self-order here."

"Sure, I will order a latte." Edward detected what he presumed to be a subtle Caribbean accent. Aaron smiled as he unzipped his jacket and laid it on the bench seat beside him.

Edward returned the smile, and in a light-hearted manner joked, "Perfect morning to take the Canada Geese along! We got frost here last night." Silence ensued and he was surprised at Aaron's response. The smile faded, and a questioning look came to his eyes. He hesitated.

"Um ... yes, sure. "There was more silence. Edward could sense the awkwardness.

"Your coat—a Canada Goose. I meant ... well, great to have a Canada Goose coat for these chilly spring mornings."

A subtle smile returned to Aaron's face. "Yes, I understand, well of course, a recent purchase ... I'm afraid I am not really up on name brands and such." He turned and headed for the front counter to place an order. "I will be right back."

As he did so, Edward glanced down. *Yeah, I was right about the shoes.* He sat back down. Aaron placed his order. He stood facing away. Edward gazed at him thoughtfully. *So why the hell does G.Q. Magazine want a discussion with me about my pocket watch?*

———◆———

"That's how I found it." Edward took a sip of his coffee. Aaron turned the pocket watch over in his hand.

"Did you ever dismantle this watch?"

"No, I haven't. When you open the cover, and look close, you can see that the small screw heads affixing the dial were soldered over, making disassembly difficult."

Aaron opened the case and looked closely. Edward thought he saw a slight nod of understanding. Perhaps more than the simple acknowledgement of the soldered screw heads. "Do you know something about this timepiece?"

Aaron shifted his gaze to Edward then back to the watch. "No, I'm afraid not." The eye movement was quick, too quick. *Maybe he does know something.*

"Your boss ... S.C.? He didn't tell you specifically why he has an interest in this timepiece?"

"No, he only showed me the photos you posted online."

"Hmm S.C. ... does S.C. have a proper name?" Edward was beginning to feel uncomfortable.

Aaron glanced up at Edward. "He does, but he prefers to remain anonymous."

Edward did not break eye contact. He reached out his hand to retrieve his watch. *Ok buddy, you've had time enough. What are you up too?*

With a slight hesitation Aaron handed the watch back to Edward.

"So …?"

Aaron swallowed; his eyes darted away for an instant. "He … my boss, would like to make you an offer."

"An offer? But I never said I wanted to sell! I'm only looking for some information. I told you—the house where I found the timepiece—on Maple Street, nothing to be learned there about the watch's history, other than perhaps it was one of many old props used in theatre productions. I'm sorry, but it appears as though you, or your boss, misunderstood my inquiries."

"No, we just … well, my boss thought he would like to make you an attractive offer, which could save a lot of time and give you a tidy profit. How does one thousand dollars sound?"

Edward hesitated. He was startled somewhat. Looking down at the watch, he turned it over and opened the case. "Yesterday I drove to London and went to a long-established jewellery store in the city. I had some dealings with the proprietor in the past, and I trust him. After a close inspection of the watch, his advice to me was to travel to New York City to visit a knowledgeable watchmaker who, as he stated, "If anyone can help you, it would be him." Edward paused, focusing on Aaron. "The money, I can always use a little extra cash, but not a necessity. Time … got lots of it now. And well, I'm starting to think that your boss, and perhaps you too, know something about this watch that I don't."

"My hope in coming here was only that a favourable transaction might be achieved between both parties. I will tell you, I have been authorized to pay you the sum of two thousand dollars for the watch. Would that seem fair?"

Edward observed Aaron was tensing up a bit. It made him think back several years ago when Carmen had interrogated him for a psychology assignment. The assignment was required for a course and involved observing and assessing human facial expressions to determine thought patterns. Edward thought the exercise was incredible stuff. He learned a lot from her over the course of that project. *Thank you, Carmen, I'm going to give this a shot!*

"I'm not sure ... So, Aaron, do you live in Toronto? The email I received stated you'd be driving from T.O.."

"Ah, yes I do." His eyes blinked twice and barely detectable jaw muscles contracted as he lightly clenched his teeth.

"I find myself in the greater Toronto area a couple of times a year at best and only know the general layout. So, in what part of that sprawling metropolis do you reside?"

"Close to the city center." Aaron stayed mostly still, with steady eye contact, but Edward detected an involuntary swallow.

"Oh, near to Rogers Centre, must be cool to catch a Jays game with free parking."

Aaron's eye muscles tensed and lost focus for a second.

Aaron spoke firmly "Yes, I take advantage whenever I can."

Edward smiled inwardly. *Ok, interrogation over.*

THE SUN BEGAN TO BRING warmth to the clear morning, but still a cool, moderate wind persisted. Edward breathed the air deep into his lungs as he pedalled away from Coffee Lodge. He hoped a good dose of fresh air would help to clear his thinking. A two thousand dollar offer to buy his newly acquired pocket watch had indeed changed his perspective. The man went no further with his offer, but he did become much more insistent, almost pushy. He even advised Edward that to accept his offer would be 'the wisest decision.' *What an odd comment.*

The offer was turned down. No names or telephone numbers were exchanged, a simple goodbye and nothing else. However, now for sure this unusual pocket watch had taken 'center stage,' and Edward James was very interested to see this drama unfold.

SEVEN

Edward rode his bike up the driveway of a small white frame house just around the corner from his own street. A blue Mazda 5 was parked in the drive, indicating that perhaps Derek would be home and have some free time. The man was always busy with some sort of project. Edward took off his helmet and hung it on the handlebars, then leaned his bike against the front of the house. He heard the faint whirring sound of a servomotor. Walking towards the front entrance, he glanced up to see the motion of a roof-mounted security camera following his movements. He waved. *What a lovely way to say good morning.*

Derek was home. Now hopefully, they could spend some time together. Edward wanted to tell him all about the pocket watch. He had already sent him via email the photos and 'information request' he previously posted online, along with a short text message last evening about his pending meeting at Coffee Lodge.

Edward and Derek were good friends. It was an unlikely pairing, which developed over ten years ago. Both had been asked to participate as panel members on a 'career night' at the local high school. They participated as part of ten or so construction trades advisors brought in to give a short talk, and answer questions for the graduating students who might be interested in their vocation. Edward, of course, spoke on welding. As a security specialist, Derek's talk was on security systems. They sat beside each other during the presentation and chatted cordially throughout the evening. Afterward, Derek asked Edward if he might be able to help him with some aluminum welding that needed to be done for his own personal use. Edward answered yes. As it turned out, they lived just around the corner from one another, and soon Edward learned Derek was quite an extraordinary person. Single, unattached, in his early 40s, a little heavy-set, average height, average features, average house and average car. Mr. Average? Well not quite.

Derek was an electronic-mechanical wizard. *Not* so average in that area at all. Many of his skills were incorporated into his occupation as a security system installer, and he embraced other passionate interests as well. Being a highly-trained volunteer firefighter for the town also inspired a keen interest in police work, most notably investigations and communications. He was a fully credited ham radio operator, with dozens of personal contacts all over the world. Derek held two college level degrees: computer programming and computer technical advancement. But the real love of his life? Edward referred to it as 'gadgets and gizmos.' Derek loved to tinker, research, build and experiment relentlessly. The man created. *Someday this guy is gonna nail it!*

Both Edward and Marie tried on several occasions to play 'the matchmaker' and set Derek up with someone who they thought might be an appropriate partner to share life's experiences. It was not to be, however. They had to admit defeat.

Edward offered this consolation to Marie: "I think as a teenager, Derek went in search of his father's old copies of Playboy magazines—as most young teenage boys will do—but couldn't find any. Instead, he had to settle for Popular Mechanics, and his fate was sealed." Marie thought this explanation to be quite probable.

Edward waited patiently at the door, as no knocking or ringing of a doorbell was required. Derek would be alerted to his presence as soon as he entered the premises. He seemed to remember a conversation about the sensitivity of the many pressure sensors Derek had positioned throughout his property. Couple that with about six scanning cameras with remote zooming, located in various strategic locations. Edward knew the capability existed for Derek to have Edward's computer-enhanced image sent worldwide instantly, on several databases, to be identified and evaluated.

Ha, he won't find much of interest there.

A high-tech series of beeps and tones sounded as the front entrance alarm deactivated and the door opened. Edward was met by the round, smiling face of his friend. "Hey, how's it going? Come in, come in. Awesome you dropped by. How'd the meeting go? You bring the watch? I'm super anxious to see it … guy from Toronto, right? What did he say? K, let's go to the kitchen."

Edward smiled at Derek's enthusiasm as they made their way down a cluttered hallway past the archway, which led to the equally cluttered living room. Boxes, cables, and electronic devices were everywhere. The plain white walls held no pictures, but instead contained a plethora of control panels, video monitors, switches and indicator lights for the exterior grounds and the rest of the entire house.

They carefully navigated their way to the kitchen. Edward scanned the room. Dishes were piled in the sink, pots and pans covered the stovetop, and empty cereal and pizza boxes lay scattered about. He winced at the sight of several discarded Kraft Dinner boxes close to a couple discarded Spaghettio cans. A bit of effort was always required here for adaptation to the surroundings. *Well, at least he's consistent.* Had the house been neat and tidy, Edward would have suspected a problem. *Nope, it's all good.* The trick, though, was to find a place to sit without getting poked, prodded or possibly shocked.

With a couple of swift manoeuvres, Derek cleared away dishes and articles from a small area on the table. Two chairs were salvaged and set in place. "Can I get you a Coke?"

"Sure, thanks." *Yes, that should be safe.* Edward hung his coat on the back of a chair. "Not working today?"

"No, I got called to a job on Sunday morning. It took about 4-5 hours, so I took today off." Derek opened the refrigerator door to grab the Cokes. Edward made a point of looking away, rather than allow himself any observation, no matter how slight, of the fridge's internal contents.

"Nice to enjoy some flexibility in your job scheduling." Derek gave Edward his drink, and they both sat down.

"Yeah sure is. I'm anxious to get some work done on my drone project. I'm hoping I could get you to do some more aluminum welding for me, in about a week or so?"

"Sure, we'll set it up." Edward took a drink and set the can back down. A smile formed on his lips. It was an involuntary action now, whenever he visited. His head slightly cocked to one side, his eyes questioning with the words flashing across his mind like a giant electronic billboard. *Why, Derek?* After 10 years of constantly trying to understand Derek's logic, his brain eventually conceded and transferred all responses directly to his autonomic nervous system. *No surprise here.* All was as it should be. Edward wondered how Derek might top the 'fingerprint scanner.' Perhaps this would be it.

"A drone project … you have your own drone?"

"Yea, delivered yesterday."

"Hmm … I'm thinking I might need one of those things. I'll talk to Marie."

Derek started to laugh. "Ha, I can't even talk you guys into getting an entry level door alarm."

"Well hey, we invested in our own 'psychological security system.'"

Now Derek was leaning back in his chair laughing heartily. His round face beaming, a tear rolled down his cheek. "I ..." he stopped to compose himself for a moment. "I told my boss about your security system: the big dog dish with the name 'Rambo' in bold letters printed on it, placed right beside the 'Welcome, please come in' mat. It cracked him up! He laughed about it forever. I think it made his day."

Edward waited for Derek to settle himself. *Now there's a happy person.* "So, your drone, in simple layman's terms, what will it do?"

Derek took a swallow of his Coke, in preparation for the pleasant task of presenting an outline of one of his projects. "Lithium-ion powered, four tilting rotors, controlled real-time by a laptop or a smartphone. Armed with a 29-mega-pixel zoom camera, still shots or high-def video, and with the aid of rooftop sensors, autopilot surveillance is possible. I'm in the process of designing and building, with your welding assistance, an entirely retractable rooftop launchpad. I'm estimating a sixty second launch sequence. I'm currently studying load factors in the event of heavy snowfall. My completed design should be ready in about two weeks. Construction time ... about a month, depending on the welding." Derek was in his element now. Edward could even feel his excitement. With brain activity in high gear, there would not be much chance in slowing him down now.

In contrast, this was not so much Edward's element, but he did manage to slide in one word: "Surveillance?"

"Absolutely! If the security system in my home is ever breached, the drone will automatically be launched. It will be able to circle the outside perimeter of my property for over 30 minutes, recording in real-time video with 360-degree orientation. Rooftop halogen lighting will be activated to illuminate objects of interest for later identification." Derek leaned back in his chair, let out a deep breath, and reached for his Coke.

Edward remained silent for a moment, trying to digest Derek's informative discourse. *A kid in a candy store.* "You know … I can set you up with an awesome, extra-huge dog dish. We'll come up with a cool name … How about 'Bruiser?'" They both started to laugh. It had a calming effect on Derek.

"So, Edward, please tell me all about this mystery watch. How'd the meeting go?"

Edward took another sip of his Coke. He leaned back and smiled at his friend. "Okay." He paused. "Derek, have you ever read *G.Q. Magazine?*"

EIGHT

"This guy Aaron, I don't think he's from Toronto … anywhere in Canada for that matter." Edward raised his tall glass of beer, took a swallow then set it back down on the granite counter top.

"Oh?" Marie sat across from him. They were again seated at their island facing the patio door in the open kitchen. A glass of red wine sat before her. She had returned home from a regular day shift about an hour ago, freshened up, and had changed into a pair of slim fitting jeans with a black light knitted V-neck sweater. She felt comfortable now. This was a regular occasion for them. They both looked forward to having a beer or a glass of wine together before supper and discussing how each other's day had been. It was something each of them valued in their relationship. Marie knew what would dominate today's discussion. It would be 'the pocket watch.' Edward had been talking almost non-stop about his meeting at Coffee Lodge this morning, and Marie had to admit the conditions surrounding this watch were becoming most unusual.

"Did you ask him?"

"I did," Edward replied, "he said yes he lives in Toronto, close to the centre of the city. But things don't quite match up."

"Match up … with what?" Marie asked.

"I … well …" Edward reached for his drink. "I did a quick evaluation." He took a long swallow and set the almost empty glass back down. *I think I'm going to need another beer.*

"What kind of evaluation?" Now seemed the appropriate time to have a sip of wine. She did and smiled with one of those 'this should be good' smiles.

"Ah … do you recall a few years back when I helped Carmen with her project for neuroscience? The one about psychological studies on facial expressions that in turn reveals internal thought patterns."

"Of course, I can recall her insistence and that as a case study you were *a pain in the butt!* Too much smiling and laughing, not taking the exercise seriously enough, however … I do believe she overcame your inconsistencies, and received an excellent grade on the assignment." Marie's smile suggested she was in her amusement mode. "You're telling me you *did* pay attention and learned something?"

"Hey! She said I was a pain in the butt? Wow … little does she understand my calculated methods of lessening and controlling stress levels. Mostly *hers,* I might add!"

"Yes, Edward, we're all guilty of underestimating your psychological prowess at times. But still … we *do* love you." Marie reached out and took Edwards hands in hers. "So, what have you learned?"

"I asked him some questions, easy general stuff. He appeared tense, hesitant, a bit uncertain or confused. Things like parking, Toronto Blue Jays, everyday things. But one thing that stands out: I told you what he looked like …"

"Umm …" Marie had sat back and was holding her wine glass by the stem. She began to oscillate the glass and gazed as the wine cascaded ever so gently. Allowing herself only a brief moment before she raised her head. "And …"

Edward continued. "So, when the guy arrives in his BMW, the first thing I notice is that he is wearing one of those down filled

'Canada Goose' bomber style jackets, you know the ones right?" Marie nodded. "So, as he takes off his coat I make a friendly comment regarding Canada geese and how it's nice to have them along on these chilly mornings—just a fun metaphor, to break the ice. Well … it went right over his head. He stared at me like I was speaking a different language, so I asked … Canada geese? Canada Goose coat? His response, "I don't pay much attention to brand names." Hmm, I'm thinking: the BMW, the jacket, Gucci's, Mephisto's … I bet I can't even pronounce the brand of underwear this guy prefers! And he doesn't pay attention to brand names … Really?"

"Well," Marie interjected. "perhaps he comes from money. You've heard the phrase, 'A royal.' Like … chauffeur drives him to father's favourite clothier. Mother has selected his hairstylist, and then he's off to the polo match, or to the family yacht for 'high tea.' Well possibly a latte, you did mention his preference. But brand names … too much bother. Better to employ people for such trivial undertakings. Keep the masses working, crucial for the family business and investments."

Marie agitated the wine in her glass with a perfected circular motion. She brought the glass to her nose and inhaled deeply. Holding the glass out at arm's length to study the colour and the legs of her vintage, she brought the glass to her lips and delicately took a sip, lightly swishing the wine in her mouth. Her head tipped back as she swallowed. "I bet your friend Aaron has access to the family's wine cellar. Now there's something to pay attention to!"

"Bravo Marie. I can tell your selected Ontario vintage has loosened you up considerably." Edward smiled at his wife. "However, I must disagree with your theory."

"How come? I kinda like my theory, and it's *fun*." Marie pouted.

"Because of his watch," Edward replied.

Marie rolled her eyes, "His watch? But of course! It would ultimately depend on his watch. What do we know about a man until we have … you never mentioned anything about his *watch*!" She slouched forward with both elbows on the counter, and her hands cradling her chin. She needed to have support, both mental and physical, for the pending narrative she must now endure. "Yes Edward, please continue."

"A Tag Heuer Aqua Racer 300, black dial."

Marie offered nothing in the way of altered facial expression. Edward resumed. "The watch is a fine, entry level, high quality mechanical timepiece with water resistance to 300 metres. It fits well with jogging attire or a business suit, compliments of selecting the black dial over the optional blue dial. Starting to get the picture, Marie?" There was a pause.

"I was starting to think you were watching too many mystery-suspense shows on TV, but actually I'm the one who does that." She allowed herself a smile. "Please go on."

"We know that Aaron prefers quality, as evident by his attire. He chose a mechanical watch over a quartz type, which shows an intellectual appreciation for excellent mechanical precision. Also, he selected a watch with high water resistance offering the possibility he finds himself in or near water frequently. The choice of a black dial over the blue dial—which I can tell you lends itself beautifully to aquatic settings—indicates that he can afford only one quality watch, and it must be suitable for both land and sea."

"Our conclusion?" Edward paused and observed as Marie settled back in her chair. She was not exactly holding her breath. "Our friend Aaron is handsome and intelligent—but take note—a bit aggressive, very untrustworthy, and, just like the rest of us mere commoners, he is required to budget his finances. And, as I said before, I don't believe he lives anywhere in Canada."

"Any ideas?" Marie was leaning forward now in anticipation.

"He's got what I believe to be—although quite subtle—a Caribbean accent and a tanned complexion … hey I might be totally off base here, but do the math."

"That's crazy Edward! You think someone would travel all the way from the Caribbean to try and buy your pocket watch?"

Edward shrugged his shoulders." I guess the bigger question … why did someone else fund this operation?"

In silence, they stared at one another. Marie felt a slight tingling in her lower abdomen, which she knew to be a deep inner presence, and it did not feel overly good.

MARIE WAS BUSY GETTING ready to leave for another day shift, going back and forth between the cupboards and the refrigerator, and then off to the dining room table to rifle through some scattered pages she had been working on the night before. She stuffed them into a leather shoulder bag, in between taking quick bites of cut up pieces of fruit from a bowl on the table. A quick glance up to the clock on the wall told her she was cutting it close this morning: it was 7:20 a.m., and 25 minutes were needed for driving time. Her shift started at 8:00 a.m. She rushed back to the kitchen to resume her assault on lunch packing.

Finding the remains of a glass of orange juice Marie downed it in one gulp. "Edward, what's the weather for today?"

Edward was sitting at the island with his laptop open before him. He held a mug of coffee in one hand. After taking a leisurely sip, he smiled at Marie as he simultaneously set his cup down and punched at the keyboard. "Here we go: sun and cloud, high 16 degrees Celsius, wind switching around to southerly 20-30 kilometres per hour, 40 percent chance of precipitation. So, a great day with seasonal temperatures with a chance for rain coming in by tomorrow afternoon, though."

"K thanks, so I'll wear a light coat." Marie resumed her scurrying about, heading off to the front hall closet for shoes and a coat. "Could you please pour me a coffee in my travel mug?" she called out over her shoulder as she left the room.

"Sure can." Edward leaned back, held his arms out wide in a big stretch. Getting up he walked to the cupboard directly above the fresh pot of coffee that sat warming on the coffee maker. He was filling her travel mug when Marie bustled back into the room, doing up her coat as she scooped up the half-eaten bowl of fruit. She found her fork amidst the scattered pages on the table. There came another quick glance up to the clock.

"You're booking a flight to New York City today?" Marie asked.

"I hope so, I was checking online. I think a one-way flight would be best. There are lots available, hotel rooms too, as midweek is favorable. Derek said he'd drive me to Detroit to catch an early morning flight and he can still be back in time to start work, no problem."

"So, you're thinking tomorrow?" Marie finished the fruit and was placing the empty bowl into the sink.

"Possibly, I still should wait until I hear from the watchmaker in New York, though. I left a message on his answering machine last night around 10:00 after I got off the phone with Derek."

"Oh, I went to bed at around 9:00 and I could hear you talking ... an hour on the phone with Derek?" Marie laughed as she slung her cooler bag and shoulder bag on one side of her body. "I couldn't do it, way too technical." She scanned the room searching for her purse and found it on the dining room chair. She hurriedly walked over and grabbed it. "Edward, my coffee, please? Walk me to the car, okay?"

"Carry on ..." Marie positioned her purse on her opposite shoulder with a quick check to verify that her keys were in the front opening. She headed out of the room to the side door that led to the attached garage, with Edward following.

"Well, we talked about my travel route in NYC," Edward reached into his back pocket and pulled out a folded sheet of paper.

He unfolded it with one hand, as he passed through the door into the garage. A motion sensor activated two overhead light panels, illuminating the garage. Marie's white, late model Honda Civic was parked closest to them beside Edward's Volkswagen. She had the rear driver's side door open and was placing all her bags on the back seat. Closing the door, she turned to Edward, reaching out for the coffee he held for her. She let out a deep sigh and took the coffee, at the same time checking the watch on her wrist.

"I'm sorry Edward. I really need to start getting up a bit earlier."

Edward chuckled. "Marie, this has been your 'modus operandi' for the past 20 years. Trust me here, change *will* come when you retire. Until then ..." He raised his shoulders, with palms turned up in a gesture of surrender and smiled at her.

"Okay. We've got a couple of minutes yet. Please, I'm sorry. I interrupted you." Marie gave him her best 'I know you understand me' smile. "Your New York itinerary?"

"Yea, should be interesting. I'll be one of the locals for a day or so." Edward held the unfolded sheet of paper out at arm's length in front of him. "Damn, no reading glasses! I think I will start wearing a monocle around my neck just for times like these. Hmm ... I think they are due for a comeback in the world of fashion. What do you say, Marie? Would I look handsome wearing a monocle?"

"Awesome Edward ... yes, it is for sure one of my long-time fantasies to see you wearing a monocle and nothing else! We'll talk about it later this evening in private. But for now, could we move this along please?"

"Er ... right. Okay. Here it is. I fly out of Detroit around 6:00 a.m. Arrive at J.F.K. New York 8:30-ish. I take the air train to Jamaica Station at Sutphin Boulevard. I catch the subway at Archer Avenue toward Court Square and transfer at Church Avenue and get off at Nassau Avenue in Brooklyn. Sound good?"

"I'd call it hectic rather than interesting." Marie leaned in through the open driver's door and placed her coffee in the centre console cup holder. She turned back out to face Edward. "And you said last night you'd also visit a bicycle store?"

"Yea, I'm looking forward to it. One of the largest cycle shops in the world, in Brooklyn. I'll have only a short walk back to the subway terminal, then a 'hop on' for a quick ride … easy. I've wanted to visit there for a long time and now's my chance. So, for sure it won't be a wasted trip."

Marie could tell Edward's enthusiasm was building. There would be no holding him back now. "So, you're going to get your phone set up for an extended data plan out of the country, right?"

"I'm setting it up today. No worries Marie. Derek and I have been through all this." Edward replied with confidence.

"And … how come no return flight?" Marie was not feeling quite the same level of confidence as her husband.

"Well, I kinda think I need to leave it open, in case the watchmaker needs an extra day or so. He might need some time to dismantle the watch. And besides, both prices are almost the same, anyway. A couple hundred bucks each way. It's somewhat off season for tourism now, so there are reasonable prices on flights and accommodations."

"But …" She knew she was overreacting, "By yourself … you might get lost."

Edward gave her a reassuring smile, as he took his cell phone from his front pocket and held it up. "GPS, no worries, and don't forget we'll be electronically connected at all times. I'll be studying the subway and air train routes for NYC today online. We can go over it this evening if you'd like."

That seemed to help. Marie let out a deep breath and leaned forward to give her husband a big hug. "Oh Edward, I gotta go. I'm running late!" She reluctantly let go and got into her car. She activated a switch overhead on the front sun visor causing the garage door to open, and then pressed the red button on the dashboard starting the engine. Next, she located the controller on the door and lowered her window. "I'll text you from work as soon as I get a chance." She blew Edward a kiss, turned back into the car, and proceeded to back out of the garage and down the driveway onto the street. Edward walked out of the garage to wave goodbye.

Marie called out, "Good luck! Hope your watch guy calls. I'll be home about 5:30. We'll text. Bye!" The car started to pull away and stopped. She leaned out again, "Oh, if you *do* book a flight for tomorrow, could you see if you can Skype Carmen?"

Edward called back. "For sure, bye." He waved as he watched her white car drive to the end of their short street. As she slowed and signalled to make the right turn that would take her to the main street of Petrolia, a white work van passed on her left, and turned down their street. As Marie's car vanished from sight, the white van pulled up to the small turn-around circle in front of their house. He could clearly make out the 'Bell' decals coloured in blue on the side panels of the truck. It had a couple of ladders strapped to the roof and bright orange pylons stacked above the rear bumper. It was a typical 'Bell' service truck that had been dispatched to address some sort of telephone issue on Sanway Court no doubt. Edward glanced down at his watch. *Hmm ... 7:30 a.m., starting bright and early this morning.*

The driver's side door of the van opened, and a man in blue coveralls and an orange vest emerged. He wore a white hard hat, with tinted safety glasses and carried a clipboard in his left hand. He gave a subtle wave as he headed towards Edward. "Morning sir." He stopped in front of him, and glanced to the front of the house to check the address, then to his clipboard. "James residence?"

"Yes, I'm Edward James, good morning. Something I can help you with?"

"We're doing a quick overall surveillance of Bell Canada customer's phone lines. I'm sure you've heard that Bell is in the process of switching all phone lines over to the new fibre optical transport system?"

Edward shrugged. "I guess so."

"Well this is a pre-scheduling to determine how many customers are in certain areas, so we can assess the amount of equipment that'll be necessary to do the work."

"Okay, so what is it you need?"

"Well, do you happen to know where your phone line exits your house? I'll be working on the collector box over there." He pointed to an upright metal box on the neighbour's property. "It would help if I could tag your line for identification."

Edward looked over his shoulder towards the side of his garage. "I think it's right there beside the gas line." They both started walking towards where Edward had indicated.

"Yup, that's it for sure."

The technician leaned down to feel the wire. "I'll tag it. I must check with a few more residents on the street. I'll need to tag some lines in the collector box too, and that'll be it." He stood and reached into his front pocket for a pen. Making a quick notation on his clipboard he nodded to Edward and started back towards his truck. "Thank you, sir, have a good day."

Edward smiled. "Hey, no problem." He walked back into the garage and pushed the button located next to a light switch. The automatic garage door started to close. *Okay, one more coffee, and then I want to do some work on my road bike. I need to make some decisions on upgrades. Decisions, decisions...* He went back into the house, with a big smile on his face.

NINE

WEDNESDAY, APRIL 30, 2014. 11:45 A.M.
BROOKLYN, NEW YORK, USA

IT TAKES GREAT SKILL, both acquired and innate, to become an accomplished watchmaker. Ultimately, he or she is involved in the creation and preservation of timepieces, which in turn monitor time. Time is as natural to us as the air we breathe or the beat of our hearts, but when asked to define it we experience uncertainty. Both the scientist and the philosopher have tried in vain to discover a definitive answer to the mysteries of time. Is it an illusion, the fourth dimension, a procession, a presence of forces and motion? The proposed theories are many, but it can be argued that none are absolute.

The phrase 'time is on my side' no longer seemed appropriate for the old watchmaker who was sitting at his work bench diligently attending to the disassembled timepiece that lay in front of him. He had extraordinary skill, steady hands, sharp eyes, and even the parts of his brain required to inspect, calculate and process information regarding the seemingly endless mechanical components were astonishingly precise. But, sadly, time was running out for Herbert Osterhagen. He was an old man now. The presence he had spent his life serving would soon demand his demise. However, for some, the passing of time brings wisdom. Herbert no longer felt the need to understand the presence of time—something he had spent most of his life in the contemplation of—now for him it seemed more like trying to understand the true meaning of 'love' or 'God.' He believed the human mind was just not capable.

What was important, though, was where he was at this moment, and what he was doing now. The separate components of the timepiece laying before him would soon be assembled and motion commenced. The balance wheel would oscillate, like a beating heart, in turn setting up a running motion within a highly complex mechanism, which would become a creation to serve the presence of time. Is this not what he was as well?

Herbert smiled as he remembered his own grandfather and the stories he had told of past generations of Osterhagens: accomplished watchmakers of acclaim and honour. He thought of his granddaughter, she was an Osterhagen, and her time to create would be soon, very soon. And if the message from Monday evening on his answering machine was … Herbert leaned back on his stool, allowing himself a short break. He knew better than to get his hopes set too high.

He took a thoughtful look around. This had been his life for many, many years. The watch shop in Brooklyn, New York had always been a small business of fine craftsmanship and integrity. Herbert lived alone in the bachelor suite in the back of the building, which had two main work areas. One housed his manufacturing equipment consisting mainly of small lathes, turning machines, drill presses and a considerable assortment of hand fabricating tools. The other room, where he sat now, was primarily used for assembly. Large skylights had been built into the roof to allow for as much natural light as possible. This room held a long chest-high workbench and the walls were entirely covered with cabinets, hanging tools and a six-foot high bookcase. An archway at the end of the room opened to the storefront entrance. Stools were positioned on either side of a wooden and glass front counter cabinet in which were displayed various assortments of used and or repaired pocket and wristwatches. The entrance area also served as the office facility. A desk bordered by a set of shelves and filing cabinets took up half of the space.

Herbert was happy here and had built up an exceptional reputation over these many years, being always busy with a passionate devotion to his work. He thought back again to his grandfather. His love for him had never faltered and the inspiration bestowed upon Herbert was indefinite.

Was he an inspiration to his own granddaughter? Herbert knew the true answer to that question would be deep in her heart. His eyes were starting to well up, *not good for watch repair*. Reaching into his pocket he pulled out a handkerchief. He missed her so much. *I will come to visit you if that message from Monday evening…*

A buzzer sounded, indicating the opening of the front door. Looking out through the archway towards the entrance area, Herbert could plainly see three tall, dark-complexioned men enter his shop. He noticed they all wore dark mirrored sunglasses, were well dressed in suit trousers and they all had on similar dark leather coats. He guessed them to be in their mid-thirties.

Herbert got up from his stool and headed to the front entrance, *not regulars*. As he approached them, one of the men came forward. He unzipped his mid-length leather coat, then placed both his hands on the display countertop and leaned in as Herbert approached. The sunglasses stayed on.

"A*r*e you e*r*be*r*t, de watchm*a*ker?" The two other men leaned back against the entrance door with their arms folded. The sunglasses stayed on.

Herbert had arrived at the front room and stood a few feet behind the counter. They seemed a lot bigger now. He picked up on the man's heavy accent right away; he thought it to be of Caribbean origin. The message in their demeanour was clear: they wanted something, and their first method of attaining it would be intimidation.

"Yes, I am, and your name?" This brought a slight twitch and straightening of the man's shoulders. *Apparently, this is not a simple question.* There was a slight hesitation. Herbert studied his own image in the man's sunglasses. He had forgotten to shave today. He turned his head sideways. Brought his hand up and lightly stroked the bristle on his chin followed by an ever so slight smile.

"It be *no* concern to you," the man answered in his thick, accented voice. The lead guy had regained his composure. "I tell you…we're ere on behalf of *a* very importan person; is name shall remain unknown. E has sen us ere to get *a* watch, an I tell you diss …" The man glanced over his shoulder in a gesture of confidence towards his two accomplices. Neither of them moved a muscle. Herbert said nothing; he only cocked his head and raised his eyebrows in question.

"We ave been tol not to leave ere wit *no* watch."

"A watch?"

"You gau *a* message on your an'ser machine Monday evening from a guy… E lives in Ontario, Canada? E wants to talk wit you abou *a* watch e got."

"I did not reply to any such message," Herbert shrugged his shoulders in a nonchalant way. His outward appearance was that of mild interest although his heart rate indicated otherwise. He focused inwards knowing well how a watchmaker always needs to be in control. His heart rate began to subside.

"Lisen, we know… dat you only use *a* automatic system to reply from your machine, bu I tell you righ now… de mon from Canada is on is way ere." The man lifted his hands from the counter top. He extended his left hand out to reveal his wristwatch, and then bent his arm back towards his body to view it. "11:35, e is on de subway now, ETA … 15 minutes." His hands went back down to the counter top.

Herbert had easily identified the man's wristwatch: *Casio G-Shock, an excellent choice for his line of work, I would say.* Allowing himself this brief distraction to try and stay calm, was not really having the desired effect.

"What is it that you are asking me to do?"

The man leaned over the counter. As he did so, he grabbed the left side of his opened coat at the zipper and opened it slowly. Herbert clearly understood the intent of this gesture. A revolver was nestled under his arm in a snug-fitting shoulder holster.

"I tink *asking* is not de righ wor to say ere." He leaned back letting his coat close to its natural position. No one spoke for several moments.

"I understand." Herbert nodded and took a deep breath.

"As I say before ... we ave been tol *not* to leave ere witout de watch."

"What is it you want me to do?"

"De mon's name is Edward James: tall, skinny guy. E's wearing jeans, sof shoes, an *a* black jacket. E carrys *a* small grey colour backpack. Look like late 40s, early 50s, but e's really 60 years ol, I never met im, but is profile say e's *a* exercise type guy."

Herbert remained silent and perfectly still, *a profile? They have a profile on this man?* His thoughts accelerated. He was confused. This sudden turn of events was completely unexpected.

"Lisen ol mon ... diss simple; do as you'ere tol. No one gets urt." The man reached into his pocket and pulled out a roll of bills. "My boss ... e is very generous when e gets wha e wans." He paused and raked his thumb through the bills showing off 50 and 100-dollar denominations, flaunting thousands of dollars before Herbert. "An ear me, e *always* gets wha e wans!"

He smiled briefly, the whiteness of his teeth stood out against the dark complexion of his skin. The correctness of his teeth caught Herbert's attention. *Even length, perfectly squared, no gaps, and no overlap ... the perfect set of teeth.* He hoped this moment of distraction, with some analytical thinking, would help to clear his mind. He remained silent.

"Okay, ere's ow it go down ..." the man stuffed the roll of bills back into his pocket. "I stay ere in de shop," he glanced over Herbert's shoulder, "right dere, in dat room behin you. I'll be jus aroun an behin dat archway lis'enin' to everyting dat's said. My friends ..." he nodded towards the door, "dey be jus across de stree in our automobile."

He rotated his head and pointed to a black Bluetooth device that hung around his left ear, "We ave good communication. Nobody leave from de back, nobody leave from de fron." He stood a little straighter, pushed his chest out a bit further, and walked around the counter and stood just inches from Herbert, looking down and directly at him. "*You*," he made a gun configuration with his right hand and jabbed his index finger hard into Herbert's left breast. Herbert winced. This would leave a dark bruise on his body. "All you ave to do is make sure de watch stays ere. Can you do dat ol' mon?" Herbert nodded but stayed quiet.

"You get nice bi of some money. Maybe spli wit Edward dude. We take de watch an leave, end of diss story." Another smile.

Herbert spoke softly. "I am feeling a chill, I need to take my medication." The mirrored sunglasses shifted to look down at the watch on his wrist again.

"You be'an sick or someting?"

"I have diabetes. My sugar count could be off, and I have a heart condition."

"Okay, bu make it quick, 5-10 minutes only. I don' wan you aving a stroke r someting." The man looked towards his colleagues and tapped against his earpiece, signalling them to leave and take their positions outside.

As the door closed behind them, Herbert turned and started back through the archway into the workshop. "My medication is in the locker at the far end of the room."

"M*a*ke diss fas!" There was impatience in the man's voice. "Remember ol mon, I'll b*e* righ e*re* watch'en an lis'nen." He positioned himself just around the backside of the archway, and leaned against the wall, not taking his eyes off the watchmaker.

Herbert made his way to the far end of the room and opened the locker door. His body was now partially shielded from the sight of the man. As he inspected the inner contents of the locker, he took a deep breath to calm himself, and glanced down at his hands. They were rock steady. *I am a watchmaker; I have control.*

The first thing he did was put on his three-quarter length, white lab coat and buttoned it up. He surveyed the top shelf of the locker. Therein was a vast assortment of drugs and medical supplies. He reached in and extracted two hermetically sealed hypodermic needles and removed them from their packaging. Grasping a 20ml vial of medication, he quickly filled both syringes to maximum capacity. Snapping the plastic protectors back in place, he inserted both needles in his right-side lab coat pocket. Herbert reached up to the far back top corner of the locker and produced a single small key.

Stepping back, he had just started to close the door, but stopped. Again, he focused on the top shelf. His eyes settled on a big plastic bottle marked 'multivitamins.' Swiftly unscrewing the lid, he procured one tablet and held it in his other hand. Now he moved back and closed the locker door. He turned and looked towards the archway. The mirrored sunglasses fixated on him. Herbert walked to the centre of the room and his workbench. There was a half-consumed bottle of water sitting beside where he had been working earlier. He nodded towards the man, unscrewed the top of the bottle and conspicuously consumed the tablet, followed by a long drink of water.

"I would like to return these disassembled watch parts back into their storage cabinet. If they remain out, dust will settle on them. I will then be required to redo a complete cleaning process on them again." Herbert gestured towards the scattered watch components.

The man shrugged his shoulders. "Wha do I ca*r*e? Bu ... if Edwa*r*d J*a*mes show up, you stop wha you*'r*e doin. Gau it?"

Herbert did not respond but went over to a tall wooden cabinet that was fixed to the wall. Taking the key that was still in his hand, he inserted it into a keyhole and opened the double style doors. The cabinet housed many shelves and sliding drawers. The largest shelf was near the bottom. From there he selected a moderate sized rectangular Tupperware-styled partitioned parts container with a snap lid. He held it in his right hand while he inserted the same key into another small locked drawer. He slid the drawer open and groped around inside it with his left hand. Suddenly Herbert felt a persistent tingling in his nasal passages. Taking a deep breath, he let his head roll back, and erupted with a loud sneeze. The parts container jerked upwards, though still clutched tightly in his grasp. His left hand fell forcefully down to his side. Herbert stepped back giving his head a good side-to-side shake as he reached under his lab coat to retrieve his handkerchief. Stepping forwards he closed the drawer and proceeded back to the workbench. He set the container down, raised his handkerchief to his nose and blew loudly.

"Hey ol mon, I n*ee*d you to ang in de*r*e. An *don* use dat handke*r*chief ag*a*in. Mon, ow d*e*sgustun!"

Herbert stared at him for a moment. The mirrored sunglasses stayed on.

TEN

Thought by many to be the financial and cultural capital of the world, New York City was alive and busy on this mid-week morning. It was thrilling for Edward to be in Brooklyn.

"I'm here on business," Edward said to a woman who had stood beside him as he purchased his pass for the air train at JFK Airport. The connotation of that statement gave him a sense of pride. He knew he was not here on business and his choice of clothing would attest to it: blue jeans, a short sleeve polo—a birthday gift Carmen sent him from Tel Aviv—a windbreaker, walking shoes and a backpack. But with a little imagination, he could see himself as a successful figure within the borders of this great city.

Edward ascended the stairs from the subway terminal to street level in Brooklyn, New York. With a spring in his step, he felt excited. The trip had gone well, with him needing to ask for directions only once, at the airport, concerning time schedules of the air train. Preliminary studies of his intended route paid off.

As he arrived at street level, he reached into his pocket for his cell phone to access the GPS function. He would need to walk approximately four blocks to arrive at the watch shop. Extending his left arm to reveal his watch, he glanced downwards: 11:45 a.m.

I should be there by noon. Edward now checked the GPS to confirm his position on Manhattan Avenue. Scheduling was on target, but he remained a bit apprehensive. His message to the watchmaker had been answered by an automated service, which only confirmed that Herbert would be there all week, during regular business hours. Adequate, but not overly reassuring. Edward thought it strange that a store owner did not speak on the phone. Perhaps he was too busy for interruptions, although *still*, it seemed to heighten the sense of mystery surrounding this pocket watch.

Edward walked along briskly. Even though he had been up since 2:00 a.m., his body felt good. A full breakfast at the airport, along with several coffees, gave him the energy needed. He was travelling light on this trip, with only a few essentials stored in his small nylon backpack which would see him through a couple of days. He packed an extra shirt, underwear, socks, and a toiletry bag, nothing fancy.

For the first time ever, and because of Carmen's insistence, Edward did a virtual tour of the street he was walking on, courtesy of Google Earth. *Wow, how cool is this? I feel as though I've been here!* He and Carmen Skyped on Monday afternoon, and she wanted to know everything about the watch. She hardly believed no information could be found on the Internet. In Carmen's world, everything that is anything can be found on the Internet; you just need to know how to search. Edward smiled; to say that Carmen was a little excited about this watch mystery would truly be an understatement. She made him promise to text her as soon as he finished his meeting with the watchmaker. Already a text message had been sent to both her and Marie confirming his safe arrival.

Marie appeared to be getting a bit enthusiastic as well, or perhaps it was more her worrying about Edward's safety. *Hard to say.* Either way, she signed up for the hour-by-hour live updates from 'The Big Apple.' *Investigative reporter Edward James on the scene …*

He was getting close. He knew he was looking for a single story, small rectangular brick structure on Nassau Avenue, set in amongst mostly two-story buildings. The building would be ahead on his right.

He spotted it, up ahead about half a block. Quickening his pace, his heart rate began to increase and not completely because of the exercise. *I sure hope he isn't gone to lunch or something ...* Edward nervously checked his watch again: 11:56 a.m. Clearly recognizing the building, it appeared ordinary; a small place, with only one front display window protected by a sliding iron-barred partition. The top third of the single steel front door consisted of similar iron-barred, protected glass. It had a flat roof, with several built-up skylights installed.

As Edward came up to the front of the shop, he tried to look inside the front window. A partially closed set of horizontal blinds obscured any possible view into the interior. Centered between the blind and the glass hung a single signboard approximately 1 foot by 3 feet in size, black with white letters which read: '*Watch Shop*'. *Hmm, not much into advertising.*

Edward stood in front of the entrance door. The top glass portion was covered by a 'store hours' sign and it read: *Monday to Saturday 9:00 a.m. - 6:00 p.m.; Sunday - closed.*

Taking a deep breath, he checked his left side pocket. The watch was securely in place. Edward turned the doorknob. With a slight push, he opened the door.

ELEVEN

Sometimes first impressions of a person stand out and stay with us for the rest of our lives. The reasons causing this phenomenon to happen might be many: perhaps the series of events leading up to the encounter were significant or the ambiance surrounding an individual was unusual. Could be our own imagination, fueled by desire, or a restless anticipation to know what will be forthcoming has framed this outcome. But always there needs to be something special, consciously or subconsciously; somehow, we are moved.

"I am Herbert Osterhagen." A German accent was apparent but word pronunciation and sound structure were precise. Edward leaned forward over the front counter to receive a firm handshake. Considering the older man's eyes, he was drawn into a faint sapphire sparkle and somewhere deep inside him, he felt something more.

"I'm Edward James. I've arrived from Ontario, Canada." They released their handshake. "I hope you received my message?"

Herbert did not answer. He turned and stepped back to the desk he was sitting at when Edward entered and to where an open laptop computer sat on top. He began striking various keys, intently focused. "You have brought in a watch for repair?" The typing ceased. He closed the lid, turning back toward the counter.

Slight confusion was Edward's reaction to the abrupt reply. "Well, I don't know ... I was hoping to gain some information on a peculiar watch I've come to possess. You were recommended to me by Colin Nash of the Nash Jewellery Store in London, Ontario."

A soft smile formed on the watchmaker's face. "When I met young Colin, I believe he was only this tall." He held his hand out to indicate an approximate height of a 4-year-old. "A fine, handsome young lad, as I recall. I had several friendly meetings with his father over the years—a good man. You then traveled from London, Ontario?"

"No, I'm from the small town of Petrolia. It's about a one-hour drive from London. You might have heard of the name?"

"The small town with the big history." Herbert gestured for Edward to sit down on the stool next to him at the counter.

He took a seat as well. "We live in a global economy that is based on oil, and as I understand, it this owes much of its origin to Petrolia. I believe some important history can be learned from that small town." Herbert smiled, "The surest way forward is to remind ourselves of what we have already learned."

Edward nodded and returned the smile. "There seems to be an underlying sense of pride within the community. I know history plays an important part in that."

"So, might the history of Petrolia be a factor in your acquisition of this so-called 'peculiar watch' that you wish to have identified?" Herbert questioned.

"Well, possibly ..." Edward reached into his pocket to retrieve the watch. "You see, I found it at a home garage sale. I was told it had been used as a prop for the local theatre where a fire broke out, and consequently the device ended up in a box filled with many other props that were salvaged. The owner of this assortment of items passed away, and two young teenagers were hired to help sell off items of the estate. I was just joking around and rummaging through the box. I kind of latched on to it. But after looking a bit more closely, I detected what I thought to be quality craftsmanship." Edward handed the watch over the counter to Herbert.

As he accepted the watch and brought it close to where he could focus, Herbert executed a sudden sharp intake of breath as he opened the cover. There was no mistaking it. *A surprise reaction?* Edward thought so, but immediately Herbert turned his head away and began a series of loud coughs.

"I am sorry. I am afraid I have caught a chill today."

Now Edward was not so sure. "Are you okay?"

"Yes, I will be fine. I may need to take some medication, though. I have it with me if needed." Herbert went back to studying the watch in silence. Edward took a moment to observe the older man. Overall, he appeared to be in good health, with an average height, slim build, and he still retained a full head of white hair. But what Edward found most exceptional was the almost intense sense of calm that seemed to radiate from him. As he slowly rotated the pocket watch gently in his hand and examined it, Edward realized he wore no glasses. Clearing his throat, Edward broke the silence.

"With the assistance of my reading glasses or a magnifier, I find it most strange that the screw heads that are affixing the dial were soldered over, and I think the technique used indicates a heat range of over 1,000 degrees Fahrenheit, as evidenced by the slight bluing of the surrounding metal." This caused an immediate reaction from Herbert. He looked up and raised an eyebrow.

"You know about soldering techniques?"

"Yes ... well a bit. I'm retired now, but my trade was welding, and throughout the course of my career, soldering applications were required of me."

"I see." Herbert's attention was unwavering. The old man gazed at Edward. Apparently, he was pondering something. He broke his thoughtful silence, "Indeed, our chosen professions have their similarities."

"I would've liked to disassemble this watch, but I thought it better to get some professional advice." Edward unzipped his jacket most of the way and then reached down to disconnect the waist strap of his backpack to facilitate its removal.

"No need to take off your pack. We will not be too long here." Edward stopped. He was a bit disappointed. "You did well to leave this timepiece untouched. I can most certainly help you in your quest for information." Herbert returned to his inspection of the watch.

"Thank you." The positive statement gave Edward some mild optimism. "Would you wish to look at the inside of this watch to help in your assessment?"

"I might possibly, but first I want to show you something." Herbert closed the cover but retained the watch in his left hand. He rose from the stool and walked over to the desk. He switched on the laptop. His left hand was now obscured from Edward's vision, concealed behind the open cover. The program took several moments to load. Herbert leaned in towards the laptop while simultaneously tapping several keys. He appeared satisfied, then straightened up and lifted the computer from the desk. It looked as though he reached reach down with his left hand to his coat pocket, although the view was again obstructed.

Turning, with the computer grasped in his right hand and the watch in his left, the watchmaker made his way back to the display counter. "Your watch." Which he offered to Edward, who accepted it, then held the timepiece out away from his body to help aid in his ability to focus. He opened the cover. *It's okay; just want to be sure …*

Herbert was watching him, the opened laptop had been set down, and the screen rotated in his direction. Edward set the watch on the counter top, and then stared at the screen. Unmistakably, he could see a large image of the pocket watch. It showed a close-up with the cover in the open position. He looked up to meet Herbert's gaze, which had never left him.

"Are you familiar with the 'zoom in' feature located on the top toolbar?" Herbert asked.

Edward's eyes returned to the screen. "Yes? But how …"

"There is an engraved inscription on the inside cover." Herbert interrupted. "It is done in a circular pattern on the outermost edge. You will need to enlarge the image until the font becomes legible."

Edward hesitated, looking at his pocket watch that lay open on the counter top. "But there's no inscription on my watch."

He gave Herbert a questioning look. "But …" A subtle raised hand by Herbert curtailed his objection. Edward resumed his scrutiny of the screen. He found the cursor and began to magnify the image. Another glance back to Herbert. No change: calm, intense. Back to the screen, the inscription came into focus. What Edward saw startled him. He inhaled sharply and held his breath, rereading again. The circular inscription etched itself permanently into his brain. It read:

> *This is a warning. You are being watched and are in danger. Stay calm. Listen very carefully to what I say. When I sneeze, make your escape.*

Edward could feel his breath releasing. A strange feeling enveloped him. He felt as if he had been transported into a dream, a dream where his own reality was in question. He needed some form of reassurance. Without it, a state of denial or perhaps a mild state of shock could be forthcoming. Never in his entire existence had he been confronted with this kind of threat, but somewhere deep inside Edward knew that his own response would be critical. The reassurance came in the form of a steady, unfaltering voice, and it sounded of complete confidence and focus.

"You may exit the page now." Edward did as requested. He closed the laptop, stared at Herbert and waited.

"The pocket watch in your possession has significance. Tell me, Edward, what is your interest in watches?"

Herbert's voice called Edward's attention back. His breathing stabilized. He paused, his voice needed to be steady. "A general interest; a hobby, I suppose." Edward really enjoyed discussing watches. Over the past several years he had attained much information on horology from books, magazines, and the Internet. It was a topic he was comfortable discussing, and comfort in any form would be welcome now.

"Several years ago, I started to save money for a mechanical watch to commemorate my recent retirement. I found out I had a keen interest in horology. I formed respect and admiration for the watchmaker and his trade." Neither broke eye contact. Edward was hoping for a response from Herbert. None came, as he seemed to be lost in thought.

"You acquired your watch?" Edward drew a blank. He glanced towards the pocket watch on the table, momentarily confused. "Your watch, for retirement?" Herbert smiled.

"Oh ... of course." Edward returned the smile sheepishly. He pulled up his sleeve to reveal his wristwatch, tilting his wrist to give Herbert a better view.

"Ah yes ... a Rolex reference No. 216570, caliber No. 3187. Excellent, an intelligent choice: an exclusive design, having expert craftsmanship and a robust movement. Knowing its integrity, this timepiece can bring you great feelings of achievement and success, when worn with respect. This most definitely is a watch to be proud of, Edward."

Edward was impressed, somewhat humbled and still afraid. Not knowing what to say, he remained silent.

Herbert took in a deep breath. He clasped his hands together and began to speak: "Your pocket watch was created during the reign of a great queen. There was a great watch that was created for this queen. These two watches were destined to cross paths. The great queen suffered an untimely death. The great watch remained. Many years passed. The queen lost her throne. The watches have not crossed paths, but their ultimate destiny remains the same. They can only meet in one place: the place where the queen has regained her throne. It is to that place where you must go, Edward, as you possess the other watch."

Herbert leaned back on his stool. He tipped his head back. Quickly reaching into his trousers' pocket, he grasped his handkerchief and brought it to his face, and erupted in a loud sneeze!

TWELVE

Edward reached over and picked up the pocket watch, snapped its cover closed, and stuffed it into the pocket of his jeans. Feeling his heart rate starting to increase and taking a deep breath, he looked to Herbert: calm, intense, the ever so slight sparkle in his blue eyes. Neither spoke. Time seemed to slow. They sat in silence. Seconds passed. Edward let out a deep breath. Herbert nodded and formed a word with his lips. Without question, the word was *go*.

Edward reached down, found the zipper tag to his windbreaker and pulled it up. He then cinched the waist strap tighter on his backpack and quickly rose from his stool, which slid behind him across the tile floor, making a loud scraping sound. Just as he started turning towards the front entrance door, an immense figure of a man rushed out from behind the archway bordering the room beyond! Edward allowed himself only a glimpse in that fraction of a second. He acknowledged a tall, dark-complexioned man wearing a leather jacket and mirrored sunglasses.

The man yelled, "E's making a run for de fron entrance. Chase im downn!"

This was it: 'the drop of the flag', 'the lift of the gate', 'the starter's gunshot'. The adrenaline surging, no turning back now! The inscription on the watchcase flashed across Edward's mind: *you are in danger.* He went full out. His last second of rational thought registered the sound of a heavy Caribbean accent.

He was now in survival mode with the front metal door half open when he felt the grasp of a powerful hand taking hold of his jacket. Yanking his arm away, Edward started to spin his whole body around through the doorway. Just as he passed through, his sleeve ripped, freeing his arm. Grasping the outer doorknob with his now freed hand, and using every bit of weight he had combined with the momentum of his spinning body, he forced the heavy metal door closed. The man could see it coming. He started to pull back his hand, but a fraction of a second too slow. A sound came, a sound Edward had never experienced before but he understood. Bones were breaking. A painful yell from the building's interior reached his ears. Glancing down, he saw the sickening sight of four long fingers, bent at an impossible angle, protruding from between the steel edge of the door and the doorframe.

There came another sound, loud shouting, and a car door slamming from across the street, just to the west. Edward turned to see two other men: tall, dark and robust, running straight for him!

Once again, a strong Caribbean accent assaulted his ears. "We gau *a* ma*r*k on im! We'll run im downn! You t*a*ke ca*r*e of de ol mon!"

Edward now found himself in an extraordinary situation, a situation that enabled him to experience a rare occurrence of human brain function. Under times of high stress, the velocity of synaptic connections can accelerate to the point at which perception appears to progress in slow motion. Such was the case now, and in less than one second, Edward had observed and assessed his assailants.

Sixty years of stored memory calculated the probability of escape. His odds did not appear too good. However, one thing stood out: *dress shoes.* Two strong, young men, well dressed in leather coats and wool pants, on any given day should easily be able to outrun him, but they both wore leather-soled dress shoes.

Edward's foot-wear: rubber-soled walkers. *Big difference, still a long shot, but game on!*

Edward sprinted east on Nassau Avenue. His peripheral vision showed a 30-metre head start. Immediately he neared his 'red zone.' In another 15 seconds, he would need to slow down or risk a complete cardiovascular shutdown. Storefronts and pedestrians became nothing but a blur. Dodging to and fro, the startled yelps and cries of people on the street rang in his ears. He glanced off arms and shoulders. Contact with a dog on a leash almost caused him to fall. The scream of the dog's owner added to the commotion in his ears. A car horn sounded, and another, but something else too: the loud sound of running footsteps. There came more screaming and yelling, and yet again another sound. He almost panicked. Laboured breathing that was not his own matched the running footsteps behind him!

Do something. Do something now!

Edward was running opposite the flow of traffic in the lane closest to him. His brain started to time the gaps between cars. He waited and counted. The breathing sounded much louder now. The heavy footsteps seemed deafening.

Wait... wait... now! He veered suddenly to the right, directly into the oncoming traffic and sounds became chaotic: screeching tires, the blasting of horns, screaming and yelling, but he got it right. With just enough space for one, it was so close, almost disaster. He had consciously darted in front of a taxicab. *These guys can drive a car.*

He hit the sidewalk on the opposite side of the street running and took his first glance back: one man down, the other helping him to his feet. The traffic had stopped dead. Soon though, they were both up and back into the chase.

Edward turned back again; 100 metres was his gain. He scanned his options ahead and spotted an entrance to what appeared to be a park. The storefronts were thinning out now, which made the park probably his best option. He needed to slow his pace, breathing was becoming difficult, and his heart rate was way too fast.

Turning into the park entrance, Edward glanced back again …75 metres. They were gaining. Running on a paved path heading towards the center of the park, his vision was of a mostly flat landscape of trees and shrubs with a small playground in the distance. Picnic tables and benches were located off the main pathways. The situation did not look good. Maybe it had been a mistake to seek refuge here without people around, and soon his body would start to fail him. He took another glance back: 50 metres and closing. They had entered the park. Edward needed something; he had been hoping for rough, dense terrain. Anything: scanning ahead, the park boundary looked to be about 1 km away. Into the distance, he searched and ran on.

Something bright orange caught his eye. Edward thought maybe orange construction fence. *Construction? How big? How much?* He knew construction sites and how they worked. His pursuers probably did not. A surge of adrenaline ran through him. He quickened his pace. Edward felt a glimmer of hope.

He was within 100 metres of the partially coloured orange fence when an arm and bucket of an excavator came into view. This would indicate a substantial volume of digging was underway. The site would be of a moderate size with possibly much more equipment, depending on the job. At 50 metres from the site, he could make out the unmistakable outline of a hydro lift, a heavy truck with a telescopic crane arm mounted on its frame. This looked familiar to Edward. There was a roadway bordering the northeast corner of the park, which was closed off for the work. It was beginning to appear more like an under-road piping replacement project. The type would either be sewer, water or gas.

He needed the answer and would need to process this information lightning quick. His eyes darted back and forth scanning, searching. He could see through the holes in the fence now.

Information. I need to know now! Looking back again almost caused him to panic. *Only 20 metres! My time is up!*

When he turned back towards the fence, he got his answer. A yellow covered pipe, approximately 25-30 metres in length lay on wooden skids parallel to the side of what would be a 2- to 4-metre deep trench. The pipe was covered with a protective plastic coating and looked to be 16-18 inches in diameter. *It's a gas line.* Edward processed the information in mere seconds. He noted thick plastic insulators, bolted and spaced evenly throughout its length. It had been prepped to be installed inside of another larger pipe that was in place under the road to act as a protective tunnel for the high-pressure gas line. Edward understood; he was looking at a road crossing, a gas piping replacement project and now it was lunchtime and the area looked abandoned.

The site was coming up fast. Edward knew what to do and where he was: home turf. The next thing he recognized confirmed it. Parked beside the pipe on the embankment was a welding rig—a one-ton pickup truck with dual wheels on the rear and a welding machine along with other tools of the trade mounted on its bed. That's where he headed, hoping to find something. Edward had always made sure he had one on his own truck when working off a welding rig, for many years. The item he was looking for had become one of his most useful tools.

But right now, he had to focus on the fence. This type of construction barrier fencing was of a standard design: a little over 2 metres high, with a steel tubing frame and integrated heavy wire mesh between the upright posts. An additional plastic webbing band about 4 feet in width and bright orange in colour was fastened to the steel mesh for greater visibility. Used primarily for semi-permanent applications, support for this type of fence is achieved by the installation of sand-filled blocks or welded flat bar, which are anchored to the bottom of the upright posts. This design provides adequate support for its purpose. However, Edward had learned when a force is applied to the barrier the base can be made to rock a bit, which causes a spring-like bending or flexing to occur.

Many years ago, Edward and a couple of his work buddies had practiced perfecting the art of scaling these temporary fences. After a few scraped shins and bruised egos, they made a discovery. If you ran full out towards the barrier at about a 45-degree angle and sprang upwards much like a high jumper would, then at the last moment as you made contact mid-span with your shoulder, and allowing a full body rotation, the fence would flex way down, and spring back. Surprisingly, it would deliver you upright on the other side, hardly missing a stride in your run. Edward remembered: *full commitment is key.*

The sound of chasing footsteps assaulted his ears just as he hit the fence! He might have over-committed, but it worked. His body over-rotating slightly on the landing caused him to fall forward, but the ground was soft, and he rolled, making a quick recovery to his feet. He did not even look back towards the yelling of the chasing men. They were held up at the fence.

Edward's eyes never stopped searching. He had to circumnavigate the trench to get to the welding rig. A quick glance affirmed his assumption that the casing pipe under the road was empty and he assessed the dimensions to be 24-28 inches in diameter. *The perfect size.* The backpack would have to come off.

His eyes scanned, searching the back of the welding rig. Did this guy have one? Many did, at least in Canada. How did young boys lose their old worn out skateboards to their welder dads? Often high-pressure pipeline welders must enter long lengths of larger diameter pipe for internal inspection or repair, and having their balanced body face down on a skateboard would allow the welder to traverse the inside of the pipe almost effortlessly. Using his hands and toes for steering and propulsion, he would soon become quite adept at this mode of transport. It had been awhile, but Edward was practised enough to be good at it.

At the rig now, he came to a stop and took his eyes off the truck for a second. He was breathing hard, his lungs felt scorched. His body needed rest. Glancing only for a moment back across the trench confirmed what he already believed. They made it over the fence and were running around the end portion of the ditch. 25 seconds, no more!

Edward became almost frantic. He saw the usual stuff: oxy-acetylene torch, propane tank with tiger torch, grinders, welding rod pail, mud boards and knee pads. *Is there one? Please! Please! Only 15 seconds!* He grabbed at a mud board leaning against the cab and flung it away. A wheel was sticking out from beneath another smaller board. *Yes!* Edward grabbed the wheel and pulled hard, freeing the device from the wood. It was a worn, somewhat burned up old skateboard with four old steel wheels. *The best kind, thank God!*

As his body twisted away from the truck bed towards the trench, something else caught Edward's eye. His brain and body were racing so fast it became an almost automatic reflex. He ceased his body rotation only long enough to grab the wire handle of an orange coloured gallon paint can. In one quick motion, the paint can was transferred to his right hand which held the skateboard as his left hand found and released the plastic holding clip on his backpack. He had one shoulder strap off as he flung his body down the embankment and skidded on his butt and the soles of his shoes down a steep 3-metre drop. Landing hard on his feet at the bottom, the backpack was already hanging on his right arm.

With 10 metres to the open casing, Edward ran hard and managed to transfer the skateboard to his left hand. In his right hand, he now clutched the backpack and the paint can. As he skidded to a stop at the opening, he heard a loud thud. The men had landed hard at the bottom of the trench with a lot of swearing. He did not even look. Positioning his body perpendicular to the pipe opening, Edward brought his right hand back as far as possible. With force, he flung the backpack and the paint can into the opening. No sooner had the throw been completed, was Edward assaulted by the sound again—like screaming in his ears! Running footsteps: close, so close. Stepping back two steps he slammed the skateboard to his chest, and lunged his body forward into the pipe opening. *Keep your shins up!*

A good analogy might be diving into a black hole. This would not be the best place to be if you suffer from claustrophobia—a restricted space. You need to stay relaxed. Echoing sounds can seem quite strange, almost eerie. Any sound coming from either end of the pipe gets amplified and reverberates in your ears. It is entirely dark. You cannot see your hands right in front of your face. There is no looking back, not even sideways. Cold, dark, impenetrable curved steel encases you. Your own breathing becomes louder than maybe ever before. In this type of environment, the senses of the human body become heightened. Both blood pressure and heart rate increase. The air you breathe smells different. Hyperventilation is possible. There can be a very real sense of isolation. For most humans, an environment of this type will initiate an innate, primordial fear. And that fear can lead to panic.

But for Edward James, gliding through a 30-metre stretch of 28-inch high-pressure piping on a skateboard gave him an almost tranquil feeling, as a result of knowledge, understanding and years of experience. He heard the commotion behind him, the cursing and groaning. Their voices and rigid body movements echoed loudly through the encasement, enveloping Edward. The men had entered the pipe and it would be a close fit. They would be slithering slowly forward on their knees, toes, and torsos. For them, this would be a slow, agonising end to the chase.

Edward's body received a much-needed rest. He even had to remind himself where he was, and what he was doing. How truly bizarre, he thought. His mind wanted to take him back to the years of welding pipeline. However, he had been flung into the middle of a spectacular 'Bond' movie. He almost did not want to leave his feeling of security inside this pipe.

Catching up to his backpack first and slowing to a stop, he took some time to flatten and stuff it between the front of his chest and the skateboard. He continued forward and came to the paint can about 20 seconds later. With no need to stop, he simply straightened the can and extended the handle out allowing it to roll along, only nudging it occasionally to keep the forward motion. He thought about the contents of the can; it was about three-quarters full of a substance called Polyken Primer, a tar-like paint reduced with methyl-hydrates to a consistency thinner than water. Its purpose was to seal off the pores of steel pipe before the application of a special plastic tape. It worked well to control corrosion on underground piping. But that is not even close to what Edward had in mind for it for now. With its black colour, strong odor and excellent ability to penetrate, Polyken Primer was very messy. Stains on clothing did not come out and direct contact with exposed skin might literally take weeks of scrubbing to remove. And soon, these guys, who Edward assumed by their sounds were far enough in not to go back, would find out all too well of its staining properties.

He almost felt sorry for them. *Well not really.* All too soon he came to the opening at the end of the casing. Rolling the can out, he then tossed his pack out. Slowing right down almost to a stop, he allowed his head and shoulders to exit the pipe. There was a drop of over a metre to the ground, but it would not be a problem. By re-positioning the skateboard to his stomach and groin area and nudging his body forward, and carefully grabbing the edge of the pipe below him—much like a gymnast would hold a parallel bar—a slight push propelled him forward, causing his body to pivot on the board. With one graceful somersault, he was out standing firmly in a squat position.

I guess I've still got it.

Okay, enough of the accolades, one more thing to do here. He listened intently. The men had to be about one-third of the way through, with no more cussing or yelling now, only heavy breathing. They would know they had now passed the point of no return. Fear would start to creep in and unsettle them.

Edward walked over and picked up the can of paint. He reached into his pocket and took hold of a quarter. Walking back to the pipe entrance he set the can down just inside the pipe end and using the 25-cent piece he pried open the lid and tossed it away. The coin went back into his pocket. Again, positioning his body perpendicular to the opening of the pipe end, he grasped the handle with his right hand; his left hand cupped the forward-tilting can. Allowing both arms to retract together, he dug in his feet to strengthen his stance, then flung the can forwards, but quickly ceased its motion abruptly. This caused the full contents of the can to gush out in a long stream of about 8 metres in length. Edward let the can fall back in a deliberate arc away from his body, not wanting one drop of this messy liquid to fall on him. Standing back, he tossed the empty can away, and walked a couple of paces to retrieve his backpack. The skateboard he left beneath the pipe opening where it would be sure to be recovered.

Turning, he looked towards the pipe one last time. The last 8 metres at the bottom of the casing was now covered in wet paint. The fumes would soon permeate the entire length of the pipe. These fumes were not overly toxic, but they would strongly enhance the reality of fear.

Edward spoke softly towards the pipe opening. It might have been possible for his pursuers to hear what he said, but doubtful. "Best of luck guys, this is well deserved I'm sure."

With that, he took off, climbing up the bank of the trench to the deserted street above. As he did so, he made a thoughtful gesture to the universe; in his mind, Edward opened the green book, and recited a familiar affirmation to himself; *I am the strength and the courage to move forward steadily through any condition, whatever it may be.* He closed the book.

His thoughts turned to leather dress shoes, completely ruined leather dress shoes to be exact.

THIRTEEN

Edward passed through a tree-lined residential area of Brooklyn, heading back in an easterly direction on a street that ran parallel to Nassau Avenue, one block south. He continued to run but at a much slower pace. He was determined to get back to Manhattan Avenue. This was the first chance in the recent turn of events where there would be time to think and take stock of his situation. It was not like Edward knew what he was doing, but he did understand he needed a plan.

Luck played a significant role in his escape. Luck: a simple, casual, everyday term we like to use repeatedly. Yet this simple word can have enormous consequences during our lives. Is luck a result of effort and determination? At what point does luck pass into the lofty regions of divine intervention? Edward enjoyed pondering questions like these, and right now he would only admit to feeling intensely alive and very lucky indeed.

He was trying hard to make sense of what transpired. The most important question: who are these people and why was his pocket watch so important to them? First the rather unusual meeting at Coffee Lodge and now this. Herbert the watchmaker—he recognized the watch, although he was not transparent or open about it at all. Why? Was he in danger too?

It was apparent to Edward that Herbert knew he was coming. He typed the message of warning on the computer image of the watch. The men had arrived at the shop before him and were waiting. How did they *know* he would be coming to visit Herbert the watchmaker on this Wednesday morning? He did not tell anyone, other than those close to him. Edward tried to think back. Yes, he mentioned to Aaron at their meeting at Coffee Lodge that he had been advised by the proprietor of the London jewellery store to seek out a watchmaker in New York. That was it—no other details. So how did they know? Did Herbert tell them? That would be unlikely. No, the more he thought about it, the more Edward thought Herbert tried to help him escape, and if this was the case, would he not have been in danger as well?

So, what's the plan?

Deeply breathing in the fresh air was not enough to clear his senses. Nothing seemed clear right now, other than he needed to stay well away from any of the men who chased him or their associates. He did not want to be recognized. His jacket had been torn, and his clothes were dirty, so the best course of action now would be to change his outward appearance. He was heading back to Manhattan Avenue where he could at least change his clothing in one of the many small stores located on the street.

Edward slowed his pace to a quick walk and then reached into his pants pocket for his cell phone. Turning it on—with the GPS function still active—he located his position. Manhattan Avenue was two blocks ahead. He would then turn right and see what he could find in stores. Turning off the phone, and stuffing it back into his pocket, he resumed running.

Edward had one pressing thought that would not leave him. *Is Herbert okay? I need to try and help him ... but how?*

He could not go back to the shop. Well possibly he could, with the police. What could he say to them that might prompt them to go and check on Herbert? *I need some advice.*

Edward ran on, thinking as he went. *Of course, Derek ... a call to Derek!* He would know what to do, and he desperately needed someone to talk to.

He looked towards the busy intersection of Manhattan Avenue, with pedestrians and traffic. It would be best not to run now and bring about unwanted attention. Yes, Derek would tell him what he should do.

———◆———

Edward walked out of a sporting goods store onto the street with a new look. He started heading east towards the intersection of Nassau Avenue. A bit farther and he would come to the subway terminal entrance he exited approximately two hours earlier. Most noticeable of his new attire was the Brooklyn Dodgers baseball cap. He chose a two-tone white with the blue peak with a blue 'B' embroidered on the front. *This'll make a great souvenir for my fun-filled, relaxing visit to Brooklyn, New York.* He also wore his red and white Oakley sunglasses. These were already in the backpack. His black nylon jacket, he tossed in a garbage can inside the store and replaced it with a similar style in red, thinking it would tie in the Oakleys. A new pair of black jeans completed the clothing transformation. Luckily the polo shirt from Carmen received no damage. And finally, he opted for a black nylon shoulder bag, in which he stashed his original jeans and the grey backpack.

He remembered a small restaurant, located a short distance away on Nassau Avenue, which he previously passed. Although he did not feel like eating, Edward realized that after the kind of activity he had been through his body needed calories and hydration, and an opportunity to relax a bit and call Derek.

As Edward crossed over the avenue and turned left to follow the street west, he extended his arm to glance at his watch: 2:15 p.m. Derek would be working now, but still available by cell phone.

The sign for the restaurant soon came into view, one block ahead on the right. The westbound traffic was getting noticeably backed up. *How do these people manage to cope with this kind of gridlock day after day?* Edward arrived at the restaurant. He gave it the 'once over.' The diner appeared good, with a standard glass front and some attractive flower arrangements displayed on the sides of the window: neat and tidy.

Edward just started to open the large glass front door when something caught his eye, flashing red and blue lights just barely discernible in the distant westerly direction. *Oh, that's why the traffic is backed up. An accident I guess.* Looking back to the entrance he opened the door fully and entered the building. The glass door started to close behind him when he froze. He stayed still for a moment, then turned back quickly, reopened the door, and stepped back onto the street. Edward stared to the west at the faint flashing lights. *Those lights ... they are maybe about one mile away. That has got to be close, real close!* He started into a brisk walk towards the flashing lights and what he hoped was *not* Herbert Osterhagen's watch shop.

Within a quarter mile of the flashing lights, he saw two police cars and an ambulance positioned directly in front of the watch shop. Edward's heart sank. Walking on the opposite side of the street, and getting closer he could see a small crowd of onlookers gathered on either side of the road, joining store owners who had stepped outside of their businesses to see what was happening. One police officer directed traffic, while another began partitioning off the front of the building with yellow caution tape. Another siren was heard and was getting louder. They were preparing to partially close off the street to vehicle traffic.

Edward stopped and stood within a small group of onlookers about fifty metres from the building. He could tell the situation was serious. The rear doors of the ambulance were open. The attendants would be inside. He waited and hoped. Edward could make out short conversations around him. Certain phrases stood out from the surrounding sounds and attracted his attention.

"Nice old man."

"Very private person."

"Excellent craftsman."

"The best rates too."

"I had trouble with my watch, that's until Herbert fixed it. Now it's great!"

"He serviced my mantle clock for free."

"He can be a bit odd at times."

"Sure hope he's gonna be okay, best damn watchmaker in New York City."

The voices continued, creating a character portrayal of the old man Edward had sat and talked with no more than two hours ago.

The door to the watch shop opened, and a police officer stood holding the door as a stretcher was wheeled out through the opening to the sidewalk towards the back of the ambulance. Edward heard the gasp of a woman who stood close to him. He focused more intently. Atop the stretcher lay a securely fastened, black bag enclosing the body. The zipper was closed. Edward watched as they loaded the stretcher into the back of the ambulance. The conversation around him ceased. Everyone stood in silence. It was all too clear to Edward:

Herbert Osterhagen, the watchmaker, is dead.

FOURTEEN

His hands trembled as he pressed the required digits from the numbers displayed on the touch screen of his cell phone. Edward returned to the small restaurant and was seated at a remote table located farthest from the entrance. He faced the door to see everyone entering the building. An untouched bowl of soup and a half-consumed glass of water lay before him on the table.

His call was answered on the fourth ring.

"Hey, Derek here." A surge of relief passed through him. Derek would be working now, and perhaps unable to answer his phone.

"Man, I'm so glad I got you."

"Edward, you sound a bit off. You okay?"

"You got a couple of minutes? There's been trouble here. I'm not sure what to do." Edward spoke in a nervous, hushed tone.

"Oh … well yeah, just give me five seconds. I need to finish this set-up on a system scan for a security install." Another worker's voice sounded in the background, as Derek discussed the procedure they were working on.

"Okay, I'm back. My co-worker can handle things for a bit." Edward heard Derek's footsteps, laboured breathing, and the closing of a vehicle door. "I'm in the work van alone now Edward. So, what's going on? Trouble?"

"Well, I'll give you a more complete, detailed description of what happened when we can sit down together, but for now I'll stick to what I think are the most important events. Trouble, *yes!* Let me start by telling you Herbert the watchmaker is dead. I think murdered. I witnessed his body, zipped up in a body bag, being loaded into the back of an ambulance."

"What? Holy shit! I don't think I want to ask you this, but are you going to tell me you and your pocket watch are in some way related to the death of this watchmaker?"

"I'm afraid so." Edward heard a sharp intake of breath on the other end of the line, followed by heavy respirations. *I'm probably not the only one shaking now. I've certainly got his full attention.*

"So … what …?"

"Let me start at the beginning." Edward paused, hopefully to let Derek settle a bit. "So, I arrive at the watch shop as scheduled and meet Herbert Osterhagen, the watchmaker. He does not admit to having received my phone message. Nevertheless, he's cordial, although quite brief and abrupt. When I show him the pocket watch he seems a bit startled, but he starts coughing, so now I'm not sure if he was genuinely startled or not. He then tells me my watch has significance and he'd like to show me something. The watchmaker sets an open laptop down in front of me and asks me to view it, making note that I'll need to zoom in to read an inscription set in fine print. On the screen is what appears to be my own pocket watch I came here to gain information on. He tells me to read the inscription located on the backside of the front cover. I do so, zooming in. As it comes into focus, I can't believe what is now before me on the screen." Edward stopped. He could no longer hear Derek's breathing. "You still with me?"

"Yes, yes! Go on. What did it say?"

"I won't soon forget. Word for word it said, 'This is a warning. You are being watched and are in danger. Stay calm. Listen very carefully to what I say. When I sneeze, make your escape.'"

"When I sneeze? Was he making a joke?" Derek sounded incredulous.

"No joke, believe me." Edward resumed. "We talked about watches for a bit. He wanted to know about my interest in them. He proceeded to tell me about the pocket watch, only it sounded more like a coded story, or a riddle of sorts. He spoke of my watch being made during a time of a great queen and how it is destined to cross paths with another watch ... A watch that was made for this great queen. The queen dies but her watch remains, and now my pocket watch is still destined to cross paths with the queen's watch, which apparently can only happen in one place. Finally, the last words spoken by Herbert to me were, 'It is to that place you must go, Edward, as you have the other watch.'"

"That's it? So, you don't know where the place is that he thinks you must go?"

"Nope. I guess he wanted me to figure it out. He said no more. He just sneezed!"

"Ah, back to the sneezing thing." Derek's voice sounded of the incredulous tone again. "Then what?"

"So, then my friend, all hell broke loose!"

"Can I heat that up for you?" Edward sat in silence staring off distantly. He had not been on the phone now for almost five minutes.

"Uh ... what? I'm sorry?"

"Your soup; you hardly touched it. I could refill and reheat it. Was everything all right?" A pleasant looking waitress smiled at Edward with a questioning look.

"Well yes, that'd be great. I'm afraid I've been distracted." He leaned back in his chair to allow the waitress access to the bowl. "The soup is excellent. Thank you." Edward returned the smile.

"No problem." In one quick motion, she retrieved the bowl and started off, striding gracefully through a pair of swinging doors into the restaurant kitchen.

Edward took a moment to admire her poise and friendliness: a cordial, ordinary, middle-aged woman. She appeared happy and content. She probably met and befriended a thousand people, working in a small restaurant in New York City. *Everyone has a story.*

Edward's own 'story' had taken a bizarre twist. The smiling waitress reminded him he too was—at least according to his own introspection—an average guy. The question arose: *Why me? What are the odds?* Was this just a bending of the law of averages, and stumbling into some crazy ongoing saga of a valuable old watch? Or could a supreme universal consciousness now be fulfilling a pre-ordained prophesy with the destiny of a 'significant pocket watch,' as Herbert the watchmaker alluded to?

How could Edward have the answer to these questions? Ultimately, he believed, it would come down to his own personal faith, which had always been to do his best.

The green book called to him again, as it always did in times of fear and uncertainty.

He looked up and saw the waitress returning to his table. Her smile, again a welcoming sight. He drew confidence from her smile and the passing thought that accompanied it: *ordinary people ... they are not ordinary. They are special.*

"Here you go, sir. I do hope you enjoy."

"Thank you." Again, Edward returned the smile.

The soup tasted delicious. He realized now how hungry he was. His conversation with Derek settled his nerves somewhat. Edward smiled to himself. It was funny; during the summation of his escape, he had needed to calm Derek down and remind him to keep breathing. But still, it had been the right thing to call Derek. They were both in agreement he should leave New York as soon as possible. Derek said he would check on travel options for Edward and get back to him soon.

Looking down to his wrist, Edward noted it was 2:38 p.m. He knew for certain both Marie and Carmen would be expecting a text from him any time now and that he would need to word the text messages carefully so as not to alarm them. Carmen would be staying up and waiting. The time would be 10:38 p.m. in Tel Aviv now. She had her studies and needed her sleep. Marie would be working. She would be off at 5:00 p.m. Undoubtedly, she would be upset, no getting around it. More importantly, Edward was starting to have some concern for her safety. It was unsettling for him that they were waiting—the men at the watch shop.

Again, how did they know I was coming? He shook his head and scooped up the last of his soup.

Derek might have an idea. He pushed his empty bowl aside, and grasped his phone in both hands, leaving his thumbs free and poised in the all too familiar communication stance of the 'new millennium.' As he sat in silence thinking about how to word his text message to Carmen, an old song from the sixties popped into his head:

> *Where have all the flowers gone?*
> *Long time passing,*
> *Where have all the flowers gone?*
> *Long time ago ...*

But in his version, the word 'flowers' was substituted with 'phone booths.' Edward sang softly to himself. His mind wandered; sixty years old and retired, was he going the way of the phone booth? It appeared to be inevitable. Was he still needed? He hoped so. *We all desperately want to be needed.*

He focused on his thumbs stumbling about the touch screen. *As long as I don't watch anyone else do this, I think I'm getting the hang of it.*

> *Carmen: I had my meeting with Herbert the watchmaker, having lunch now, will be leaving early for home. I have a lot to tell you. He gave me some information, but we still need to do more research on our own, had some excitement too. Maybe we can Skype later, on Thursday. All the best with your studies. Bye.*

Edward sent the text off. *Should do. One down, one to go ...* His phone vibrated; incoming call with Derek's number on the screen.

"Derek, thanks for the callback. So, what's the travel plan?"

"Oh yeah, no prob ... looking good." Edward could tell he was still a little revved up. "I really don't want you showing yourself at the airport. This might be some kind of gang activity. If so, the airport might be one of two places where they might expect you to turn up."

"Right, the airport makes sense ... you think the security there won't be sufficient?"

"I'd rather you stay out of sight, as best you can."

"Ok, what's the other place?"

"The police station."

"I'm struggling with this Derek. Would it not be better if I went to the cops and told them what happened? I think Herbert was murdered!" Edward used hushed tones, so as not to be overheard. "Do they not need to know I could be involved?"

"Maybe ..." There was a pause on the other end. Derek would be thinking this through carefully. He resumed, "Let's back up a bit. You *assume* he was murdered, but didn't you say he was coughing and sneezing?"

"Well yes, but people don't generally die from coughing and sneezing!"

"Fair enough. Could you identify any of the three men who chased you—you told me they all wore mirrored sunglasses."

"No, I can't identify any of them."

"Edward, I think if you went to the police now, you might be putting yourself in harm's way. The police would not be able to provide you with protection in a city the size of New York ... listen, I have some contacts, via my ham radio aficionados and fire department personnel. I can for certain find out what happened at the watch shop. It may take several days, though. But, who's to say you can't contact the police in Brooklyn at a later date, if you're needed for their investigation. We need to think about your safety first."

Edward thought Derek was right, but it wasn't helping to ease the sense of helplessness he felt.

"Derek, you said *gang* activity. Doesn't fit with the first guy Aaron in Petrolia. Aren't gangs usually within the boundary of a city?"

"Yea you might be right ... I'm not sure. I intend to ask around."

"Is there ..." Edward hesitated, he was searching, and it kind of frightened him. "Is there such a thing as a ... 'Caribbean Mafia?'"

"I don't know. I can understand why you're asking. But let's wait on that one." Derek's voice quivered slightly.

"Derek, I'm concerned for Marie's safety. Somehow, they knew when I'd be at Herbert's watch shop. Any ideas?" There was only silence on the phone.

"To be honest, I didn't think about that. But yeah, man ... weird." More silence. "So, the only people who knew your itinerary were me, Marie and Carmen?"

"Yes, no one else and I can't imagine why they might tell anyone else."

"Hmm ... Edward, anything different or unusual at your house recently? Like a contractor or someone doing work at your place?"

"No … nothing. I've been home by myself."

"How about any servicing of your computers or cell phones?"

"Nope, they're all fine…" Edward's cell phone dinged, indicating an incoming text message.

"Hang on a second Derek, my phone dinged, let me check …" He read a short reply from Carmen saying: *K, we'll Skype on Thursday!*

"I'm back. Yeah, that was Carmen. She responded to a text I sent her before you called." Edward thought for a moment. "I got an urge to call her. We never talk on the phone anymore, and I'd prefer we did, especially in a situation like this. Now it's mostly texting. I miss the old phones I guess. I was even thinking about how phone booths don't exist anymore. While I …" Edward stopped! He said nothing.

"Hey, you still there?" Concern sounded in Derek's voice.

"A phone service truck!" he paused again. "Right after Marie left for work, 7:30 Monday morning, a worker pulls up in front of our house and tells me he's doing an assessment to schedule some pending work on the phone lines on our street. He asks to see where my phone line exits the house. I show him and he tags it. I closed up the garage door and went back into the house …"

"What kind of work? Did he say?" Derek impatiently interjected.

"Ah … fiber optics. Yes, he said Bell was in the process of converting all existing lines over to fiber optics and our street would be coming up to have the work performed."

"Done!" The heightened sense of confidence in Derek's voice was unmistakable.

"Done? What do you mean?"

"Your street … it's already been done! Fiber optic lines were installed on your street when they did my street two years ago. Your phone's been tapped!" At Derek's last words Edward experienced both relief and a quickening sense of fear.

"Derek, I need to get home! I'm frightened for Marie. I don't want her to be alone!"

"Absolutely, she can stay with me. I'm off work shortly. I'll stop by your place right from work. I'll take care of the phone line."

"Thank you so much Derek. I don't know what …" Edward was more than thankful to have Derek as a close friend.

"Hey, I'm here for you. It's gonna be okay. Right now, though, I need you to get your butt in a cab. Go to Newark, New Jersey. You'll buy an Amtrak ticket to Detroit Michigan. Train leaves at 4:35 p.m. You'll have two transfers: first one in Washington, D.C., second one in Toledo, Ohio. Then a bus takes you to Detroit Michigan. I'll be waiting to pick you up at 1:00 p.m. tomorrow."

"Wow, excellent work Derek. I'm on my way." Edward reached into his pocket for his money clip. "Derek, thanks again. But … can I ask another favour of you?"

"Shoot!"

"Well … I think we need to tread lightly here. I'll call Marie and explain things as gently as I can. Would you mind taking her out for dinner tonight? On me of course. We've done well, I think, in solving part of the mystery—I mean with the phone line thing—but Marie…well, that's another matter. Derek, as your friend, I need to warn you …"

Edward took a deep breath, "Marie's not going to be happy!"

EDWARD AWOKE TO the light, rhythmic 'clickety clack' sound of the Amtrak train wheels. He looked at his watch, 6:45 a.m. The train would be arriving in Toledo, Ohio at 9:00 a.m. After a one-hour layover, a bus would take him to Detroit, Michigan, where he would meet with Derek. The trip was long, so he slept on and off through the night. It was quiet, with only about twelve or so other passengers travelling in his car. He had been able to use two seats as a small bed, using his shoulder bag as a makeshift pillow.

A short time after he boarded for the first leg of his journey he called Marie. She had returned home from work and Derek was waiting for her. Edward received a text from him earlier at 4:15 p.m. stating that his suspicion about the phone line was correct. It required gaining access to the 'collector box' in the neighbour's yard. He did so and removed the bug which was an 'inductance type', which are easy to install and remove.

Edward talked with Marie for 15 to 20 minutes. He did his best to play things down and reassure her everything would be all right. He tried to emphasize Derek had contacts with the fire department and would obtain police information about the incident at the watch shop. Edward had been somewhat surprised at Marie's controlled demeanour and cognition. Not until later, did he realize her training as a healthcare professional was taking over.

A practicing R.N. could be confronted with life and death situations on an almost daily basis. Facts and information always take precedence over everything else; learned knowledge and skill follow, and finally compassion and understanding.

Marie appeared to be focused in the first stage; that is, until Edward mentioned to her it would be best if she were to stay with Derek at his place until he got home.

"What! Are you kidding me?" Facts and information were no longer taking precedence. Full-blown emotion was in charge now. "Let's see … my odds for living a long, happy life? I'm thinking life would be better to get kidnapped by these thugs from New York! We can give them the watch, and everything's back to normal."

"Now … Derek's place? I'll get more radiation and magnetic resonance than if I were strapped naked to a running x-ray machine and left for a day inside of an MRI machine continually scanning me! The man breeds bacteria in his fridge most haven't seen before. Strains of viruses can be found in his house that doctors have never studied. They reside in all the packing and boxes coming from Indonesia, Burma … where ever! Remember the huge, weird looking spider that hitched a ride from Pakistan? I'll bet he's still got it! Perhaps he named it. I wonder if he ever finished the collar he said he was going to make!"

"Really Edward? I always thought you loved and cared for me!"

Edward smiled. He began searching in his backpack to locate his toiletry bag. It was nice to see Marie still had her feisty charm and humour.

They finally came to an agreement. The dinner out 'tipped the scales'. However, she insisted on bringing her own bedding, a full can of disinfectant spray and an assortment of fruit-double bagged for breakfast in the morning.

"Do you think Derek will be offended?" she asked.

Edward's reply, "Many have tried, but all have failed!"

With his toiletry bag under his arm, he started off to use the facilities at the rear of the train car. Afterwards, a large coffee and a breakfast sandwich would be in order.

———•———

As Edward sat in the dining car eating his sandwich and sipping his coffee, he began thinking back again to his meeting with Herbert. Going over the previous events last night, however, he couldn't put things together in any way that made complete sense. Considering what happened, he thought he owed it to Herbert to do his best, and perhaps try to make sure the watch fulfilled its destiny if indeed there was such a *destiny* for his pocket watch. Herbert had helped him to escape and it cost him his life.

I want to help. What were you trying to tell me, Herbert?

Was he forgetting something? Edward recited the watchmaker's discourse softly, as best as he could remember. "Your pocket watch was created during the reign of a great queen. There was a great watch that was created for this queen. These two watches were destined to cross paths. The great queen died suddenly …" or 'untimely' I think he said. "The great watch remained. Many years passed. The queen lost her throne." *This is where it got even weirder …* "The watches have not crossed paths, but their ultimate destiny remains the same. They can only meet in one place: the place where the queen has regained her throne." *I don't get It … how does the Queen regain her throne? I thought she was dead!* "It is to that place where you must go, Edward."

He sat in silence. *I'm missing something.* Did he not remember correctly? He thought he did. Right in the inscription Herbert had written, 'Listen very carefully to what I say.' And he had. *What else did Herbert say? I think …* "Your pocket watch has significance," *followed by,* "Tell me, Edward, what is your interest in watches?" *Does this mean anything? After that, I told Herbert about my own retirement watch.* It now appeared to Edward that Herbert had been trying to calm him down.

Or perhaps… He needed to understand a bit about my own knowledge of watches before he continued. This seemed reasonable to Edward. *If true, then Herbert believed I was capable of understanding what he was about to tell me. And what was that? So here we are back to the beginning.*

Edward brought along a pad and pencil in his backpack. As soon as his sandwich was finished, he began jotting down all the points he could recall from the conversation. At about halfway through, his cell phone dinged, indicating an incoming text message. Pulling his phone from the pocket of his jeans he immediately brought up the text message. It was from Marie. Edward started to chuckle as he read the text:

> *Good morning Edward. How was your night? Pleasant journey? I'm now trying to recall how I let you*

talk me into staying at Derek's house. I survived, but it required sharing my accommodation with a drone hanging about chest high in the center of the room. Derek is working on it. I happened to wake up around 1:00 a.m. and I was convinced it was Derek's pet spider from Pakistan. I think my scream woke the neighbourhood. Didn't seem to bother Derek though. Soon, I'll need to experience firsthand the resident bathroom. Right about now, the spider from Pakistan looks rather tame. I'll let you know if I survive!

Edward began laughing. Tears started forming in his eyes. He went back to his note pad, but the tears were making it difficult to continue. He wrote out the word *Queen*. The word blurred. A single teardrop fell directly onto the page just as he silently thanked Marie for her assistance.

You're an immense help right now. He laughed again.

The word *'Queen'* was now both blurred and smudged. *Marie, Marie! Look what you've done to the Queen. Marie ... Ma ...* he stopped dead. He wasn't breathing.

That's it! The Queen ... of course! The Great Queen! Marie, Marie Antoinette!

His hands started shaking. He remembered he read the story before. *Yes, a great watch had been commissioned for a Great Queen! And the great watch had a nickname!*

Now it made sense, he understood what Herbert said! He grabbed up his phone and started hammering keys into the Google search engine: *Watch built for Marie Antoinette. Named: The Queen*

The first page of relevant sites popped up on the screen. Edward quickly scrolled down the page. He stopped at a Wikipedia link and tapped with his index finger. The page came up. He enlarged the screen and started reading. *Damn, no reading glasses again.*

He stared at the page in almost total disbelief as he scrolled through it. When he finished, he started over: *Watch commissioned for Marie Antoinette in the year 1783. The Breguet No. 160, also known as 'The Queen…'*

He finished reading the page for the second time. Now he just sat in silence staring at the screen. He thought about his daughter Carmen. The hair started rising on the back of his neck.

What are the chances …?

FIFTEEN

THURSDAY, MAY 1, 2014. 9:15 P.M.
UNIVERSITY OF TEL AVIV CAMPUS, ISRAEL

ANOTHER BEAUTIFUL, warm evening in Tel Aviv and the stars were shining brightly in the clear night sky. A warm breeze caressed her skin and gently tossed her long blonde hair. Often when walking about the university grounds on nights like this she could be seen coming to a halt, and while gazing up at the stars, with her athletically toned body silhouetted against the shimmering light, she might twirl, reaching her arms wide, in a way of embracing all that she found beautiful in the world. To an interested observer, it might appear she was the beauty to be admired. But Carmen James knew all too well the poise, the grace, and even an opportunity to be here now, did not just happen. These things came because of dedication, devotion and extreme commitment from herself, her parents and many others. Beauty is a creation she was grateful to be a part of. Her deepest desire was to help preserve it. The basis of her life choices and why she lived here now attested to this.

Tonight, however, Carmen would not stop to admire the tranquility of this lovely evening. Excitement filled the air, a diversion if you will. She left the studio, located in the recreation centre, after having finished a ballet class. Carmen was excited. A full hour of pointe class had not done much to lessen her exuberance. She still had an hour and a half to wait. Her dad would be just getting back home from Brooklyn, New York. The eight-hour time change meant she would be up well past midnight, but it did not matter. She would not be able to sleep anyway. He said in his text they had more research to do, and some excitement had transpired. What kind of excitement? The waiting was driving her nuts. Their Skype time was set for 11:00 p.m., which would be 3:00 p.m. back home. That left time for a shower and a snack.

The university grounds were well lit. Other students made their way from classes. Carmen felt safe here. It had been a difficult decision to come to Israel to do her graduate studies in environmental science. She had been here about six months, and although challenging, she had confidence in her choice. To her it seemed this country had a heightened sense of seriousness. She thought in part it was because of how the people struggled to obtain and preserve their independence. There also seemed here an intellectual diversity that permeated almost all facets of existence, and Carmen's research indicated the environmental commitment and technologies in this country were second to none.

She thought of the University of Tel Aviv, as an excellent choice to obtain a diverse, international perspective for environmental studies. With some reservations her parents agreed, but their separation was not easy. They were a close family, maybe too close. Growing up as an only child would contribute to this. With no siblings, Carmen received the attention. She needed to be on her own now and prove to herself she could be independently strong. She had a life of challenges ahead, and although at times a little scary, Carmen believed she could face them.

As an undergrad studying psychology, Carmen thought she had an understanding of the role parents play in their children's development, with a parent's love for their children being the most determining factor. For her, she understood love to be a unity with no boundaries. In that sense, Carmen did not feel now or ever completely alone.

As she approached the pathway leading to the entrance of her residence, Carmen made a silent wish to herself that her mom, her dad, or perhaps both, would come for a visit soon. A short break, coming up for Independence Day and Remembrance Day was pending. *Couldn't hurt to ask*, she missed them so much.

"Whoa ... that's *sooo* intense!"

Carmen sat at a desk in her dorm room. An opened laptop set before her, displayed the image of her mom and dad in real time. They were Skyping. Carmen had been riveted to the screen for the last 15 minutes with full concentration as she sat processing the information in almost total disbelief.

"Well, I did have about 19 hours on the train ride back to recover." Edward's voice sounded somewhat compressed and electronically shallow.

"I ..." Carmen paused. "I wasn't referring to the New York thing—it's that Mom had to stay at Derek's place! I've heard stories ..." She held a straight face, but her lower lip started to quiver and her eyes sparkled.

Marie reacted first. She leaned close to her husband, put her arm around his neck in a headlock position and started to squeeze.

"I bet none of the stories you heard tell of the inner sanctum of the man's bathroom."

Carmen shook her head as she bit down on her quivering lip.

"I'm probably the only survivor who experienced it. And out of pure love for my family, I must spare you the details." Marie loosened her grip.

That was it—Carmen broke first, and her laughter was contagious. Her dad followed and her mom joined in. The headlock turned into a hug as tears started streaming down Marie's cheeks.

Many times, Carmen watched some of her favourite professors use humour in their lectures. She now understood how the human brain, at times, thrived on a positive diversion. Learning and reasoning became easier and ultimately more efficient. It released tension for the family; a shared comfort between them that transcended great distance.

"So, Dad …" Carmen tried to compose herself. "I always thought when you were off to work, it was a time of perseverance and dedication to support your family. I didn't know you spent your days goofing around, trying to perfect the technique of tumbling over construction fences!"

The laughter continued. Edward shrugged his shoulders. "Who's to say that goofing around can't pay off eventually?"

"Lucky for you." Marie gave her husband a quick kiss on his cheek, lifted her arm from his shoulders, and straightened up.

"Sounds like … without the construction site, you were toast!" Carmen was now preparing for some analytical discussion.

"Well, a wise old man—my dad—once told me, everyone needs a little luck sometimes. Ask me now, and I'll say, he spoke the truth," Edward smiled.

Carmen took a moment to recall her deceased grandpa. He lived on in her too. She pictured what the old watchmaker might have looked like. He could be similar in many ways to her own grandfather. Had he been kind, smart, and funny too? She hoped so. *Maybe he had grandchildren of his own,* she wondered…

"The watchmaker, Herbert Osterhagen, and your description of what he said about the two watches. It's not making sense to me."

Carmen leaned back in her chair. She gazed around her room lost in thought. Her eyes settled where they most often did in times of contemplation: to a framed print of an 'oil on canvas' by Edgar Degas: *Two Dancers on a Stage*, which her mom and dad had ordered and framed. The gift had been waiting for her when she moved into residence. The picture measured a large 60 cm x 40 cm. As her room was small, she reserved the largest portion of open wall for it. Two ballet dancers were portrayed in the picture; two personalities, both of which told of the beauty in human form, but each in their own way.

Carmen had to make a difficult choice in choosing her own way when she decided not to pursue a professional career in ballet. It was almost heartbreaking. However, she ultimately had made the right choice. Now, with focus and determination, she would, in her own way, try to preserve and restore a different beauty that could be timeless, much like the beautiful art of ballet. She turned back to the smiling faces of her mom and dad, *thank-you*.

She resumed her previous thoughts and began to play back in her mind the logistics of Herbert's discourse with her father.

"Okay ... so we have your watch created during the time of a great queen, and we know a great watch was created for this great Queen." Carmen paused.

"There are two watches. Apparently, they have a predetermined destiny, although we're not told what. Then, this great Queen dies ... *untimely*, he said. We don't know her name, but we must assume that for some reason she died at an early age. The great watch survived, however, and its destiny—which would include your watch—remains until this day. But here's where I'm confused, if Herbert related this sequence of events in chronological order, and it appears he did, then ..." again Carmen paused for a bit longer. She stared upwards into space, completely lost in her thoughts.

"When the watchmaker said, 'Many years passed,' followed by, 'The Queen lost her throne,' well ... that appears out of context, unless ... Herbert either referred to the Queen in a symbolic manner, or ... might there be two Queens?" Her gaze went back to her parents' image on the screen. However, she did not want an answer yet. Leaning forward she gazed at her father.

"It sounds like Herbert Osterhagen, an exceptionally intelligent man, might have been asking you to do something in a way that the man listening in the back room would not understand." Carmen leaned back in her chair, but her gaze did not falter. She awaited an answer.

But the answer came slowly. Even through the digitally pixelated image on the screen, it was clear that Edward had been moved by his daughter's intellect.

"Wow, you *do* retain and process information rather well."

Carmen laughed with a shrug. "Believe me, I get lots of practice around here."

Edward continued. "You're absolutely on the right track. Yes indeed, Herbert did, in fact, speak to me in somewhat coded terms. I'm sure he was convinced, after knowing the depth of my interest in watches, I'd understand the real meaning of what he said."

Now Edward shuffled a little uneasily. "But I have to admit, I struggled with it, over and over."

He laughed. "I think Herbert underestimated my inabilities. However, finally, your wonderful mother helped me out!"

"What?" Marie abruptly leaned away from her husband so that she could stare directly at him. "This is news to me!" She lifted her hands and shoulders in a bewildering gesture and turned back to face their computer screen. "Glad I could help?"

Both Carmen and Marie looked at Edward for his reply.

"I thought it best I present my findings with us together. I've told no one else. Carmen, can you do a quick Google Search on your phone now for me please?"

"Okay." Carmen grabbed her phone and activated Google.

"Go ahead." She focused on her dad impatiently.

"For you and your mom, I'd like you to read a brief summary on Wikipedia. Type in: 'The Queen, watch for Marie Antoinette.'"

Carmen felt her breathing stop! *He just said Marie Antoinette!*

It was the first listed site. Before selecting, she scanned the first two lines beginning the excerpt; *The Breguet No. 160 grand complication more commonly known as the Marie Antoinette or 'The Queen' is a case watch designed by Swiss watchmaker ...*

Before she tapped the link on her phone, she raised her head. She still did not breathe. The two lines she had read started to overwhelm her. Somehow, she knew by simply tapping her finger on a Google link a revelation of immense importance would be presented. Carmen stared into her father's eyes as her finger descended gently to the screen. She took a deep breath, looked down at the screen and began reading the summary out loud:

"Marie Antoinette watch ..." she paused. "The Breguet No. 160 grand complication, more commonly known as the Marie-Antoinette or the Queen, is a case watch designed by Swiss watchmaker Abraham-Louis Breguet. Work on the watch began in 1782 and was completed by Breguet's son in 1827, four years after Breguet's death." Carmen blinked hard at the dates.

"The watch is thought to have been commissioned in 1783 by Count Hans Axel von Fersen, an admirer and alleged lover of the French Queen, Marie Antoinette. The watch was to contain every watch function known at that time, including a clock, perpetual calendar, minute repeater, thermometer, chronograph, power reserve, pare-chute, chime, and an independent second hand. The watch is encased in gold, with a clear face that shows the complicated movement of the gears inside. Breguet used sapphires in the mechanism to decrease friction." Carmen absorbed every word, processing each detail. An intricate mental image began to form.

"Marie Antoinette never lived to see the watch, as it was completed 34 years after she had been executed." The unfolding story enticed Carmen.

"This watch was part of the watch collection at the L.A. Mayer Institute for Islamic Art in Jerusalem, having been donated as part of the David Lionel Salomon's collection. It was stolen by renowned master-thief Na'aman Diller with many other watches in 1983—although it was recovered in 2007. As of 2013, the watch was valued at …" Carmen gasped, "$30 million!"

My dad's pocket watch … is it somehow connected to this? Oh my god!

"I think we're fine to stop there," Edward interjected and waited in a brief moment of silence. He continued.

"I have one more important fact to add… The Queen has since been returned to the museum in Jerusalem." They sat in contemplative silence.

Marie was the first to speak. "The place where the Queen has regained her throne."

Carmen quickly followed with, "It is to that place where you must go Edward." She looked intently at her mother, and to her father and continued.

"And one more astonishing fact … I'm sure Herbert Osterhagen was unaware your daughter is close by to *that* place—the place where you *must go*." Her voice reverberated in an excited tone, but she waited and focused on her mother.

"We owe it to the memory of Herbert; don't you think Mom?"

Marie glanced at Edward, and back at Carmen. A grim smile was settling on her face.

"I know when I'm outnumbered. You two are good … very good. I think it would be easier to stop a herd of wild buffaloes!" She partially turned and faced her husband.

"How did you word it … 'I thought it best that I present my findings with us together?'" Marie began a subtle nodding of her head with a loving look at her daughter and Edward.

"So … how exactly did I help you in solving this puzzle?"

Carmen thought she was going to burst. She couldn't even focus as her dad started talking.

This is just … unbelievably awesome!

SIXTEEN

THURSDAY, MAY 1, 2014. 6:00 P.M.
PETROLIA, ONTARIO, CANADA

"There must be another woman! Please, be honest with me." Marie had her back to him and was busy chopping vegetables for a stir-fry on the kitchen counter-top. Edward sat at the island in the centre of the room, facing the patio doors. He had just said goodbye to Derek on the phone. He set the handheld receiver down on the counter-top.

"What?" He could not see her face. He waited, unsure how to respond.

"I mean ... that must be it." Edward noticed her shoulders slouching forwards. "I overheard you ask Derek if I could stay again with him; this time for up to a week!" Now her head was shaking side to side. "I don't think you love me anymore, Edward."

With a soft smile of understanding on his face, he got up, walked over to Marie and pressed his body up close behind her. His arms cradled her as his hands clasped lightly around her slender waist. He gently squeezed and kissed her neck. She set her knife down, lifted her head up, and then leaned back to welcome the embrace. Her body trembled ever so slightly as she stifled a sob. Neither spoke.

Marie needed reassurance. She felt isolated. Edward needed to slow down and give her that reassurance. They both sought understanding and sometimes that is best found in loving silence. Moments passed. Marie was the first to speak.

"I know I'm being selfish. I really want to go with you!"

There was a long pause. Edward finally spoke. "I wish you could come with me too, and I haven't been sensitive to your feelings. I'm sorry."

Edward released his embrace. Marie turned to face her husband. As she gazed up at him, with her eyes brightly shimmering in tears, Edward smiled. "There could never be another woman." This brought a smile from Marie.

"Oh, Edward I'm being silly and seeking attention."

"You deserve all the attention I give you, and so much more. That's the reason; there could *never* be another. Our two worlds collided Marie. I'm afraid we're gonna have to make the best of it."

This brought a bigger smile to her face, which caused a tear to fall from her eye and cascade down her cheek. Edward leaned in and kissed it away.

"Hey, you need some help with those vegetables?" He turned towards the sink and reached his upturned palm towards a soap dispenser and washed his hands under the faucet. "Just give me a minute here."

"Yes sure, that would be good." She was still smiling as she turned back to the vegetables on the counter and proceeded to set up another cutting board and knife beside her. Edward dried his hands with a towel and shuffled in next to her. He reached over and took a large onion, which was sitting before him.

"Here, let me do the onion."

"Oh thanks, that would be great."

"Well, you know what they say … at least I think they say …" He started to laugh. "A family that cries together, stays to…" Marie jabbed him with her elbow.

"Too funny!" They both began cutting their vegetables in a contented silence. "Edward, what do you think has to happen to make—as you said—'two worlds collide?'"

"Like, with me and you? "He responded.

"Well, I was thinking about us when you said it, but now I'm thinking about the two watches—yours and 'The Queen.' Could they really have a destiny, and if so, who or what will bring them together?"

Edward had found a paper towel and was wiping his burning, runny eyes. "It would take a much greater intellect than I possess to answer that question, Marie."

"I mean, what a coincidence you would be the person to find this pocket watch which has been lost away in this part of the world for so many years. Now, it will travel to Jerusalem, to what … fulfill a destiny? Your daughter is studying at the University of Tel Aviv. She has a four-day holiday coming up." Marie stared directly at Edward. "How many stars need to be aligned to make 'two worlds collide?'" She took a deep breath. "If you take out the word coincidence, the scenario seems almost frightening, and I'm not even referring to what happened in New York."

Edward returned her gaze, steady and focused. He was silent, lost in thought. He finally spoke. "Watches are the keepers of time. Not too long ago I read a quote from Albert Einstein: '*Time is only necessary to keep all things from happening at once.*'"

Edward felt almost helpless. Marie was asking for reassurance. He could only offer her this: "Perhaps the stars have *always* been aligned."

———◆———

"Mmm … a lovely wine, an excellent selection to pair with our stir-fry."

"Thank you." Edward raised his long-stemmed Bordeaux-styled glass and sampled the vintage. He nodded in approval. "I'll try and make some room where I can stow away a bottle or two of wine from Israel for us to enjoy together upon my return. They have some excellent varietals, which are indigenous to the region." He looked at his wife. They were seated at the island across from each other. Marie had placed a lighted candle between them as a centrepiece. Soft jazz music was playing in the background. The flickering flame of the candle caused the soft, ambient light to play across her features. Edward could not turn away. She was so beautiful in this moment.

His voice was low, but he put deliberate emphasis on his next two words, "*It sucks!*"

Marie shrugged. Edward glanced down at his plate. "Can't you find *someone* to take your shift for a week?"

"On such short notice, the answer's no. Only in an absolute emergency, you know that. We've been through this before. It's only a week." She gave him a thoughtful look. "This is an adventure best suited for you and your daughter. Carmen is over the moon with excitement about this watch. I can't even hope to relate to that kind of enthusiasm…but *you* can."

Edward raised his head. "I …"

"I'll be fine." She paused. "But I need you to promise me something …" There was a serious tone to her voice. "If *anything*, no matter how small should happen or even seem out of place, you need to promise me, Edward, that you will call the police and let them handle it." Her eyes were fixed on him.

"Of course, Marie, I understand the seriousness here. You have my word."

"I believe you, Edward. But I fear for Carmen. She is an intelligent young woman. However, I feel her enthusiasm and passion for adventure could leave her vulnerable."

"I have worked in the medical profession for many years. I witnessed first hand how many people in this world cause harm to others to get what they want. It is a sad, unforgiving reality. Carmen does not yet possess the life experience to fully comprehend this." Again, Marie stopped. Her expression softened. "I'm not asking for you and Carmen to stop living your lives the way you want to. But please … please be careful."

"I will." Edward watched Marie take another sip of her wine.

Setting her glass back down, she continued. "I have a three-day weekend ahead of me and I'll need to keep busy, so I formulated a plan." Edward raised his eyebrows. He took a bite of his stir-fry and waited for Marie to continue. "I'm going to make an attempt and do some much-needed cleaning at Derek's place." This brought an amused smile from her husband.

"I'll be bringing my own cleaning supplies. Does Derek own a vacuum cleaner?"

"Ah, well …" Edward thought for a moment. "Yes and no."

Marie cocked her head to one side in a quizzical manner. "I was hoping for a yes *or* no answer. Not a yes *and* no answer! This shouldn't be an overly difficult question. Oh, wait … are you confused Edward, because I used the words *cleaning* and *Derek* in the same sentence?"

Edward broke out in laughter. This caused him to start choking on food that was still in his mouth, which launched a violent coughing attack that lasted a good twenty seconds. It only took Marie a matter of moments to determine he had indeed cleared his airway and would make a full recovery. She gave her husband a satisfied smile. Yes, it did seem fair now that he too might share in some of the suffering. Her suffering was the dreaded contemplation of a week with Derek. Edward had stopped coughing and was now clearing his throat continuously. Reaching for his glass he took a drink. Marie noted his face colour now matched the colour of the wine almost perfectly. She took a sip. Savoring the taste, she sat back, knowing it was not nice—but she couldn't help herself—chuckling inwardly and enjoying the moment, she stated, "I guess that *was* a difficult question. You alright? Can I get you anything?" The prim smile was still on her face.

"Yes ... no, I'm okay. Excuse me for that Marie." Edward inhaled deeply and could continue. "About six months ago I stopped by to say hello to Derek. He had his vacuum cleaner up on a workbench. It was mostly dismantled."

"Oh, so Derek was fixing his vacuum cleaner ... maybe I haven't been giving credit where credit is due?" Marie gave her husband a hopeful look.

Edward smiled and shook his head. "Well no, actually he took it apart because he wanted to use the motor for another application."

"Ha, silly me! For something of much greater importance, I'm sure?"

"Well, that would depend upon whose perspective we choose to endorse."

"How about Derek's? I love to be entertained." Marie smirked.

"He used the motor from his vacuum cleaner to make an automated can crusher for his pop cans." Edward could not help but detect the ever-growing expression of disbelief on Marie's face.

He continued. "It's cool. The device crushes and stores the empty cans in a cylindrical paper sleeve that measures about 14 inches in length. The sleeve reaches full capacity at 24 cans. You then remove the filled sleeve from the machine, fold the paper on each end, much the same as you do when rolling coins, and *voila*! Into the recycle bin at 1/20th the volume. A cleaner, happier environment, don't you think, Marie?"

Marie did not know what to say. Most times when they were either with or discussing Derek, she never knew whether to laugh or cry. Ultimately, though, she understood him to be a kind person, who happened to be very smart in some areas and lacking in others. "I'll be looking forward to an in-home demonstration. Did he name this invention?"

"He calls it 'The Quantum Crusher.'"

"'The Quantum Crusher.' I like it! So, we need to take our vacuum cleaner over to his place. Derek can help clean up the environment; I can help to clean up his home. We have a deal!" Marie raised her glass in confirmation. "I haven't enjoyed a can of pop in a long while. Hey, life is still good!" They clinked their wine glasses together; each took a drink and went back to eating their meal and discussing their itineraries for the following day.

———◆———

As they were finishing their meal, Edward's phone dinged with a text message from Derek. He took a minute to read it. "Well Marie, here's my itinerary."

"Our very own private travel agent has it confirmed?" Marie smiled as she scooped up the last of the food on her plate.

"'Derek's tech travel' sorted it all out." Edward laughed. "He insisted on setting up my itinerary on his own computer. 'The only way to be totally secure' I think he said. And, as well, somehow he knows where to score the best prices." Reaching into the breast pocket of his shirt, he removed a pair of reading glasses and put them on. "Oh … this is excellent: I fly out of Sarnia tomorrow at 1:00 p.m. There's a short layover in Toronto, then a direct flight to Tel Aviv. Arrival time: 10:00 a.m. Saturday morning."

Edward glanced up to Marie, "Unfortunately, I can't pick up Carmen on Saturday, as she is meeting with one of her professors. However, as you heard her mention, she can still have four days away by doing some advanced studies before she leaves. I'll take a Sherut taxi to Jerusalem, where I have a room booked at the Prima Royale Hotel. An 'econo box' rental will be waiting for me, complete with GPS plugin. Let's see …" Edward glanced down at his watch as he was doing some calculations in his head. "Yes, I should have the better part of the afternoon to walk through the Old City for some sightseeing. Then, the following day I'll be up early for the drive to the University of Tel Aviv. I'll pick up Carmen on Sunday morning May 4th at 9:00 for the start of her four-day break."

He stopped talking and peered over his glasses at his wife. He took a deep breath and set down his phone, and took off his reading glasses. With focused intensity, he leaned in and held his arms up and forward with his hands configured as if holding on to a steering wheel at the 3 and 9 o'clock positions. His thumbs he kept free and began flexing them alternately back and forth while maneuvering the imaginary steering wheel ever so slightly to and fro.

"Vroom … vroom …" Edward's concentration was intense.

"Watch out, Edward! Geez, you almost ran over your wine glass. That's *real* crystal!"

"Sorry dear, but I had to swerve for an oncoming tour bus, a camel and a donkey cart all without slowing down, so as not to get rear ended by the diesel spewing truck hitched to my back bumper! Whew, that was close."

"Oh Edward, truly you are my hero. How do you do it?"

"It's all in the thumbs, Marie. You need to co-ordinate the sound of the car horn with honed driving skills. Beep … beep!"

"As they say, 'When in Rome …'"

Marie cut in. "Could you teach me to … wow … 'do as the Romans do' and drive like *that?*" She gave her husband one of her favorite amused looks.

Edward leaned back and relaxed on the wheel for a bit, but he dared not turn away from the road, not even for a moment. "I'm sorry Marie but … well, I think it's something you're born with … like the 'superhero' thing." He suddenly had to swerve again, but this time he stayed well clear of his wine glass.

"Hmm …" Marie sadly nodded her head. "I understand. Do you think it might be possible for my *superhero* to find a parking spot for his 'econo box' so that he might use his *super powers* to help with the dishes?"

"Vroom … vroom …" He had to overcome distractions from his wife, but Edward remained focused. His eyes began darting to the sides of the road. "Could be a tall order Marie, always a challenge in this part of the world … oh wait … beep, beep … brakes … vroom, vroom … beep, beep … gotta be quick … vroom, vroom … very quick … nailed it! Yes!"

Edward leaned back, dropped his arms and let out a deep breath. He went through the motions of releasing the seat belt and shutting the engine down.

"I'm there for you, Marie." Edward proudly pulled his shoulders back in a big stretch.

"Wow, I'm impressed! Let's get these dishes done super fast. We've still got half a bottle of wine to finish." Marie paused. She had a twinkle in her eye. "Maybe you have some other super powers yet to be embraced?" There was silence.

Marie leaned forward. "Why Edward … is that a *superhero* blush I'm seeing? Superheroes blush too?"

"I'm afraid not Marie." Edward smiled as he rose from the island carrying his empty plate along with flatware and a water glass. "That would be the light from the candle passing through the wine in my glass and causing a refraction of colour. Most notably, in the wavelength range of 610-620 nanometres causing a soft reddish-orange hue to be observed upon my features."

He laughed as he placed the dishes in the sink. "You need to understand, Marie, that *superheroes* can be academically inspired as well."

Marie joined Edward at the sink with her own empty dishes in hand. "Does this mean there will be no more *super powers* from you tonight?" She had a sad look on her face.

Edward stopped for a thoughtful moment. "Please don't despair Marie, and don't give up hope. It may appear rather odd, but I've had an affinity for phone booths as of late," Edward mused.

"Hmm ... more wine Edward?"

He smiled, "You'll need to hold that thought for a bit. I must scoot over to Derek's for a quick visit when we're done the dishes. I'm going to drop off the pocket watch."

"How come?" Marie opened the door of the dishwasher that was to the left of the sink and began rinsing off the dishes.

"He's remodeling a travel case that was made for an old compass. He's using special memory foam and needs the watch to form the impression. Also, I'll get my credit card back from him."

"Everything is booked and paid for?" Marie asked.

"Pretty much. I'll be leaving my phone with him tonight as well. He's installing a new SIM card and data plan. He'll charge it to my phone account."

"Wow. We're fortunate to have his support. Sounds like you two have got all the bases covered. So, who's driving you to Sarnia Airport tomorrow?" Marie was placing the dishes in the dishwasher as Edward started filling the sink with water to wash a couple of pans and cutting boards.

"Okay, so here's the drill." He smiled, "'the drill,' is what Derek called it. Must be the fireman, police thing, I guess." Marie returned his smile nervously.

"Like I said, I drop off the watch and phone tonight. I'll take a back way and use the rear entrance. I'll do the same thing tomorrow morning to retrieve the items. We load your bags, and my luggage too, into your Honda, then ... oops, almost forgot, and our vacuum cleaner." Edward chuckled. Marie kept silent, still looking nervous. "Then I'll call a mechanic friend of mine at the service center in the east end of town to get permission to leave your car parked there for as long as we need."

"Then we'll lock up the house, and you'll drive me to Sarnia Airport. We'll leave here at 11:30 a.m. My flight out is 12:45 p.m. When you return to Petrolia at 1:30ish, drive to the east end and park your car at the service garage. Leave your stuff and lock up. I hope it's not raining. Our local forecast for tomorrow is rain ending at noon, then sun and cloud, 15 degrees Celsius. So hopefully an enjoyable walk for you to the center of town. Give Derek a call on his cell. He'll meet you at Tim Hortons for lunch. After lunch, give him your key fob and head out on foot for his place. He'll meet you there with your stuff. You'll need to be indoctrinated on his security access codes and fingerprint scan procedure. Derek also advised us—Carmen as well—that until we learn more about the situation, we need to 'watch our backs' at all times."

Marie was drying the last pot. She kept going over and over it. She had her head down as she continued to rub with the towel. Edward noticed her silence. He knew she was frightened. Walking over to her, he put his arms around her and gently hugged her. She let the pot hang limply at her side.

"Hey, you've got quite a shine happening on that stainless-steel Marie." They stayed silent in their embrace. "Oh, one more thing from Derek; he informed me that the drone is now relocated to his room." Edward stepped back and looked down at Marie with a loving smile.

When she gazed up at him, he could see her eyes were again filled with tears. She tried to return his smile. It did not quite happen. "I want you to have a great, wonderful time with our daughter on her break. I can't wait to hear all about the adventure." Now she could smile. "Bring me back something nice?"

Edward leaned forward and kissed Marie on her lips. He softly broke away and whispered in her ear. "Again, I will say it. You have my word. I promise."

THE WEATHER FORECAST for Friday morning was correct. As Marie pressed the control on her sun visor, she and Edward were met with the sound of thunder and heavy pelting rain when the garage door opened. Sure enough, Southern Ontario was receiving a typical spring thunderstorm.

"Radar is showing the system should be moved well off by 12:00 p.m." Edward had backed the Honda into the garage after he had returned from Derek's place to facilitate the loading up of the car.

"Good, either way, I'll wear my nylon rain jacket with a hood just in case." Marie drove out of the garage and pushed the control again to close the door, and she started a brief checklist. "So, everything you need is in your carry on?"

"Yup, been over it twice."

"Passport, boarding passes, money, credit card, sunglasses, reading glasses, phone … and of course the infamous pocket watch?"

"Gee, if I forgot the watch, would that constitute an emergency? You'd need to catch the first flight out and bring it to us."

"Nice try, Edward. Anyhow, I'm attending a week-long date with our good friend Derek. Wouldn't wanna miss *that!*" Marie smiled only briefly. She had to set the wiper blades to high speed to keep up with the driving rain. Already her side and back windows were blurred with streaming water. She stopped at the stop sign at the end of their street and proceeded to make the right turn that would lead her to Petrolia Line. She had to strain to see the road in front of her. "Maybe we should book you on a boat bound for Israel?'" she joked.

"If it doesn't stop raining within the next 40 days, I'll heed your advice. I should be in the appropriate place, don't you think?"

Marie laughed as she reached forward to select the defrost control which was located on the center console. The windows were starting to fog up with the high humidity.

The next stop sign was at Petrolia Line, the town's main street. She put on her right turn signal and carefully scanned for oncoming traffic. There were several cars parked along the side of the road to her left, which somewhat obstructed the view of oncoming traffic. She waited patiently for a few cars, and then turned right onto the street. Once safely turned and heading west, she routinely glanced in her rear-view mirror and saw, but only partially, through her rain-streaked rear window the car which had been parked second in line along the side of the road also pulled out with headlights on and proceeded west. It was a fair distance behind her. This was a busy street. Marie did not give it a second thought. But perhaps she might have had she been able to see clearly out of her rear window.

Almost certainly a late model, white, 3 series BMW would warrant a second look.

SEVENTEEN

SATURDAY, MAY 3, 2014. 11:45 A.M.
PRIMA ROYALE HOTEL JERUSALEM ISRAEL

"Shalom ..." Edward stood in front of the reception desk in the lobby of the Prima Royale Hotel. He smiled and addressed a beautiful young woman who stood behind the glass-topped counter. "Edward James ... I believe I have a reservation?"

"Shalom, Mr. James," she returned the smile—speaking in excellent English, typical of young, professional Jewish people in this part of the world. Her deep, dark eyes held fast for a lingering moment, then averted to the angled computer screen positioned to her right. Edward felt his breath catch slightly and thought how effortless it is for natural beauty to overload the senses. Her dress attire was business professional, a navy coloured, shapely fitted skirt and blazer with a soft off-white top. Her perfectly straight, full bang, shoulder-length bob seemed to have the depth of infinite shades of black as it gently swayed with her movements and refracted the ambient lighting. Classic, elegant features set on pure olive skin and the subtle use of red lip-gloss on her full lips was exquisite. But her large, dark coloured eyes enveloped Edward. He had seen it before in this place—this country. Women and men—young and old—their eyes showed sadness, joy, and understanding.

At first, Edward had thought he was responding to culture shock. Yes, the first time here, bringing Carmen to University, he found himself intrigued by all the sights and sounds of a foreign country. It had heightened his senses. Many would say—with age comes beauty, and much of this land and its culture, portray a history—not merely hundreds of years, as in most modern Western cultures, but thousands of years. The great Western civilizations of the world owe much of their foundational religious and social structure to these ancient surrounding regions.

Edward recalled a statement he had read in a book written by a spiritual sage; he could not remember the name. In reference to the inhabitants of Israel, it read: *The Jewish people are symbolic to the evolution of the conscientiousness, or soul of mankind.* He thought it quite an astounding claim. Was it true? Considering the vast amount of world media coverage allotted to such a small country, it seemed probable. Whatever the reason, Edward could not deny his feelings. Maybe it was indeed heightened senses or perhaps just a lifetime of religious, social conditioning which made him overly sensitive to these people and their culture. He did not know for sure.

"Yes, you are reserved for 5 nights with an option of extending for an additional 3 days." Her soft voice lured him back from thoughts of a thousand years. He had been watching without focus her slender fingers dancing across the keyboard of the computer. He looked up at her smiling face. Again, her eyes drew him in. *The Sirens are calling…* Edward had to pause. *No … it's so much more than that.* The sadness, the joy, the deep-seated understanding he saw in her eyes portrayed a timeless beauty, which somehow appeared to make a moment of understanding infinite.

"Welcome to Jerusalem, Mr. James."

"Thank you." He reluctantly composed himself.

"Your accommodation with us will be a deluxe room, two double beds. Your reservation states another guest?" She glanced back to her computer screen briefly.

"That's correct. My daughter Carmen will be staying with me until Wednesday. I'll be driving to Tel Aviv tomorrow morning to pick her up." Edward almost winced as he said the word 'driving.' He inwardly shrugged off the apprehension he had when confronting the task of driving a vehicle in a foreign land. Besides, he *had* been practicing with Marie the night before.

"And yes, we contacted a rental agency. They have a sub-compact vehicle reserved in your name. Following a confirmation call from us, they will deliver the car at your convenience. Let's see …" Again, she focused on the computer screen followed by a quick flurry of typing. "Yes, your room is ready now. It will be nice, having an early check-in after a long flight. Could I please copy your credit card information to put on file for the duration of your stay?"

Edward dug into his pocket for his money clip to retrieve his card. "Yes, for sure." He handed her the card.

"Will this be your first time visiting Jerusalem?" the young woman questioned as she typed in the credit card numbers.

"No, second time actually. About six months ago my wife and I traveled here to Israel, to enroll our daughter Carmen at the University of Tel Aviv. We had a week to tour the country as well, and spent several days in Jerusalem. A wonderful time for us."

"This has been our first real separation as a family, and it's been a little tough. With the two holidays here now, and Carmen having four days off, and I had no immediate commitments, so I'm here for a short visit. My wife has work responsibilities at home, so unfortunately she couldn't make it." He accepted his card back.

"That is so thoughtful of you to travel all the way from Canada to be with your daughter. It sounds like you have a good family relationship." The sincerity in her voice brought out a warm smile from Edward. When it came right down to the most important things in life, he knew how fortunate he was.

"Carmen will be really looking forward to returning to Jerusalem. She was moved by this city."

Her eyes brightened to the passionate reference to her city. She reached up with her right hand to the lapel of her blazer and glanced down. She returned his gaze. "I'm sorry, I forgot to wear my name tag today," she paused, "I'm Meira." She raised her eyebrows with a hopeful smile.

"Nice to meet you Meira, please … call us Edward and Carmen," he returned the smile.

"Okay thank you. Maybe Carmen and I will get some time to chat and talk about her studies and how she's getting along. I recently graduated from the University of Tel Aviv myself. I would enjoy hearing her thoughts on our two diverse cities. Also, we can talk about Canada too. I hope I get the opportunity to visit there some day."

Edward pondered for a moment. He gazed once again upon this beautiful woman who stood before him and again wilfully descended into her deep dark eyes. Almost like a reflection, he saw his own daughter Carmen. The skin, hair and eye colour were different, but somehow it did not matter, much of Carmen was there. In a distant land, tens of thousands of miles from her own homeland, in a culture born from thousands of years in a different, tumultuous history—symbolically, she existed.

Ultimately, I think we're all the same. You just need to look closely enough to see it.

Edward extended the handle of his carry-on luggage bag and started towards the elevator within a lovely hotel, in what may be regarded as one of the holiest cities in the world. His thoughts were of reverence.

Edward intently studied the screen of his laptop placed in front of him on the table. He sat in the small restaurant of the Prima Royale Hotel and was taking advantage of the free Wi-Fi service while awaiting his lunch order.

Feeling refreshed after a shower and a short power nap, he took a sip from a tall glass of Carlsberg and glanced around. At 1:30 p.m. the cafe was busy with approximately 25 people having lunch. Obviously, this was a popular restaurant. *Always a good sign,* Edward mused. He observed the majority to be locals or at least thought them to be, as they were fluent in Hebrew. Also, there was a mix of Caucasians, couples and a few singles as well. The soft audible murmur of Italian, French, and English resounded.

Catching his eye through a transparent glass window off to the side was a quick reminder of where he was. Two men dressed in the traditional Ultra-Orthodox or Hassidim Jewish fashion of black suits, hats, and shoes, wearing full beards, with one long curled strand of hair in contrast to a short-cropped style on each side of their face, known as side-locks, strolled past. *Theologians, perhaps?* Edward wondered.

How do they manage the oppressive seasonal heat of this climate dressed like that? One can't help but marvel at the human spirit.

A waiter arrived carrying a tray with Edwards's order of a 'ham and swiss' with salad on the side. "Here you are sir," he smiled as he set the dishes down on the table. "Will you need anything else for now?"

"No, that's great, thank you." Edward returned the smile as he repositioned his laptop to finish reading the article on the screen. He watched the young man leave, then focused back to what he had been reading: a brief history of the L.A. Mayer Institute for Islamic Art Museum, quite an interesting read.

He reviewed it again, reading softly to himself, "The museum was established in 1974, founded by Vera Bryce Solomons, the daughter of Sir David Lionel Solomons, a notable scientist with a primary interest in electricity on which he authored several published works and pamphlets. He succeeded to the Baronetcy and held many political positions. Sir David had a great passion for horology and became *the* leading authority on the lifetime of the famed watchmaker Abraham Louis Breguet. In 1921, he self-published a major work on Breguet's life and career. Throughout his own lifetime, Solomon amassed the world's largest private collection of Breguet watches and clocks." Edward took a bite from his sandwich and continued. "The collection was comprised of 124 pieces including the two watches considered to be the pinnacle of Breguet's art: the 'Marie Antoinette' No. 160 and the 'Duc De Praslin' No. 92."

Edward had read in detail about the 'Marie Antoinette' watch and her mysteries, but he now learned the 'Duc De Praslin' had also been stolen from a museum in Paris, France, and then later retrieved.

Wow! Lots happening in the world of watchmaking in the 19th century. He took a long sip of his beer. *Let's see … to narrow it down …* He read on in silence now.

> *After his death in 1925, 57 of Solomon's best Breguet pieces, which included the 'Marie Antoinette' watch, were bequeathed to the museum that his daughter had founded and named in memory of one of her former professors—Leo Aryeh Mayer.*

And then … Edward mused as he chomped away at his salad. *What really put this museum on the horological global map*:

> *On April 15, 1983, the L.A. Mayer Institute was burglarized, and 106 rare timepieces were stolen, including the entire Solomon Collection. The multi-*

million-dollar theft was Israel's largest ever robbery. At this time, the 'Marie Antoinette' watch alone was valued at US 30 million dollars.

The case remained unsolved for more than 20 years, until in August 2006 the museum was contacted by a Tel Aviv antiques appraiser who informed them that some of the stolen items were being held by a lawyer whose client had inherited them from her deceased husband. She wished to sell them back to the museum. The police were contacted, and the client was identified as Nili Shamrat, the widow of a famed burglar Naaman Diller. Further investigations led to Israeli, French, and American investigators recovering 96 of the 106 rare timepieces that were stolen in 1983. From the testimony of Nili Shamrat, based on her dying husband's confession, it was believed that Naaman Dillar was successful in this burglary mainly because of an inoperative security alarm system, and the inadequate placement of the night watch security guard.

Edward closed his laptop. Finishing the last of his sandwich, he reached into his pocket for his cell phone and proceeded to scroll through the contacts list until he found the entry for L.A. Mayer Museum. He was staring at the telephone number when the waiter returned.

"Can I get you anything else, sir? Was everything okay?"

"Very good ... no, just the bill thanks." Edward added, "I'll pay with a credit card."

"Certainly, I can bring the machine to your table," the waiter turned and started to walk away when Edward called out to him.

"On second thought ... let's just put it on my room tab, number 316, Edward James."

"Yes, of course, sir." the waiter called back "I will return shortly for you to sign."

Edward gave him a friendly wave, then looked back to his phone and selected the number. It started to ring. Nervous tension started to rise with each successive ring. *A place with such an intriguing history and home to a timepiece collection that could rival any in the world, and now my acquired pocket watch has led me here, to this almost mystical domain of barons and queens. Does the secret of my watch lie deep in their dim and secluded past?* Edward felt a deep sense of intrigue and romanticism.

"Shalom ... L.A. Mayer Institute for Islamic Art. Jessica speaking."

EIGHTEEN

SUNDAY, MAY 4, 2014. 8:30 A.M.
PRIMA ROYALE HOTEL JERUSALEM, ISRAEL, (MEMORIAL DAY)

It was a bright, clear morning with a comfortable temperature of 26 degrees Celsius. Edward sat sideways on the driver's side of his sub-compact rental car. With the door open, his feet rested on the pavement of a parking spot in front of the Prima Royale Hotel. He had his reading glasses on and studied the portable GPS unit that came with the car. The destination *University of Tel Aviv* had been entered and he was trying to save to his own memory the major waypoints of the forthcoming road trip.

About six months ago, accompanied by Marie and Carmen, he had travelled these roads; they were straight forward, consisting mostly of interstate type four-lane highways. The route entailed travelling on #50 to #443 and then following #1 into the city. This would be the quickest way, depending on traffic of course, which Edward hoped would not be too heavy given the holiday and lack of work-related commuting. There was another more scenic route connecting the two cities a bit farther south. Perhaps they could travel that way when he brought Carmen back again in four days' time. She gave him directions to her residence for when he arrived on campus. Assuming her dad would not remember from six months ago was a correct assumption. Edward reached into his jean pocket to confirm he carried the directions with him. Short-term memory loss was becoming apparent, and he did not like it. *Hmm ... maybe I can work to make this degenerative process more selective. Marie always seems to be telling me I'm quite accomplished at selective hearing. So ... yeah, the talent's there ... I'm thinking just a redirection of focus.* He removed his reading glasses and tucked them into his shirt pocket.

Edward was anxious to leave. He did not inform Carmen yet about his quick call to the museum. Jessica—the woman he spoke with on the phone—said that although the Institute would be closed due to the holiday, she would be there in the afternoon. "It might be an appropriate time for you to come," she had offered. Edward agreed.

He would tell Carmen about the arrangement when they met. She was way too excited already, and he had lots to relate on their hour-long drive back to the hotel, and of course she would want to study the watch. It lay packed in its box on the passenger seat.

He swivelled back around and positioned the GPS on the top left of the windshield using the suction-cup mounting device. He carefully routed the power cable, closed the car door, and fastened his seat belt. Edward had already gone over the switches and controls with the rental car representative after he filled out the required paperwork. Now, he took a moment to re-familiarize himself as he started the vehicle. There was not much to it, really. The rental was a small white sub-compact with a manual transmission and little in the way of comfort options. Radio and air conditioning were included. The options list did, however, match the price, and Edward was not complaining.

As he checked through the basic controls and switches, he sent a 'thank-you' thought to Derek for setting him up so well on this trip. That is, until he got to the horn. He pressed it again to make sure he had pushed correctly.

He called out, "Derek! What have you given me? This isn't a horn! It's a squeaky toy. Nobody's gonna get out of my way when I lay on this! They will only point at me and laugh." Sighing, he pressed one more time and groaned, "It's a good thing I brought a hat and dark glasses; I don't want to be recognized by anybody when I'm tooting this baby toy around the city." Edward smiled sadly as he put the car into reverse and backed out of the parking spot. Selecting first gear, he accelerated out onto the street and called out his open window hoping somehow Derek might be listening, "Hey, just kidding buddy. I owe you, man!" With two more slaps on the horn, a quick shift into second gear and a smile on his face, Edward was off to pick up his kid. And he could not wait.

CARMEN PACED BACK and forth on the walkway in front of the Broshim Dormitory. She had a small suitcase set off to the side of the front entrance. It was quiet at the residence this morning, owing to the event of a national holiday. On most mornings except Saturdays, the Sabbath, there was a constant activity of cars, buses, and students in motion. Carmen's building was one of the first to be completed in an ambitious development of new residences for the Tel Aviv University campus. This showed evidence of just how big a business it was becoming to draw students of both national and international status. The project was nearing completion, but still generated activity. The completed buildings were excellent accommodations of a modern design, with many attractive features and amenities. Included with her own private quarters and shared bathroom, were rooms with lots of natural light and study alcoves dispersed throughout the building. Carmen found it a comfortable place to be and the food in the cafeteria was excellent.

Carmen tipped up her Ray Bans and glanced at her watch: 9:35 a.m. She had her hair tied back in a ponytail and wore slim-fitting denim capris, an unbuttoned collared shirt with sleeves rolled up to three-quarter length, and a snug fitting camisole top underneath. A brown vinyl and leather-accented, medium-sized satchel hung over her left shoulder. Stylish natural leather sandals with rubber soles completed her attire. The outfit, combined with incessant pacing and emphasized by the dark aviator sunglasses spoke of a young, fit, attractive woman ready for adventure.

Carmen looked at her watch again: 9:36. *Six minutes late Dad!* She could see down the road in the direction he would be coming from and had been intently watching the sparse traffic for the last 10 minutes. He did not tell her what kind of vehicle he had rented.

Just then a tiny white car came into view. As it got closer she could vaguely make out the sole occupant who was wearing sports sunglasses and a ball cap; she turned away, *nope, not dad's style.* A squeaky sounding 'toot-toot' of a car horn brought her attention back to the little white car. *No way …* It turned in and pulled up in front of her residence. Right before it came to a stop, she looked in through the passenger-side window. Beneath the ball cap brim and the red and white Oakleys, she saw a broad grin beaming at her that Carmen knew could only belong to one man.

"Daddy!" She raced around to the driver's-side door and began hopping up and down with exuberant vibrancy, impatiently waiting for the door to open. Edward applied the e-brake and turned off the ignition. He reached for the door handle and stopped. He wanted to take in the moment. His daughter had her fists clenched tightly and was bouncing up and down. Edward could not wait any longer. He opened the door.

"Hey, Carmen! Can I have some of that energy? I sure could use it." He rose up out of the car into a loving father-daughter embrace—the kind you wished would never end. They clung to each other. No words were spoken. None needed to be. They hugged. They remembered. All too soon they stood back holding each other at arm's length, glad that dark glasses covered their misting eyes.

"Thanks Dad, for being here. I wish Mom was here too."

"Me too. She sends her love." Edward paused, and then broke out into a grin as he gave her shoulders a squeeze. "Her love comes with a set of instructions, however …" Carmen cocked her head to the side, let go of her dad and stepped back slightly.

"I bet I know," she laughed. "Be careful!"

"Extra careful! I think were her words: please keep me posted and up to date via email, phone, Skype … whatever, right to the point where it starts to become annoying." Edward winced.

"Mom's relentless. Our adventure will need to be safe, healthy and thoroughly reported, or else!" She giggled as she ran for her suitcase.

Edward could see his daughter's energy was starting to build again. He leaned back into the car and released the trunk latch. Carmen walked over, tossed her luggage in, closed the lid, and started towards the passenger door. "Hey Dad! Sweet ride! Wanna like … cruise some of the hot beach strips here in the Veev before we head to the hotel in J-Ru?"

"Yea Carm, thanks. Derek set me up fine. Sounds cool. Turns out, though, we kinda got an appointment this aft to bring a certain watch to a certain museum to score some info goin down on that piece." Edward did not have to wait long for the predictable reaction. They leaned over the car facing each other. He smiled as he watched her fists clench again.

"Yes … yes! Did you bring it? Okay!" She flung open the car door.

"In the box on your seat Carmen."

She had her door closed, seat belt on, Ray Bans lifted and perched on top of her head, and had the box open before Edward sat down. Once his seat belt was fastened, his door closed and the engine running, he leaned over and pointed out to Carmen the tiny clasp that would open the cover of the watch, which she now had cradled in her hands. Completely engrossed in what she was studying, Edward could hear her uttering soft, almost inaudible exclamations of "Awesome! Wow!"

"Here we go." They departed from the front of the residence and headed back on the road en-route to Jerusalem. He gave the horn a couple of cheerful pats as he settled in behind the wheel. It was great to be with his daughter again. Carmen looked up. She seemed to be calming down and redirecting her energy more towards concentration now.

"Dad, tell me all that's happened in detail. I want to hear all about it. We've got an hour drive ahead of us."

"Okay, sure ... here goes: It was the annual garage sale in Petrolia. I hadn't yet been to Brad's for a hotdog ..." Carmen sat up abruptly and stared over at her father.

"Oh, come on, that hurts. I meant detail about the watch! You know how much I look forward to those hot dogs every year. That was cruel!"

Edward gave Carmen his best 'guess I'm guilty' gesture. "Sorry, just trying to set the right ambiance."

"Okay ... so, how were they?"

"Excellent of course. I had two this year on your behalf. I mean, well I was thinking of you when I ate them," he smiled proudly.

"Oh, that was so very thoughtful of you," Carmen smirked.

"Thank you, but let me continue ... I was riding my mountain bike ... a great morning for a ride ..."

"Dad! We only have an hour!" She glared at him in a stern manner.

"Okay, okay! Just kidding."

"Oh ... and Dad, could you please try and not use that horn too much, especially when my sunglasses are up like this?" Carmen paused for effect. "I'm getting to know people in this country now. I might be recognized!"

EDWARD IMPARTED HIS narrative, and it lasted for over an hour. He found a space to park on the street around the corner of the Prima Royale Hotel at approximately 10:45 a.m. He now had Carmen up to date on all that had transpired over the last several days regarding the watch. They were both anxious about this afternoon and the pending visit to the museum.

"After we get you settled in, we can have an early lunch, and you can fill me in on the details of 'life as a foreign student.'" Edward smiled as he popped the trunk latch and they both exited the car. Carmen grabbed her suitcase from the trunk and extended the handle as her dad locked up the car. They headed towards the hotel main entrance, about 50 metres away, located on the corner.

"Oh, Carmen, a lovely young woman works here at the reception desk. Her name is Meira. I met her yesterday at check in. We chatted for a bit. She told me that she's looking forward to meeting you."

"Oh, what a beautiful name." Carmen assessed the exterior of the hotel as they approached. "This looks really nice … in a lovely area, too."

Edward nodded. "Nice inside too."

As they rounded the corner, the flashing lights of a police cruiser parked directly in front of the entrance greeted them. The car was empty.

"Hmm … you get a deal on this place?" Carmen mused as they started through the doors.

"Well yes, actually Derek …"

"Ah, Derek! Say no more, please."

They both laughed as they entered. Edward caught Meira's eye. She stood behind the reception desk in conversation with a police officer. He could not help but notice a frown come over her face when she spotted him. As they approached the desk, Meira seemed to excuse herself from the officer. They were speaking in Hebrew. A look of concern came over her face as she addressed them.

"Edward, a moment, please? I am sorry." She forced a weak smile, looking towards Carmen, "I am Meira. You would be Carmen?"

"Yes, pleased to meet you, Meira." She gave her father a quick, uneasy glance.

"Excuse me, but the manager has asked to see you both in his office." Meira picked up a desk phone and hurriedly spoke in Hebrew. Carmen leaned close to her dad's ear. "I think she said, 'they are here now.'" Edward nodded and started to get an apprehensive feeling as he observed the police officer staring at them. *Something is definitely wrong here ...*

"It is that door over there to the left." Meira put the phone down and gestured towards a paneled door. Edward turned to Carmen, trying to appear reassuring as he nodded towards the door. Meira offered another nervous smile as they started towards the office. Edward was about to knock when the door opened. A man of medium build and height, with peppered grey hair and wearing a dark blue suit, greeted them. He smiled and held out his hand. Edward felt a firm handshake. "Hello Mr. James and daughter Carmen, I am David Agar, the hotel manager." He offered a light handshake to Carmen. He spoke excellent English.

"Please, just Edward and Carmen is fine," Edward politely offered.

"Yes, thank you, come in and have a seat." The manager responded as he closed the door behind them. Edward and Carmen sat in two leather chairs positioned in front of the desk. He walked around the desk and sat in his chair. The small office had one small window that let in some natural light. A bookcase filled up the opposite wall, and a brightly coloured abstract 'oil on canvas' hung directly behind the desk. David had a serious expression on his face as he began to speak. "I am very sorry to inform you Edward and Carmen that it appears there has been some trouble with your room."

Edward glanced to Carmen, then back to the manager, with a questioning expression on his face. "Trouble?"

"One of our cleaning staff was walking down the third-floor hallway one hour ago when she noticed the door to your room open slightly. This in itself was not so troubling; however, as she passed close to the door, she heard an electronic beeping sound coming from inside the room. Thinking it might be an unattended alarm clock or a telephone handset left on, she thought to knock loudly and call into the room. Upon getting no response, and opening the door, she saw that the suite was in complete disarray. Drawers had been left open with clothes and personal items thrown across the floor. The mattress cover had literally been torn off with the top mattress tossed to the side, which had, in turn, knocked the telephone from its base." David Agar took a moment to glance down at a paper on his desk.

Carmen suddenly grabbed her dad's arm and blurted out, "Someone has broken into our room?" They turned to each other, a bewildering look etched on both their faces.

"I am afraid so Carmen." His expression did not alter as he scanned the paper again. "At 9:42 a.m. the cleaning woman called my office, and I went up to the room immediately. A quick inspection revealed that the room safe had also been tampered with. We then left the room and called the police. They arrived 15 minutes later." The manager clasped his hands together and leaned back in his chair. "I am so sorry Edward and Carmen." He waited a moment knowing they would need a bit of time to get over the initial shock.

He continued, "I understand this is most unsettling. You will, of course, be given a new room with an upgrade and have our most sincere apologies."

Carmen still squeezed her father's arm. Edward was ever so slightly shaking his head from side to side, still somewhat bewildered. He spoke uneasily, "Should we be going up to the room to check my things and to see if anything's missing?"

David responded, "I would have to ask you to please wait for a bit. Two uniformed officers are on the premises now, and as I understand an inspector will be arriving shortly. He will want to talk to you personally and ask a few questions."

"Of course, no problem." Edward glanced over to Carmen and saw she had a puzzled expression.

"Inspector?" She queried, addressing the manager.

"Yes," he answered. "As you and your father come from another country and this incident happened in a hotel it will be classified under the general heading of tourism, which as I am sure you are aware generates much revenue for our country. Consequently, acts of this nature are taken very seriously by our government." The manager offered his first attempt at a smile. "I have been told the inspector will be here soon. Until then I would like to ask of you to wait in our conference room. It will be a most suitable, private location in which to speak with the inspector." His smile looked much brighter now. "I will have Meira escort you to the room and take an order for any beverages of your choice."

Edward and Carmen both nodded. "Yes, sure, okay," they both softly replied at the same time. The initial shock was subsiding. The eyes of father and daughter met in an almost secretive understanding, an understanding that by now they both mentally processed. There could be only one reason for the break-in, and their thoughts were simultaneous: *It must be the watch!*

NINETEEN

THE CONFERENCE ROOM at the Prima Royale Hotel was of a typical design: long and narrow, built to accommodate one table with 20 leather chairs. The room had been decorated in soft colours, with attractive non-imposing art adorning the walls. Edward and Carmen sat facing each other at the end of the table closest to the door, which had been left partially open. They both had a soft drink can, and an ice-filled glass in front of them that a waiter from the restaurant had recently delivered with coasters and napkins. Neither said much since leaving the lobby with Meira, who was again very apologetic. The time was not right for casual girl-to-girl chitchat. Even so, Carmen had a pleasant feeling about her. She looked forward to having some time with Meira under better circumstances.

"I was thinking…" Carmen popped the tab on her root beer. Edward followed suit with his Coke. He raised his eyebrows in anticipation. "You're retired now. I'm an adult, enrolled in graduate school. I think now is the time for you to be honest with me."

Edward had been pouring his soda. He stopped and stared closely at his daughter. He did not say anything.

"I mean, I'm thinking … you were more than a welder. Like a double agent or something." She paused, "Does Canada have like a C.I.A. thing going on ... 'Spy Mounties' maybe?" She did not wait for a reply. "Let's get some perspective here: In the last several days you have been solicited by a covert man with a Caribbean accent, had your phone tapped, you are jet-setting to various exotic locations around the world, your life has been threatened by big, menacing thugs and now your hotel room was broken into and trashed. Let's not forget that backing you up is a genius type techno gismo geek who is supplying you with the latest technology in SIM cards, GPS, etcetera ... as well as taking care of flights, hotel accommodations, rental cars ..."

Carmen stopped. "Well okay, the rental car doesn't quite go with the picture, but hey ... Canadians *do* tend to be moderately practical." Somehow Edward managed to keep a straight face.

Carmen continued with a mischievous sparkle in her green eyes. "All that's left to complete the profile is for Mom to show up wearing a Dior gown with a 25-karat Cartier diamond necklace, looking stunning as she hangs off your arm while attending the opera or playing the casino. I hope the thieves spared your tuxedo when they wasted the hotel room!" Carmen leaned back in her chair and took a long sip of her root beer. "So, father ... the truth please?"

Edward understood the 'cover.' Again, his daughter was using humour when she had to use her brain for a new or unusual task. Wanting to participate, he felt up for the challenge.

Shaking his head slowly and shifting his gaze downward in a submissive gesture he said, "The truth can hurt Carmen," he hesitantly looked up into her eyes. "A long time ago, when you were young ... I should never have kept this from you for so long. I'm sorry. Yes, I was indeed more than just a welder." Edward waited until he saw Carmen shift uncomfortably in her chair. He gazed downward again, and finally raising his head up with a most convincingly sad voice he stated, "I was also a plumber."

Carmen gasped in horror. "A plumber!"

"Yes, it is true, as you have now become an adult I will tell you, and I'm not overly proud of it." A look of shame came over his face. "There were times when my pants and undershorts were riding low, and my t-shirt did not completely cover, well ... kneeling down with pipe wrench in hand, I guess the view from behind ... not too pretty."

"Oh, my god!" Carmen clasped her hands over her open mouth. "At such a young tender age—*post-traumatic stress disorder* pending!"

In the silence, his daughter's beautiful green eyes studied him. With a questioning expression, she asked, "Daddy, what have we gotten ourselves into?"

Edward shrugged, "We can only do our best. We need to figure this out. I hope by this afternoon we'll have some answers."

Carmen glanced at the door and back to her dad. "What are we going to tell the inspector when he comes?"

Edward sat thinking. "I'm not sure what would be the best. You got any ideas?"

"Well ... let's see. It's doubtful the inspector would know anything about the pocket watch. He will, though, I'm sure, have some knowledge of the L.A. Mayer Museum and its relation to watch antiquities. However, our problem is we've learned almost nothing about this watch other than it might be tied to some kind of strange prophecy and that a bunch of criminals are trying to steal it." Now it was Carmen who shrugged her shoulders as her father stretched out his leg sideways to gain access to the pocket of his jeans. He took out his cell phone.

"Tell you what." Edward turned on the phone. "I'll give Derek a call. I think we should get his opinion. Possibly he has some info on the New York thing. It could shed some light."

"You do realize it's only 6:00 a.m. in Petrolia now?" Carmen glanced at her watch.

"Right, yeah, it's okay, Derek's an early riser. He'll be getting up about now."

"Mom is off this weekend. She won't be getting up for at least an hour or so." Carmen shuffled in her chair. "Dad, she's not going to take this well."

Edward nodded. He was trying to think of the best way to handle it.

"I don't want to upset Mom." Carmen bit down on her lower lip.

"Okay ... I'll ask Derek not to tell her about the break-in. I'll speak to her myself right after our visit to the museum. Hopefully, by then, there will be some better news to share. That could help smooth things over." He offered Carmen a weak smile and began dialling.

"You're not calling the house number, are you?" Edward stopped. "Mom will get up if she hears a long-distance ring. Better to call his cell."

"Good *call* Carmen. No pun intended, right?" He gave her a nod, hit cancel, and started over.

Derek picked up on the third ring. "Yo Edward ... How's things in the Middle East?"

"Hey Derek, glad you're awake. How are you guys doing?"

"We're okay. Marie is sleeping, probably tired. She's been working her butt off around here. Wow, I got floor and counter top space extreme! I'm thinkin I've now got room to start up a couple of new projects."

Edward could envision Derek beaming on the other end. "I'm sure that's what she had in mind." They both chuckled. "Listen, Derek, Carmen is with me now at the Prima Royale. Thanks for setting everything up."

"Hey, no prob ... everything checked out okay?"

"Well, yes, up until a short time ago." Edward hesitated. "I'm afraid we've had a bit of trouble ..."

"Trouble ... again? Man, Edward, you're beginning to get a reputation!" An increase in breathing intensity could be heard coming from Derek. "Are you guys ok? What happened?"

"We're okay, just fine." Edward smiled at Carmen who mouthed the words 'Hi Derek.' "Carmen says hi."

"Hi to Carmen." It helped to restore Derek's breathing somewhat.

Edward resumed. "We just got here from Tel Aviv this morning and were confronted by the hotel manager. Our room was broken into."

"Anything taken?" Derek was starting to rev up again.

"Well, no ... at least I don't think so. We haven't been up to the room yet. We're waiting now for a police inspector to talk to us and bring us up to date on the damage. I didn't leave anything of value in the room. Well ... I did put my passport in the safe." With silence on the line, Edward could almost hear Derek thinking.

"It's gotta be about the watch, you took it with you right?" The uneasiness in Derek's voice was evident.

"Yes, only clothes and toiletry items were left in my room." Edward paused. "However, my five bladed razors ... those things are like getting super expensive. Do you think ...?" That brought an amusing smile from Carmen who patiently studied the melting ice in her glass.

"Yea right, Edward. Was the lock mechanism on the door damaged?" Derek was on a mission now and not about to slow down.

"Didn't sound like it; apparently, a cleaning person heard a beeping sound coming through the opened door and went in to investigate. The phone had been knocked off the hook, and the place was trashed."

"Okay, so I'm guessing if the lock wasn't damaged there had to be adequate technology available to open the locked door ... a card insert, right?"

"Yes, and it closed behind me and locked automatically."

"Right, so I think we can tentatively tie it to the phone tapping and our friends from New York." Silence resumed on the phone line. Edward did not want to interrupt Derek's train of thought. He knew the wheels would be turning.

"Edward, I'm fairly sure you were followed. Your flights and accommodations were all made here on this end. Definitely secure. Your cell phone is and will be okay if you don't let it out of your sight. Make sure you change out the SIM card in Carmen's phone with the one I gave you." Derek stopped. He added, "I'm sure I don't need to tell you again: watch your backs."

Edward could sense an uneasiness in his own voice. "Derek ... you got anything more on the New York thing?"

"Not yet. I'm hoping today some time."

"I was thinking we might learn something that could help us during the upcoming interview with the police, and also later this afternoon when we will be meeting with someone at the museum. Thing is ..." He halted for a moment, before continuing, "Carmen and I are not too sure about what to say and do under these new circumstances."

Derek's response was delayed. "I get what you mean. As far as the police are concerned, I don't think you should tell them about New York. Mention the word *murder*, and I can guarantee you fireworks will start going off. And even then, if you say that your newly acquired pocket watch might in some way be connected to the Marie Antoinette watch and the biggest heist in the country's history, well ... look out! You'll probably never see your watch again. As for the museum, I say let them come to you. They're the ones who should have the knowledge to tell you what you need to know."

Edward looked over at Carmen who was staring at him intently. She would already have determined by the look on his face that Derek had given them their answer.

He held the eye contact with his daughter as he spoke. "That makes a lot of sense. Thanks."

"Hey, no sweat, I'm with you on this."

"Derek, this latest turn of events is going to be tough on Marie. Carmen and I thought it might be best if we spoke to her in person, hopefully with some better news. Later this afternoon after our museum visit, we could Skype."

"Okay, I got your back on this one. Should work out. I'll be leaving shortly for the office warehouse. I'm restocking my work van today. I won't be home for some time, around 2:00 p.m. or so. What I can do is leave a note to Marie telling her you called and will be in touch with her later today."

"That sounds perfect!" Edward was a bit more relaxed now. "Derek, again—thanks, buddy."

"Hey, you got it. Tell Carmen to enjoy the museum. You guys can figure it out." He laughed, "With her brains and your good looks ... no wait, sorry that should be with her brains and *her* good looks ... Oh, I don't know. Anyhow, you guys rock! Later Edward."

"Later Derek."

As he pressed the 'end call' button and smiled at Carmen, Edward thought he felt better overall. However, what Derek had last said in the context of light passing humour stayed with him in a most unsettling way.

Just how was *it* to be figured out? Edward wondered.

EDWARD AND CARMEN SAW a medium-sized man enter the conference room. He had a fair complexion, black wavy hair and sported a close-cut, well-trimmed moustache that took away from a rather large nose. His dark eyes had a bright, piercing quality. Carmen was drawn to the quality of his perfectly fitting lightweight wool suit done in beige, accompanied by a subtle pink shirt and a deep cobalt blue silk tie. She suddenly felt under-dressed for the occasion.

Edward was admiring the two-toned steel and rose gold rectangular curved case of a vintage styled Girard-Perregaux wristwatch fastened to the man's wrist with a cognac alligator strap. It had a soft, creamy white dial on which were traditional Arabic numbers, and dauphin hands, also created in rose gold. *Very, very nice.*

"Hello Mr. James and daughter Carmen, I would like to introduce myself. I am Inspector Claude Gadgét." The French accent was unmistakable but pronunciation was very precise in a confident voice. He had an air of dignity about him and his posture appeared effortless and perfect. Both Edward and Carmen rose from their chairs as the inspector extended a warm handshake to them. "Please …" he gestured for them to resume sitting as he stepped back to close the door. He smiled as he pulled out the chair from the head of the table, unbuttoned his suit jacket and sat down.

"Thank you for your patience. I am sure this event is most unfortunate for you both. We should not be too long here. I am sure you will be happy to resume your holiday." He turned towards Carmen. "I understand, Carmen, you are an undergraduate from Canada doing your first year of graduate studies at the University of Tel Aviv."

Right off she could sense his underlying focus and intensity. *Be careful. There's not a lot getting past this guy.* "Yes, I am pursuing a degree in Environmental Science," Carmen smiled. *He doesn't blink much either.* Gadgét took some time. An ever so slight furrow appeared on his brow. His gaze did not falter.

"Carmen, this country is attracting an increasing number of foreign students each year. I believe there are many reasons for this. However, I think the most notable is its unique international status. This is a country in a land of ancient written history. It is an excellent combination for worldly scholars such as yourself." Carmen thought she might be blushing. No one had ever actually called her a 'worldly scholar.' *Maybe this guy's okay, even if he is a bit intense.*

She smiled. "I'm getting along well and picking up on the Hebrew language a bit too. I believe it was the right choice for me to come here to study."

"I am glad for you Carmen. I myself made a choice to come here from another country. I was born and raised in Paris, France. I am sure you picked up on my accent. I have been fortunate to learn many languages. It is most necessary in my line of work. My accent, though!" He laughed softly and raised his hands up in a gesture of acceptance. "It is always here to say from where I came."

Inspector Gadgét turned in his chair to address Edward. "You have taken the opportunity of the short holiday Edward … do you mind if I call you Edward?"

"No, that's fine" Edward responded.

"You came to visit Carmen; that is excellent. Your wife, I understand, is predisposed with work obligations and had to remain in Canada." He was sincere and his eyes did not waiver.

Edward held his gaze. *This guy just got here, and he has a case file on us already!* "Yes, it's unfortunate for us. Nevertheless, I am recently retired and no longer assume those responsibilities myself."

"Ah, congratulations on your retirement Edward. May I ask what your occupation was?"

"High-pressure pipe welding."

"A trade that requires a high level of skill. Yes, that helps to explain your affinity for fine craftsmanship." Inspector Gadgét offered a confident smile.

Edward responded with a puzzling glance to the inspector, then over to Carmen. She just raised her eyebrows and tipped her hands up in a 'beats me' gesture. A little pensive, he turned back to Gadgét.

"I see, Edward, you dress in a comfortable casual style, yet you wear an expensive watch. The model you chose is in the 'Professional Series' from one of the finest watch companies in the world and offers excellent value for dollar. It is my deduction Edward that although your acquisition of this timepiece is to mark an important achievement, I presume that for you it is not a status symbol. Rather, I believe you can relate on a practical level to the skill and precision required for the creation of such an excellent mechanical device." Claude Gadgét leaned back in his chair. For the first time, he seemed to relax his intensity. "Please forgive me, Edward and Carmen, for my redundancies. It is my job to observe. I cannot seem to help myself." He offered an apologetic smile.

Edward showed the appearance of approval. "I believe you are accurate in your deductions inspector, and I will take that as a compliment. Thank you."

Gadgét slightly bowed his head. "If I might now fill you in on our progress with the investigation." It was back to business for the inspector, glancing back and forth between Edward and Carmen as he spoke. "We determined that a person or persons gained access to the building by a rear entrance. The key lock mechanism on the door shows signs of having been tampered with. Several digital video monitors are in service on the property, both inside and out. We are currently in the process of obtaining data that will be scrutinized back at headquarters. I have been to the room. It is most probable the room was ransacked with the intent of finding something specific. I personally believe this to be a professional operation." Inspector Gadgét paused. He continued to look from Edward to Carmen. His focus intensified. "The hotel room safe in the hall closet was scoped." Again, a brief silence resumed.

Edward shifted uneasily. "Scoped?"

The inspector responded, "Yes, a small hole is drilled through the encasement and a tiny fibre-optic illuminated 'scope' is inserted. It is attached to a small viewer. This allows the thief to inspect what is secured within the safe, thus determining if any further action is required."

"There was only my passport which I locked in the safe before I left the room this morning ... nothing else of exceptional value in the room either."

The furrows deepened on his brow. Claude Gadgét now leaned forward. "It would appear your passport was not the object of desire for the intruders."

Both Edward and Carmen knew for sure where this conversation was headed. Gadgét's poignant stare now shifted back and forth between them continuously in preparation for his next question. This man could read faces, and he would know that quite often the truth can be found more in what you see than what you hear. "Perhaps in your possession Edward is something you might have considered leaving in your room, which could be of significant interest to someone?"

Unfortunately for Inspector Claude Gadgét, he was at a disadvantage, and he knew it. He just did not know how much. He had made the best of an unfortunate seating arrangement, which made it difficult to analyze two subjects simultaneously. What he could not foresee, however, was that before him sat two students of psychology who had been informed of his pending arrival, and unknowingly he had given them time to prepare for it.

There were no slips, no stumbles, not one involuntary twitch, not even the bat of an eyelid as they both focused on him unwaveringly.

Edward replied, "If not the watch I'm wearing on my wrist, then perhaps this is a case of mistaken identity." He broke eye contact with the inspector and turned to Carmen. She met his gaze before addressing Inspector Gadgét, giving him an affirmative nod.

The inspector said nothing. The silence was stifling. Looking from one to the other, he finally conceded. "It does happen upon occasion." He reached into the inside breast pocket of his suit coat and retrieved two cards and handed them each one. "I would like to leave you my numbers where I can be reached. I am sorry for the inconvenience. We will most certainly do our best to identify the perpetrators. Please, if anything else happens, contact me immediately." The inspector rose from his chair. Edward and Carmen did the same. "I do hope you enjoy your holiday together."

"Thank you," Edward responded.

"Nice to meet you, Inspector," Carmen added. He re-buttoned his suit coat and extended his hand again for warm handshakes. Grasping her purse on the table, Carmen lifted it to her waist, opened the zipper, and carefully tucked the inspector's card right next to the case of the pocket watch, which was nestled securely within. Re-closing the purse, she looked up to find his eyes fixed upon her. Carmen smiled confidently. This time she saw an ever so slight uncertainty in his penetrating stare. *Inspector Gadgét, I believe we have a stalemate.* She slung the purse over her shoulder.

The inspector turned. He opened the door and held it for Carmen and Edward to pass through. His free hand found the light switch near the door and was just about to depress it when he stopped and turned back to focus again into the room. His eyes scanned the table before him. The two remaining pop cans sat close together, situated further down the long table. The two tall glasses sat upon damp napkins directly where Edward and Carmen had been sitting. He observed these glasses with more interest now. Each had about one or two inches of tinted water in the bottom. The ice had long since melted. Inspector Claude Gadgét thoughtfully turned back to the door and spoke quietly to himself, "Perhaps I have been guilty of an oversight." He hesitated, "This conference is over," he flicked the switch, plunging the room into darkness, "for now!"

TWENTY

The early lunch Edward proposed needed to be re-scheduled as just 'lunch.' When it did not happen within a reasonable time frame, they re-scheduled yet again and re-classified as a 'late lunch.' Nevertheless, when they did finally eat the food was delicious. Also, Edward and Carmen had a chance to be alone to plan their late afternoon itinerary.

Consequently, 1:45 p.m. found them on a 15-minute walk down lovely tree-lined streets on route to the L.A. Mayer Museum. Dealing with the authorities had been a lengthy process, as well as repacking all of Edward's belongings and getting settled into the new room: a larger suite situated on the top floor, where access to a lovely rooftop lounge was just up a short flight of stairs.

Meira and David were helpful and accommodating, even going as far as having their lunch delivered to them on the rooftop lounge, compliments of the hotel. They greatly appreciated the gesture, a much-needed recovery break. Enjoying their food and drinks while taking in the excellent view, Edward and Carmen discussed the possibilities of their visit to the museum. They agreed to take Derek's advice and 'let them come to you.' Most of the personal information on what transpired regarding the watch could always be disclosed later if necessary.

For now, the scenario would be: Edward found an old watch at a garage sale in Petrolia. Thinking it might be of excellent quality he went to a jewellery store in London, Ontario. His assumption about the quality was confirmed. Through online browsing, Edward had learned a little about L.A. Mayer Museum and its expert knowledge of antique timepieces. He planned to visit his daughter who is studying in Tel Aviv, and things were favourable for the 'two for one' scenario.

After establishing their 'game plan', Carmen searched walking directions to the museum while Edward called once more to confirm their arrival. He spoke again with Jessica. She would watch for them at the front entrance at 2:00 p.m.

It was sunny and warm, so Edward opted for cargo- styled shorts, a polo shirt and sandals to accommodate the hot temperatures. He wore his Oakleys but without a hat this time. Carmen remained dressed the same as earlier.

Walking along, they chatted about Carmen's university studies and things back home, which helped to ease the noticeably increasing tension they experienced as they got closer to their destination. They also began to discuss a tentative itinerary for the next day, hoping they could revisit the Old City and enjoy falafels for lunch.

When they walked around a bend in the street, the impressive architecture of the L.A. Mayer Museum came into view; a building made up of three rectangular shapes. The two-tiered centre block housed the main entrance above street level and was framed by five-domed archways, which were accessed by cement steps. Behind the archways were the glass entrance doors and glass window panels. The two side blocks, or wings of the building, were set forwards with narrow vertical glass panels evenly spaced on the front. The entire structure consisted mainly of sandstone brick, typical of the city of Jerusalem. A large header across the top of the centre block, painted in red, contrasted sharply against the light beige walls. It contained what appeared to be an abstract symbol of a timepiece dial in the centre and lettering on either side. As they approached, Edward and Carmen took in the beautiful details of the building. Getting even closer, the writing on the nearest side of the dial appeared to be in Arabic, the far side in English. Carmen was the first to make out the printing in English. She read the words aloud, "The Mystery of Lost Time."

"Hmm ... that certainly seems appropriate for us right now," Edward mused.

"Looks like we might be at the right place," Carmen laughed.

They arrived at the front of the building and turned into an opening in an iron fence and proceeded up the cement stairs leading to the entrance. Carmen tried the glass door and found it locked. She removed her sunglasses, opened her purse and set them inside. Cupping her hands on the side of her head to shield her eyes from the light, she pressed her face close to the glass and peered inside. In a moment, her vision began to adjust.

"See anything?" Edward arrived at her side.

"No ... oh wait ... yes." Carmen tapped loudly on the glass with one hand. "She saw me! She's coming."

"Must be Jessica," Edward responded.

Carmen stepped back just as a young woman could be seen through the glass releasing the lock. The door opened to a smiling face.

"Hi, and good afternoon. You must be Edward and Carmen?" They both nodded. "Please, come in. My name is Jessica." She held the door for them to enter. Edward removed his sunglasses and tucked them into his shirt pocket as they went through the door.

Jessica had a tiny frame and long dark hair pulled back in a nicely maintained ponytail. Her complexion was fair; it looked as though her skin did not get much sun exposure. She wore slim-fitting black dress pants, a loose collared white blouse, and black kitten-heel pumps. With her black plastic framed eyeglasses, Edward thought she fit the historian stereotype perfectly. Carmen concurred;

however, she thought her eyes would distinguish her from others. They were a crystal blue colour and even through her glasses, a sparkle seemed to radiate. A look that Hollywood film directors and producers exploited with great success, albeit often with the use of tinted contact lenses.

"As you know, the museum is closed today. I am here to catch up on some paperwork." Jessica turned slightly as she continued to escort them through an archway leading to a small left corner alcove. To the right was another archway, partially covered with a curtain of richly textured tapestry.

A modern low-profile table surrounded by six chairs of varying styles for lounging and reading took up most of the space. A natural wood rack stood on the far wall, which held pamphlets and magazines pertaining to the museum. Three framed photographs hung on the back wall. They were pictures showing the founding of the Institute. A corner shelf in matching wood held two hand-painted vases against the nearest wall. This made for a casual, comfortable setting.

Jessica stopped and addressed them. "We can relax here and talk." She motioned towards two high-back armless chairs positioned nearest them and facing the back wall.

"Thank you," Edward responded. "As I said when we spoke on the phone, we're hoping we can get some information on a pocket watch I recently came into possession of." He and Carmen remained standing. They exchanged glances, both a little dubious of this young woman's qualifications. They would have been more reassured to be meeting with someone older and more experienced. Jessica appeared to pick up on their uncertainty.

"There are several people employed here at the museum who are well qualified to assist you. Being that I am here today and not too busy, I gladly offer my services. I hope I can be of help." She gave them a reassuring smile. "I hold a degree in horology as well as many years of extensive study in the related history of timepieces."

Edward and Carmen were feeling a bit more at ease now. They moved closer to the chairs. Jessica's smile brightened. "Edward, I believe you said you were going to walk here from your hotel, and I know its quite warm today. Could I interest you both in a nice tall glass of lemon iced tea? I am going to enjoy one myself. I just made some fresh before you arrived."

"Thanks for the offer Jessica, but I think I'll pass. I just finished a beer back at the hotel." He glanced towards Carmen. "Maybe Carmen?"

"Do you like iced tea, Carmen?" Jessica showed a hopeful expression on her face. Carmen had learned many people in Middle Eastern regions placed importance on the partaking of tea. For some, it represented a ritual of kindness and acceptance. Carmen felt somewhat obliged.

"Yes, I do. Thank you. I would like some tea." She returned the smile.

"Edward, anything else? Some water, or a soft drink?"

"I'm okay. Thanks again."

"Okay, well please …" Jessica gestured again towards the chairs. "I will be only a minute. Make yourselves comfortable." She exited the room through the partially drawn tapestry curtain behind Edward and Carmen. They settled into their seats.

Jessica returned several minutes later carrying a tray on which two tall glasses of iced tea balanced. A medium-sized leather purse was now slung over her shoulder. She gracefully stepped to the side and placed one glass before Carmen and the other opposite her. In another fluid motion, Jessica set the tray off to the side as she manoeuvred around the table and took a seat in a leatherette tub chair facing them.

"There we are." Jessica had her bright smile on them as she set her purse on the table beside her and promptly opened it. "I could not find any napkins in our kitchenette. I am sure I have some here we can use ... yes, here we are." She proceeded to pull out two napkins, one of which she handed to Carmen.

"Thank you, Jessica, this looks refreshing." Carmen immediately lifted the glass to her lips and took a sip. "Mmm ... very good, do you use honey and lemon?"

She could not help but notice the full thickness and silky texture of the napkin. She set it on the table and placed the cold glass on top of it. A picture of an old carriage was stamped on one corner, and underneath was something printed in Hebrew. Previously, Carmen thought the time had arrived for her to start the arduous task of trying to learn written Hebrew and the Arabic languages.

"Yes, that is correct, and thank you," Jessica replied. "I do make iced tea often. I find the beverage helps me cope with the warm climate."

She took a sip of her tea, set it down on her napkin and proceeded to direct her attention towards Edward. "So ... shall we talk about your watch? If you are interested, I would be happy to show you our excellent collection of timepieces after we are finished here."

"That would be great. We'd really like to see the exhibits." Both Edward and Carmen were starting to feel excitement building.

Edward sat up in his chair. Carmen took another sip of her tea. "I guess I don't have too much to tell you. I'm not a collector of antiques at all, so my knowledge is quite limited with regards to old timepieces. However, before you examine the watch I will tell you how I found it."

As Edward related the story of acquiring the watch, Jessica listened intently. Carmen sipped at her tea. He told her of his discovery at the garage sale, with a brief outline of Petrolia—its history and the theatre fire, which resulted in the salvaged box of props where he discovered the watch. Edward then spoke of his inquiries at the jewellery store in London, being careful to omit the owner's recommendation for him to go and see a watchmaker in New York.

He mentioned his futile online search for information and finished by stating his intent to visit Carmen on this long weekend, who currently attended the University of Tel Aviv.

Edward offered a hopeful smile. "I embrace an interest in watches, having perused many websites on the topic for several years. In doing so, I read of the expertise of this museum on horological antiquities." He gave a slight shrug of his shoulders, "Thought it might be worth a shot." He nodded at Carmen, indicating a pre-arranged signal to retrieve the watch from her purse.

Jessica leaned forward in her chair and focused in eager anticipation of seeing the timepiece. "I think I can understand your enthusiasm for watches Edward," she smiled. "I have been admiring the one you are wearing. I love it when I get the opportunity to observe Rolex design and their superb quality."

Edward smiled in appreciation of Jessica's comment. "From a layman's perspective, of course, I can detect a certain build quality in this pocket watch as well."

Carmen reached into her purse, which hung on her shoulder, then held the watch case in both hands. Edward gestured for her to give it to Jessica. She complied and as she extended her arm she experienced an odd heaviness in her limbs.

Jessica held the case and opened the lid. *That's weird ... I don't remember giving it to her!* Carmen saw her remove the watch from the case. *Are her hands trembling? I don't know ... my heart. It's beating way too fast! Something is closing around me!* She saw a rapid dark movement to her right, coming from behind them. There came a different sound; something was very wrong. She felt dizzy. She had to force her head to turn. In a blur, she watched her dad's elbow swing directly back behind him in great force. A loud whooshing sound filled her ears as the dark figure fell back through the archway behind them.

What was that? Why is my dad slouching down in his chair? More noises came to her ears. They seemed to echo. First Carmen heard a gasp followed by an, "Oh my god!" A female's voice. *Jessica ... what's wrong?*

Her father was yelling, "Carmen! Carmen!"

Why are you yelling? Why aren't you moving? The sounds of her father's voice echoed all around her, yet his lips did not move. Carmen forced herself to focus. She looked directly at him. *Why do you keep yelling? There's something in your neck.* She stared harder at a hypodermic needle. At first, she had no comprehension. Then it hit her hard. She started to panic. "It's a needle! Jabbed in your neck!" she screamed.

The yelling sounded louder now, and even a bit clearer, "Run Carmen! Please, please ... run Carmen!"

Survival mode took over. Carmen was at war with a mentally and physically confused body. Every thought, every movement had to be forcefully willed from the depth of her being. Somehow, she stood up and looked over the table as her iced tea glass shattered in an explosion of liquid, glass, and ice. Oddly there came a pang of regret for knocking over her glass and ruining such a lovely napkin.

She was at the archway, which loomed like a tunnel before her. She crawled on her hands and knees like a child. *Daddy has stopped. He's stopped yelling at me. I'm glad. That scares me. He never yells at me like that. Someone has hurt him! This is so wrong! Help ... I will find someone to help us...but not here, outside!* Carmen made her way to the heavy glass doors of the front entrance. She managed to pull herself up. Her brain told her she was pulling on the handle. *It's locked!* Panic started to build. *You're inside. The lock! Where? You watched her do it. There!* Her hand found the latch. It turned. Again, she tried to open the door. Harder and harder she pulled. There was no movement.

Someone started to cry. It was her. She sank slowly to her knees. *I'm sorry Daddy. Something is wrong. I can't do it.* Carmen forced her head to turn back. She wanted to call out again to her dad, but her head could only go halfway. Through tear-filled eyes, she stared at the wall beside the entrance doors. No help would be coming.

Something appeared through the watery lenses of her eyes. At first, nothing registered. Then something came from her subconscious—a resolution—and with it a surge of adrenaline. She crawled to the wall. Her body weight fell against the shiny round metal disk; the 'handicap button' located 1 metre from the floor. With a loud click, the front door opened. Carmen was out.

The sudden shock of the external heat helped. She made it to the handrail on the stairs and descended them on her knees. At the opening of the gate on the sidewalk, Carmen pulled herself up. The sun blinded her. She called out for help, but no sound of her voice could be heard. With only one thing left to do, she let go of the gate railing and ran for help. At first, Carmen had the feeling of running free. However, the bright sunlight started to diminish, and she began to fall with it. Colours started flashing out of the darkness as she fell. *Why haven't I hit the pavement yet?*

There only remained a soft green glow and the sense of being a young child. She went back to a time when her father tossed her up high in the air. With no fear, she fell back down to the strong, reassuring cradle of his arms. Carmen felt safe.

TWENTY-ONE

The Dream

Carmen does not know if she is sitting, standing or lying down. There is a green hard cover book before her. It opens to a full-page colour photograph—the portrait of a handsome young man. He has blonde hair and a matching beard. She is staring into his soft hazel green eyes. An emerald radiance envelops her.

Carmen is frightened, and she trembles. She feels a gentle touch on her shoulder. "Be not afraid. You shall not be harmed." She is confused. *The touch, the voice ... but I am alone.*

"You are not alone." The portrait of the man had not moved, yet his presence is being heard and felt. "You are under the influence of a high dosage of medication. The effects of the drug shall soon pass, and although your conscious retention of our meeting will be only realized on a subconscious level, I will tell you it is crucial that you are here."

Carmen remembers. "Something terrible happened. My father ... he is hurt, or maybe worse. He needs me! I was running for help." She starts to cry. The book before her grows larger. The touch on her shoulder is even softer and gentler now.

"Your father was called. He has known me, in his heart, for much of his life. He answered a call."

Carmen stops crying. She wants to understand. "What was he asked to do?"

"He retrieved and delivered a device. I am the creator of this device; a timepiece of great importance."

Carmen notices she is no longer trembling. Somehow his presence surrounds her with peace and tranquility. She continues to search in his eyes, which are captured on the coloured plate of the still page. "Why am I here?"

"You also have been called. I am grateful to acknowledge your assistance in a series of events, which have been required to ultimately deliver the timepiece to a particular place and to ensure its safety. It shall remain in that place until its day of recovery."

"Carmen, be not afraid."

The green book closes.

TWENTY-TWO

He followed them for approximately 15 minutes from the front of the Prima Royale Hotel to this place: a museum. He read the English words mounted on the building, 'Museum for Islamic Art.' Positioned across the top of the structure to the left of a circular illustration were the words 'The Mystery of Lost Time.' A young woman from inside had unlocked the front entrance and allowed them to enter. This did not look good. He understood why they were here, and having more people involved would complicate things.

Across the street from the museum, and positioned a short way down the road, he watched and waited. Not wanting to appear too conspicuous, his clothing consisted of lightweight running attire. Knee-length shorts with a semi-mesh muscle shirt exposed the fit, toned body of a sprinter. He wore a small nylon satchel across his body with a light strap fastened at the waist. Dark sports sunglasses, headband, and ear buds completed the disguise.

The truth was though, Aaron Dekr loved running. Although no longer competitive, he still trained for the 100 metre—his best defence against the stresses of life, and as of late there were many. He was not happy, as all it seemed to be about now was waiting. Opening his satchel, he withdrew a cell phone and initiated a call. He spoke quickly in hushed tones then returned the phone to the bag.

His 'cover' was excellent. With water, an energy bar and by executing a few stretches now and then, he would be okay to stay here for maybe 15 minutes before anyone might become suspicious.

Aaron was getting impatient. Things had not gone well. He failed in Petrolia. Edward James had been underestimated in New York, the hotel break-in netted them nothing, and now Edward had involved his daughter Carmen and museum personnel. Time would be running out. He was beginning to obtain a much clearer understanding of what his boss's capabilities were, and he did not like it. He needed to think clearly, knowing that opportunities do not always present themselves. *Sometimes you must force the issue.*

Aaron grabbed his water bottle and took a long drink. Returning it to the bag, he began a series of stretches, all the while keeping a sharp eye on the front of the building. He mentally weighed his options. Overall, his immediate future did not seem too favourable, and the stretching did little to alleviate his building stress.

He witnessed movement at the front entrance of the museum. The door opened. Aaron stopped and stared harder. No one walked out of the entrance. The door was being held open automatically. He waited and saw no activity. *What's going on? Why is no one coming out?* Just as it began to close, something caught his eye on the stairway; someone was crawling down the steps. *What the hell?* From where he stood 200 metres away, he could not see the bottom half of the entrance. Now it became apparent that this person must have crawled through the doorway. It took him only a matter of seconds to distinguish the long blonde ponytail belonging to Edward's daughter Carmen.

He instinctively started to move towards the museum but stopped when another movement on the street came into his peripheral vision. What appeared to be an older man was walking, entering the bend in the sidewalk, which would soon bring him into view of the museum. Aaron checked himself. He moved back to the shelter of some trees. *I'm better to wait.*

It was very unsettling for him to watch the young woman frantically struggling on her hands and knees. She made it to the gap in the iron fence and pulled herself up into a crooked standing position. Aaron shifted his eyes towards the pedestrian. He rounded the bend and was now in view of the front of the building. He caught sight of the woman clutching the fence. His pace quickened. The man could see something was not right. Carmen James staggered to and fro, barely able to stand. He was less than 50 metres from her. Suddenly she let go of the railing and stumbled headlong onto the sidewalk directly towards him. Her legs, however, did not support her. After four or five shaky running steps, she began to fall. The man started running. He caught her in his arms a second before she would have hit the pavement.

Aaron let out a deep breath. He clenched his fists tightly at his side. An intense anger welled up inside him. *What have they done to her? Where is her father?* He thought back to the brief profile he had been given on her. *Carmen James is an innocent, intelligent, young woman. She is undeserving of this! Someone has got to them!* Aaron looked on helplessly as the man attended to her unconscious body. He placed her purse under her head and was checking for a pulse on her neck and then leaned in close, with his ear to her face, undoubtedly listening for breathing. Aaron felt a surge of relief. *This man knows what he is doing.*

Holding her hand, the man reached into his pocket for his cell phone. His call took only a matter of seconds. Now it was just waiting. He continued to kneel by her side.

Aaron let his fists relax as he observed several people approach the scene, bystanders and residents curious about what had happened. He retreated back a little further. It would be prudent not to be involved. Out of the corner of his eye, Aaron thought he caught a glimpse of a shadowed figure lingering behind the glass of the front entrance. When he turned to get a better look, the figure vanished. He returned his gaze back to the commotion on the sidewalk.

A siren sounded in the distance. Aaron would need to wait for a bit. This latest development certainly changed things. Now he must try his best to be patient.

A slight change in the activity across the street occurred. The onlookers were moving and their voices got louder. Focusing between their shuffling legs, Aaron noticed movement from the incapacitated young women. It looked as though she was regaining consciousness. A couple of minutes later the man who attended to her helped her to her feet. He pointed towards the museum and spoke rapidly to the bystanders in Hebrew. With her arm around his neck, Carmen James shakily made her way back through the gate towards the entrance. A woman assisted on her other side, as they climbed the stairs slowly and made their way to the front door. They helped her back into the museum.

This, Aaron thought, was a bit odd. Perhaps she had asked to be taken back in because of her father. Several moments later the woman who helped came out and walked down to the sidewalk and joined the other bystanders.

The siren grew louder. Aaron had only to wait another two or three minutes before the flashing lights came into view as an ambulance pulled up in front of the building. As one siren shut down, another different sounding one wailed in the near proximity. As two attendants ran into the entrance, a separate set of flashing lights came into the street. A police car came screeching to a halt right behind the ambulance. Two uniformed officers got out and promptly made their way into the building. This was Aaron's cue to leave. It would be too risky to remain here.

Swiftly and silently, Aaron distanced himself from the museum. When far enough away he started to run, quickening his pace, going faster and faster, until he sprinted full out. He knew all too well how dangerous uneven pavement or concrete can be for a sprinter; a trip or a fall at these speeds would have dire consequences. But right now, it seemed worth the risk.

For Aaron Dekr, running fast was his best defense against stress, and at this moment, his stress level was near the bursting point.

TWENTY-THREE

CARMEN OPENED HER eyes to a concerned, caring face of an older gentleman. She thought she had been dreaming, and there was a sense of tranquility that must have been in the dream, although she could not remember.

"Ha kol beseder?" He asked in a calm voice.

Carmen did not respond; confusion still enveloped her.

"Is everything okay?" He offered in clear, concise English with a familiar Hebrew accent.

She nodded. "I ... I'm not sure." Carmen tried to look around. Everything was spinning. She realized she was lying on the sidewalk, the man kneeling over her. Other people stood around. They stared at her and spoke in Hebrew. Only a few words were discernible to her: 'sick girl' and 'falling down.' Carmen started to realize they were talking about her. *What happened to me?* Carmen's thinking was foggy and disjointed.

"It appears you became sick. You fell down on the sidewalk." The man held her hand. "Luckily, I was out for a walk. Just as I came around the bend, I saw you clinging to the iron fence in front of the museum. I could tell something was wrong ..."

"The museum!" The word triggered an immediate response. "My father has been hurt! I need to help him! Please!" Carmen tried to sit up. "We were in the museum!" Things started to spin as dizziness took over.

The man squeezed her hand. "Yes, I will help you, but I think you need to lay back for a bit." He held his other hand behind her head as she settled back down. Her breathing increased, and if not for the disorientation, she might have started to panic.

"I will ask you to be calm. Can you tell me your name?" He gave her a caring smile.

"My name is Carmen ... Carmen James. My father is Edward James. We were at the museum." Her anxiety was building again. She tried to suppress the sensation and remained prone.

"Carmen, I am Amnon Gosser. I live nearby in the area. I also happen to be the curator of this museum." His brow furrowed, although the kindness remained. "Today is a holiday, and the museum is closed. When you said you were *at* the museum, might you be referring only to the outside?"

Carmen knew her brain was not working right, as processing information was difficult. "Amnon, can you help me sit up? I need to start moving a bit."

"Yes, of course." Amnon nestled his hand under her back and helped her to a sitting position. Carmen waited for the dizziness to clear. When it finally did, she recovered somewhat.

"We were inside. A woman let us in. Her name is ..." Carmen took a moment. "Jessica."

"Jessica?" Amnon showed concern. "Jessica Smythe?"

Carmen hardly listened. She was frightened. "Something happened. I got dizzy, then ... my dad ... Amnon, please! Can you take me back? We need to help my dad!" Carmen started crying. She could not help it.

"But Carmen, the museum is ..." Amnon stopped. "Yes, I have my keys, and it will be better for you inside where the temperature is much cooler, and you can drink some water. I called for help.

When they arrive, we can meet them inside." He gave her a reassuring smile. "Do you think you can stand?"

Carmen nodded, which caused several tears to cascade down her cheeks. Determination overcame her fear and confusion. She struggled to her feet, and with Amnon and another woman's assistance, she made her way back to the entrance of the museum.

Amnon unlocked the front door. He left Carmen in the other woman's care, while he went inside and disabled the alarm. There was no sign of anyone on the ground floor. He returned quickly to get her. He pushed the handicap button on his way. The door opened, and the three of them made their way inside. Amnon motioned towards a pair of leatherette chairs, positioned against the wall close to the entrance. After Carmen settled in one of the chairs, he thanked the woman and asked if she would mind waiting outside to direct the ambulance attendants when they arrived. The woman said yes. She smiled and put her hand on Carmen's shoulder. There was warmth and caring in her lingering touch. "Shalom."

"Thank you," Carmen replied. The woman turned and walked away.

Amnon thanked her as she left. He turned to Carmen, "Will you be okay to sit alone for a bit? I will get you some water."

"Thank you, yes." She did her best to put on a brave face. Amnon briskly walked away through the archway where Jessica had led them earlier. Watching him made her feel frightened again. *What happened to us?* She tried to remember.

Amnon returned with a bottle of water. He cracked open the lid and handed it to Carmen. She was able to unscrew the top and take a long drink. The cold water tasted refreshing. She took another sip and then screwed the lid back on. Amnon watched her intently. He could see she was still frightened. Her hands trembled as she manipulated the water bottle.

"I broke my glass of ice tea!" Carmen blurted out. "In there!" She pointed to the archway where Amnon just came from. "I think there was something wrong with the tea."

Amnon had a worried expression on his face. "You had tea? There in the alcove?"

"Jessica gave it to me." Carmen's eyes started to well up again as she stared at Amnon. "But there was someone else!" Amnon put his hand on Carmen's shoulder to try and comfort her. He thought she might be going into shock. He thought for a moment.

"Carmen, can you recall the approximate time you had the tea?"

"I'm not sure ... what time is it now?"

Amnon glanced at his watch, "2:35."

"Wait ... the time was 2:00 when Jessica would be watching for us. Yes! She unlocked the door and let us in!"

The appearance of Amnon's face was unsettling. "But Jessica is ..." He stopped to think. "Carmen, I would like to ask that you wait again. I wish to get for you a cold compress to put on your forehead." He gave her a forced smile as he turned and went back again through the archway. He stopped to observe the alcove briefly. Everything seemed in order with the table and chairs all in their proper place and the tabletop clean and tidy.

Amnon started to turn towards the partially covered archway en route to the kitchenette when something caught his eye: a slight glistening of refracted light, from a tiny object under the chair closest to him. He had to focus carefully, and as his angle of vision changed he lost sight of it. Kneeling, he searched under the chair and finally found it, carefully retrieving the object for inspection. Between his thumb and forefinger, he held a small shard of broken glass. With his other hand, he gently patted around the wood flooring. It was damp to the touch.

Amnon got slowly to his feet, lost in thought. *What on earth has happened here?*

The cool, moist towel felt revitalising against her forehead as she leaned back in the chair. Carmen was presently the centre of attention as two police officers and two paramedics hovered over her. Amnon stood back and talked on his cell phone. Her train of thought started to improve. However, the fear and uneasiness did not abate, especially after talking with Amnon and learning her father and Jessica were no longer in the building.

"Your body temperature and breathing are okay. Blood pressure and pulse rate are a bit high, though." The young female paramedic undid the Velcro band attached to Carmen's arm.

Her male assistant explained, "We think you should come to the hospital. A doctor will want to do a blood test. Oxygen on the ride will feel nice too." They both gave her encouraging smiles.

"Okay, thanks." Carmen looked questioningly to the two male police officers. They exchanged glances with each other and then one of them left Carmen's side to speak with Amnon Gosser.

"We will meet you at the hospital, Miss James," the remaining officer said. "A missing person's report will need to be filed. For that, we require a statement from you and Mr. Gosser." He was quick to notice a look of panic come over Carmen when he spoke the words 'missing persons.' He reached out as he bent down and held her hand in both of his. "We will do our best to find your father and the young woman."

Carmen was grateful to these kind people. She nodded, knowing they cared.

Amnon finished on the phone. He and the officer had a few words and then they both started back towards Carmen. As they approached, the officer accompanying her straightened up and stepped back. The paramedics repacked their instruments and quietly conferred with one another in Hebrew.

Carmen removed the compress from her forehead and turned towards Amnon who stood before her. He gazed down with a sad, thoughtful smile. "If you would like, I can come and be with you at the hospital. I have only to wait just a bit to give my statement to the police and share a few words with the security guard who is on duty."

Carmen liked Amnon Gosser very much. He understood she was alone and was doing his best to make things better. "Thank you, I'll be okay. You need to be here." Carmen hesitated. A puzzled expression crossed her face. "Amnon, I don't recall seeing a security guard here before, when my dad and I met with Jessica."

Amnon did not answer her immediately. He looked at the police officers, then back to Carmen. "I am afraid the security guard on duty stayed on the lower level of the museum. He said he spoke with Jessica and knew she would be working for a while here on the ground floor. Jessica told him she would contact him when she was leaving."

"Oh." Carmen was thinking much clearer now, but her thought process was still off. She tried shaking her head from side to side hoping that something inside her brain might clear. "My dad spoke to her twice on the phone about getting some information on an antique watch. She was expecting us. When we got here today, Jessica told us she held a degree in horology and studied history for many years. Jessica said she would try to help us." Carmen was confused. "Amnon, did Jessica lie to us?"

"I do not know her well enough to answer your question fully." Amnon stopped. Carmen could tell he was troubled.

He continued. "Jessica started working for us 3 months ago, to do some volunteer work at the institute. We agreed to employ her for 10-15 hours a week. Her work here has been more than satisfactory. Jessica is a shy, reserved young woman, and I have come to consider her exceptionally bright. She is passionate for antiquities, especially old watches. I am not aware of her past studies or of her having a degree in horology," Amnon paused. He let his gaze fall to the floor. He sadly shook his head. "This is quite disturbing for me. I do not understand."

The room went silent. Amnon raised his head. He glanced around at the others then back to Carmen. "I just got off the phone with our security dispatcher. Twenty minutes ago, he received a call from Jessica. He said she sounded frantic over the phone. She told him she needed to leave the museum for a family emergency and that she forgot to inform the guard on the lower level. Jessica said she locked up but mentioned nothing else."

Carmen had a realization: she was not the only one who was worried.

"Carmen, I believe you shall recover completely with no permanent effects." A female doctor stood beside Carmen's hospital bed in a curtained off cubicle in the emergency ward of the Shaare Zedek Medical Center. Carmen was lying in a semi-upright position. She had been here for about an hour, and this was the second time the young Jewish doctor had consulted with her. "Your blood tests indicate you have traces of Midazolam in your system." She held a clipboard in front of her, with a pen poised, ready to take down any necessary notations. "Can you recall how much tea you were served and the amount you drank?"

Carmen thought she was almost back to normal now. However, her memory was still quite fragmented. "It's hard for me to remember … I think a tall, slender glass, mostly full … I drank about a third to half of it? Not sure." The doctor gave her a reassuring smile.

"That's okay, you are doing fine." She made a brief note. "The reason I ask, Carmen, is that knowing the amount of the drug you ingested is critical." The doctor raised her eyebrows in an almost amusing gesture. "We have all enjoyed movies, where the camera zooms in on a pill capsule being pulled apart and the contents are emptied into a coffee mug or martini glass. Then after a quick sip or two, the victim becomes dizzy and lapses into unconsciousness, only to awaken a half hour later, a little bewildered, but nonetheless ready for action again." She laughed softly. "I'm afraid—in the real world—it is a bit more complicated." She glanced back down to the clipboard momentarily.

She focused back on Carmen with a serious, thoughtful expression. "Let me start out by saying that whoever determined the dosage to be mixed into your tea seems to have measured the dosage right, either by luck or by intelligence." She paused. "Maybe a bit of both."

"You see, Carmen, it takes a powerful drug to render a human being unconscious. Also, people react differently under various conditions. Many variables need to be considered. The science of this is called anesthesiology, and as I am sure you understand, years of study and indoctrination are needed to become competent in this field."

Carmen focused on what the doctor was saying, bringing her some relief, which helped lessen the building anxiety.

"I told you what happened at the museum. My dad … there was a needle in his neck. Do you think …?"

The doctor's expression became much softer now. "Carmen, I cannot make assumptions. I will only say that the administration of a drug into soft muscle tissue of the neck would possibly lessen some of the variables affecting the total outcome of the dosage. For example, in your case the food in your stomach from lunch would have slowed down the release of the drug to your brain, which, in conjunction with your excellent physical fitness, made it possible for you to initiate limited movement. That is what I mean by a variable, and you can see how it would affect making an accurate calculation of the amount of drug being used." She could see Carmen's eyes were starting to well up. The doctor softly put her hand on her shoulder. "I *do* hope the administrator of these drugs chose wisely in *both* cases."

Carmen started to cry. It was a release for her, and the doctor understood. She set her pen and clipboard at the end of the mattress and depressed the switch to elevate the bed. She leaned in close to offer Carmen a hug. Carmen accepted. She nestled her face just above the woman's breast and wept. The only sound in the room was the convulsive sobs of a patient crying into the gentle embrace of her doctor. This sounded for some time until the crying eventually softened and stopped. They parted their embrace.

The doctor sat on the edge of the bed and looked into a young woman's tear-filled eyes. "Carmen, I am a doctor in a troubled land. I have witnessed much stress and violence. I believe in my heart that we all want peace and to love one another, but somehow the fighting and the violence continue. I am blessed with the opportunity to heal the sick and tend to the injured. I am grateful, yet I believe it is not enough." She stopped. An understanding smile formed on her face. "It is *hope* that makes our world a beautiful place. And I can tell you are a strong young woman, Carmen. I want you to have *hope*. That is enough." She retrieved her pen and clipboard and rose from the bed.

She gazed down at Carmen and smiled. "Just a little helper, though ... I'm prescribing a mild sedative for you—Lorazepam—to make things easier for the next few days and to help ensure you get the proper rest you need." She walked to the end of the bed and drew open the curtain. Turning back, she said, "Goodbye, Carmen."

Through tear-filled eyes, Carmen beheld a memorable vision: a smiling doctor with a wet lab coat. Carmen did not answer. Instead, she silently mouthed the word 'thank you.' Their eyes locked together for a lingering moment. The doctor nodded and left to attend to another patient.

"The number you are trying to reach is currently unavailable." The automated voice sounded cold and devoid of sensitivity. It was worth a try but what she had expected; her dad could not be reached by his cell. Carmen put her phone back in her purse and waited.

The sedative she took began taking effect and it helped a lot. The nurse gave her a 2-day supply, with a prescription for more if needed. She had been asked to come to this room and wait for a police officer who needed to get a statement from her. The room was a small place for meetings. Doctors used the place to confer with patients or other medical personnel in private. It had no windows or pictures on the walls; everything was plain and simple. There was a table with four vinyl chairs, a cabinet, and counter-top, on which sat a small computer and not much else. Carmen sat alone in one of the chairs facing the door. She thought how the uninspiring décor suited her feelings perfectly regarding her upcoming meeting with the police. This time there would be no calling Derek or setting up a plan with her dad. This time it would be just her and the officer. She already decided the time was now to be open and honest. The circumstances warranted that. The police would need to be told everything and anything that might help them find her father. Carmen held inside a slight twinge of guilt. *I hope the officer who sees me isn't ...* She heard a soft knock at the door. It opened. *Inspector Claude Gadgét ... So much for wishful thinking.* Now the guilt increased. *Well, at least he's smiling. A little forced perhaps, but a smile nonetheless.*

"Hello, Carmen." The inspector entered the room and closed the door behind him. He stood motionless, with his hands clasped together and a concerned expression on his face as he looked down at her. "This is not a pleasant way for us to be spending our holiday." Claude Gadgét waited a moment longer before pulling out a chair. He unbuttoned the single front button of his beige suit coat and sat down.

Carmen found his attire to be every bit as lovely as it had been this morning, and it added some much-needed colour and texture to a rather bleak room.

"Please, tell me how you are Carmen."

"I'm feeling much better. We need to find my father." Carmen was trying to rush things. She could not seem to help it.

"I understand Carmen, and I am glad you are recovered." The inspector reached into an inside breast pocket of his suit coat and retrieved a small recording device. He set it on the table in front of them. "I thought it best we meet here at the hospital in private, rather than at the police station. We can have you back to your hotel much quicker this way." He motioned towards the recorder. "I need to ask if you would mind if I record our conversation, which will allow you to make a verbal statement that is required to file a missing person's report and is best for liability reasons."

Carmen witnessed a slight change in his expression. She did not understand what he meant by 'liability reasons.' The inspector read her puzzled appearance and responded, "Sad for me to say, Carmen, but it is not advisable that a police officer be alone in a room with a subject." Claude Gadgét shrugged his shoulders in acceptance, and his eyes showed sadness. "This is the way of the world now. We no longer trust one another." He reached out and lifted the recorder. "This electronic device is needed to ensure our trust. Well … at least some of it." Inspector Gadgét was silent as he looked into her eyes. Carmen understood. She nodded her acceptance of his request.

He turned the device on and set it back down on the table. He leaned back in his chair. His gaze did not alter. "I have been to the museum. You and your father did not trust me, Carmen. And if I may reiterate, it appears to be the accepted response for the way we live today; however, I would like to hear, of your own volition, why you were not open and honest with me about the watch, which, as I understand, has been stolen."

Carmen did not like the situation. This was not supposed to be part of the adventure. She felt guilty, sad and frightened, all at the same time. Right now, crying might be an option. *But he turned on that damn recorder.* The thought of that sparked a bit of anger too. Now it was *her* who had to explain everything and make things right. *Not telling the cops was Derek's idea!* She wanted to grab her cell phone, dial up Derek's number and say *Here ... this guy will tell you all about it!*

However, that is not what she did. *Wow, sometimes being an adult really sucks!*

Instead, Carmen put on the bravest face she could find and held eye contact with Inspector Claude Gadgét. "I apologize for the mistrust and any inconvenience we may have caused, Inspector. Overall, I think I can use one word to sum up why we were not, as you phrased it, 'open and honest.' The one word is 'afraid.' We were *afraid* the watch would be taken away before we had a chance to learn anything about it. You see, we have learned there might be a connection between our watch and the Marie Antoinette watch, thus raising the possibility of the timepiece being part of the great robbery at the L.A. Mayer Museum in 1988."

Inspector Claude Gadgét studied her intently. He remained silent. He was waiting and the tension was building. Carmen had a resource to deal with it, though.

She leaned in closer to the recorder. "However, there is much more to the story." She saw his eyebrows rise in anticipation. "I think I should start at the beginning ..." Carmen did not change her expression or alter her gaze.

"Do you like garage sales and hot dogs, Inspector?"

A smile spread across his face. "Actually, I do."

TWENTY-FOUR

Inspector Claude Gadgét was a skilled driver. The perfect balance of caution, aggression, and concentration resulted in smooth, seamless transit to the Prima Royale Hotel. Carmen sat in the passenger seat of his unmarked police vehicle and admired his confidence behind the wheel as they flowed through traffic. He could even multitask, as evident by communications with other police officers via radio and cell phone, all the while dodging between and around the constant stream of obstacles in their path. No doubt much of his expertise had come from many years of police work in Paris and Jerusalem. He chatted freely with Carmen. It put her more at ease and gave her a feeling of security knowing he was trying to help her.

"I will be returning to the police station directly after I deliver you to your hotel, Carmen." The inspector kept his eyes focused on the road. "I can have the missing person reports ready shortly. Also, I will be sending off a fax to the NYC Police Department." He glanced down at his watch. "It is Sunday morning in New York City now. I would not expect to receive information regarding the possible homicide in Brooklyn until Monday at the earliest."

They arrived on the street of the Prima Royale Hotel. Claude Gadgét pulled up to the front entrance and stopped. He put the car in park and swivelled in his seat to face Carmen. "Thank you for disclosing the information in such explicit detail. I *do* understand why you and your father chose to remain silent about the pocket watch." He gave her a soft smile. "And although your firefighting friend Derek sounds intelligent and quite interesting, I would ask if you need further advice on any undertaking with regards to this case to please call me at any time. Do you still have my card?"

Carmen nodded. "Yes, thank you, Inspector." She unbuckled her seatbelt and opened the door.

"It sounds like your father is a resourceful man. We need to believe he is okay. It appears the thieves got what they wanted. Hopefully, the personal threat to you and your father is no longer standing. However, I still want you to be careful. I will be working late tonight on this. You need to get some rest, Carmen. We can talk tomorrow." His reassuring smile helped. She stepped out of the car.

"I will Inspector. Thank you." She closed the passenger door and entered the hotel.

Inspector Claude Gadgét drove out to the street and was gone.

CARMEN WANTED DESPERATELY to talk to her mom but dreaded the thought of making the call. The hot shower had felt warm and relaxing. Still bundled up in the hotel bathrobe, she picked up the room phone and dialled the front desk. Meira had finished her day shift and Carmen was glad for it, not wanting to talk to anyone right now about what had happened. Well, excluding her mother, of course. Yes, she needed to make *that* call soon. First, though, she would order something light to eat. It would be here by the time she finished on the phone.

The male receptionist picked up on the third ring. Carmen promptly asked for room service and ordered homemade vegetable soup, a whole-wheat bun, and ice water. The delivery time would be approximately 20 minutes. She hung up the phone and went to change and brush her hair.

She returned several minutes later wearing a loose-fitting t-shirt and long sweat pants. Sitting down on the desk chair she reached for the phone and stopped. *I forgot something.* Carmen walked to the bathroom and returned carrying a box of Kleenex tissues. *I think I'm gonna need these.*

TWENTY-FIVE

SUNDAY, MAY 4, 2014. 11:00 A.M.
PETROLIA, ONTARIO, CANADA

D<small>EREK HAD STUCK</small> the note on the front of the coffee maker. In scratchy handwriting, it read:

> Hey, gone for most of the day, will be home late afternoon. Edward called and asked for some advice, said they will call you this aft after museum visit. Have a great day! Derek.

Marie pulled the note off the coffee maker at around 7:30 a.m. She reread it now and glanced up at the clock on the kitchen wall: 11:00 a.m. That would be 6:00 p.m. in Jerusalem. *They should have called me by now ... and what was the advice they needed from Derek so early this morning?* Marie felt anxious, but she did not want to worry. Keeping busy would be key, and truth be told she had much to do to fulfill her commitment to house cleaning.

She looked back to the coffee maker, which glittered in the sunlight streaming in through the crystal-clear glass of the window. Her gaze meandered down the length of the spotless countertop, taking in the balanced juxtaposition of an equally clean toaster and kettle set in amongst various kitchen requirements.

Marie turned and walked over to the refrigerator and opened the door. She shuddered at the thought of what had assaulted her senses when she did this for the first time yesterday. *What a difference a full day can make.* A clean, fresh smell emanated from within, where ultra-shiny shelves and compartments awaited the safe, hygienic storage of foodstuffs. The fridge was essentially empty now. Nothing could be salvaged, save for an almost full box of Coca-Cola. She discarded the cardboard and placed the cans neatly on a lower shelf. A water pitcher sat within easy access, filled with filtered ice water. She removed the jug, closed the door, and walked over to the kitchen table where she filled her empty glass.

After returning the jug, Marie came back to the table to sit for a few minutes. She smiled to herself as she gazed around. This room had been an enormous one-day challenge. With still plenty more to do in other rooms and only a short amount of time, she honestly felt up for the task mainly because she might have convinced Derek to keep his home this way. To her, that in itself was inspirational.

Marie had done what most people would think to be utterly inconceivable: instill in Derek an unequivocal desire to keep his home clean and tidy.

Marie took a long sip of her ice water. *Edward is going to be so proud of me!* She stared off into space as she recalled her accomplishment. *I believe I saw genuine fear in Derek's eyes! Carmen will be impressed.*

She set her ice water down and took some time to relive the experience. Yesterday she made a plan. After all, what good would it be to invest a tremendous amount of time and effort into the cleaning and organizing of someone's house only to have them mess everything up again in a shorter time than it took her to do the cleaning?

As a healthcare professional, over the years Marie had amassed considerable knowledge on the hygienic quality of the home environment and the detrimental side effects of an unclean atmosphere within. It would be a simple matter of enlightening Derek with the cold hard facts.

Marie initiated the implementation of her plan with a delicious home cooked meal of salad, spaghetti and meat sauce, served in the comfortable setting of a newly cleaned and organized kitchen. Derek was impressed. He told Marie his kitchen never looked this good. Also, Derek loved homemade spaghetti. Maybe he would skip the salad.

Marie used this seemingly innocent gesture to launch into her oral conviction, which hopefully would enable Derek to 'see the light' and alter his errant ways.

She started out softly, explaining the vitamins and minerals required to maintain a healthy human body. *And yes, it is important to eat your salad, as it contains many nutrients vital to good health that are not found in spaghetti and meat sauce.* Marie recalled a bit of impatient grumbling at this point. However, Derek complied and hurriedly consumed his salad.

Then came the time to build her case. She explained about mold and mildew, and although she imparted, quite emphatically, the seriousness of these toxins, Derek was more interested in when he could eat his spaghetti.

However, Marie was determined. "Derek, can you understand that breathing these toxins in your home can actually cause spores of these contaminants to literally grow in your lungs? And this condition can lead to respiratory failure and ultimately death!"

Marie subtly shook her head as she took another sip of ice water. Trying hard to remember, she thought Derek's response had been a raised eyebrow. No worries, though, she saved the best for last, and to disclose the information while he ate his supper would surely bring about the desired effect.

"Derek, have you ever heard of dust mites?" He did not answer. His mouth was full of spaghetti noodles, most of which seemed to be hanging down to his chin. He only nodded. "I have a magnified picture of one of these scary looking creatures here on my phone. Take a look." Marie handed her cell phone across the table to him. He studied the magnified image while chewing his food. Marie continued to narrate, "These creatures, by the millions, can take up residence in the unclean home and cause many forms of serious illnesses that are most often thought to be allergic reactions. Severe respiratory problems and flu-like symptoms are all too common. You see, these microscopic mites thrive in moist, humid environments and they live off our dead skin particles."

Marie smiled grimly to herself now, as she remembered taking a long pause and watching Derek take another mouthful of spaghetti while he intently studied the image on the screen. She purposely refrained from taking as much as one bite of her own meal lest she lose her appetite because of what she intended to say.

She continued. "But here's the real disgusting part; it's not the dust mites themselves that are the threat to our health. It is their waste ... their poop. We ingest their poop, and we become sick!"

Rethinking last night's conversation was unsettling for Marie. It was out of character for her to possibly ruin a person's meal just to get a point across. However, extreme circumstances required extreme measures, and she knew for certain most people would agree that the state of Derek's house was an extreme circumstance. Her worry about jeopardizing his meal, however, was unwarranted. He did not so much bat an eyelid, due no doubt to his being preoccupied with his meal. Undeterred, Marie pressed on with determination. She had yet to reveal the 'ace up her sleeve.'

"In mattresses, pillows, and cushions is where they prefer to dwell. Remember I said they like a warm, humid environment?" Derek nodded without looking up.

"Do you think that you, like most people, sometimes sleep with your mouth open?"

This was the 'closer', the fruition of a well-executed plan that would connect with Derek. Marie recalled how he stopped chewing and looked up at her. There were still several noodles hanging out of the corner of his mouth. "Do you mean they go into our mouths when we sleep?"

"Yes, they do! Your nostrils and ear canals as well."

"And ..." Marie remembered clearly his long pause and his sudden change of expression as the realization clicked. "And when they're in there they might ..."

"Yup, you got it!"

"Oh, that's gross!" Derek sat motionless.

Marie eagerly anticipated this stage. Here she could use her knowledge and professionalism to carefully guide Derek to an understanding of how he could realize a healthier, happier home environment using her as his number one consultant. It did not, however, happen quite that way.

Marie got up from the kitchen table and walked over to the kitchen sink, where she placed her empty glass. She gazed out the window into the backyard, not looking for anything in particular but taking in the ambiance as she recreated what came next.

Derek studied the image of the creature. He resumed chewing. The hanging noodles disappeared from the corner of his mouth. His fork slowly began twirling amidst the food on his plate, gaining momentum until a sizeable portion of spaghetti was captured. He transported it to his waiting mouth. More noodles fell to his chin. Derek's expression had not altered until it now finally began to soften. Looking up he leaned forward, handing the cell phone back across the table.

Marie would remember the next image forever. His round face had transformed into a beaming smile, highlighted with spaghetti noodles and sauce as he leaned back in his chair. The noodles were soon consumed and the sauce wiped clean with a napkin. He set his fork aside and clasped his hands together.

"Marie! Do you know what I'm going to do?" Excitement was contained in his voice. Marie only raised her eyebrows in bewildered anticipation. Derek's excited behaviour did not match the response she expected.

"I'm going to dig up my old high school microscope! It's excellent quality. Haven't used the thing in years, though. I'll dust her off and take it to bed with me tonight. How cool, to see one of these dust mite fellows up close and personal!"

Derek forgot all about his spaghetti. Marie was at a loss for words.

She turned away from the kitchen window and stood in the centre of the room, lost in thought. She remembered smiling a lot while eating her salad. Derek started back into his meal with vigour for both the food and his newfound dust mite project. The man was amazing, unbelievable even.

Marie did not take well to defeat. Somewhere deep down she found reserves to fight against it. Something from within made her mind wander throughout the rest of their meal as Derek incessantly rambled on about technical specifications of microscopes and the modifications he had made to his own device. She could not remember one fact from his discourse.

She did, however, remember in explicit detail where her mind wandered. Marie's memory took her to a hospital emergency room where she was assisting in surgery. These rooms are sterile environments where she had worked many times. The cool temperature, hats, booties, gloves, and scrubs were all in place to protect the patient from contamination. Her mind forwarded to the cleaning of Derek's refrigerator. She watched herself open the door for the first time, then quickly close it. When she returned she wore latex gloves, a hospital surgery hat, and a mask. This was for her own protection against mold, spores, and mildew. Next, her mind went back about a year to her own living room. Edward was sitting in his favourite lounge chair by the front bay window watching a video on his laptop. Marie recalled stopping abruptly behind him as she walked past. Something caught her eye: the clothing of the people on the screen. They were dressed like surgeons and nurses would be when performing an operation. They were, however, not in a hospital setting but rather a manufacturing facility. After asking her husband what they were doing, Edward explained to her the video showed the manufacturing company Casio demonstrating the assembly of wristwatches. The reason the people in the video were dressed like that was to prohibit organic contamination from entering the precise mechanical and electronic mechanisms.

The one final memory was nothing more than a brief statement about Derek mentioned by Edward about two weeks ago. Marie did not think much of it at the time. However, she did think of it more seriously last night, with it becoming the final stop of her mind's wandering.

As Marie stood in the centre of the kitchen floor, she took some time to look around and to reaffirm to herself something she had known for a long time. *For me, it's never really been about victory or defeat.* No, for Marie life was about the health and well-being of herself and others. Helping those in need came as natural to her as breathing. All the rest was just 'preparation.'

She would at times though indulge herself in 'the sweet taste of victory.' This time it manifested itself as a joyous tingle throughout her body as she replayed the 'final act' of last nights' meal with Derek.

"Marie, I know you're not finished eating yet, but would you mind if I begin cleaning up the dishes now?" He started towards the sink with his empty plate. "I'm kinda anxious to find my microscope. It could take a while. I got it packed away somewhere downstairs."

"No, of course not, Derek. I can tell you're excited about getting back to using it after this many years. Don't worry about the dishes. There aren't many. I can handle things."

"Okay, thanks!" He gave her a big grin as he put his plate in the sink. Turning swiftly, he began exiting the room.

Marie called out. "Ah, Derek …" He stopped in his tracks. "I have a quick question."

"Sure." His attention focused on Marie.

She wanted to slow him down, so she took her time and pretended to be thinking. "Edward and I were talking over dinner a while back. He mentioned to me you were planning to create an actual retina scanner for your own security use." Marie could see his face brightening as his focus intensified. He took a step closer. "I would like to know … does not the making of such a device involve complicated and somewhat delicate electronic components?"

"Sure does! Absolutely!" He took another step closer. "Been doing a lot of research. I'm almost there. I think I can … no … I know I can. I'm gonna build it!"

Marie could almost feel his heart rate increasing. She changed direction. "Derek, do you know of the manufacturing company Casio?" He slowed for a moment, gave her a quizzical smile and replied. "Yea, of course, they make digital quartz watches. My work watch is a Casio G-Shock. Awesome—owned it for over 3 years now. Been to hell and back with that baby … hasn't missed a beat. But why …?"

Marie cut in. "I remember Edward showing me a video of the Casio manufacturing company building watches and thought it strange that all of the employees in that video were dressed like I am when I work in the OR. I thought we were the only ones required to maintain a sterile dress code. Then Edward explained to me how delicate electronics and ultra-intricate mechanical parts require almost the same level of ambient, sterile control as hospital operating rooms do. He said that even their breath could cause damage, if not for the masks." Marie paused. She focused intently on Derek. "I had no idea ..." she stopped talking. There was no need to say anything further.

It was at that moment when the fear registered in Derek's eyes. His rosy face colour drained away. The smile disappeared. His head dipped, and his gaze dropped to the floor. When he lifted his face and looked at Marie, she remembered thinking, *His fear is gone, but I believe he's going to cry!*

Derek walked slowly to the table and sat down. He leaned forward. "Sometimes I can be really stupid. 'I can't see the forest for the trees.' How can I ever hope to design and create the stuff I want to when I live and build in this kind of environment?" He stopped. Marie stayed silent. Several moments passed. "I always knew this day would come." He shook his head. "I'm such an amateur." He hung his head.

Now he was hurting. Marie reached across and warmly took one of his hands in hers. "Edward said something else when he talked about the retina scanner. He told me, 'I believe Derek can and will build that thing, but it won't stop there. The sky's the limit for what this man can do.'"

"Derek, we're proud of you. Even Carmen maintains you can be weird, but in a cool way." A smile started to appear, a smile that just could not stay away from his face for long.

"Thanks, Marie." He made eye contact again. "You know all the stuff you said about electronics and sterile workplaces? Well, truth is ... I've known about it for a long time. But I guess I pushed it away."

"Look, the way I live is not nice—well the messy living part anyway. I'm always in such a rush that I don't take time to think about it." Derek waited and took a deep breath. "I realize now that if I want to move forward from here there needs to be changes made. As the saying goes, 'It's time to clean up my act.'"

"Literally!" Marie could not pass on that one.

Derek uttered a soft laugh as he rose from the table and walked over to a drawer which he opened and removed a pad and pencil. "I'm going to build myself a proper workshop downstairs. But first I need some advice from you on a whole bunch of other stuff to clean this place up." He smiled and sat down again. "What would you suggest?"

Marie did not move from the centre of the kitchen. She did not want to initiate any movement that might take away from reliving the moment. She felt her eyes start to mist over, as they had last evening. The tingle remained. *Ah … the sweet taste of victory can be so lovely!*

Derek had not even flinched when Marie suggested a highly recommended cleaning professional come to his house once a week. Marie followed up with advice on getting a new mattress and pillows with antibacterial covers. Also, an upgrade to the furnace filter would be in order, along with a Swiss made air purifier; which uses water as the filtering medium.

And finally, and this brought a smile to her face as she recalled her final suggestion, "Derek, you will need to buy a high-quality vacuum cleaner. One that has a Hepa filter for its secondary filtering stage." She had deliberately paused. "And under no circumstances are you *ever* to take the motor out for any reason!"

A howl of laughter burst from Derek, which he managed to suppress only long enough to utter a few words. "But you said you really *like* my can crusher!" His laughter resumed. Marie had to join in when she saw tears rolling down his rosy cheeks.

And now Marie laughed again as she stood in the kitchen recalling the moment.

Just then the home phone rang in the living room and startled her. Immediately she registered the two-toned ring of a long-distance call. *Oh, that will be Edward and Carmen!* Marie was bursting with excitement. She raced to the adjoining room and scooped up the receiver from its cradle and brought it to her ear. "Hello?" There came no immediate answer. "Hello?" she tried again as she let out a breath.

"Mom ..." The pause and the sound of the voice on the other end were enough to tell Marie something was not right.

"Carmen, are you okay? Is everything alright?"

Marie stood motionless in the room as she pressed the phone to her ear and listened. Her shoulders sank. A slight trembling began in her hands as she bit down on her lower lip. Her cheeks started to glisten from traces of tears as they fell.

She remained silent. This voice speaking to her from far away in a distant land seized her heart. With tear-filled eyes, she gazed at the surrounding walls. Her world was crumbling down around her.

When she spoke, her own voice sounded strange to her. "I'm booking a flight to Tel Aviv. I will be in Jerusalem as soon as I can. I love you."

A nurse receives training about how to deal with emergency situations. Many are put to the test often in their careers and sometimes in their personal lives.

Marie James stopped crying. She forced herself to put one foot in front of the other as she retrieved her cell phone. It had never been about victory or defeat. That is not what was important to her.

She dialed Derek's number. *Besides, the sweet taste of victory is soon diminished.*

TWENTY-SIX

SUNDAY, MAY 4, 2014. 6:00 P.M.
JERUSALEM, ISRAEL

He always made her his number one priority. For as long as she could remember, she only had to call out for him and he would be there. As she grew older and more independent, the electronic lifeline of her cell phone enabled his support, understanding, and sharing of everything important to her any time she needed.

Carmen never questioned if it was supposed to be this way. Now her dad was gone, and she had so many questions she needed help with, *but Dad isn't here to help me now!*

She sat alone at the desk in the hotel room and stared at the recently delivered food. Over and over she recreated the day's events in her mind and tried to make sense of everything, but Carmen was unsuccessful, ending up in tears when recalling the heartbreaking phone call to her mom. She finally put a stop to the cycle when she remembered the words spoken to her by the kind doctor: 'I want for you to have hope, Carmen.'

She could do that. Carmen took in a deep breath and let it out. She reached for the Kleenex box on the desk and withdrew a tissue to dab her puffy eyes and blow her nose. *I'll have to avoid all mirrors for a while!* She discarded the tissue into the nearby wastebasket and noticed it overflowed with them. *Okay, enough is enough! Yes, I can and will have hope!*

Carmen lifted the cover off her tray of food. The soup smelled good. She began eating, all the while thinking of her mom. It came as no surprise she would be coming here immediately. Carmen understood the phone call had been devastating. Carmen also knew her mom as a fighter. Carmen had been raised by parents with opposing personalities. Her father was philosophical. He preferred reasoning above all else, as his ultimate defense against an imperfect world. Her mother differed, being a giving person who did what was needed to try and make the world a better place for herself, her family and others by being resourceful and practical.

Carmen believed she derived traits from both her mom and dad and that always gave her confidence.

It would be difficult. Carmen and her mom had never faced this kind of uncertainty before. They did have each other, though, as well as some thoughtful, intelligent people who would be doing their best to help them.

Carmen tore her bun apart and spread butter on each half. She swiftly consumed one portion and reached for her full glass of ice water. Thinking back to her hospital visit, Carmen recalled how the nurse insisted she keep well hydrated for the next few days to flush her system out. She thought perhaps an iced tea would have gone well with dinner. *I'm not quite ready to try that just yet.* Carmen grimaced and hoped she would not develop some taste aversion to iced tea. *Jessica's tea tasted good. If I ever meet her again, I'll have to get the recipe!* Carmen caught herself smiling at her somewhat twisted joke and the thought of how humour can help, even at the worst of times.

She took a long drink of the cold water. The ice clinked against the side of the glass as she set it back down on the desk.

The sound triggered something within. Suddenly, Carmen was drawn into a vivid flashback. She remembered in slow motion the tall glass of iced tea shatter. Liquid, ice, and glass exploding across the table. And once again she felt the confused sense of guilt for having ruined such a lovely napkin, saturated and covered in broken bits of glass. The flashback ended abruptly. However, a small image remained for a fraction of a second, much like a retinal image can continue briefly even after we close our eyes. Psychologists call this phenomenon an 'after image.'

The 'after image' her memory retained was the black carriage printed in the corner of the napkin. It had remained untouched.

Carmen sat motionless, staring ahead, lost in thought. *I remember those napkins—the excellent quality.* She recalled the softness and the thickness. *That's not the kind of thing most women carry around in their purse.* She brought the image of the small carriage to her mind. *Would it be a high-end business, which might have napkins printed with their logo ... a restaurant?*

Carmen got up and started pacing around the room, thinking hard. *Okay, if I went out dining in a cool, expensive restaurant, there's just no way I would scam a couple of napkins and stuff them in my purse. Not a chance ... too tacky. Maybe ... so ... yea, might Jessica have a part-time job in a classy restaurant ...? That would be ok.*

Carmen walked to the far end of the L-shaped suite. From beside the second bed, against the wall, she retrieved her overnight suitcase and tossed it up on the bed, undid the zipper and pulled out her laptop. She opened and turned the device on while making her way back to the desk.

After a bit of rearranging, she brought Google up on the screen while eating her soup. Entering the words *Restaurants in Jerusalem/Carriage Logo* delivered up a list of sites. Carmen finished her soup and started down the list. By the third link, she spotted the symbol. When the site loaded, she found it at the top of a webpage for a restaurant named Montefiore, located in the Mishkenot Sha'ananim District. The photos showed a lovely area located on a hilltop overlooking the southwest side of the Old City Wall. A windmill was also located there, which seemed to be a historic landmark, set in amongst many well-kept buildings, in a picturesque, terraced landscape.

Carmen scrolled through numerous pictures on the photo gallery before opening a new window. She then entered the restaurant's name in Google Maps. When the map view came up, she studied it and determined the distance from her hotel to be only a few kilometres.

She glanced at her watch: 6:50 p.m. It had been a long, hard, exhausting day. She was tired and needed her rest. She grabbed the remaining half of her bun and took a bite. The food, however, seemed to help. What could she do? Was this important? Did it mean anything? Her brain kept asking questions, as she recalled the day's events and finished off the last of her bun.

Her final thought before taking the last drink of ice water was of her dad. *Oh ... I so hope he is okay.* The hurt began to well up again. Her eyes started misting. She wanted to cry.

No! Not again! Carmen shut her laptop with a determined force and stood up. *I gotta try this! Okay ... The Montefiore Restaurant in the Mishkenot Sha'ananim District. Let's go!*

She picked up the room phone and dialed the front desk. The call was promptly answered. "Hello, this is Carmen James in 817. I would like a taxi at the front entrance in 10 minutes please."

OKAY, SO I'M HERE NOW, *enjoying a nice $25.00 salad with more ice water. Now what?* She took in her surroundings. The Montefiore had an attractive décor with a beautiful view towards the Old City walls. *I could see coming back here with Mom and Dad for some* *serious Italian cuisine.* Carmen smiled. *And their budget would allow me to order more than just salad!*

The restaurant was quite busy, and Carmen felt somewhat self-conscious sitting alone and pretending to be enjoying herself. However, the salad tasted excellent, and it gave her time to think. *What am I even looking for? Too bad I didn't have more time to spend watching detective shows. Then I might know what to do.*

She played out a couple of options in her head. *Okay let's try the honest approach: I ask to speak with the manager. Then I say ... "Hi, my name is Carmen. I was assaulted earlier today along with my father, who is now missing, it happened at L.A. Mayer Museum, and I'm wondering ... is there a Jessica that works here? Black hair, blue eyes, glasses, small stature, I think a few years older than me. She was involved and I would really like to speak with her."* Carmen smirked to herself. *Yea that should work ... Not!*

Well, maybe I need to be more creative ... Carmen pondered for a moment as she lifted her ice water and took a drink. She picked up the napkin that lay beside the glass and examined it. *Yup, the same napkin for sure.* Returning the glass to the table, she watched a waitress walk by.

I could talk with one of the waitresses: Hi, I'm Carmen. I met a lovely young woman earlier today, and she was kind enough to give me one of your beautiful napkins. Her name is Jessica. I thought she might work here. I'm hoping to see her again." Carmen started giggling as she thought about the response *that* would get her. *Wow ... that is so lame! She gave me a napkin? The waitress is gonna think I'm desperate! She'll expect me to hit on her!*

Carmen knew she needed to end this train of thought before she broke into full-out laughter, which would undoubtedly gain a lot of unwanted attention. Luckily, the ice water saved her. The frequent consumption of which was making its presence known. She grinned as she dabbed at her mouth with the napkin before grabbing her purse and standing up.

The washroom sign, with a direction arrow, was located towards the back of the restaurant. Carmen made her way to the sign and through a short passageway. She then turned right down a short hallway. The washrooms were located on the left of an intersecting corridor. Carmen entered through a door marked with a universal sign for women. The men's washroom was further down on the same side.

Several minutes later Carmen opened the door to return to her table. Just as she stepped through the doorway, she caught a fleeting glimpse of a figure disappearing through a door on the other side of the hallway a short distance down on her left side. It had only been a second; however, her brain set off an alarm. The figure appeared slender with dark hair. Carmen stopped. The door closed behind her, as she stood motionless in the deserted corridor.

Could that have been Jessica? She craned her neck towards the door through which the person had gone, almost directly opposite from the entrance to the men's washroom. There was a sign framed on the door. Carmen glanced around. It was quiet. She took several steps towards the door to study the sign more closely. Her thought was that the room would be off limits to customers otherwise an English translation would be offered. She debated what to do.

Looking all around, Carmen silently made her way closer to the door. She wanted to know. All was quiet as she grasped the door handle. Holding her breath and with a final look around she quietly turned the doorknob. Leaning forward, she pushed open the door only a crack and peered in. The first objects that came into view were a stackable table and chairs positioned in front of a refrigerator and counter tops with cupboards. *It's a lunchroom.* Carmen let out her breath. The room appeared empty. Her eyesight travelled down past the table and chairs. She opened the door a bit more.

A movement caught her eye. At the far end of the room, past some benches and another door—which she thought to be an employee washroom—a figure was taking something like an envelope from a cubby unit mounted on the far wall. Carmen could not see well enough through the small opening in the door to make a positive identification, and the person stood with their back to her. Although she did determine it was a woman of small build, with black hair. Her heart pounded. *This might be Jessica!*

Carmen took a quick peek over her shoulder. Still nothing: all quiet. She turned back and pushed the door open further. Just as she did, the person turned away from the cubby and moved towards a heavy steel door and began to open it. Carmen got a quick side profile glance at the woman. She took in a sharp breath. *No glasses, but that looks like Jessica!* No sooner had she uttered the thought to herself than the woman disappeared through the door, which rapidly closed behind her. For a brief second Carmen saw the fading daylight from outside. *She's gone! Now what?*

Carmen felt a twinge of fear coarse through her body as she slipped into the room and softly closed the door behind her. *I'm not supposed to be in here!* She walked the length of the room and went to the heavy steel door. She opened it and peered outside. Carmen saw a small walkway leading to a cement, descending stairway. She could see nothing beyond that. The woman would have already traversed the stairs and be out of sight.

Carmen was about to run out after her. However, she checked herself. *I can't leave here without paying. Damn!* She turned back into the room. The door closed. *I might still be able to catch up!* As fast as possible she reached into her purse for her wallet. She found the bills she needed. Clutching 120 Shekels in her hand, she closed her bag preparing to leave. Something caught her eye—a glimmer from small rectangular bronze coloured name tags labeling each cubby slot. Carmen stopped to think. *Which box did she take something from?*

She hurriedly surveyed the wall structure's three rows of boxes and ten units per row. The woman had been standing well towards the left end, not bending down or stretching up. *It had to be the middle row—left end, for sure.* Carmen scanned the labels, looking for Jessica's name. She could not find it and then took about three seconds to check the name tags under every box. *There's no Jessica here.* She focused one final time on the labels. This time one name stood out. It was third in from the end, and more importantly the two names on either side were male. *'Rachel Cohen.'* Carmen mentally registered the name.

Precious seconds had passed. *I gotta go! If she's walking, I have a chance! Driving—probably not.*

Carmen flew out of the room, down the corridor and back into the restaurant, no longer caring what attention she drew to herself! Nothing was quiet or reserved in her demeanor now. It was all or nothing.

The room full of people stopped what they were doing and gaped, as a tall, young woman in tight-fitting jeans, a loose-fitting top and purple Pumas streaked past them, barely slowing down to toss money on her table. She narrowly dodged a startled waitress, and was gone.

Carmen skidded to a stop at the front entrance only long enough to yank open the door. She knew she needed to go left and down. The buildings, roads, and walkways in this area were built on terraces to accommodate the sloping hillside, and this resulted in many stairways going from one level to another.

Carmen ran the entire exterior length of the building to her left along a terrace, which brought her to a corner door; the same one she opened from the inside only moments before. There was now only one way to descend the stairway at the end of the terrace, opposite the door. She took the stairs in two steps, landing on the service road below. The option now was left or right.

Carmen stopped, her breathing coming fast. The light was fading. A choice needed to be made. She stared hard to the right, focusing on about 100 metres of pavement before the roadway turned. Nothing could be seen besides parked cars along the bordering stone wall. She turned to the left. Here the road continued in a straight line for approximately 200 metres. Possibly she saw something move, or perhaps not. It was getting too dark to tell for sure.

It took only a split second for the uncertainty to help make her decision. She held her purse tightly to her side, as she started to run left. Carmen was an excellent runner and the pavement was smooth and flat, which suited her long strides perfectly.

Professionally trained dancers are some of the most underrated athletes in the world. The physical training required for many forms of dance at a professional level is astounding. One attendance to a ballet in any one of many countries throughout the world can be quite rewarding to anyone interested in athleticism, and although Carmen chose not to pursue a professional career in ballet, she underwent numerous years of intensive training. Her desire to stay involved never lessened. At 23 years old, and in excellent physical condition, when her adrenaline kicked in, Carmen James was indeed a 'force to contend with.'

She calculated a time deficit of about 60 seconds to the woman from when she exited the door. With no cars driving on the road, it was probable she would be on foot, and even if she walked at a brisk pace, Carmen figured about 25 seconds of full out running would close the gap. Providing, of course, the right direction had been chosen. She was about to find out.

Her adrenaline surged. It took about 5 seconds to reach top speed. Her heart rate spiked. She stared straight ahead without focusing. Her breathing came deep and fast. Her toes swept across the pavement in a blur. At 20 seconds, her body was at full anaerobic efficiency. Ten seconds more and muscle fatigue would prevail, when her system responded to the inevitable oxygen deficit. At 25 seconds, a moving figure materialized before her. Carmen slowed. She became very much aware of her body's requirement for oxygen.

Her chest heaved. Through her open mouth, she inhaled air as fast as possible. At 35 seconds Carmen slowed to a fast walk, and her vision became steady.

Seventy-five metres ahead was the woman. She turned off the road on the right side, and started descending another flight of stairs. Carmen increased her pace a little. She squinted in the semi-darkness. Only 25 metres separated them now. Her breathing had stabilized. She called out.

"Jessica! Jessica is that you?"

The woman froze at the top of the stairs and spun around to face Carmen.

It's her!

They were much closer now. "It's me, Carmen!" There could be no mistaking the shock on Jessica's face. They were now only 10 metres apart, "Jessica stop! What's going on?"

Now it was Carmen who was shocked at what happened next. Jessica frantically turned and fled down the stairs!

Carmen was bewildered and confused. *What just happened?* She almost came to a complete stop before her startled brain processed the information. *What the…*

Carmen gave chase. She hit the stairs running! *It's not going to be that easy, girl!*

TWENTY-SEVEN

SUNDAY, MAY 4, 2014. 5:00 P.M.
JERUSALEM, ISRAEL

OLD STONE WALLS, in a dark cellar-type room, surrounded the cot upon which he lay. Edward opened his eyes and stared up in confusion at a bare, cement ceiling. An attempt to raise himself up to a sitting position brought a searing pain to his head. He settled back to a lying position. The pain in his head eased somewhat. Rolling slightly side-to-side enabled him to survey his surroundings. *What is this place? What's happened to me?*

There was not much to see. Edward lay on a fold-out cot in the middle of an otherwise empty small room. A cement floor and low ceiling with four stone and mortar walls formed the layout. Beyond his feet, an old black, wooden door under which was a rather wide gap allowed the only light. He saw no fixtures or switches, only bare walls.

In complete silence, Edward listened to his breathing as he began to remember. *In the museum ... someone behind me ... my neck. I think I hit somebody. I couldn't move my arms or legs. Then ... Carmen! Oh, my God!* He felt fear, which intensified to panic. Disregarding the pain in his head, Edward sat up. His eyes darted frantically around the room. He swung his legs around and tried to stand. He fell face first onto the floor, and then struggled to get on his hands and knees. *Oh please ... please ... let her be unharmed. Carmen, I'm sorry. What have I gotten us into?*

Something caught his eye; Edward faced away from the door. In the dim light, he focused on two items beyond the head of the cot and crawled towards them: a one-litre bottle of water and an empty gallon pail. He picked up the plastic bottle. The seal had not been broken. The throbbing pain in his head continued as the panic subsided- not, however, the overall angst. His mind began contemplating the idea of prison cells. He guessed what the bucket was for. Sitting on the floor, he swivelled towards the door, unsealed the water bottle, and began drinking.

Am I a prisoner? He stared towards the door. Taking another long drink, he saw his hands shaking. *But why ... I must think they got what they wanted. What the hell is so important about that damn watch!*

Edward thought to glance at his own watch. The illuminated hands told him he had been unconscious for nearly two hours. Checking his pockets confirmed no items were stolen and the contents of his wallet revealed nothing missing, including money. He pulled out his cell phone and tried to turn it on. There was no power. He assumed the battery was drained.

I need to check that door. Edward took another drink. The water appeared to be helping. He began feeling a bit stronger. After tucking the items back into his pockets and setting the bottle down, he grabbed the cot for support and shakily got to his feet. He remained there for a time, breathing deeply. The pain in his head had not improved, and the sudden surge of blood after standing did not help. Nevertheless, he moved forward until he grasped the doorknob. Turning and pulling only verified his assumption. Indeed, he was a prisoner. *Why are you doing this? Who are you? Don't you have what you want? My daughter ...* Again, panic began to consume him.

"So help me, if you hurt her in any way, I'll ..." it was the first time since regaining consciousness Edward spoke out loud. He felt a rage building. The panic lessened, replaced by anger. He swore out loud as he grabbed the door handle with both hands and yanked hard. The whole door shook and rattled loosely as Edward continued his vain attempt for freedom. He did not stop until he fell to his knees from exhaustion. He held tightly to the handle with both hands. The fire raging within him burned down and tears began falling to quench the flames. Through tear filled eyes he gazed upwards.

"Please ... please don't harm my daughter."

Edward stayed in this position for some time allowing his breathing to return to normal. He hung his head in despair, uncertainty clouding his thoughts.

Finally, pulling down on the door handle for support, he got to his feet. In doing so, he became consciously aware of how loose the door was in its frame. Once standing, Edward focused to his right and inspected how the panel was mounted. Through the faint light, he could make out only two hinges and a mounting design where one side of the mounting plates lay exposed to the inside of the room. He let go of the doorknob and moved in for a closer look. Each hinge contained only two of the three required 'Phillips type' screws. Edward wedged his fingertips between the wood frame and the door panel to check the tightness. By pulling, he could make the plates rock to and fro. *Probably the frame will be showing signs of rot as well.*

Edward stood back for a moment. His body was regaining strength. He turned and made his way back to the cot and sat down on its edge. Reaching over for the water bottle, he took another long drink. After setting the bottle down, he massaged his temples to lessen the pain. It helped a bit.

His night vision had adjusted to the dim light, allowing him to see well. He looked again towards the door as he reached into the pocket of his shorts. Hopefully his nail clipper would still be there. It was. Edward held the device up and thoughtfully gazed at it. This was the one tool always on his person. Over many years it became for him a 'Swiss Army knife' but at one-tenth the size.

Construction workers need to be resourceful, as often improvisation and creativity are required to get the job done in a changing environment with limited tools at hand. Edward had found a surprising number of uses for such an ingenious little device. He used it to cut, pry, file and slice on numerous occasions. It had become his preferred tool to be used as a tire iron for the removal and installation of his bicycle tires. And of course, a pretty good manicure was at hand anytime he liked.

With nostalgia, Edward thought back several years to a comment Carmen said to him when he was emptying his pockets at an airport security check en-route to a family holiday. She stood behind him in line and watched as he placed his money clip, a few coins, and his nail clipper into the usual plastic bin. She spoke in a soft voice, "Dad … if these airline security people only knew what you can do with that nail clipper, there's no way you're getting through!" Carmen started to giggle.

Marie stood in front of him and had overheard the comment. She turned with a serious expression on her face and whispered, "All it's gonna take is the threat of having the pilot's fingernails cut and filed to the quick and done—this plane's going to Cuba!"

She paused. "Oh wait … never mind, that's where we're going anyway!" The three of them burst out laughing. Edward recalled the people around them and how they stared. *They probably wondered why we were so happy.* Edward sat in silence. *Can we ever go back?* The once pleasant memory was now bittersweet.

Edward was afraid, afraid for himself and his family.

He returned his attention to the clipper and dismantled it by extracting the main pin, which he tucked safely away in his pocket. The top lever bar was now separate from the V-shaped blades. He then wedged it in tightly between the two blades to form a small T-shaped makeshift screwdriver, which he knew from experience would fit nicely into the large 'Phillips' screw heads.

Edward got up and walked to the door to test out his newly assembled tool on the hinge at eye level. Both screws could be turned. He stood back. It would be better to remove the bottom hinge first. His head still throbbed, making concentration difficult. He bit down hard on his lip as he lowered to one knee. He tested the two lower screws and found them to be about the same as above.

Edward leaned back and gazed up at the old black door. *What are you hiding from me?*

Again: "I am the strength and the courage to move forward steadily, through any condition, whatever it may be." The green book stayed close to him always, especially when he needed it most.

He put his head down and got to work, with the soft sound of positive affirmations echoing off the walls.

TWENTY-EIGHT

'It's not going to be that easy, girl'—a statement Carmen might just as easily have directed at herself. She had almost lost sight of Jessica already, and she was tired. It did not take long for her to realize how nimble and quick Jessica was on her feet. By the third descending stairway, Jessica was almost out of sight. Carmen could not keep up and darkness was impending, making running treacherous as she negotiated the cement stairs and stone-walled pathways that descended the hill. Finally, the slope ended. Carmen emerged on a path from dense trees and bushes. She could make out the sound of traffic and found herself on the sidewalk of a paved road. Her heart pounded.

She looked around frantically and spotted Jessica about 40 metres up the road running hard. There was no time to spare. Carmen realized this would be her chance to catch up. Right where Jessica ran now, the road became a short stone bridge. Carmen confirmed there was not an exit off the straight road for at least another 150 metres. An opportunity presented itself.

Adrenaline kicked in and once again Carmen demanded 100 percent physical commitment from her body. This time, however, she needed to enter the mental state of 'mind-over-matter' and disregard the pain in her lungs and muscles. The sight of her prey looming larger with every long stride urged her on. The sounds of traffic and blaring car horns assaulted her ears and added to the invigoration.

Jessica jerked her head around in fear. She witnessed how rapidly Carmen was gaining on her. She tried to run faster, knowing how vulnerable she was in a straight line. They were coming to the end of the bridge, and the sidewalk on the left side of the road would soon end as the roadway divided.

The wall of the Old City loomed a dark grey off to the right in the impending darkness. Jessica needed to be on the other side of *that* wall. To do so would mean crossing the busy two-lane highway, ascending more stairs, and traversing a pathway leading to the Zion Gate. Once through, a right turn would bring her to the familiar streets and alleyways of the Jewish Quarter. Safety for her would be on the other side of the wall.

She jerked her head to the right repeatedly, in a frenzied manner, as she ran!

What is she doing? Carmen was no more than 15 metres from her, and the fork in the road was coming up in about 100 metres. The sidewalk would end soon. *She's looking at traffic. Oh, my god, no!* Carmen tried to scream her name. She did not have the breath for it, though, and there would not be another chance. Jessica lunged herself out into the street! The sound of screeching tires filled the air followed by horns and angry yelling. In the time it took Carmen to stop and blink her eyes, Jessica stood motionless on the other side of the road staring at her. Their eyes locked. *You could have been killed, and for what?*

One car was sideways in the middle of the road. Traffic had stopped, and for a moment there was an eerie silence. As Carmen stepped out onto the road, a strange feeling came over her. She stared at Jessica. Somehow, there came an understanding: an understanding of total commitment on the other side of the road. She did not understand why, but she intended to find out.

The silence broke. A car door opened and angry voices resounded. Carmen called out between heaving breaths, "Jessica stop! I need …"

The connection dissipated. Jessica turned and fled towards a stone stairway. Carmen did not hesitate. She darted across the road in full view of the angry motorists. It was hard for her to make out what they were yelling in Hebrew. But she felt certain it was not nice.

Jessica ascended the stairs. Carmen needed to keep her in sight. They were only 10 metres apart. When Carmen started to climb the steps, Jessica was at the top. She managed to keep her in sight by taking two steps at a time. The stairway curved to the left, which led them to a path darkened by thick trees and shrubs. Carmen could hardly see. The traffic sounds and angry yelling diminished. She only heard pounding feet on the path and her own heavy breathing. She wanted to call out again but lacked the energy. The path finally broke from the dense trees, allowing more ambient light. Carmen saw Jessica 20 metres ahead. Again, she had lost some ground. Her body was weakening. The only hope now would be for Jessica to start tiring. The path came to a fork. Jessica veered right, which turned them towards the Old City wall.

Running at twilight, shrouded in the stone-cold shadows of an ancient old wall on a bordering desolate pathway, with the foreboding grey color growing ever larger before her, a chilling sensation enveloped Carmen. Her mind began flashing imagery of death and destruction from years past, within and around this stone barrier. She understood how walls such as this are built out of fear, and throughout recorded history the inhabitants behind these walls had known fear. *Why is the Old City of Jerusalem always in such a state of unrest?* Carmen could almost feel their misery.

Their path curved and followed along the outside of the wall. They were running right beside it. Carmen tried hard to close the gap. She failed; her body was fatigued.

One hundred metres brought them to a structural change in the wall. Carmen remembered from looking at a previous map it was the Zion Gate: one of the several entrances into the Old City. *She's going inside.*

They came up to a point where a road with sparse traffic intersected the pathway. Jessica veered left and passed through a large walled gate into the Old City, startling several pedestrians as she darted across the narrow roadway.

This *does not* look good. If Carmen's memory served correct, this was the Jewish Quarter. They were on a wide sidewalk now, but she surmised they would soon be in narrow, twisting alleys.

She did not have to wait long. A solid stone wall bordered their left side, intermittent with barred windows and doors of small shops, which all blurred past. As Jessica ran under an archway, Carmen saw her turn to look back. The gap remained 20 metres. Carmen realized then it might as well have been 20 kilometres, for right after the small archway they entered a labyrinth of stone passageways that became increasingly narrow. Two turns later Jessica disappeared.

The chase ended. Carmen slowed. Guessing at one more turn brought her into an open courtyard where any one of four possible passages intersected. Carmen came to a stop at the center of it. She bent forward in complete exhaustion and breathed deeply as the pounding of her heart subsided. She stayed this way for several minutes before straightening up.

Looking around, the first thing she noticed was how dark and quiet it had become. *Man, this is creepy. Not a place for me to be alone at night.* Carmen thought back. She only made three recent turns and had confidence in finding her way back to the gate.

As Carmen began retracing her steps, a thought occurred to her; *Jessica knows this place. She had me beat when she got across that road. Damn! Well, I gave it my best shot.* She began to quicken her pace to a fast walk. *I gotta get my butt outta here!*

THE TAXI PULLED UP in front of the Prima Royale Hotel at 9:05 p.m. Carmen thanked the driver, "Toda rabah," and handed him some money. The driver nodded.

"Bevakasha," he replied. Carmen stepped out of the back of the cab and with a small 'thank you' wave of her hand she closed the car door and entered the hotel.

It was quiet in the lobby. Carmen nodded to the male attendant at reception and walked over to the elevator doors. There was no waiting, and in only a few minutes she entered her room on the eighth floor. After locking the door, she walked over to the desk and set down her purse.

Next up was a trip to the washroom. Carmen found herself standing in front of the mirror as she turned on the light switch. "Oh, my God!" She gasped at her reflection. "I don't think I've been following the doctor's orders! What had she said? 'To ensure you get the proper rest you need'?"

Right, well this is scary—dark circles under bloodshot eyes, tangled hair, sweat all over my face and neck. Lucky for that taxi driver it's dark out. Man, he would've had nightmares! Carmen gave herself a tired smile. *We gotta submerse you in a hot bubble bath. Wow, what a train wreck!*

Approximately one hour later Carmen emerged from her bath wearing a nightshirt and shorts, with her hair in a single braid. Somehow, she managed to stay awake, and it was well worth it, as the bath helped relax her fatigued muscles.

Her eyes fell to the complimentary water bottle sitting on the television stand. She retrieved it, walked over and opened her purse, and extracted a pill from the small packet the nurse had given her. Now she would get the rest she needed. Popping the pill in her mouth, Carmen tipped back her head and downed half the bottle.

She made a mental note to buy some more bottled water to have in the room. Maybe a few energy bars and some snacks would be good too. For now, though, it was off to bed. A good night's sleep had become priority number one.

With the lights turned off and covers pulled up, Carmen snuggled into the soft, warm bed. She would not last long. Her body was so exhausted, it seemed to melt into the pillow top mattress as she turned on her side, closed her eyes and whispered a soft goodnight to her dad. *I don't know how yet, but I'm going to try again tomorrow. There's nothing more I can do tonight.* A soft smile spread across her face. *I love you, Dad.* She started to drift off.

"Or can I!" Carmen opened her eyes and rolled onto her back. A name popped into her head: *Rachel Cohen*. She stared wide-eyed at the ceiling for several moments. It was from the bronze nametag on the cubby unit at the restaurant. She had completely forgotten about it. "I need to know!"

Carmen had to will her tired body from the comfort that cradled her. It was truly an act of love, and love has no weaknesses.

She threw back the covers and swung herself out of bed. In the darkness, she made her way to the desk and opened her laptop. The soft glow from the screen illuminated her face as she sat down and began typing.

If you have a face, a name, and access to the Internet, you can source information on anyone if your subject is associated with any of the worldwide social networks. And it seems most young adults of the new millennium are.

Carmen began her search with the largest network. She logged into her own Facebook account and entered a search for the name *Rachel Cohen*. In seconds, an extensive list came up. Next, she refined her search, and typing *Jerusalem* in the Location bar brought up a narrowed list of seven *Rachel Cohens*. Beside each person was a small photo. Carmen studied the small pictures as she scrolled through the list. At the fifth Rachel she stopped, *I think we got our girl!*

Clicking on the photo presented a profile page. Here Carmen had access to limited, general information about Rachel Cohen and the opportunity to study two photos. The first: a larger version of the smaller profile picture. The other was a cover photo, which spread across the top of the page. It showed a young woman standing in a scenic photo with picturesque buildings against a landscape of lush green meadows in the background. It looked European.

Carmen studied the images closely, paying attention to body size, hair and eye colour. *Okay, there are no glasses, but for sure ... either I'm looking at an identical twin sister, or that's the woman from the museum I know as Jessica!*

Next, she read the concise list of information on Rachel Cohen:

-Lives in: Jerusalem

-Studied at: Alfred Helwig School of Watchmaking in Glashütte Germany

-Born: May 11, 1991

Carmen leaned back in her chair as she took a moment to process the information. As she scanned the screen again, a smile came to her when she read the Facebook prompt:

Do you know Rachel Cohen? Send her a message.

Ah, no thanks. Somehow, I don't think that's gonna work. For some reason, she doesn't seem to like me.

Carmen leaned in again and focused on the screen. She opened a new tab, which activated the Google search engine. This time she typed in:

Rachel Cohen Alfred Helwig School of Watchmaking.

Almost immediately a page of multiple links came up. The first three sites listed had Rachel's name associated with the school's name printed in English in bold print. The brief descriptions, however, were all in German. Carmen did not understand the language, although the second site listed caught her eye because of a word used common to German and English: *Prestige*. She chose the site and clicked on it.

When the site came up, it was clearly in German. Although she did not comprehend it yet, Carmen scrolled the page and briefly assessed it. The article appeared to be taken from a school newsletter. At the bottom was a picture of Rachel standing with an elderly man and a middle-aged person who appeared to be handing her an award. Carmen focused on the top of the screen to locate the translate icon. The screen went blank as the search engine analyzed and processed the request. It took about ten seconds.

Carmen waited. She knew from experience that translations on web pages were not always grammatically correct; however, with a little logical figuring a satisfactory result would be achieved.

The page came up again. Scrolling a bit brought her back to the picture. She wanted to read the descriptive paragraph below it. She examined the photo one more time before she began reading. Her eyes opened wider as she leaned in closer to the screen. Her breathing halted with one sharp intake of air. All was quiet. The only light in the room was the L.E.D. display of the computer screen, which cast an eerie glow onto her motionless features. Seconds passed. A strange look came over her face. Carmen let out her breath. Her eyes blinked hard several times as she scanned the photo again.

Carmen's voice broke the silence, as she began to reread the paragraph to herself.

"Rachel Cohen receives the prestigious award of distinction presented to her by the Dean of Alfred Helwig School of Watchmaking for graduating top of her class—year 2013. Rachel descends from a long line of horologists dating back well into the 16th century and is the sole remaining heir of her generation to the Osterhagen watchmaking legacy." Carmen paused. She felt the hairs on the back of her neck begin to rise as she read the last sentence. "Shown here with her proud grandfather, distinguished New York City watchmaker Herbert Osterhagen."

Carmen averted her eyes from the screen. She gazed around the darkened room. An unsettling fear began to permeate the air. She reached for her purse and opened it to find the card. In a few seconds, she held the room phone to her ear and dialed the cell number for Chief Inspector Claude Gadgét.

TWENTY-NINE

FRIDAY DECEMBER 28, 2012. 1:00 P.M.
GRAND CAYMAN ISLAND

Twenty-two-year-old Rachel Cohen sat on a beach towel she had spread out on the bow of a small sailboat, which her parents rented for an excursion earlier that afternoon. Gazing out at the sapphire water surrounding her, Rachel marvelled at the beauty of the Caribbean. She was spending her Christmas break from school in the Cayman Islands with her parents. Returning to Germany in the New Year would mark her final semester of a 3-year program in watchmaking. She was excited to be graduating soon. For now, though, it felt wonderful to be with her mom and dad. They spent the last several days doing fun activities. The highlights included tasting her first rum cocktail at Rum Point and several kilometres offshore from there the magical opportunity to cradle large stingrays in her arms in their natural habitat. On Christmas Day, they snorkelled with the beautiful fish in and around the coral and rock formations of lovely Smith's Cove, and now today they were doing their own sailing excursion.

Rachel peered out over the starboard side. They were about 2 kilometres offshore of Grand Cayman Island. She believed she was falling in love. This place seemed like paradise. She learned how the three islands that make up the Cayman Islands are directed by the British Government and are known as Overseas Territories. They have political and economic stability and tax neutrality, which has contributed to making the Cayman Islands one of the largest financial centers in the world. This in turn has resulted in possibly the highest standard of living in the Caribbean.

Rachel smiled to herself as she thought back to her dad's comment upon their arrival. "Rachel you're going to notice the people here smile a lot and always appear happy. It's because they don't have to pay any tax!"

Rachel recalled her response. "Dad … haven't you told me many times that money doesn't guarantee happiness?"

Her dad chuckled and said, "Does this mean you actually listened to me through all those years of your youth? I guess I need to know what I might be held accountable for, now that you're all grown up." He gave her a warm, loving smile with a playful wink to her mom.

Rachel thought there existed here a heart-warming friendliness that was special. She would not soon forget it, and the place would always be trying to call her back. Her gaze travelled dreamily along the shore taking in the beautiful scenery. *I'm a lucky girl.*

As an only child growing up, Rachel never felt alone. Her mom and dad always made her feel like she was the centre of their world and her grandfather, or 'Opa' as she liked to call him, became her best friend. Although her life had been split between living in the United States and Israel, her grandfather made it his number one priority to be with his only granddaughter whenever he could.

From him came her love of watchmaking. She showed interest and fascination in watchmaking from a young age, and her grandfather spent countless hours sharing and teaching her from his years of cumulative knowledge in the field of horology. She especially loved how he would talk about the past and tell all about her great grandfathers and their numerous accomplishments and traditions in watchmaking. Rachel understood early on that she was the only remaining Osterhagen of her generation and also realized that somehow in her genetic makeup a certain trait or gift had been passed down.

Watchmaking came naturally to her. She exhibited excellent fine-motor skills, along with a brain that processed and calculated analytical information extremely well. Her dream was to design and build high quality timepieces. With her grandfather's guidance and support, Rachel was well on her way to attaining the necessary skills and knowledge to fulfill her goal. Regarding education, Rachel held an undergraduate degree in computer design, which included an additional course in CNC machine technology and a minor in mathematics. Her 3-year watchmaking program in Germany was now 80 percent complete and of her own volition she studied the history of horology for many years.

Rachel formed a deep-rooted passion for watchmaking and someday hoped to restore the Osterhagen name to its rightful place among the world's best in horology. As she gazed out over the water, Rachel envisioned the day when Osterhagen timepieces would once again garner world-renowned respect from great watchmakers and critics alike, along with such iconic names as: A. Lange and Sohne, Patek Philippe, Vacheron Constantin and Breguet. She had thought out this dream a thousand times.

To most, her goal might seem next to impossible; however, Rachel had a secret. For many generations, the secret of a unique watch had been passed down—a mysterious timepiece commissioned in part to the Osterhagen Watch Company in the early 1600s. Although this remarkable watch had been lost, a book, showing in detail the specifications and movement of this most unusual device, which incorporated an unknown technology of extraordinary potential, remained. Rachel had been given access to the book, which resided in her grandfather's possession for a long time. Secretly, she photographed and made a digital copy and transferred it to a small USB key, which she carried with her always.

Looking towards the stern, Rachel exchanged smiles with her mom and dad. They were relaxing as they piloted the small sailboat in a good stiff breeze over the open water. Looking up, she spotted a big cloud forming and blocking out the sun, so she would not need her sunglasses any longer. Spying her satchel containing a laptop and a few personal items, Rachel got to her feet carefully and made her way along the gunwale on the port side towards the back of the boat to retrieve her bag. She still wore her life jacket over her bathing suit.

Rachel did not feel overly confident about this sailing adventure. She figured her mom and dad must have stretched the truth a bit to rent this boat. They never owned a sailboat themselves. Their limited experience came from a close friend in New York who enjoyed sailing and took them out on a number of occasions. Her dad obtained a small craft boating license, although that was many years ago, raising the likelihood of his forgetting much of what he had learned. Instinctive prudence told her to keep the floatation device on.

Rachel walked to the rear of the boat beside her mom and dad. Her mother reached out to her with a quick hug. "Oh Rachel, it's just so beautiful here, don't you think?" She gazed into her daughter's eyes with a radiant smile as the warm breeze played on her face and hair.

"I do. I kind of wish our time together here on these islands would never end." Rachel laughed as she bent down and picked up her tote bag. "But reality is ... back to school for me in less than a week." She smiled. "I'm going to take advantage of the cloud cover and review some watch stuff on my laptop."

Her mother turned and gave her smiling husband an understanding look. It was no secret just how much their daughter loved her studies in horology. Although the genetic influence seemed to skip a generation, Rachel was an Osterhagen thru and thru. As she gazed at her only child making her way back to the bow of the boat and resettle with the open laptop upon her beach towel, a sense of pride flowed through her. A genuine spirit of the family legacy was innate within her daughter. The intelligence, the determination, the skill; it was all there, developing into a creative, passionate force which was and had been shared by Rachel's grandfather, his father, and the many Osterhagen watchmakers gone before. Where would this lead her? Might she be the one to resurrect the Osterhagen Watch Company?

As her mother, she shared in Rachel's dream to bring the company back to the world someday. It often brought her to think of a comment made by her father—Rachel's grandfather—Herbert. Close to this time of the year at Christmas they were observing a young three-year-old Rachel trying to assemble a plastic toy clock given to her by her grandfather. A toy designed for a child of at least twice her age, but nevertheless she gave it most of her attention, while a lovely dollhouse with all its furnishings and residents sat alone in the corner.

As he watched his granddaughter, Herbert made the comment, "I think it conceivable that one day it will be women who lead the way in the field of watchmaking." He did not elaborate further as he studied her intently.

Seeing her daughter focusing on the screen of her laptop, her father's words seemed especially significant. She reached over and took hold of her husband's hand and leaned in close to him. They were happy and so very proud of their daughter.

Rachel perused some school notes. She wanted to be well prepared for a practical assignment scheduled for the new year. Soon, however, her mind wandered. Maybe the tropical setting or being on holidays promoted a bit of day dreaming, and usually for Rachel that meant thinking about the special watch and how someday she would become famous as the person who would bequeath to the world an innovative technology that might ultimately change everything for the better.

She reached into her satchel and pulled out a rubber-coated USB memory key. Separating the device, she plugged it into her laptop. Within seconds, the first of many images came up. She was careful to keep the screen facing away from the back of the boat. Her grandfather had been very insistent about not breathing a word to anyone, including her own parents, regarding this unique timepiece. It was to be an absolute secret between the two of them. Rachel knew he would not be pleased if he ever found out she made a digital copy of the book.

Never had it been her intent to deceive Opa; she loved him too much for that. However, in the last few years she could see him becoming more and more forgetful about things like where he put his hat or what day it was. Rachel smiled inwardly. *He may not remember what he had for lunch an hour ago, or even if he ate lunch at all! But never has he forgotten the assembly sequence or identification of even one of a hundred or so components within a watch movement, even right down to the exact model and movement calibre numbers of literally hundreds of timepieces. Incredible!*

Rachel's smile turned to a look of concern. She understood her grandfather was not well. He had for a long time suffered from a form of mental illness. She was not told exactly what, and she never had the heart to ask. He took medication to keep it under control. That was enough for her; he was a wonderful grandfather. Because of these and other medical concerns, Rachel decided to photograph the old book. Her opportunity came easily, as quite often now her grandfather would nod off to sleep in the middle of the day, sometimes for up to an hour, with no forewarning. He was on several different medications for many various ailments, and Rachel knew his body was getting tired. During one of their recent visits together she simply asked to see the book and soon enough she had used her phone to take the required pictures as her Opa dozed in a recliner chair.

Rachel looked up from the laptop for a moment, and watched as the shoreline appeared to glide past her. It made her think of the slow and consistent passage of time, never stopping. She felt an ache in the centre of her being as her gaze fell upon an old fallen tree in the distance. It gently glided past and out of sight.

Her inspiration and best friend for as long as she could remember was tired. The day loomed when he would become like the fallen tree. Her Opa would no longer be there for her. The shoreline blurred. Her eyes no longer focused properly through a wet film. The scenery became abstract.

Rachel devoted most of her life to study. She possessed the knowledge and skill to fix a broken watch and bring its pulse back and offer new life to an ageing timepiece. Never though, in all her years of study, had she learned how to fix a broken heart.

―――◆―――

As she had been so many times before, Rachel was completely engrossed in her study of the images on the screen. She knew all the drawings, their specifications and notations by memory. From time to time her mind would wander. She would find herself conjuring up images of the world-wide success of the newly formed Osterhagen Watch Company, which held the patents on a technology that would revolutionize not only horology but also major industry in general. As CEO of the company, Rachel Cohen might well become one of the most influential persons of her era. So much, could she do.

Though, it would be very difficult, maybe even impossible, without the watch. It had been lost now for hundreds of years. Her grandfather spent much of his lifetime searching in vain. What could she do now? As Rachel studied a drawing and notation on split magnetism she wondered; after graduation, she might find some time to enrol in some physics classes. That would be a good start. Perhaps then she would gain the knowledge required to solve the mystery on her own. She was young and educated. *Why not? I will uphold the honour and tradition of the Osterhagen name. This is something I must do ...*

"Rachel! Rachel!" The sound of her father's loud urgent voice jolted her out of the deep mental zone she had been absorbed in for the last half an hour. "Rachel! The weather is turning!"

Rachel had not been aware how dark it had suddenly become. A cold gust of wind lashed across her face.

"Rachel, you need to get to the back of the boat with us!" Her mother sounded frantic. Fear gripped Rachel as she became aware of her surroundings. The sea had changed to a dark ominous colour and swells were developing. The small boat began to rock side to side. A few large drops of rain hit her face hard, as the wind got stronger. She looked up; the sky appeared black and angry. Her father yelled to her mother. He was shouting about a high current and sail tension, trying to be heard over the loud flapping of the sails. More raindrops hit her head as she yanked the memory stick from the laptop and stuffed it into her bag. Slamming the lid closed she held her computer and bag in one hand as she tried to stand.

A loud moaning sound came from across the water, as the yelling increased in the boat. Rachel felt panicked. It was hard to stand. Her mother screamed, "Rachel, Rachel, get down! Get down!"

She was so frightened, she could not think. Her body moved two steps and froze; she was afraid to bend down to try and grasp the small rail along the gunwale. The boat began moving more forcefully as the loud roar from the wind assaulted her ears. Wild with fear, she stared at her parents. Her mother stretched out her hand as her father fought to control the boat, which heeled way over.

Rachel's mother screamed out her name again, but Rachel could not move. She saw terror in her mother's eyes when their gazes locked. A sudden calm in the wind allowed the boat to begin righting itself, as the rubbing sound of slack, loose rigging sounded. Rachel was less than two metres from the safety of the stern. She forced two more shaky steps towards her mother's outstretched arm when a low whining sound started to build. A few ominous moments later their small craft was struck by a powerful wind shift from the opposite direction. The wind shrieked as the slack in the sail wretched and slammed with great force against its rigging. The vessel violently heeled over as a loud tearing sound screeched in the wind. The excess slack in the sail provided too much momentum for the changing force and the rope cleat holding the boom in place let go with a loud snap. The boom swung wildly across the deck and struck Rachel, just above her hipbone! Air was driven from her lungs in one hard blow, which swept her cleanly off the gunwale into a dangerous sea.

Rachel was in a fight for her life! She gasped for air, trying to stay alive.

In some kind of strange nightmare, her mother was screaming, her father yelling, "Rachel! Swim to shore! Swim to shore! Rachel, Rachel!" Over and over came the sounds, the wind, the rain, the waves, the gasping for air, and the strong taste of salt water. "Rachel, Rachel!" She could hardly breathe.

The voices faded. She rose and fell. Everything looked dark, even though it was only late afternoon. A hard driving rain ensued, and she could barely see.

"Swim to shore! Swim to shore!" The sound cut through the deafening roar of the wind. *Is the wind talking to me? Is God the wind?*

She started coughing up seawater, feeling a searing pain in her chest and throat. Her breathing was stabilizing. She noticed her legs were kicking and her arms were rotating in a swimming motion.

The voices from her mother and father were gone now. Through the wind and the rain, a small red light flickered off to her left. It began fading farther and farther away with each rise and fall of the waves. To her right a vast darkness loomed, indicating land.

Over and over, over and over, Rachel kept telling herself as she veered in the direction of land. *Over and over, one arm over, the other arm over. Over and over...* Rachel willed herself on.

The wind continued telling her, "Rachel, swim to shore. Swim to shore." And for one hour it did not stop until a big wave with a powerful surge landed her exhausted body on the sanctuary of a soft, sandy beach. Rachel crawled forwards and fell into unconsciousness.

Less than an hour later, the violent storm ended, giving way to a breathtaking, sparkling turquoise sea.

Rachel Cohen was spotted lying on the beach by a middle-aged couple who came out for a romantic, arm-in-arm stroll, on a gorgeous, desolate beach to watch a spectacular sunset in paradise.

Rachel was revived and taken to safety.

A search and rescue effort had been organized for the missing sailboat and its two occupants.

The next day it was reported: The vessel had capsized.

There were no survivors.

THIRTY

SUNDAY MAY 4, 2014. 10:15 P.M.
JERUSALEM, ISRAEL

"Hello Carmen, this is Chief Inspector Claude Gadgét."

"Hi Inspector, I thought it best to contact you. I have some additional information I think you should know."

"Carmen, I am a bit surprised to hear from you at this late hour. I assumed you would be resting after your exhausting day. Are you okay?"

"I'm okay, thank you Inspector. I'm in my hotel room and hope to be resting soon."

"Very good. I finished up for the night at the station, and I am in the car heading home to enjoy the rest of the holiday. Ha, ha ... I think I will have an hour and a half left to celebrate." His good humour put Carmen at ease. "What is it you would like me to know?"

"Well ..." Carmen took in a deep breath and began. "I'll try to keep this short. I had a bit of a flashback about an hour or so after you dropped me off." Carmen paused to collect her thoughts. "It was about a logo printed on the corner of two high quality paper napkins. Jessica took them from her purse to set our iced teas on." Again, Carmen paused.

Inspector Gadgét responded to her hesitation. "Yes Carmen, I can hear you fine, please continue … the napkins?"

"Well, this might sound silly … I guess, a girl thing … but it seems a bit unusual to me for a woman to carry that kind of napkin around in her purse. I mean … they sure looked like the type usually found in expensive restaurants or classy bars and it's so not cool for a respectable woman to scam something like that for later use. Unless, well … I thought she might have a part time job in a nice place, then it would be fine … no big deal … a little employee perk. Can you see my logic Inspector?"

The inspector did not respond immediately. Instead he took his phone briefly from his ear and increased the audio output. Carmen had his full attention. "I understand. Please continue."

"Well, I searched Google for restaurants with the logo, hoping to spot it somewhere on the list of suggested sites."

The inspector interjected, "May I ask what the logo was, Carmen?"

"The logo was of an old carriage."

"Thank you, please go on."

"Yes … so soon enough I found a picture of what appeared to be the same logo displayed on a website for a restaurant called Montefiore in the Mishkenot Sha'ananim District."

"I know the restaurant, Carmen."

"Long story short, I got a cab and went there, ate half a salad and had some ice water. I went to the ladies' room in the back of the building. When I came out I saw a woman entering a room across the hall. She looked like Jessica, so I peeked into where she had entered. The woman grabbed something out of a cubby on the wall, and then left out a back door of the building. I couldn't follow her right away, as I had to pay my bill."

"I did notice though, a nametag below the open slot where I thought she had taken something a moment before. I made a mental note, and rushed back to pay my bill, and left the building. Luckily, I chose the right direction to go, and she was on foot. After a lot of running, I caught up to her. When I called Jessica's name, she turned to face me. We were quite close together. It was definitely her. I called out I wanted her to wait, but instead she ran down some stairs. I chased her as best as I could. It was getting dark and the terrain was difficult. I eventually lost her in the Jewish Quarter of the Old City." Carmen stopped to let her tired body catch up to her racing thoughts. It felt exhausting reliving the chase.

The inspector commented; "I think I can picture where you ran if you entered at the Zion Gate. You had a lot of elevation change with a busy highway to cross as well. That was a lot of running."

Carmen continued. "Yes, Inspector we entered at the Zion Gate. Fortunately, I found a taxi to bring me back here to the hotel. I got cleaned up and was almost asleep when the name I had seen on the cubby came to me. I decided to check it out on Facebook, about 15 minutes ago."

"What was the name Carmen?"

"Rachel Cohen." Carmen felt a shiver run up her back. She stared at the picture on the screen. "I found her picture and profile. A school she had attended was listed, so I Googled it with the name Rachel Cohen." Carmen stopped to think of the best way to word the information.

"Inspector, my laptop is turned on and I am looking at a translated article taken from what appears to be a school newsletter from the Alfred Helwig School of Watchmaking in Germany. I am looking at a photograph in which the woman I have known as Jessica is being presented with an award by the Dean of the school. Alongside her and the Dean is a much older man."

"Inspector, I would like to read to you the translated caption below the photo." Silence ensued for several moments. Carmen was about to say something when Claude Gadgét spoke up.

"Yes Carmen, I am sorry. I have pulled my auto into a parking spot so I can give you my full attention. Please go ahead and read me the caption."

Carmen took in a breath. "Rachel Cohen receives the prestigious award of distinction, presented to her by the Dean of Alfred Helwig School of Watchmaking, for graduating at the top of her class—year 2013. Rachel descends from a long line of horologists dating back into the 16th century and is the sole remaining heir of her generation to the Osterhagen watchmaking legacy." Carmen took in another deep breath, "Shown here with her proud grandfather, distinguished New York City watchmaker Herbert Osterhagen."

No sound came for many seconds until Carmen discerned a low audible whistle, followed by the inspector's voice. "Carmen, the mystery surrounding your father's pocket watch grows deeper by the hour. The watchmaker from New York has a connection with the L.A. Mayer Museum, whereby in a somewhat mysterious presentation, he summoned your father to that place. This could be a most important lead in finding your father. Most excellent work! This name will be valuable in locating Jessica's home residence, which up to now we have been unable to determine. Also, we can run a profile on Rachel Cohen and her grandfather, Herbert Osterhagen, both here and through the NYPD, I expect to be in contact with them tomorrow."

The inspector took a moment. "Carmen, I need to ask you to text me either your cell number or an email address. I have a couple of pictures to send you. Please remember, Carmen, this is extremely confidential, but I need you to witness them for your own safety."

"Of course, I will text you both. What are the pictures of?"

"We sorted through video content of six different surveillance cameras for the hotel break-in and the assault at the L.A. Mayer

Museum. The pictures are not clear enough for positive identification purposes; however, a certain male suspect has been caught on camera outside of both buildings at the estimated time of each of the crimes. It appears he stood watch for both operations. Although the photos are a bit grainy, I would like for you to study them. I would describe him as about 26 years old, 185 centimetres tall, dark hair, 90 kilos and fit. He has tanned coloured skin; I am thinking his ethnic background is bi-racial."

"I am hoping you are out of danger now, Carmen, as the criminals have obtained what they want. However, I do not like to make assumptions I cannot back up with evidence. So please, I ask of you to stay calm. Get your rest, but do not let your guard down, and be careful. If you think you see this man, I want to know."

"Of course, Inspector."

"I will send these pictures to you from my home later this evening. You can access them in the morning. I will be detained at a meeting early tomorrow, and unavailable for contact until after 12:30 p.m. However, I have voicemail or you can always call the station."

"That sounds okay. I think I might sleep til then anyway." Carmen was more relaxed now, and a wave of tiredness passed over her. She was glad she had called Inspector Claude Gadgét. He made her feel safe.

"One more thing, Carmen; I wish to tell you about a strange coincidence I had this evening."

"Oh?" The short response with raised eyebrows was the best she could offer. Her body demanded sleep.

"As police officers on duty, whether in our autos or at the station, we frequently monitor the police band on our radios. About the time of sunset this evening, I listened in on a call from a patrol car that had been dispatched to Hebron Road between the Jaffa and Zion Gates for a traffic violation." There was a pause. Carmen became more alert.

"Let me try to translate from Hebrew to English, Carmen, what the officer was told by some very angry motorists: 'Two crazy women were running east on Hebron Road between Jaffa and Zion Gates. One of the women might easily have been killed as she ran directly into traffic to escape a crazy woman chasing her.' Unbelievably no injuries were reported, but the near collision of several vehicles stopped and backed up all traffic for quite some time." Claude Gadgét paused before continuing. "After what you told me Carmen, do you not see the coincidence?"

"Coincidence, Inspector?" Carmen was now quite nervous.

"Yes Carmen, I thought it through and concluded that it can only be a strange coincidence. The police officer was told the women were crazy, and yet again the word crazy was directed to the woman who did the chasing. As I have mentioned before Carmen, it is in my job description to observe, and I know that you are *not* crazy. My observation of you has shown the probability of above average intelligence, but most definitely, and I repeat ... not crazy. So ... I will stand behind my deduction: a most extraordinary coincidence. I will investigate this incident no further."

Interrupting complete silence on the phone line, Carmen spoke first, "Thank you, Inspector."

"Whatever for, Carmen?"

"The compliment."

"You are welcome; it is well deserved." Chief Inspector Claude Gadgét ended the call. He put his car in gear and accelerated back out to the roadway.

After hanging up, Carmen returned a text message to the inspector with her email address and cellphone number. She closed her laptop, got up from the desk and headed for her bed in the darkness. She spoke softly as she went. "Mom and Derek ... I'll call you guys tomorrow." She climbed into bed. Ever so quietly she breathed, "Night Daddy."

She was asleep before her head hit the pillow.

For the first few moments after she opened her eyes, Carmen was disoriented. All too quickly, though, the hurt of yesterday flooded her thoughts. *No, it wasn't a nightmare.*

She glanced at the digital alarm clock: 11:04 a.m. She had slept for over 12 hours. After a long stretch, she pulled back the covers and climbed out of bed. Some light filtered into the room through the closed curtains. Carmen walked over and pulled open the drapes. She had to squint her eyes as bright sunlight flooded the room. Another beautiful, sunny day in Jerusalem.

She stretched again, aware of soreness in her legs from the hard running last evening. A few short steps to the desk and she had her phone in hand. It was still on silent mode, the way she always kept it to prevent disruption during classes at university. It became a habit. Most professors were adamant about restricting cell phone use during their lectures, so most students kept their phones on silent and checked them often for missed calls or messages. Carmen had two messages: one from her mom, the other from Inspector Claude Gadgét with photo attachments. She read her mom's first.

> *Carmen, I hope you're okay. I booked a flight for Israel tomorrow. I fly out of London Mon. May 5th, 7:00 p.m. Leave T.O. 9:30 p.m. Arrive Tel Aviv Tues. May 6th, 1:00 p.m. local time. Hope we can talk tomorrow. Luv Mom. <3*

Carmen thought for a moment after reading the message. She wanted to call Derek's place soon to give them an update on what she had discovered about Jessica/Rachel. It would be early back home in Petrolia: 4:00 a.m. *Ok, I'll dress and prepare for the day, then call Derek on his cell in half an hour. He gets up real early. I can call Mom about 3 hours later. That should work.*

Next, she checked out the text from the inspector; it was only a brief message: *Photos I want you to view,* accompanied by four frames. Carmen enlarged each picture separately and zoomed in and out as she studied them carefully. They looked like normal security photos shot from cameras placed above street level, the likes of which she had seen on news channels before. All four were of the same man. The images were quite grainy and in black and white. After shuffling back and forth Carmen thought she had the camera locations nailed down to three: outside at the front of her hotel, through a glass door at the rear of the hotel, and finally two pictures from across the street at the museum. She thought back to the inspector's description of the man, as she tried to piece together for herself a detailed outline.

Let's see, we got sunglasses in all four pics. Tall, dark medium length hair, yes—tanned complexion … hard to say. Well, yea, I think the inspector's probably right. What else did he say? Carmen thought for a moment, *ethnic background—bi-racial … gee … cops are good at this.* She continued to go back and forth between photos. She narrowed her scope down to the two photos from the museum. The subject was dressed in running attire: a sleeveless shirt, shorts and running shoes. *And … the other thing he said—and fit?*

Carmen focused on one of the two pictures now, the one with the best image of the man's physique. *Whoa … this guy looks like he's ripped!* She lingered a bit too long, her gaze transfixed upon the screen.

"Carmen James! You're checking him out!" she reprimanded herself loudly. She shut down her phone, although not before stealing one last glance.

He's probably some low-life steroid junkie who makes a miserable living breaking into hotels and creeping on people! She shuddered in disgust.

Carmen glanced towards the TV stand, and walked over to retrieve what remained of the complimentary bottle of water. Returning to the desk with it, she opened her purse and looked through it. Carmen still had a half-eaten power bar, which she grabbed along with her small packet of pills from the hospital. Her plan was to stay on the pills for one more day. They helped to control her emotions, and today might be quite difficult if it meant sitting around waiting and thinking about her dad.

She popped a pill into her mouth and followed it with a drink of water. She had the power bar consumed in less than 30 seconds. The water finished soon after. Carmen disappeared into the bathroom to prepare for her day.

Twenty minutes and several trips to her overnight suitcase later, Carmen found herself standing in front of a full-length mirror a revived woman. No more dark circles appeared under bloodshot, puffy eyes. The long sleep had done wonders, and with the help of some expertly applied make-up complimenting the soft wavy curls formed from the braid in her naturally highlighted blonde hair, Carmen was back.

Feeling good about herself and the way she looked would help her through the day. Carmen opted for high-rise denim shorts and tan sandals. Tucked into her shorts, a loose fitting white blouse, which showed a touch of bare shoulder. For an accent, she chose her blue leather charm bracelet, then sat down to paint her toenails to match the bracelet. She had brought some nail polish along hoping she would find time to do them, and the diversion would help keep depressing thoughts at bay.

Carmen glanced at her watch on the desk. It showed 11:35 a.m. She had finished her nails. They would dry while she talked on the phone to Derek. She wiggled her toes. It felt nice to make her feet pretty. Although sometimes she thought it a little *preppy*, it was a fun thing to do.

Carmen picked up her phone. *Sorry if I wake you Derek, but I really need to talk to someone from back home and you're the guy.*

She had the desk chair turned sideways and her long legs were stretched out in front of her. The call rang on the other end. She wiggled her toes again and admired her handiwork. The call was answered on the forth ring.

"Hey, Carmen."

"Hi Derek, did I wake you up?"

"No, no ... had to be up for work; I'm going in early and checking out at noon so I can give your mom a ride to London. I'm glad you called. You got the text from your mom about her flight plans?"

"I did Derek, yes. Is Mom okay? How's she doing?"

"Under the circumstances, I'd say okay ... but she's hurting deep down." After a brief silence, he added, "How are you doing, Carmen? Marie told me about the attack. Are you feeling better after the drug thing?"

"Yes, much. I went to the hospital where a nice doctor told me I was lucky. I'm taking some sedative medication now; I think it helps a lot. I wish Mom and I were together today so we could help each other. Is she sleeping?"

"I think so. She had a rough night, though. I heard her up pacing."

"I'm glad you're with her. Thanks, Derek."

"Hey, I'll do what I can. No problem, Carmen. This is getting weird, and well ... we're all scared, but I know your dad ... he's a tough and capable person. He's gonna take care of himself ... Okay?"

"I believe you, Derek. And the weird part? I need to talk to you ... it's got even weirder ..."

Derek did not respond immediately. After a few seconds, he stated, "I was going to call you too, Carmen, with some strange news. But you go ahead."

Carmen heard Derek's breathing quicken. Her heartbeat matched his mounting excitement as she began, "I'll not go into detail over the phone, so I'll keep it short. Okay, so it turns out that Jessica from the museum is not really Jessica; who she *is*, in fact, is Rachel Cohen, granddaughter of Herbert Osterhagen, the watchmaker from Brooklyn, New York!"

"Wow!" Derek sounded intrigued. "Yea, the New York thing … well get this. The dead body your dad saw being carried out of Herbert Osterhagen's watch shop?" Derek paused for emphasis. "It *wasn't* Herbert the watchmaker like we thought … it was some Caribbean thug, some criminal bad ass with a record as long as your arm."

"Herbert Osterhagen's *not* dead?" Carmen cut in.

"Yea, apparently what went down … and keep in mind, Carmen, this info isn't official. It comes from a couple of firefighters—friends of mine in New York. They're saying Herbert called the cops himself and reported that a guy collapsed in his shop. So … the cops come and remove the body and take a statement. They return the next day for some more information, Herbert is gone. Autopsy is done on the body and the cause of death is reported as drug overdose. So, the cops obtain a warrant and search the watch shop, and guess what they find … hypodermic needles and the same drug, in various forms. Herbert Osterhagen the watchmaker is now *wanted* on suspicion of murder!"

As Carmen listened she glanced down and noticed her hand was shaking. She took some deep breaths to try and control the building anxiety. Derek continued, "And get this … did your dad mention how he slammed the heavy door on the guy's hand when making his escape from the shop?"

"Yea ..." her own voice sounded far off. "He said for sure the man's hand would be badly broken."

"Well ... either before or during the autopsy, the doctors found the broken bones of the hand had been previously set with a splint and wrapped in gauze and tensor bandages in a professional way." Derek stopped to take a breath. "How weird is that?"

Carmen felt herself starting to cry. She had spent the last half an hour making herself look pretty. Now it was starting all over. She bit down hard on her lip. No, it would not be happening again.

Anger started to build and the crying stopped. "Derek, what the hell is going on here? Why are we involved? This is *not* who we are!"

"I'm sorry Carmen, this really sucks."

"Derek, the needles, the drugs, I think he is here. Herbert Osterhagen is alive and here with his granddaughter, Rachel Cohen!" A chilling fear even anger could not block out permeated her.

"Derek, I need to send this information off to the police inspector right away. Anything else?"

"No that's it from my end."

"If you see Mom before you leave could you fill her in and say I'll give her a call in about three hours from now? I want to go to a store to pick up a few things."

"No problem ... and Carmen ... I think it's gonna get better."

"Thanks for what you're doing for us, Derek."

"Hey, it works both ways. We'll talk soon. Bye."

"Bye, Derek."

As soon as Carmen ended the call she began composing a text. As she watched her thumbs fly across the keyboard, it was noticeable; her hands no longer shook.

At present, Chief Inspector Claude Gadgét was the best sedative she had to calm herself down.

"Carmen, I am so sorry." Meira leaned over the reception counter at the Prima Royale Hotel. She had both of Carmen's hands clasped in hers as she stared hopefully into her eyes. "If there is anything, anything at all we can do to help ... I want you to know, we are here for you."

"Thank you Meira, that's very kind." Carmen had spent the last 10 minutes talking with the receptionist and filling her in on what had happened at the museum. It was plain to see she was shaken by the news.

"I am looking forward to meeting your mother. I wish it were under better circumstances. She is arriving tomorrow afternoon?"

"Yes, she is scheduled to arrive in Tel Aviv at 1:00 p.m. I'm going to be calling her today and we'll talk about her travel arrangements."

"If you need, I can reserve a taxi or set you up with train and bus schedules."

"Okay, thanks Meira. I'll let you know if we need anything." Carmen smiled. She liked Meira and hoped soon things would work out and the two of them might have some time to hang out. "What I need now though, is directions to the nearest store where I might buy some bottled water, some energy bars and a few snacks. I think a walk would be good for me to sort things through."

Meira smiled in return. "This is such a lovely area to walk and it is a beautiful day." She continued on, "There is a small store about 5 minutes from here, where you can purchase what you need. It will be easy; turn right from our hotel to the next crossing street and go right. You will pass a bank on your side of the road ... look for the store; it has a black awning and stairs." Meira grinned, "Easy for sure ... right, right—then on the right."

"Sounds hard to screw up!" Carmen laughed. "And if I get lost, I always have GPS on my phone to find my way back." She patted her purse affectionately.

Meira was concerned. "Carmen, please take care of yourself. You have the hotel's phone number, yes?"

"I do … in my contacts." Carmen replied.

Meira grabbed a small card from a rack, turned it over and wrote a number down. She handed the card to Carmen. "My cell number … if you need it, or anytime you want to talk."

Carmen acknowledged the heartwarming gesture and smiled, "Toda rabah." She tucked the card into her purse as she turned and walked to the front entrance and headed out through the door. She turned right and, looking back, gave Meira a small wave through the glass. The smiling face of the kind, young woman lingered with her as she began her walk.

As she came up to the first intersecting street, Carmen realized she was squinting in the bright sun. Her sunglasses were still in her purse hanging on her left shoulder. Stopping for a moment and turning to the left she let the bag slide down her arm. As she began to undo the zipper something caught her eye: a man. He stood on the other side of the road, across from the Prima Royale Hotel. Her heart thumped and her body froze. Carmen shifted her gaze towards him. He was turned away, not moving and holding a phone to his ear.

Oh, my god, it's him! Carmen's pulse raced. She could hardly breathe. *Wait I'm not sure … but he fits the pictures. My God, no!* Carmen started to panic. Her hands were shaking. *I can't go back towards him to the hotel. I can't run … I don't know … I can't think what to do!* She began fumbling with the zipper. With her purse still open, she reached for her phone. *Inspector Gadgét … no, no, he's in a meeting. I can't just stand here!* Carmen became aware of her breathing, coming hard now. She began hyperventilating. *Do something!* She fumbled for her sunglasses and scanned the crossroad in front of her: a busier street. Other people were walking, much more traffic. *People! Yes, go towards them. You won't be alone!* Carmen put on the glasses, stuffed the case back into her purse and started walking. It helped; the hard breathing began to subside, although she was still too terrified to look back.

If he doesn't know that I think he's following me, and people are around, maybe I can get to the store.

As Carmen walked briskly, she couldn't help but experience that most unsettling sensation of 'someone is watching you.' She felt her ears burning and her scalp seemed to be tightening around her head.

She arrived at the main intersection—the next of her right turns. The traffic became more constant and lots of people were around. This helped reassure her. The panic subsided, leaving a trembling fear in its wake.

She thought about Inspector Claude Gadgét. *I wish I could call him now ... another half hour or so ... he'll be done his meeting.* Carmen remembered some of his words, *'I ask of you to stay calm. Get your rest, but do not let your guard down and be careful.'* As she recited his words to herself it was almost like he was with her. *Only half an hour ... I can talk to him then. He will help me. I can stay calm, Inspector, and I am being careful ... lots of people are around.*

Her thoughts went to something else he had said, *'I am hoping Carmen, that you are out of danger now as the criminals have obtained what they want.'* A bit of comfort came from this thought, although it was swiftly replaced with confusion, as the reality of how perplexing this whole series of events had become.

Carmen made the right turn at the intersection. She wanted to turn and see if the man followed behind her but she was too frightened. It would not be much further now to the store and she would find out then.

Her pace had quickened and she consciously had to tell herself to slow down. It would not help to make it appear as though she was running away, which might provoke the man into some form of action.

So, what does he want from me? I don't have the damn watch, buddy! And either you or somebody—watchmaker and granddaugh-

ter I guess, kidnapped my father, so what's the deal? Carmen fought the urge to start crying again while thinking of her dad.

She was so scared. Instead she visualized her call to the police inspector. He would help her; Carmen had a direct line to his cell phone. He could arrest this guy and that would be the lead that would guide them to her father.

This last thought jolted Carmen to a stark reality. It almost made her stop dead in the road and turn to face her pursuer. *Catching this guy might be crucial; it could lead us to my dad!*

Carmen's mind raced. *What can I do?* The gripping fear surrounding her began to dissipate in the face of a burning love for her father. An opportunity to help find her dad presented itself here and now. She had to do something about it. *C'mon, Carmen. Think!*

She scanned the street well ahead, as the bank from Meira's directions came into view on her right. A couple of seconds passed and she spotted the black awning and stairs leading up to the storefront.

Still thinking hard, the wooden stairs passed beneath her feet and she opened the door to enter the small grocery store. *Okay, I'm not thinking hard enough ... Let's mix up the brain functions a little: perhaps I've got this all wrong ... our friend, the 'steroid junkie' is shy ... maybe things have been a little off on the scoreboard as of late and he's looking for a hot date. Hey, I might be his type. I stay fit ... long legs, blonde hair ... we could do some sensual jogging together, even ...*

Carmen had entered through a glass door. To the left of the door, a large window that had several advertisements on the glass would conceal her enough to allow her to look out from the storefront without being seen from the street. She nodded to the storekeeper who was busy stocking shelves. About three other people were also in the store.

Carmen tipped her sunglasses up to the top of her head as she headed to the left window. She pretended to be perusing some items on a small shelf below while she peered out to the street and waited.

Nearly two minutes passed until she saw him. He was across the street and walking in her direction. He stopped about 30 metres from the store and took a cell phone from his pocket and put it to his ear. Carmen saw him clearly now. She took in a sharp breath. The gripping fear returned, although she was not completely sure it was only fear. *Wow! This guy doesn't exactly fly in under the radar! Criminals look like that? I'm in Jerusalem, not Hollywood!*

She took in the tall, athletic build, with the dark styled hair and golden-brown complexion. He wore off-white chinos and brown sandals. His shirt, un-tucked and collared with elbow length sleeves in a captivating teal green colour, she guessed was silk by the way the fabric shimmered in the sunlight and swayed in the light breeze. An attractive pair of brown tinted sunglasses matched perfectly with a braided leather bracelet he wore on his right arm. The total look: quality, modern-casual.

Carmen had to literally pull her eyes away. *Okay Carmen, enough staring. And remember the date thing was a joke right … just a little humour to make your brain start working. Now think!*

She left the window and went in search of bottled water, located in a cooler near the back of the store. She concentrated as she passed some nutrition bars. Stopping, she began sorting through the selection. As she did, a thought came to mind of having something to eat now. It would be a good idea if she had to run again. A rush of panic surged through her body at the mere thought of running again.

I can't outrun this guy! Chasing Jessica is one thing, but I'm not … Carmen's thought patterns shifted direction. She held an energy bar in front of her and appeared to be examining it, but without focus. She was mentally in another place. Several minutes passed. Carmen looked up and cocked her head with an intense expression on her face as her voice sounded, only loud enough for her to hear. "Was I shown some valuable street smarts last night?"

She glanced around at the walls inside the store looking for a clock, and spotted one on the wall behind the cash register. Taking a few steps and leaning slightly gave her visual access: 12:10 p.m. Carmen had not bothered with her watch today, as it did not seem likely to her that the time would be a factor. However, it was now important for her to know exactly when the inspector could be reached. His voice again rang in her ears, *'Do not let your guard down and be careful.'*

I will Inspector. I'll be sure to have people around me always.

Carmen was very nervous as she reached out and grabbed three energy bars, not even paying attention to what kind they were. She hurried to the back of the store and procured two 500 ml bottles of water and then made her way back to the middle of the store to the cash register, where a woman rang in her purchases. After thanking the cashier, Carmen tucked her wallet back into her purse along with the purchased items and checked the weight of her bag by swaying it back and forth while holding firmly on the handles. She opened her purse again and took out her phone. Activating the GPS, Carmen made her way towards the door. Before exiting the building, she typed in her destination: *Zion Gate*.

Carmen lowered her sunglasses and descended the stairs. She glanced to her left without moving her head. He had retreated back down the street; however, she witnessed an ever so slight lift of his head when he spotted her.

Okay Steroid, you probably don't need the exercise, but it's a beautiful day. How about joining me for a walk?

Carmen turned right on the sidewalk that followed the road. She was unsettled. Her hands started shaking again. Studying the map on her phone, she talked silently to Chief Inspector Claude Gadgét as she walked. *I think this is gonna take about 30 minutes, Inspector. I will walk only on busy roads with lots of people. I can scream very loud when I want to. You can ask my mom and dad when you talk to them; they'll back me up on this!*

Humour was a positive thing for Carmen. Once again, she used it to stimulate her thought process and clear her head. She managed only a tight smile now though, thinking of how her parents might well have suffered hearing loss because of her.

Humour; it can be a good thing. Would it be enough to see her through this? She was doubtful. Her pace quickened.

LESS THAN 16 HOURS AGO, Carmen had passed under this same gate and entered the Old City of Jerusalem. This time, however, the circumstances were different. She was leading now. The walk had taken 25 minutes. There had been no running on dark paths, only walking on main roads with constant vehicle and pedestrian traffic. It might have been, under different circumstances, quite enjoyable given the beautiful weather and scenery. She had not once turned back to confirm his presence, lest he might suspect she knew he was following her. A strange feeling and not at all a comforting one, having someone stalking you. However, Carmen dealt with it. She relied on instinct, being aware of her surroundings and making sure there were always people nearby to assist her if necessary.

Carmen turned right into the Jewish Quarter and spotted the familiar landmarks from the night before. Once she passed under the narrow archway leading into the tight labyrinth of alleyways, things would start to happen quickly. It would be just under five minutes until she arrived at that place. This allowed some time to study her GPS. Although the narrow corridors were not all shown in detail, it was still enough information to confirm the possibility of things going according to plan. Carmen checked her phone: 12:35 p.m. Inspector Claude Gadgét should be accessible now.

The call would be made in approximately 10 minutes. She desperately hoped he was good to his word and available for contact.

The archway came into view. Carmen took a deep breath to try and calm herself; she stayed focused, trying not to let fear paralyze her now. She realized staying in control and being confident would be her only recourse.

Have I not felt this way many times before? She relived an analogy, an analogy of an illuminated ballerina standing alone on a stage in front of hundreds of people waiting for the first note of a music score to commence. *She* was *that* ballerina. Beneath the classic poise, a pounding heart and a trembling fear made every cell in her body vibrate in anticipation.

The first note struck as Carmen passed under the narrow archway. The trembling fear released; it became energy and passion.

The dance had begun.

THIRTY-ONE

SUNDAY MAY 4, 2014. 6:30 P.M.
JERUSALEM, ISRAEL

The last of the screws were withdrawn. Edward had been working at the arduous task for over an hour, and his head still pounded. Painful blisters formed on several of his fingers, and a nauseating sense of weakness permeated his body. He thought about lying back down on the cot to rest. Reflection upon the situation, however, advised him against it. He might not get a second chance. He had no idea who or what was behind the door, and figured it would be best to press on.

The old hinges made indentations in the doorframe, which held the panel in place. Edward gathered up the four long screws and walked over to the corner to set them out of the way. He reached into the pocket of his shorts and retrieved the pin for the nail clipper. Reassembling the device, he stowed it away again in his pocket and stepped back towards the door.

Removing the screws had kept his mind occupied, which in turn somewhat repressed his feelings. Now, as he stood before the door, he sensed nervousness and fear beginning to rise again. He thought of Carmen, which helped renew his purpose.

Edward took a deep breath and firmly grasped the edge of the door between the hinges. He yanked hard on the heavy door, breaking it free with a snapping sound. Tugging at the panel, it slid away from the frame and the full opening was uncovered. After carefully leaning it against the wall, Edward stood back and peered out.

He looked up at a short stone stairway, which led to a long cement hallway. There was no sound or movement beyond the stairs. He stepped out of the room and stood at the foot of the stairway to get a better view of his surroundings. Light appeared to be coming from under three of the four closed doors and what appeared to be an open archway near the end of the corridor. Beyond the archway, he made out a single door. The doors were spaced evenly along the hall. The closest door was one of two located on the wall to his right, and on his left, was only a single door, a bit farther down towards the archway.

It appeared to be a timeworn building—perhaps a basement or cellar below ground level. Edward could only make out a single light fixture on the ceiling with exposed wiring, which led off to somewhere on the right. It contained no light bulb, only an empty socket. Mounted on each side of the walls were several old wrought iron sconces holding half-burned candles. Even through the dim light, Edward had no difficulty seeing, as his eyes adjusted well due to the considerable time he had spent in a much darker room.

Edward quietly ascended the stairs to explore his new surroundings. His soft-soled sandals did not make a sound. The silence seemed to amplify his pounding heart, reverberating in his head. He came to the first door on his right and grasped the old brass doorknob. No light emitted from under the door, as he turned the knob. Edward partially opened the door and peeked inside. Satisfied there was no movement within, he entered the room.

A quick survey revealed a toilet facility. It was quite dark with no windows, only vacant cement walls. The contents of the room were sparse: a composting, waterless toilet sat in one corner of the small room, and in the other, a small cabinet with an attached mirror, upon which was a steel washing basin. On the floor beside it sat a half-gallon plastic water jug. No faucets of any kind were present, although the remnants of old water lines could be seen entering the room from the ceiling above and hanging midway down the wall where they had been capped off. Just like in the hallway, a single cord of wiring originating from above the ceiling routed on the bare cement to the center of the room to a fixture with no light bulb, and then across to the wall of the door frame where it descended to a box with a switch that had been removed and covered over. Edward gave the room a final scan, taking in a few more items: a plastic 5-gallon pail on the floor beside the toilet, which he assumed contained peat moss or a similar substance for the compostable toilet, and beside that an open box of miscellaneous items. He thought he spotted rolls of toilet paper, tissues and paper towels, and some aerosol cans.

As he closed the door and turned towards the next room down the hallway on the opposite side, he thought he might be getting a better understanding of where he was—in an old building—hundreds of years old—likely in the Old City of Jerusalem.

He came to the next door and carefully opened it. This one, however, did have some light escaping from underneath. Edward peered in through a small opening and noticed no sound or movement. Opening the door farther, he saw a window in the center of the back wall located close to the ceiling. He was definitely in a basement. Dim light filtered in through an old paint-peeled wooden framed window that had exterior bars affixed on its frame. Dirt and grime made the glass almost opaque, and a closer inspection was required to identify all the items in the sparsely furnished room. Under the window, perpendicular to the wall, lay another fold-up sleeping cot, although this one appeared larger than the one Edward had been lying on. On the cot were a pillow and a couple of blankets and sheets folded at the end. Beside the cot was a small night table, upon which stood a kerosene-type lantern. A tall dresser located in the right corner held a small open topped wooden box containing a few toiletry items: a hairbrush, comb, razors and what looked like a shaving cream aerosol, soap and deodorant, with a small portable mirror laying flat alongside. In the left corner, from a coat rack hung a light jacket and sweaters. Beside them, leaning against the wall, a single folding chair.

Edward closed the door. The last two rooms he inspected were both minimally furnished, yet looked as though they might have been recently used. He thought this might be someone's short term or occasional residence, as indicated by the lack of personal items and furnishings. The barred window in the bedroom unsettled him.

He proceeded down the corridor. As he approached the archway, he thought he heard a faint sound above the beating of his heart. Edward stopped and listened. *It sounds like ticking…* He moved closer until he stood only a metre from the archway and the door facing it. The sound became louder from behind the closed door: a ticking noise, but more than one. *Clocks?* Edward took two more steps. He was in front of the panel now and looking at light coming from below. *Someone might be in this room!*

He froze, unsure what to do. Edward was afraid. He had no weapon, nothing to defend himself with. Peeking in through the archway, he determined the room to be an old, seldom used kitchen with a dirty, barred window. A wooden table, arranged with two chairs, a countertop and sink, made up the furnishings. An old gas or propane stove was positioned off to the side. Another empty light fixture, with a covered switch and an electrical box was mounted near the floor. Overall, the room appeared abandoned, as though it had not been used for years.

Edward thought to try and find a knife or something solid. However, there were no drawers or cupboards to search. The counter top had open shelves beneath, but they were empty.

Wasting no time, Edward moved towards the door at the end of the corridor. He thought it would most likely be the exit or entrance for the basement, given the rectangular layout of the building. Edward needed to know if he had a way out. He quietly made his way to the end of the hallway.

He used the same practiced technique to slightly open the door. Fortunately, it also was not locked. Again, he heard no sound or noticed any movement. This time, however, he stood sideways in the event someone came up to him from behind. Once satisfied there was no threat presented, Edward opened the door wider. As he did, a whisper of fresh air touched his face. His assumption had been correct; beyond the door, a set of six or seven cement steps led up to the ground level with an iron-gate entrance. He could see above the top step, where the gate was closed off with a heavy chain and fastened with a padlock.

Edward cautiously walked towards the stairs. Leaving the door ajar, he silently climbed the stairs to the metal gate. He inspected the lock and chain: a combination style device and the gate itself was strong and well anchored into the cement. There would be no walking out of here—at least not now.

Pressing his face tight against the bars, Edward saw the outside light fading as long shadows stretched across the cobblestones. The building was located on a narrow street facing the back of a large stone structure across the road. It was quiet, with only the sound of a few car horns in the distance. He could see little to either side, as the stone and mortar walls of the set back gate entrance blocked his view.

Edward believed he was in a separate lower flat of a larger building, and although not certain, he felt the location probably was within the walls of the Old City as he had suspected. He stayed pressed against the bars for a few moments, hoping someone might walk by. No one did.

Anxiety had made him forget about his headache and sore fingers, but now his discomfort returned. It came as a reminder for him to keep moving, moving towards his only option—back down. Pulling his face off the bars, Edward experienced the disparity of imprisonment, as he grasped the bars tightly. Never had he been incarcerated. *Is this what it's like to be alone and afraid?* He let go of the gate, took a deep breath, and retraced his steps.

Listening to the ticking sounds, Edward lightly held the old brass doorknob and his breath. Ever so slowly he turned his hand until the mechanism reached its stop. Gently, he pushed inwards until a tiny slit of light escaped the room. With one eye close to the opening, Edward peered in.

More light came from the room, and the ticking sound grew louder with the slight opening, indicating the presence of clocks inside. He could see only the left side of a well-lit room and saw a wall lined with shelves, upon which sat a number of clocks and other various timepieces. There were also assorted tools and parts bins within view. At the back of the room, he noticed a clean, barred window under which was a high standing workbench and accompanying stool. The workbench extended beyond his vision. Under it were two car batteries with connecting cables, tied to a controller unit set on the wall above. One cable extended to a small opening in the window frame, two others were mounted along the wall to power the lighting. Edward thought it was a solar panel energy system, and opened the door farther to inspect the right side of the room.

As the rest of the view unfolded before him, he hardly noticed another similar window come into sight, or how the workbench extended from one wall to the other and contained many more tools and parts bins, as well as two intensely bright lights on pivoting, extendable arms—hovering overhead. Edward's attention was captivated by something else.

Almost in the corner of the room, sitting on another stool, hunched forward with his back to him, sat an older man engrossed in a task. Edward held his breath, as he opened the door farther to get a better look. The dry hinges creaked. Edward froze. The man lifted his head and spun around.

Edward gasped and stared in disbelief. The man wore a loupe to magnify one side of his vision, but there was no mistaking the silver hair or the single blue coloured eye fixed on him.

"My God … Herbert Osterhagen!"

THIRTY-TWO

"Ah Edward ... Nice to see you again! Come ... sit." Herbert Osterhagen lifted the loupe from one eye to his forehead and gestured with a free hand towards the empty stool. "Let us discuss horology ... watches ... timepieces. I have much to repair. Always so much to do ... but I could take a break now." He gestured again as Edward had not moved. "Please, pull up a stool."

Edward cautiously entered the room. He stared at the old watchmaker, startled and bewildered. He spoke as he moved forward slowly. "I ... I'm confused. I didn't expect to ever see you again. I thought ... I assumed you were dead!"

Herbert gave him a subtle smile. "Simply a case of mistaken identity; most understandable in your situation."

Herbert paused as Edward stopped beside the stool. "And I have been waiting to tell you, Edward ... The Brooklyn Dodgers baseball cap suits you well."

Edward's thoughts were spinning as he recalled standing among the small crowd of people across from the watch shop, watching a dead body being loaded into the ambulance. "That would mean you ..."

"A necessary course of action I'm afraid." Herbert gestured again to the stool.

Edward sat down and took a moment to arrange his thoughts. "You were at the museum ... Herbert. Where is my daughter Carmen?" Edward glared at the old man. His anger rose, "I need to know she is safe."

Herbert nodded and held a serious look of understanding. "Yes, I was at the museum Edward. I have every reason to believe your daughter is safe. She left the building, using her own strength. In a small dosage—mostly Versed—as I used in her case, would have worn off quickly."

Edward absorbed the statement, and it brought about a slight sense of comfort, although it did little to subdue his growing impatience. "You need to tell me now ... what the hell is this all about!" The surge of temper brought on a wave of pain to his head. He brought up a hand and massaged his forehead, trying to get some relief.

Herbert Osterhagen responded to the indication and reached into a drawer under the workbench. "Your head is hurting Edward. I am very sorry." He leaned over and offered him a pill container. He swivelled around and opened the lid of a plastic cooler sitting on the floor. He produced an unopened bottle of water and handed it to Edward. "Two of those will relieve the pain."

Edward examined the plastic container: prescription Tylenol 3s. The generous act helped to calm him a bit as he opened the bottle and verified the type of pills. He tossed two of them into his mouth. Tipping his head back, he downed half the bottle of water. Nodding a 'thank-you', he returned the container to Herbert, who lingered as he placed it back into the drawer.

He raised his head up with a sad expression. "I would like to apologize, Edward. I am truly sorry for what happened. First and most important, I need you to understand; Rachel had no previous knowledge regarding the assault on you and your daughter. I must take full responsibility for that." Herbert cast his gaze downward.

"Rachel?" Edward responded with uncertainty.

"Ah, yes ..." Herbert lifted his head. "The young woman at the museum you know as Jessica ... her real name is Rachel. Rachel Cohen. She is my granddaughter."

"This is all about the watch I found in Petrolia, isn't it?"

"Yes, it is." He stared directly at Edward with an unwavering focus.

Edward continued. "Why is it so important? One person has died and others have been stalked, harassed and assaulted!"

Herbert did not respond immediately. Sorrow came over him as he stared at Edward. "I have deceived you and brought pain and anguish to your family. For that, I am sorry. I hope you can forgive me." He paused. "The answer to your question is not easily forthcoming. I will tell you what I can about the watch and its importance to me when the time is appropriate."

"When the time is appropriate?" Edward felt apprehensive. "What's wrong with right now?"

"I need to get back to my watch repair."

He witnessed a change settle over the old watchmaker. His eyes glazed over, and in an almost nervous manner, he frequently shifted his gaze. Nevertheless, Edward pressed him. "Why are you holding me prisoner, Herbert? You have what you want. You stole the watch from me. What is left to do?"

Herbert regained some alertness. His gaze fixed steadily for a moment. "You must understand Edward ... from the moment you left my shop in New York, the watch was not yours. A significant importance is attached to it, which you may never understand." The old man lowered his gaze and stayed silent.

"There are bars on the windows, and the entrance gate is locked. I want to leave right now!" Edward's voice rose. "I want to find my daughter and see for myself she is alright!" He stood and walked over to the old watchmaker who had not acknowledged him. Edward put his hands firmly on the old man's shoulders and shook him. "I need the combination to the lock on the front gate!"

When Herbert Osterhagen looked up into Edward's angry eyes, he faltered. The nervous appearance returned. "I am sorry I do not remember it."

"What do you mean you don't remember it?" Edward shouted, his body shaking.

"It is my memory … It has been a long time since I have been here. I do not always know … I think I might have forgotten to take my medication."

"Is it not written down somewhere? Do you have a phone?" Edward's anger had not subsided. He would wring it out of the old man.

No response, just a nervous faltering stare. Edward took a deep breath to control his emotions. He was beginning to think something was off. Herbert Osterhagen's demeanour had shifted. His grip softened, and he let go of Herbert's shoulders and stepped back. He asked in a quiet voice, "Do you think you might remember soon?"

Herbert nodded slightly. "I would like to resume my watch repair now. I have much work to do."

Perhaps from knowledge gained by taking psychology night courses over the years, or maybe from the many discussions with his wife Marie about her involvement with the mentally afflicted in her own profession, Edward could tell Herbert Osterhagen gained mental stability from his love of watchmaking. He would leave him alone and try again later. "I think you need to resume your work, Herbert." Edward witnessed a sparkle returning to those crystal blue eyes. Herbert lowered the loupe and turned back to the bench.

Edward stood motionless behind the old watchmaker's shoulder for a good length of time. He was witnessing something special. The skill of the man prevailed. The hesitation and the nervousness had completely disappeared. It had given way to a calm dexterity of pinpoint accuracy. Herbert Osterhagen became the master of his domain. A countless number of parts, some so tiny they could not even be discerned by the naked eye, were positioned in the assembly process of a watch movement. Edward watched with both awe and respect until the movement was nearly assembled.

When he glanced up, he noticed the outside light had faded. It would now be quite dark in the rest of the flat. He spotted a kerosene lantern, like the one in the bedroom, on a small table near the door, with a trigger styled butane lighter lying beside it. Picking up both items, he quietly left.

Edward returned 20 minutes later and found Herbert winding and setting the wristwatch he had assembled. Edward had gone through each of the rooms in the flat searching for a way out or for some tools to force the lock at the front entrance, but he failed on both counts. Edward did, however, open the sliding wooden framed window in the kitchen. At least this brought some fresh air into the flat, which was almost entirely in darkness except for the battery powered lighting in the watch repair room.

Edward hoped this might be an appropriate time to engage Herbert and possibly encourage him to recall the combination of the lock. He thought about using a softer approach, which would undoubtedly keep the watchmaker more relaxed.

Herbert remained intently focused on the timepiece. Edward wondered if he even knew he had left the room and returned. Edward surveyed the repair room closely. He did not want to start opening drawers, so he stayed occupied just observing. Most of what he saw were tools and parts for watchmaking. They would not help him force a lock or cut a chain.

Edward walked over to the stool and sat down. He remained quiet for a while and noticed his headache had diminished. This helped a great deal in his thought process. Picking up his bottle of water from the workbench, he took a drink and said, "Herbert, I enjoyed watching you work."

Herbert looked up and swivelled his chair slightly towards him, the loupe no longer mounted on his head. He smiled. "I can understand how watchmaking would be of interest to someone like you."

"Perhaps someday I will get an opportunity to learn more, but for now, Herbert, please … can you try to remember the combination to the lock? I really need those numbers. I want to leave now. I am concerned for my daughter's well-being."

"Carmen is okay!" A female voice sounded from directly behind Edward. He spun his stool around. "I just saw her 20 minutes ago, and she's fine."

Edward stared. Rachel Cohen stood in the doorway.

THIRTY-THREE

The words spoken by the young woman standing in the doorway embraced Edward. As he stared at her, a great weight lifted from his shoulders, and the sound of her words flowed into every cell of his body like a soothing caress. *Carmen is okay! She is fine! Thank-you, thank-you.*

Even without her eyeglasses, Edward knew she was the woman from the museum: Jessica. The soft flickering light from the candles in the hallway outlined her features in a ghostly manner in the darkened part of the room. She appeared quite fatigued and her breathing sounded deep.

"Did you talk with Carmen?" Edward asked hopefully.

"No, but I saw her close enough to tell she's alright." Rachel shifted her gaze towards her grandfather and Edward did not press any further. He was so happy his daughter was safe.

"Opa, I thought Edward would be gone by now. He looks fine. Why is he still here?" She looked troubled, glancing back and forth between the two men.

Herbert did not speak. Edward said. "Rachel …" he waited a moment. "I guess we were not properly introduced, but I suppose I know who you really are now … and I'm pretty sure I can help you out with your question."

Their eyes met, and Rachel held his gaze steady as he resumed. "I woke up inside a locked room. All the windows are protected with iron bars, and the only access to this flat is through a solid steel gate, which is secured with a chain and padlock combination, and it would seem your grandfather can't recall the numbers to open the lock. Hence, I'm still here."

Rachel's look softened. She gazed at her grandfather as she replied to Edward, "That would be my fault. This has been an exhausting day … I was planning to write the numbers down for him, but I forgot. Opa hasn't been here for quite some time, and I replaced the old lock with a new one. At best, he maybe heard me say the number once. I'm sorry."

She turned towards Edward. "I am also very sorry for what happened to you and Carmen." Edward witnessed a distraught expression as she moved closer to him and continued. "I was not fully aware of the situation. I should have been more prepared."

She glanced over to Herbert. "My grandfather is a good man, Edward. I hope you will give me some time to explain things and hopefully I can help you understand." She focused on Edward again. "I want you to know I will accept full responsibility for the actions taken against you and your daughter. I put your watch in a place of safekeeping, and I intend to return it to you as soon as I can. If you wish to go to the police, I will understand. I ask only that if you do, please bring me along."

Edward looked from grandfather to granddaughter. Things had changed. He no longer felt threatened. Carmen was okay and he would be fine. Would this be the end of it?

He gazed back and forth between them, as he considered his situation. "I travelled a great distance, and although I enjoyed a brief visit with my daughter, I really hoped to gain some information on what appeared to be an interesting old pocket watch." He paused and then continued. "It seems; however, all my expended time and effort has been in vain. I lost the watch and gained no information on it at all." He raised his eyebrows in a hopeful expression and focused on Rachel. "Is it possible for you to be truthful and explain to me what is so special about an old watch I found at a garage sale in Petrolia, Canada?"

Silence permeated the room. Rachel dropped her gaze and began to slowly rock her head from side to side as she undid a zipper on the purse hanging from her shoulder. She lifted her head, and Edward saw her eyes filled with tears.

As she turned from him to her grandfather, several tears fell down her cheek. "Opa, what have we done? These people could have been killed! And for what ... a lie?" Her voice cracked. Emotions made it difficult for her to speak. "We broke the law. You will probably be taken away. We will be apart, possibly forever. You haven't been taking your medications, why?"

She stopped talking for a moment. Taking several staggered breaths, she sniffled and used the back of her hand to wipe away tears. "Edward asked me to be truthful with him, and I want to be. But it is most difficult, as I know *you* have not been truthful with me, Opa. What can I tell him that is not a lie?"

Herbert Osterhagen broke from his passive state. "Rachel, I do not understand. Why do you say this?" Edward saw hurt in the old man's eyes. He looked from grandfather to granddaughter, watching her hesitate as she reached into her purse.

"I told Edward I was not prepared. Had I received some information I requested from a friend a few hours earlier, things would have turned out quite differently." She pulled out an old leather-bound notebook and stared at it silently as she held it up.

"Rachel, why did you take the book?" Herbert leaned towards her now. His gaze fixated on the notebook.

Rachel addressed her grandfather. "When you called me from New York and said you wanted to come and see me, I knew something changed; you were acting strangely." She paused, as she held the book towards him. "When I realized you had this book with you, I decided to do something I'd been thinking about for a while, so I borrowed it for what I hoped would only be a couple of hours. Unfortunately, it turned out to be longer than I expected."

"No! No Rachel, you should not have taken the book!" Herbert suddenly became agitated. "I fear our trust is broken! I told you many, many times this was to be our secret!"

"I'm sorry Opa, I did what I needed to do." She held a sad, thoughtful gaze with her grandfather.

"No Rachel! You do not understand. There is much more I can tell you. But now is not the time." Herbert was visibly upset.

Rachel did her best to speak through sobbing breaths. "I think I understand why you did this, Opa. It makes me sad, but I will always love you." Her tear-filled eyes turned towards Edward. "I need to make this right."

Edward glanced back and forth between them, feeling uncertain. He turned towards Rachel, as she began speaking to him. "You asked about the watch you found?" She uttered a soft, hurtful laugh. "Perhaps you would like to study it in depth, as I have done for many years. It always inspired me … a favourite childhood fairy tale that I thought would someday come true." Her eyes lowered to the book held affectionately in her grasp. "I think it's time to let go."

Neither of them noticed Herbert swivel a bit on his stool and with a shaking hand reach into a small drawer below his bench. He picked up a small cylindrical object and held it firmly concealed in the palm of his hand. He turned back around just as Rachel made a gesture towards Edward. In one quick movement, she tossed the book to him. "I hope you find some enjoyment in it."

Edward had barely caught the book when he was startled by a sharp intake of breath. In a blur, his peripheral vision caught a mass moving towards him. He instinctively leaned back. Herbert gave a loud yell as he lunged towards him. "No! No!"

The old man moved quickly, but Edward was faster. He leaned just far enough for Herbert's lunge to miss its mark. The unchecked momentum caused the old man's stool to tip, sending him careening past his target. Rachel looked up and took a step forwards to try and intervene. Herbert's body weight glanced off Edward's knees, which caused him to fall backward off his stool and crash hard on the floor. A loud scream shook the room, as Herbert crashed headlong into Rachel causing her to crumble under his weight. It was all over in seconds. Edward hit his shoulder hard on the cement floor. Otherwise unhurt, he rolled out from under the stool to see Rachel pinned under her grandfather. She did not move.

"Herbert! Rachel!" Edward quickly got to his feet. He leaned down and grasped under the old man's shoulders. He could feel him breathing heavily.

"Herbert! Can you hear me? We need to get you up!" Rachel was still not moving. After the scream, she went silent, and Edward could see her eyes remained closed. He needed to get Herbert off her.

"Herbert! Can you move?" He got no response, only heavy breathing. He shifted his grip to one side of Herbert's body and pulled up hard, rolling his body away from Rachel. Herbert's eyes were only half open; he was dazed from the fall.

"Herbert, can you hear me?" Edward called out again. Herbert's eyes flickered. A few moments passed until he opened them wide. At first, he was confused, until he recognized the concerned face of the man kneeling over him.

"Edward ... Rachel?" Herbert lay sprawled out on his back with his arm still covering Rachel's leg.

"Rachel is beside you, Herbert. I think she's unconscious. We need to get you up. Can you move?"

"Unconscious?" Herbert began to move.

"Yes, I think …" He stopped mid-sentence. Herbert moved his arm, uncovering Rachel's leg.

Edward paled. He felt sick and could not breathe.

He stared in horror at the fully depressed hypodermic needle embedded in Rachel Cohen's leg.

THIRTY-FOUR

"Oh, what have I done? What have I done?" Herbert Osterhagen kneeled above his granddaughter's still figure. He removed the needle from her leg and held it in his hand. Edward placed his hand on her neck checking for a pulse. With little medical knowledge, his observations would be estimates at best.

"Her breathing is shallow, and I feel a light, rapid pulse. What was the drug, Herbert?"

Herbert did not respond. "Herbert, what drug did you put in the needle?" Edward tried again, raising his voice.

This time Herbert lifted his head. Edward noticed the man's hands shook and he looked dazed. Edward thought he might be going into shock. "The drug was a mixture … mostly Ketamine. But, no … no … the dosage was too much for her small body. This cannot be happening!" Herbert stared at Edward with a lost, pleading stare.

"Ok, Herbert let's get you up, and I'll try to find help." As Edward stood, he noticed his shoulder still hurt. He got behind Herbert and, lifting under his arms, got him to his feet and over to the stool.

Before he sat down, Herbert opened the drawer beneath the bench and returned the needle. Edward waited for him to close the drawer and then got him settled on the stool. "Are you okay to sit? I'll be right back." Edward waited for a nod from Herbert, then turned and quickly left the room. He crossed his fingers, as he made his way through the door and up the cement stairs to the front gate. "Damn … she locked the gate behind her!" He gave a sharp tug on the lock. It was definitely locked.

Okay, now what? He stood still as he thought. *A phone! Maybe Rachel has a cell phone!*

Edward hurried back to the watch repair room. Herbert had not moved. He sat slumped on his stool staring down at Rachel's limp body. "Herbert, the front gate is still locked. I'm trying to get help for you and Rachel."

Herbert raised his head. "Is there a phone tucked away some place?" Herbert did not reply, he simply held Edwards gaze for a moment then slowly lowered his eyes back to Rachel.

"Herbert, I'm going to search inside Rachel's purse for her cell." He waited for a few seconds. Again, no sound from Herbert. He did not move.

Edward knelt and removed the strap from her shoulder, freeing the handbag. He held the open purse towards the lights above the workbench and sorted through it, finding only a wallet, make-up case, napkins, a pen, a set of keys, etcetera. One thing stood out: an envelope, with the inscription: *'The Israel Museum, Jerusalem'* printed on the top left corner. No phone.

As he closed the purse, he thought to check her pants pockets. He knew Carmen often carried her cell in her pocket for easy access, and where she could feel the vibrating signal against her leg. No phone. *Why doesn't she carry a cell phone?*

Edward glanced towards Herbert. "Herbert, Rachel doesn't have a phone. Are you sure there isn't one here?" He waited; again, no response, just a blank stare. "Please, Herbert, we need help for Rachel. If you can think of anything—another phone, a battery for my phone, anything …" Herbert sadly turned away from him, back to his granddaughter.

Edward got to his feet and walked over to the door, setting the handbag down on the nearby table, and lit the lantern. He grasped the handle and turned towards Herbert. "I'm going to yell out through a window in the kitchen. Maybe someone will hear me." Herbert's only response was another sad look. "I'll return soon. I want to move Rachel to the cot with some blankets to keep her comfortable."

Edward left. Earlier, he had found some good-sized candles in the box with the toilet supplies and placed them in the bedroom and the kitchen. He lit two candles in the bedroom and arranged them on the dresser and proceeded to set up the cot with a bottom sheet and removing the remaining sheet and blanket. Placing them on the floor beside the dresser, he grabbed the folding chair, along with the lantern, and headed back out of the room to the kitchen. Edward opened the window and placed the chair near it, and after lighting two more candles, he climbed up. Sliding the window open farther, he could just get his head through the window frame and press his face between the bars.

Edward listened. All was quiet, save for the distant sound of the occasional car horn. He took in a deep breath and broke the stillness of the night with his cries for help. "Hello! Hello! Anybody! Help! We need help! Please! Hello …"

He heard the eerie echo of his own voice each time he paused to take a breath. "Hello! Please send help! Urgent! Hello! Anybody …"

Edward kept trying. He would call out for about 15 seconds then stop and listen. He tried cupping his hands around his mouth, fashioned in a horn shape to amplify his voice. "Shalom! Shalom! Hello! Send help! Emergency! Help! Help!"

Minutes passed and nothing. His throat became sore, and soon after his voice was hoarse. The power of Edward's voice diminished. After another 5 minutes of yelling, he was finished.

Edward clung to the bars and lowered his head in defeat. Alone, he listened to the sound of the ticking clocks from across the hall. Time was crucial, and its sound seemed cold and uncaring, marching steadily onward.

How critical is Rachel's condition? I wish I knew more.

Edward thought about Marie. He so desperately wished she were here. He took his wife for granted many times and always relied on her for any medical crisis. She had asked him many times to take some first aid and medical courses, in case of an emergency. But always he refused; he could not find the time, always being too busy with other commitments.

Again, he was faced with the demands of time, but these demands might determine the fate of a young woman. This time, Edward James had run out of choices. The irony hurt.

———◆———

SITTING BESIDE THE cot in the foldout chair, Edward held Rachel's wrist firmly, checking her pulse against elapsed seconds on his watch. This would be about the tenth time over the last several hours. Nothing changed: pulse rapid, and breathing shallow. After he carried her to the bedroom, laid her down with a pillow, sheet and light blanket, he had returned every fifteen minutes to check on her.

Herbert seemed to calm a bit with Rachel out of sight. Edward insisted he take a Tylenol and asked him to try and relax. Edward promised to keep him informed. After awhile, Herbert settled and returned to his watch repair, which seemed the best therapy. The last time Edward returned, Herbert had his head lowered on his arms and was fast asleep. The medication helped him rest.

Edward leaned back in the chair and stretched. He had been sitting watching Rachel for well over an hour. His overall feeling about the situation was not good. She showed no signs of waking. He tried calling her name and rocking her gently from side to side. Nothing changed. He felt helpless and afraid for this young woman. He tried again yelling out from the kitchen window until his voice failed. Once more, the effort was in vain.

In the silence of the night, Edward gazed at Rachel and did his best to try and rationalize the situation. Deep down, he believed there had been no malicious intent by either the young woman or by her grandfather. It appeared they were trying to protect or preserve something in which they sincerely believed in. Also evident was that Herbert suffered psychological issues, which had not been stabilized with prescribed medication, resulting in a dangerous combination and leaving them in this precarious situation.

The needle had been meant for him. He was bigger and stronger. Who or what decides fate? Was he guilty of medical incompetence? Edward knew he could beat himself up over this. He also understood negativity would not improve their predicament.

Edward continued to think it through and finally quieted his conscience with a positive affirmation. *I can and will do my best; it is my promise to do so.*

With a lingering look at Rachel, Edward rose from the chair and headed back to the workshop where he found Herbert still sleeping. Walking softly around the room to stretch his legs, he spotted the leather handbook on the floor, almost out of sight, under the workbench. He retrieved it.

Standing silently, he opened the cover and perused the pages. It did not take long for him to realize the book contained detailed drawings and accompanying descriptions, written in what he assumed was German, about the pocket watch he had found.

As he studied the images, he realized he was looking at no ordinary watch movement. A rotation or a motion appeared to be indicated by arrows. It came from an unusual source, which he thought to be cylindrical magnets. What did it mean? Edward flipped to a page showing the strange symbols on the dial. He studied them from a unique perspective. His mind swirled with thoughts of ancient powers and mysticism: Mayan legends and Atlanteans, possible builders of The Great Pyramids of Giza.

What's its significance? Edward was completely lost in his thoughts when a voice startled him.

"I think I can trust you, Edward."

Edward flinched and looked up. "Herbert, you're awake."

The old man had tears in his eyes. "I have given you much reason to hate me Edward, yet you do not. You are doing your best to save my granddaughter and me from my foolishness." A tear cascaded down his cheek. "You have been checking on Rachel?"

"I sat with her over the last hour and witnessed no change."

"I am afraid she needs medical attention we cannot give her. We can only hope and pray destiny will be kind in its course." Herbert lowered his head in silence.

Edward said nothing. He felt sad for Rachel's grandfather. He did notice, however, a mental improvement in him resulting, no doubt, from the medication and the hour-long sleep.

Herbert lifted his head and resumed. "I made mistakes … I miscalculated. Now I fear time is running out. I must trust you, Edward."

Edward closed the handbook and handed it to Herbert, who held the book in both hands and gazed down with reverence. Edward could feel the passion. Something told him this would be what he had travelled thousands of miles to hear. He waited.

Herbert flipped through the pages of the book. Minutes passed until he closed the cover and placed it on the workbench. When he turned back, his tears were gone. A small sparkle appeared in his blue eyes.

He spoke. "What you came upon by chance at a garage sale in your hometown of Petrolia was a significant find, and now becomes part of a story which began hundreds of years ago in the town of Glashütte, Germany."

Herbert paused and took a moment to collect his thoughts. "Ultimately, this is a story about honour." A small smile appeared on his face, although his intensity did not waiver. He held Edward's eyes forcefully. "From what I have witnessed, I believe you are capable of upholding this virtue. I can tell you, Edward, this story has never been told to anyone other than an Osterhagen for over 200 years." He reached into his pocket and pulled out what looked like a large brass coin. Leaning forward he handed the object to Edward.

Edward examined the item. He instinctively reached into his shirt pocket for his reading glasses. *Damn! I only have my Oakleys. I asked Carmen to put them in her purse before we went to the museum.* He sheepishly extended his arm out for a better view and focused on a decorative token made of brass, about the size of a dollar coin. On one side was a stamped five-digit number—00511, and on the other side was an engraved company logo written in German: 'Osterhagener Uhrenmanufaktur, Seit 1728.' Edward turned it over several times before handing it back to Herbert.

"I can see you are without your proper glasses, Edward. Let me explain what this is before I begin."

"This is what was recognized by the craftsmen of the Osterhagen Watch Company of many years past as a claim token. It is one half of a matching pair. These tokens served the same purpose as the standard paper claim slip of today. The number stamped on one side, 00511, was the claim number for work performed on the pocket watch you found, Edward. However, the owner of the watch who held the matching claim token never returned to pick up his watch."

Herbert expected to see signs of uncertainty on Edward's face. "So how does it come to pass that over 200 years later you stumble upon this very pocket watch? And why might this be of importance to anyone?" Herbert stopped briefly and continued.

"I must start at the beginning of the story, a story that has been passed down through the generations of the Osterhagen family."

"I first heard this story as a young boy. It was told to me by my grandfather at a time when he believed I would someday become a watchmaker, following the tradition of many Osterhagens before me."

Herbert rolled the brass token in his fingers and gazed down at it. "You will have observed the engraving on the other side of this …" He angled the appropriate side towards Edward. "Translated from German it reads: 'Osterhagen Watch Company founded 1728.' My great, great grandfather, Hans Wilhelm Osterhagen, founded the company. I was told he was young, but also exceedingly precocious. It is the date 1738 that is significant in our story. The growing watchmaking business thrived, and Hans Osterhagen was gaining a reputation for excellent quality and craftsmanship throughout Europe. One day during that year a gentleman of fine repute, known to the high courts in many lands, called upon the small shop of the Osterhagen Watch Company. He wanted to have built for him some parts, which he himself would be assembling. He returned at a later date and received the parts he commissioned."

"Months passed until he returned. This time with an assembled pocket watch. He asked only for some final engraving to be done on the case and cover. It was said that at the conclusion of this visit he insisted on paying in advance, and the sum he offered Hans Osterhagen easily exceeded 10 times the quoted cost. Of course, his generous proposal was refuted. However, he insisted that the money be accepted, as he had an important request."

Herbert paused in quiet thought. "I believe I can still recall the words spoken by the gentleman to my great, great grandfather

Hans Osterhagen, as told to me by my grandfather many years later: 'This is a watch of great significance. Greater than even the finest watches of our time, including the famed watch commissioned for Marie Antoinette. You are a young watchmaker with commendable skill, Hans Osterhagen, but I am also going to call upon your honour. I ask of you, no matter what may befall, to take great care of this timepiece and guard its secrets.'" Herbert rolled the token through his fingers again. "After he was given his claim token, which matches this one, he left never to be heard from again."

Edward stayed silent. Herbert had captured his complete attention. He took a moment and continued. "Following the completed work, the pocket watch was stored and locked away, awaiting the day when its owner might return to claim it. Weeks turned into months. Often Hans Osterhagen would check on the timepiece, but this became less frequent with the passage of time. Then one day after several years, Hans Osterhagen checked on the timepiece and noticed something odd. It appeared that the single hand of the watch had moved from its original position. Knowing the watch had been touched only by him, he was curious indeed. To satisfy his curiosity, he took it upon himself to partially dismantle the timepiece. He removed four slotted screws, and the single hand, which allowed him to lift the dial. What was revealed to him by doing so, he found astounding. The watch had movement! The most astonishing fact was that the timepiece had never been wound or even moved for months, and as you know Edward, the watch has no crown for winding."

"I am sure you can well imagine how shocking a discovery this must have been to witness an entirely new technology such as this." Again, Herbert fell silent. He put the token on the bench in front of him and picked up the old leather handbook once more.

"Hans Osterhagen told no one of this discovery for many, many years. He did, however, devote much of his spare time to studying and learning all he could from it. He made sketches, notes, and blueprints, which are documented in this book."

Herbert raised the book in his hand and thoughtfully glanced at it. "Finally, he reassembled the watch and soldered the slotted screw heads to make further disassembly quite difficult. I believe Edward, my great, great grandfather must have understood what had been asked of him in the name of honour, and he fulfilled his promise. The mystery of this timepiece remained just that—a mystery—a mystery held within the confines of the Osterhagen family for a sizable number of years."

"When Hans Osterhagen died, the onus of caring for the watch passed on to my great grandfather and eventually my grandfather. Many years passed, and the Osterhagen Watch Company enjoyed success, and in 1881 the company relocated to a larger facility. Consequently, the business suffered temporary disarray as all tools, equipment, and storage containers needed to be moved. Also, a new apprentice had been hired to help with the increased workload. On a busy day of moving, he was working alone at the old location when a man came by to pick up a watch which had been commissioned months before. This man was in a great hurry as he was leaving Germany for the Ukraine or Poland. He was an oil rigger. At that time, oil riggers were in high demand due to their expertise in the building and operations of drilling platforms used for extracting crude oil. The value of oil was fast becoming realized."

A thoughtful smile appeared on Herbert's face. "I will tell you Edward, it was later discovered the man—the oil rigger who ordered the watch—came from a small town in Canada known then as 'Petrolea.'"

Edward felt goosebumps, as a shiver coursed through his body. *Here's the connection!* He finally understood where the fascinating story was going. He nodded, leaning closer, eagerly awaiting the details.

Herbert resumed. "As I am sure you have guessed, Edward, the apprentice made a mistake and somehow gave away the pocket watch entrusted to the Osterhagen Watch Company so many years before, to the wrong person! It is incredibly hard to imagine just how this could possibly have happened! However, upon further investigation which lasted for many years, a better understanding was acquired."

Herbert reached towards the bench and picked up the brass token with his free hand and held it up. "Edward, you saw the number stamped on this claim token, 00511, and I told you this is the claim token for the pocket watch you found in Petrolia; indeed, that is correct." Herbert held up the token. "The matching token to this one with the number 00511 was never brought to the Osterhagen Watch Company. You see ... shortly after the error was made, a close examination of the token that *was* brought in showed signs of damage. Although that actual token was eventually lost, it was told to me it had suffered a sharp blow of some kind, which left a crease in the metal directly between the last two digits. After close observation, it was discovered the actual number of the token submitted by the man was in fact 00517 and not number 00511 as the inexperienced apprentice believed. Furthermore, it became known to the Osterhagen family after many years of searching that it would be most probable that the man who picked up the pocket watch was indeed not the same oil rigger who initially commissioned his timepiece from the company."

"You see, oil drilling was a precarious occupation, with many injuries and deaths among the brave workers who pioneered oil development. As it turned out, there had been news of an accident happening on an oil rig in Oelhiem, which is just south of where the Osterhagen Watch Company was located in Glashütte. It was believed—and I now can personally confirm this from my own investigations—that the oil rigger from Petrolia who commissioned his watch a few months before the terrible mistake happened was indeed killed in an accident in Oelheim, Germany." Herbert paused for a long breath. Edward did not speak.

"Now it is easy to paint a picture of how these events most likely unfolded … an oil rigger from Petrolia, Canada comes to Germany to work on oil exploration rigs. He is making good money, and when he learns he is close to a world-class watchmaking region he orders a fine timepiece. A tragic accident occurs, and he is killed. Probably the token he received from the Osterhagen Watch Company, which he always keeps on his person, is damaged in the incident that takes his life. His co-workers assume the responsibility for funeral arrangements and the gathering of his personal belongings to be sent back to family or loved ones in Petrolia. The damaged token is found on his person, and it is apparent that a timepiece must be picked up as part of his personal possessions."

"It came to pass that the oil exploration at Oelheim was not overly successful. So, the drilling operation was ceased and moved to a new location in another country. Undoubtedly a co-worker went to pick up the watch right before, or during, the exodus from Germany. Finally, a travelling case would have been packed and sent to the oil rigger's home in Petrolia." Herbert turned and placed both items back on his workbench.

He looked at Edward. "We must now use our imagination, Edward, to fill in for so many years until the day just over one week ago when you first grasped the lost pocket watch in your hand."

THIRTY-FIVE

MONDAY MAY 5, 2014. 12:35 P.M.
JERUSALEM, ISRAEL

The Dance

As a rule, professionally trained dancers are flexible. They spend countless hours stretching and developing their muscles to synchronize with rhythmic impulses from the brain to form seemingly effortless, flowing movement to music. Carmen James was no stranger to this discipline, as she had quite literally grown up on the ballet barre.

She formulated a plan, and its precise execution would rely on flexibility, focus, and timing—all standard requirements for classical ballet.

As she passed beneath the stone archway in the Jewish Quarter of the Old City of Jerusalem, her concentration became intense. Carmen was the principal in this production; her male partner was behind. She would lead, and he would follow. She had mentally gone over the choreography many times. It made perfect sense. His movements would be her cues, as hers would be his.

Tchaikovsky's *Swan Lake* began. The music enveloped her as she moved forward. What young ballerina has never aspired to dance the lead role in *Swan Lake?* It was her way; Carmen would give this dance her all.

She initiated a sequence of pre-meditated movements by opening her purse and taking out her water bottle. Coming to a stop, she unscrewed the lid and took a drink. The success of her plan hinged on the fact that her pursuer did not realize he was being led to the very same courtyard Carmen herself had despondently stood in 14 hours earlier. And this is where flexibility and focus came in. Carmen needed to know exactly how far he followed behind her without conspicuously turning to look. The rear facing view she offered him, dressed in sandals and tight fitting high-rise shorts, should definitely not be recommended when fleeing a male stalker, but Carmen required a split-second diversion. She would be counting on her ability to focus her eyesight quickly, even with her head completely inverted and close to the ground.

With her legs set shoulder width apart, in one quick motion she screwed the lid back in place and moved the plastic bottle downwards towards her purse. It looked as though the bottle struck the top of her purse, falling from her grasp. Her aim was good; it fell directly in front and between her legs. Effortlessly bending at the waist, she moved swiftly. In one brief moment, she bent over and grasped the bottle with her head only inches from the ground. Carmen then took only a fraction of a second to steal an inverted glance. The green shirt and chinos registered as being about 50 metres behind her. She was not sure if she witnessed a small start in his gait as well; *Don't get the wrong idea, buddy!*

Carmen slipped the water bottle back into her purse and grabbed her compact mirror. She left the bag unzipped and waited. She needed him about 20 metres closer. Two turns were coming up, and he had to be able to keep her in sight.

The first turn to the left was not far ahead. Carmen started walking, although at a slightly slower pace. She arrived at the corner. The passageways became narrow and enclosed on both sides by stone walls. She made the turn, and after several steps opened her compact. The next turn went right, and it was imperative that he see her make it. They were mostly shaded from the sun here so there would be minimal refraction on the mirror, which she hoped would give the visual confirmation she needed. After that, a long passageway would tell him she had made the next left which led to the courtyard, exactly as she did when following Jessica/Rachel the night before.

Carmen carefully positioned the mirror against the front left side of her purse, which along with her thumb obscured it almost entirely. She took a few practice looks and slowed down. He would need to be only 25 metres or so behind to see her turning. If he lost sight of her, he would probably speed up, and Carmen did not want that to happen.

It's all about timing, Carmen. How often had she heard that phrase spoken to her from dance instructors or choreographers?

She came to the beginning of the turn, with no sight of him in the mirror. *Come on steroid! You're missing your cue! I can't stop and wait … I'm almost …* There it was, a quick flash of a green shirt in the corner of the mirror! Carmen took two more steps around the corner, then closed the compact and lowered it back into her purse. Taking a deep breath and holding her bag tightly, she sprinted forwards as hard as possible. For the second time in as many days, Carmen ran as quickly as she could, barely being able to slow enough to make the next left which would lead her into the courtyard. She felt her shoulder scrape against a stone wall, and she careened off it in a frantic effort to stay upright. People walked about, casually entering and leaving the open space of the stone yard. Startled, they stared at the crazy woman rushing into the courtyard running full out and dodging people in her path.

Carmen! You're really starting to get a reputation in this town! She veered hard to the right, heading for the next opening to the courtyard.

If she ran quick enough and the limited information on the GPS proved accurate, she just needed to keep turning right until the entrance behind her came up. At that point, she would have doubled back on her pursuer.

Then the hunter becomes the hunted. The Black Swan pas de deux was now on stage.

She passed within the square for only seconds until again the narrow alleyways closed in around her. Luckily, no pedestrians were on her chosen path. She mentally 'crossed her fingers' that no one would open a gate or step out in front of her. The narrowness made her speed appear even faster, as the stone walls flashed by at a dizzying pace. Carmen was breathing hard; her body would soon force her to slow down. The next right came up, and she almost slid out as her sandals lost their grip, but this time she had her hands out to bounce off the wall at the apex of the turn, hardly slowing.

Almost there! Push! Push! The alleyway became familiar. The map had been right. The first entrance to the courtyard measured only 50 metres ahead. Ten more seconds and she skidded to a stop right before the corner. Her chest heaved as she gasped for breath and reached back into her purse for her compact mirror. The square would be easily visible from here. However, she could not risk being seen if he happened to be facing her direction.

Carmen opened the compact and angled it with only a small amount of mirror surface jutting out into the alleyway leading to the courtyard. It took only seconds for her to focus and adjust the angle. Her eyes captured the teal green shirt and off-white chinos instantly. He stood with his back to her just past the end of the alley into the courtyard, and he had his cell phone to his ear while looking from side to side.

Yes! Nailed it! Carmen felt like she had performed a flawless performance up until now, and she was about to begin her favourite and the most stunning part of the ballet The Black Swan: Odile's Coda.

Closing the mirror and placing it back into her purse, she grabbed her phone and peeked around the corner. Now all she needed to do was keep him in sight. The rest would be up to Chief Inspector Claude Gadgét.

This was the stunning part; the Old City of Jerusalem is approximately one square kilometre in size and is surrounded by high stone walls. There are only nine gates through which one must pass to enter or leave the Old City. They are rarely locked or barricaded. However, it would be a simple matter to have a police patrol car waiting at the appropriate gate to apprehend a tall, dark complexioned male, wearing a teal green shirt with off-white chinos and sandals—a man wanted in connection with a break and enter at the Prima Royale Hotel.

Carmen's breathing stabilized. Adrenaline still pumped, and she could feel the tremor of excitement. She knew the whole audience was focused on her, silently waiting for her next move. This was her moment in the ballet. Keeping an eye on him, she pressed the switch to activate her phone. She allowed adequate time for the inspector to be available, and now she knew he would be so pleased with her.

Why, he might even ... Carmen blinked at the screen on her phone and gasped in disbelief. *No! No! No! This can't be happening ... No!* But it was happening—she read the words *low battery shutting down.* The screen went black. Frantically she pressed repeatedly! The screen stayed black. *My God, I forgot to charge my phone!*

In the space of two seconds, Carmen's brain went from meticulous focus into survival mode. It was like having a sound problem, a lighting problem and a missed cue instantaneously. *The ballet! It must continue. The audience is waiting, and they know the script;*

he will lead you to your father ... There's no time, he'll turn around in seconds! Don't think ... move!

With the accomplished grace of a principal ballerina, she moved forward swiftly and silently towards the courtyard. She tucked her phone into her pocket, and the purse was zipped and sliding down to her right hand as she went forward. Again, Carmen tested its weight, as she had done in the small grocery store.

This time, however, she did not think of self-defence. More specifically, Carmen thought of a course she had taken many years earlier with two girlfriends on how to defend against, and incapacitate, a male attacker. The learned move she favoured was a blow to the temple area of the head with a weighted object, causing immediate unconsciousness.

Her eyes were fixated on his back, as she moved on her toes ever closer. He took his phone from his ear and lowered his arm, putting it in his pocket. Carmen sensed her time was running out; he would turn back towards her any second. *Please wait ... give me three seconds!* He looked around again; this would be his last look. Carmen followed his line of vision. Many people were scattered about. She was prepared to scream at the top of her lungs to get their attention if need be. *So close! So close!* She grasped the purse with both hands and rotated it back to the right side of her body.

Her time was up! He moved his lower body in preparation to turn around, but Carmen was there, her swing already in motion. He probably heard the sharp exhale of her breath as she put every ounce of energy into the attack. It must have been an automatic reflex that made him straighten up slightly. The corner of Carmen's weighted purse barely missed its mark, catching him just below the temple on his upper jawbone, causing his head to jerk violently. He emitted a loud, startled groan and fell sideways, but regained his balance quickly and turned towards her. Carmen rotated the bag back and swung wildly again. Suddenly, the bag's momentum halted in mid-swing, and she could not move her arms! In a split second, faster than she could see, he had grasped both her wrists and held her in a firm grip.

Carmen took in a deep breath preparing to scream, but she did not do it. She did not know why.

The man's sunglasses had been ripped away, and Carmen looked up into his eyes. Blood flowed down the right side of his face. She expected to see violence and hatred before her. But there was neither.

"Carmen, I am going to let go of your arms. Do not try to hit me again!"

Carmen picked up a slight Caribbean accent. She had trouble seeing his eyes, as her vision blurred. It happened so fast, and now it was over. Tears streamed down her face. He let go of her arms.

She blurted out, "You know my name! Why have you been following me? Who are you?"

He kept his eyes on her and stepped back. "I am Aaron."

The curtain fell.

THIRTY-SIX

MONDAY MAY 5, 2014. 2:00 A.M.
OLD CITY JERUSALEM, ISRAEL

Edward awoke with a sore neck, having fallen asleep after returning to the bedroom and checking on Rachel. He had been asleep for several hours. Straightening up on the uncomfortable folding chair, he rubbed his neck muscles and rolled his head in circles. The movement helped, and the pain began to subside. He turned to Rachel. She had been unconscious for a long time and showed no signs of improvement. Nevertheless, he performed his usual routine: taking her pulse, listening for breathing, and feeling her forehead for any signs of fever. Nothing had changed; Rachel still registered a weak, rapid pulse—at least so it seemed to him—and her breathing was short and laboured, with no sign of fever. Edward took her hand and gently squeezed. He believed humans could transfer energy by touch, and now it was all he had to offer. He could not think of a time in his life when he felt more helpless.

Before he left Herbert to come and check on Rachel, he asked him where they were located. Herbert's reply was 'a desolate area in the Old City.' Those words rang in Edward's ears now, adding to his dismay.

He sat in quiet contemplation amidst the soft, flickering candlelight; the flames cast dancing shadows on the old stone walls, which surrounded him. He held a young woman's hand. She lay unconscious before him, in an ancient city of reverence. He knew people came by the thousands on pilgrimage to this place to pay homage to a great unknown. Edward gazed up from Rachel to the dark walls surrounding him as he recalled a passage from the Bible. *I have set watchmen upon thy walls O Jerusalem, which shall never hold their peace day or night* ... Were they still present? He was so close to the walls now. Could they not hear his cries for help?

Yes ... a great unknown. By being here in Jerusalem, was he, in fact, nearer to the unknown? *I don't know. I can only believe if I choose to.*

Edward did believe in spirituality. He thought humankind must be spiritual in nature for the basic reason we are inherently seeking to comprehend that which we do not understand.

"I think. Therefore I am." Edward quoted philosopher René Descartes. He thought about—as he had done countless times before—what he liked to call the mystery of human existence. *We possess an awareness of being, yet we do not know who or what we really are! Would not our unceasing, relentless quest for defining who we are be a true definition of spirituality?* Edward thought so.

He looked from the shadowy walls back to Rachel. His heart ached. His thoughts were prayers, and his prayers were thoughts. Was there a difference?

His mind travelled great distances through time, calling upon the genesis of his own beliefs, hopes, and dreams. The green book lay open before him, guiding him with affirmations, as it always guided him in his own quest for understanding. He asked for help from the great unknown.

In the quiet shadows of an old stone-walled room somewhere within the confines of the walls of ancient Jerusalem, Edward James sat beside a young woman and prayed to God.

"You have returned, Edward. How is Rachel?" Herbert heard Edward walk into the room while he was working on a watch movement that lay in pieces before him. He swivelled around on his stool.

"She's the same. I detected no change. I'm afraid I fell asleep for several hours. I awoke some time ago and sat with her. I am very concerned, Herbert. Can you think of anything we can do that might help her?"

Herbert lowered his head, with his gaze cast downward. "The drug in her system is a mixture of my own personal prescribed medications. What Rachel really needs is a blood transfusion followed by an intravenous supplement." Herbert raised his head. "I do not possess the equipment or the medications required to accomplish that."

"I'll try again soon to call for help."

"It is late, Edward, and as I told you this is a remote area. Even if your call is heard, it would be difficult for anyone to pinpoint our location due to the constant echoing of sounds off the stone buildings. Adding to that, distress calls in English might be ignored all together because of misunderstanding."

Herbert stopped, and Edward watched him swallow hard. "You and Rachel did nothing to deserve this. I am a stupid old man! Thank you, Edward, for watching over her. I should be at Rachel's side, but I cannot bear to see her like this." His head dropped downwards again.

Edward thought he was beginning to see a pattern of body movements and expressions from Herbert, indications of a possible relapse into another unstable mental condition. He remembered how Rachel asked Herbert why he was without his medications. The answer to her question now seemed obvious. Edward also knew if Herbert was rested enough, and focused on his watchmaking, his mental infirmities were significantly reduced, if not temporarily eliminated.

Edward was looking at Herbert's sad expression, slumped shoulders, and the ever so slight tremor in his hands. He needed to engage the old watchmaker. "Herbert, I was hoping to ask you a question about the Osterhagen Watch Company."

Herbert lifted his head. His eyes had started to glaze over, although now Edward detected a hint of sparkle returning.

"I wanted to ask ... whatever became of the Osterhagen Watch Company? I mean ... I never came across the name in my readings of watch history. It sounded from your story that the company had the potential to become one of the watchmaking giants of today. I understand there was much turmoil in Germany leading up to the East-West split in the 1940s, but that didn't happen until much later. So, why did the Osterhagen Watch Company fail?"

Herbert's shoulders lifted, and his posture straightened. He sat motionless, staring at Edward. Finally, he broke eye contact and swivelled his stool around so he could reach down and open the cooler beside him. He extracted two bottles of water and closed the lid. He straightened up, turned back and handed Edward a bottle. "I have no food to offer you, Edward."

Edward cracked open the bottle, tipped it back and took a long drink. "Thanks, I'm ok. I'll sustain myself on the reserves I've been building up around my mid-section," he retorted.

"From what I'm seeing, I fear I'm better prepared for survival in that area." There came no smile, only a slight expression of amusement as Herbert took a drink of his own water. He set it on the workbench and answered Edward.

"Responding to your question, Edward, is painful. I am an old man now, but I still believe one day the Osterhagen Watch Company shall exist again." Sadness sounded in Herbert's voice.

"Not long after the mysterious pocket watch was lost, my grandfather opened the new shop. It was much larger and better equipped. A great deal of money had been invested in the best equipment and machinery. It became the new Osterhagen Watch Company, and things were looking promising. Unfortunately, only a few exceptional new timepieces were completed when an incident occurred, and a fire broke out in the main building. No one was injured, but sadly much was lost, and due to financial commitments, the company could not recover. Everything had to be sold."

Herbert shrugged his shoulders in a gesture of despair. "Call it bad luck or fate … whatever the reason the family company has not been rebuilt, I cannot say. Although I believe it is not for a lack of trying. Myself, my father and my grandfather before him all devoted tremendous time and effort to attaining the goal of bringing back the company. There were, however, always obstacles, financial or political, which were insurmountable." He tightened his mouth and stared off into the space around him. After a moment, he settled his gaze back on Edward.

"I will never give up hope … Yes, my hope for the company is Rachel. She may become the reborn Osterhagen Watch Company. She is very talented and passionate about watchmaking, and I believe there is still time for me to help her …" Herbert stopped.

He raised his arms and brought his hands to either side of his face. He tipped his head low. "Oh … but now, see what I have done! Is this fate? Bad luck … or am I just a senseless, evil man?" Herbert's pain was evident. "What do you believe, Edward?"

Edward did not answer immediately. He thought carefully as he stared into the old man's eyes.

"Herbert, I've always considered myself to be a reasoning person. I can never tell you what is right or wrong; good or evil—that is a truth only you can answer for yourself. I can only tell you what I can understand in my own life experience."

Edward paused. He wanted to choose his words with care. "Ultimately, I believe it is *intent* which defines who we are and is the true measure of our worth. I do not believe Herbert, that your overall intention was to bring hurt or suffering to Rachel, myself or anyone else. I think your intentions were to honour or protect a commitment you made, and you believe in."

Shared silence ensued between the two men. Neither spoke for some time.

Herbert's hands dropped to his side. He nodded his head slightly as he stared thoughtfully at Edward. "I should have trusted you from the beginning."

Edward knew he had received a compliment from a special man. "You can now."

Herbert turned on his stool and reached for his water. He took a drink and returned the bottle to the bench. "Edward, I can tell that you and I share a passion for philosophy. Perhaps together we might share in a discussion about timekeeping."

"I think I would greatly enjoy that, Herbert. However, I feel my contribution will be minimal, especially if we get on the topic of atomic clocks, quantum physics, cesium atoms and such."

Herbert smiled. "I will tell you, Edward, being a horologist almost my entire life, I built and repaired clocks and watches that number in the thousands. I have always been proud to consider myself a keeper of time … yet if someone walked in here now and set an atomic clock before me, my first question to him undoubtedly would be: 'Where do I wind this device?'"

Edward let out a soft laugh. He smiled inwardly knowing he was helping Herbert. For the first time, it felt like they were friends having an interesting conversation.

"Well, at least you would be able to tell what it was. I'd be thinking—some kind of atomic bomb or something."

"You would not be far off, they are much of the same technology." Herbert clasped his hands under his chin, striking a classic, intellectual pose.

"In comparison, Edward, our chosen professions are similar in many ways. We are humble artisans, if you will, providing a service.

We can and do take pride in our attention to detail and overall craftsmanship. A significant difference, however, is that you can understand and see a clear picture of what it is you actually do. As a high-pressure welding technician, you fabricate transport systems and related integral components, mostly in the form of piping. You can study the processes of the various products and chemicals, which would be transported to make the required products. The many different metals and alloys that you must weld together can also be studied and understood within the science of metallurgy. Overall, as I am sure you have done in your career, a good evaluation and understanding can be deduced of your vocation."

Edward was impressed with the ease and eloquence radiating from Herbert Osterhagen. Not to mention his intelligence. He nodded. "Your description indicates a high level of importance to my profession."

"Well deserved, Edward. You play a role in providing us with fuel and lubricants for our vehicles, heat and air conditioning systems for our homes, and piping systems to generate electricity. We are so dependent on the vinyl and plastics we use … the list goes on Why, even many of the clothes we wear can be tracked to oil production requiring high-pressure piping systems."

Edward smiled. "Thank you, but please stop, I'm feeling way too important. I can honestly say, though, in comparison, I am humbled in witnessing the creations of master watchmakers, many of which leave me breathless."

Herbert lowered his hands. Edward noted a fleeting joyful look. "Perhaps that is something we have … What we as watchmakers do *not* have, I am afraid, is a clear understanding of what it is we actually do."

"How do you mean, Herbert?"

"I told you I consider myself a keeper of time. So, when I ask myself the question: what exactly *is* time? The answer eludes me."

"I think I hear what you're saying ... so many different answers to consider. I believe our shared perception of time is definitely at odds with the laws of physics."

"Yes indeed, Edward. I believe my watchmaking ancestors had no need to concern themselves with this question. Going back to the mid-17th century, evidence points to a much more contented view of the meaning of time. Synchronicity, as stated by Sir Isaac Newton, reassured man that any two events could be recorded as being simultaneous no matter where, at the same moment and anywhere in the universe. They took comfort in seeing the sun rise and set or observing lunar cycles, knowing they would always be able to rely on measured time in accordance with these absolutes. It told them where they were and for how long they had been there. They had a constant to rely on as a standard against which everything else could be measured.

Edward nodded. "And then along came the 20th century ..."

"Yes, right around the year 1915, a new and radical theory was introduced to the scientific community. The theory was 'General Relativity' and its creator as I am sure you know was Albert Einstein. Since then it seems we lost our conception of time, and we are having great difficulty coming to terms with the theory."

Edward gave his shoulders a slight shrug. "I guess we were quite comfortable for a long time after learning the world is *not* flat."

"I believe your analogy contains some humorous reality, Edward." Herbert nodded his approval. "Einstein's theory must have been just as shocking to the world at the time. In his own words, he is believed to have insisted that time, our most precious commodity, is an illusion. What we came to believe in as an absolute was no longer such; time was, in fact, relative to velocity and gravitational pull, thereby he introduced us to our new and only constant: the speed of light."

"And I can understand ..." Edward quipped, "Herbert, I don't know how many times I sat- hand in hand with my family admiring the spectacular view of a beautiful sunset and stating to them: 'Isn't the speed of light spectacular …? Behold!'"

Edward witnessed a smile spread across Herbert's face, which turned into a laugh; a small one, but nevertheless it made him feel good to know they were connecting.

"Ha Edward, yes not nearly as easily understood. So now we have been told time will slow down for mass the faster it goes through space, relative to other objects whose time will appear to increase. Gravitational pull has a similar effect. Mass and distance also must change to accommodate increasing velocity." Herbert brought his hand up to cradle his chin. "Now I am afraid this becomes a real mental workout. Do you know of Einstein's twin paradox, Edward?"

"Yes, I read about it some years back. Let's see … the hypothetical story of two twins who wish to visit a distant planet that is six light years away. They build a spacecraft, which can travel close to the speed of light. One twin makes the journey, the other stays on earth and waits. They both use precise clocks to measure total time. When the travelling twin returns from the planet, the earth clock shows the time registered 20 years for the return trip. However, the clock on the spaceship shows it only took the twin 16 years of travel to complete the journey. The reason being his velocity—time slowed for him. Therefore, he aged four years less than the twin who remained on earth!" Edward grimaced, "Incomprehensible?"

"For many of us, I believe so, Edward … I suppose back in the early 1900s this probably sounded to some like nothing more than a fanciful story. Some time later, though, with the invention of atomic clocks, in conjunction with air and space travel, the theory of general relativity has proven itself accurate. And of course, today we all see the theory in practice. Satellites in orbit send signals to earth and continually have to adjust for time dilation because of differing velocity and gravitational pull relative to the receiving devices on earth, such as a GPS, which requires precise time measurements to calculate positioning." Herbert stopped for a breath. "So where does this leave us now?"

He continued. "As time dilation is proven to be relative, how might we define time today? Is there really a past, present, and future where time flows between or is time its own dimension set on a four-dimensional grid that we enter or exit like we do a building ... And what of our own brain? Do we not possess a kind of primordial clock, which measures day and night, summer and winter? Does this mean different kinds of time exist?" Herbert shrugged and raised his hands, palms open. "So, if I believe myself to be a keeper of time, should it be so difficult for me to say what it is exactly that I keep?"

Edward contemplated. He had tried to understand the paradox of time. It seemed to him the more he learned the more confusing things became. Nevertheless, Edward offered Herbert this thought. "You're not alone in this unsettling mystery, Herbert. I read something to the effect that both physicists and philosophers are now collaborating, looking for answers to these very questions. Not a likely pairing, I'm sure."

"Ha, thank you, Edward. I guess it is true, I am not the only one hurting." Herbert gave him a wry smile.

"Also, Herbert, perhaps you can take solace in knowing what you create and maintain is not only about time."

"How so, Edward?"

"Well, I've come to understand, since owning a fine mechanical timepiece ..." Edward raised his arm up a bit and gazed down at his watch. "That it represents so much more to me than merely having something to tell time with." Edward hesitated. "Please correct me if I'm wrong, Herbert, but is not the basic technology in this watch more than 250 years old?"

Herbert nodded. "That is true, Edward; the basic design is lever escapement, regulated by a balance wheel. This technology has been with us for a long time."

"I ask myself ... why is it a watch with dated technology can seem so excellent to me and make me feel honoured to wear it? For only to display time accurately, would not the modern quartz, radio controlled, satellite signal or smart watch technologies be much better choices? Why do I so admire the mechanical watch—the kind found almost exclusively in this room, and in your shop in New York?"

A perceptive smile appeared on Herbert's face. "I believe, too, it is not just about telling time. Or maybe ... can time be measured in a timeless way?"

"Wow! That's an intriguing question, Herbert."

"I think you are telling me something I always believed, Edward; a mechanical timepiece can quite literally become a part of you. The watch you so admire is a precise, masterful complexity of components moving in harmony. Without movement from you, however, either by winding the crown or motion from your wrist, the timepiece will cease to operate. Thus, you are connected with it and can remain so for many years to come. Your watch is becoming a part of you; something that is not partial to wearing a battery-powered watch of today's modern technology, I am afraid."

Herbert offered a thoughtful smile. "So together, in a timeless fashion, with your mechanical watch you can embrace the ever-pervasive dimension of time." Herbert displayed a satisfied look.

Edward sat transfixed in admiration of the watchmaker. He had so many more questions to ask, but they could wait, as he had not checked on Rachel for a while. Thinking of questions, one which was bothering him came to mind. Why did Rachel insist Herbert had been lying to her? Edward was told the story about the pocket watch and knew about the book. Was there something else, something about the story that was not true? He pushed away the thought. *Now isn't the time ...*

He got up from his stool. "Thank you, Herbert, I hope we can continue our talk later. I want to check on Rachel and sit with her for a bit."

Herbert nodded continuously, staring off towards the wall. "I think I will get back to my watch repair."

As Edward walked towards the door, another question popped into his head. It would probably be a short answer, so he went ahead and asked. "Herbert, you said the Osterhagen Watch Company managed to complete only a few new watches. I was wondering ... did any of them survive to the present day?"

Herbert had rotated on his stool towards his bench. He turned back. "There is only one that I know of. If you get a chance ... it is on display as part of the timepiece collection in the L.A. Mayer Museum. The watch was one of the models from the new location."

The mention of the L.A. Mayer Museum gave Edward a start. He thought of Rachel working there under a false name. *So many questions.*

Edward nodded. "I'm sure it's a beautiful watch." He turned towards the door but halted as Herbert continued.

"The watch can be identified by an engraving on the case. It was the first new model, and the timepiece was created as a tribute to the gentleman who built the pocket watch you found in Petrolia."

Edward jerked his head towards Herbert. He waited for a second to register what Herbert had said. "Herbert ... what is the name of the watch?"

Herbert turned completely back and faced Edward with a serious levelling stare. "The watch is engraved with the name: Saint Germain."

Edward's breath caught in his throat. He felt faint. He stared open mouthed at Herbert. Silence pounded in his ears, and his voice sounded like a whisper. "You said Saint Germain! The gentleman was him ...?"

Herbert nodded and said nothing.

Edward only stared, trying to understand the words Herbert had spoken. He could manage only three words, and he spoke them from the depths of his soul.

"Oh, my God!"

THIRTY-SEVEN

Carmen's head was spinning. She was upset and afraid. People in the courtyard stopped and stared. She ignored them and tried to pull herself together. *Aaron ... Aaron!* She remembered this name.

"You're the person who met my father at the coffee shop in Petrolia. You wanted to buy the pocket watch. Dad had no intention of selling the watch. He only wanted to learn more about it." Carmen stopped to think. "You were representing someone else? Someone who offered several thousand dollars to buy it!"

"That is correct. I wish our meeting had gone better; it might have solved a lot of problems." He steadily stared at her.

"Problems?" Carmen lifted her sunglasses to the top of her head and wiped the tears from her cheek with the back of her hand. She was 'not buying it'. "From where I'm standing ... what I'm thinking is ... that you *are* a big part of the problem! I'm guessing you want the watch, that you and another low life tried to steal it. Well ... guess what? I don't have the damn thing! My dad is missing. He might be hurt, even ... " She felt the tears starting to well up again. However, anger overruled her urge to cry. "Do *you* know where my father is? Why are you stalking me? You are breaking the law!

The police have you on surveillance video! What the hell do you *want*!" Carmen bit down hard on her lip. Her whole body shook.

Aaron took a step towards her. He did not break eye contact. "Please, I apologize for frightening you. This is not my intent, nor has it ever been my intent to harm you or your father. Carmen ... I was not sure until now your father was even missing. If you would give me a chance to tell you what I know ... I believe there is more going on here than each of us realizes. I want to ask you to trust me." He wiped the right side of his eye to clear away blood, which began to impair his vision. He held Carmen's gaze.

Carmen dismissed an ever so slight pang of guilt for causing his injury and retorted, "Trust you? What, so you can have the watch and then maybe kill us both?"

"Listen ... if I wished to cause physical harm to either you or your father I could easily have done that. I did not."

He paused, "Yes, I do want to find the watch, but not for the reasons you might think." Aaron broke their gaze. He looked around, spotted his sunglasses on the ground and walked over to pick them up. He studied them, lost in thought. They were undamaged. He walked back close to Carmen and raised his head. "Please Carmen ... I ask of you that we find a place where we might sit down, and I can try to explain to you my involvement in this. I cannot do it here, standing in the hot sun, and I need to get cleaned up." His focus into her eyes was unwavering.

Listening to him talk helped dissipate Carmen's anger, but it left her unsure and confused. *I don't know what to do.*

She saw a single drop of blood fall from his cheek. Her eyes followed, as it hit the soft shimmering fabric of his shirt and spread to form a perfect circle of dark red. Suddenly, a strange feeling came over her. *I've been here before! I'm reliving this very moment!* She knew the phenomenon; it was called déjà vu, and even though she studied about it in psychology class, the sensation always unnerved her.

This time, however, there seemed to be an added element; the colour of his shirt triggered a memory, a memory of colour—the colour emerald green. Was this a recent dream? Carmen was not sure, but calmness enveloped her. Seconds passed; it could well have been minutes. She was not sure.

The spell broke when she looked up at Aaron. Her fear subsided, and she no longer shook.

"Ok ... I know a place, but first I need to use your phone to send a text message."

CARMEN SAT ALONE at a secluded table in the Montefiore Restaurant. Aaron had gone to the restroom to clean and inspect his injury. A waiter brought two glasses of ice water and menus. She took a sip and gazed around the relatively quiet room, presently holding only about six or eight patrons. Carmen grabbed her purse from the chair and rummaged through her bag. She found a couple of bandages and set them in front of her as she hung her purse on the back of the chair.

She remained mostly calm, and this surprised her. Carmen had made certain she always had people around or nearby. The walk to the restaurant was uneventful; they spoke only casually about traffic and a few interesting sights, and she kept a close eye on him. Aaron did not strike her as being overly aggressive or even impatient, but she had no intention of letting her guard down.

One interesting point that stuck in her mind, however, was that he did not even try to read the text she had sent. He merely handed her his phone with no questions asked, and waited patiently until she finished, then took his phone back and immediately put into his pocket. *For sure, he'll read the message in the washroom. Is he trying to make me think that he trusts me?*

Her eyes caught sight of him returning, and for a brief second, she was fixated. *Carmen! Stop staring!* Purposely shifting her gaze away, she reached for her water and took another drink. He returned to the table holding a folded-up paper towel to the side of his head, evidence that the bleeding had not stopped completely. As he sat down, Carmen held up the bandages.

"I found these ... can I take a peek?"

He nodded. "Thanks, I cleaned the cut well, but it started bleeding again, I'm afraid."

Carmen rose from her chair and walked beside him. She leaned in close as he lifted the makeshift compress away. A close inspection revealed a deep abrasive gash, about a centimetre long, oozing blood. She stepped and reached for her purse, opening it again to remove a small package of Kleenex tissues, from which she extracted one, and then set the rest of them on the table. Stepping back to Aaron she lightly dabbed the wound, then took his wrist and guided his hand to the side of his head so he could hold the tissue in place while she opened the bandage packaging.

Carmen felt a slight quiver run through her due to his proximity, which did not help her concentration. Hurriedly, she thought of some humour to try and keep from blushing. "It's a weeping abrasion; dress it with salve when you get a chance, and it should heal up just fine ... not too sure about my purse, though!" Aaron tried to look up at her, but she pressed firmly at the edges of the bandage on his head. Before he could reply, Carmen scooped up the soiled Kleenex and paper towel, grabbed her purse, and moved gracefully away to the ladies' room to dispose of them and freshen up.

"Thank you," he called out after her. She lifted her free hand in acknowledgment and disappeared.

When Carmen returned a brief time later, Aaron had his cell phone placed directly in front of him. It was turned off. She sat down and spoke first. "Did you decide what you want to order?"

"Yes ... yourself?"

"The vegetable soup of the day with a whole-wheat bun sounds excellent." Carmen offered a subtle smile, as a waiter came to take their order.

"May I order for both of us, Carmen?" Aaron asked her. She nodded. "Yes, we would both like the soup of the day with a whole-wheat bun." Aaron picked up his closed menu to assist the waiter; Carmen did the same.

A few moments later, Carmen broke the silence. "Did you read the text I sent from your phone?"

He did not even blink when he replied, "Not yet. I was going to ask you if you thought I should."

Carmen was surprised, although she did not let her expression reveal anything. "I believe that would be for the best. I want you to understand where I'm coming from."

Aaron said nothing as his eyes left hers and fell upon the cell phone. After turning the device on, his thumb slid across the screen several times to bring up the text. Carmen studied him closely for any signs of anger or contempt. She saw none. When he finished reading and looked up, she spotted a hint of sadness in his eyes.

"Is this a text to the police?"

Carmen hesitated. "The text was sent to Chief Inspector Claude Gadgét. His car is parked a short distance from here. Undoubtedly, the police have been watching us since we left the Old City."

Aaron broke her gaze, and with a solemn expression gazed around the room in silence. Carmen waited. Finally, his eyes reconnected with hers. "I think I would have done the same thing if I were in your position ... although probably not as creatively." He focused downwards and activated the screen on his phone again and began reading. This time loud enough for Carmen to hear, "Carmen here. Leaving Zion Gate for my favourite restaurant nearby. I met a person I recognized, and he offered lunch. I think it's best you're not invited, but I'll tell you all about it in one hour.

No RSVP." Aaron set his phone back down and lifted his eyes to hers. "I guess this was to be expected ... your university grades are indicative of this level of ingenuity."

"What!" Carmen was startled. "What do you know about my grades?"

Aaron did not flinch. "Carmen listen ... you must understand; I was given a profile on you and your family." His eyes faltered. "This is not something I am proud of. I do not generally spy on people... but things are what they are. There is a lot I want to tell you." He paused, "Please be patient."

Carmen settled. She gave him a slight nod.

"Before I begin, I would like to ask ... well ... reading your profile, it does not seem likely you would be the type of person who would try to hurt another. Why did you hit me—because of anger ... fear perhaps?"

Carmen's eyes now faltered. "I guess it was a spontaneous thing. My phone died right when I needed to call the inspector. I wanted you to be apprehended by the police and questioned with the hope of getting information to help find my father. I think if you hadn't moved a bit, you would've been knocked unconscious long enough for me to make the call. I would have used your phone."

Aaron shook his head. A long silence ensued. "You knew I was following you? I'm sure you figured out by now, I am not very good at this sort of thing."

"Yea, I guess I was kinda thinking you sucked at it, but it's not exactly my thing either."

"You appear to be a fast learner."

Carmen smiled inwardly. She was feeling better about this guy. "So ... Aaron. It seems that somehow you became involved with this watch thing. You show up in Petrolia from who knows where— my dad thinks the Caribbean—to buy the watch for somebody else. I'm not sure about New York, but you managed to follow my father here to Jerusalem, where you tried to steal the watch you could not buy. Your presence at the museum when my dad went missing was also recorded. I'm thinking you still don't possess the watch, yet you are still being very persistent. You feel a need to follow me around, and I'd like to know why."

Aaron was about to reply when the waiter returned with their order. They both sat in silence until the food was set before them. They thanked him as he left. Carmen spoke first again. "I think the last 2 days have probably been the craziest in my entire life, and I hardly had a chance to eat anything. This soup smells absolutely delicious, and I'm like … starving!"

"Yes, it does smell good. This is a nice restaurant with a stunning view. Although, I sort of noticed some of the staff here have been, well … kind of staring at you in a peculiar way. Are they surprised to see you?" Aaron unfolded his napkin and set it on his lap.

Carmen raised her head. She had already begun eating. "Umm …I'm sure it's got to do with the generous tip I left last time for a $25.00 salad I hardly touched!" She grimaced as she thought back.

"Oh." Aaron did not press any further and began eating.

They sat quietly eating. Carmen sensed the awkwardness. She took a break and had a sip of water. "I think the situation might be better for you now that I've contacted the inspector." Aaron said nothing. She continued. "You asked me to trust you. If I take your words to have good intentions, then I believe this is the best way."

Carmen paused, holding his gaze. "Inspector Claude Gadgét is a man I believe to be both fair and intelligent. As you can see, he is not storming in here to arrest you. Why …? Because I asked him not to. That indicates to me that he can show respect to others, plus … I think he kinda likes me." Carmen grinned. "In a professional way, of course. Well …" She giggled. "Anyhow what I'm trying to say is it might be better if I talk to him about you first. You get it?" She looked back down to her soup and dipped her spoon into the bowl. "Okay, you've got the floor. Explain to me why I should trust you, and please, if you can, help me find my dad."

Aaron replied. "I understand what you are implying. I have made some mistakes, and it is my responsibility to face the consequences. What you're saying is fair. I will do my best to explain. First, though, I will finish my soup."

By now Carmen was convinced she was not sitting across from some common thug. What she was seeing in him were proper manners and an evolved state of refinement. *He doesn't even slurp his soup! Really, you can tell a lot about a person by the way they eat their soup. Hmm ... I've always been bad for slurping, as I'm sure he's now aware.*

The silence pressed on Carmen mainly because she wanted to hear his story. *I wonder if he's going to eat the rest of his whole-wheat bun?* She cast a quick gaze towards it.

As Aaron straightened up, he caught Carmen's subtle glance at his plate. He picked up his napkin and wiped the corners of his mouth and then set it down again, folded on the table. He took his empty bowl and accompanying plate and set them off to the side. Glancing down to the plate containing the half dinner roll, he commented, "I consumed a hearty breakfast this morning, and I'm afraid I am quite full. Would you ..." Aaron gestured towards the food. "You finished yours."

Carmen did not hesitate. "Sure, thanks. They're *so* fresh." She snatched up the plate as soon as he offered it to her and had the bun almost entirely buttered before he replied with a courteous "You're welcome."

Aaron took a sip of his water, and after setting the glass down, he settled back in his chair. "Thank you for waiting. You have been patient." She nodded as she finished the last bite of the bun. "In response to your question of why I feel a persistent need to follow you around ... well as I told you, this is a job. And, I wanted to accomplish what we are doing right now."

"Ah, you wanted to ask me to lunch ... I can understand that. Some guys are not too comfortable with making the first move ...

too much pressure. A bit extreme I guess ... but look, here we are!" Carmen offered him a prim smile.

Aaron did not return the smile, but Carmen detected a little sparkle in his eyes. "I believe we need to talk. When you came out of the museum yesterday, I knew something had gone terribly wrong, but before I could help you another man had assisted. I assumed you became sick or were drugged and perhaps the same happened to your father, so now both he and the watch are missing. This has become serious very quickly."

He stopped for a moment. "I am not exactly sure how, but I think I can help, and perhaps we still have a chance of controlling where the watch ends up."

Carmen sat up and leaned forward. "I didn't realize until yesterday just how dangerous this had become. Before the museum visit ..." She watched closely for his reaction to her next comment. "A man was killed in Brooklyn ... I think, because of the watch! Apparently, the police have suspicions of murder."

A jerk reaction came from Aaron. "Oh ... I wasn't informed. I was not sent to New York. My instructions were to stay in Petrolia ... and was only later told there had been complications and that your father left the city with the watch. My instructions were to follow, observe, and try to find an opportunity to obtain it."

"So, you weren't one of the thugs who chased my dad through Brooklyn ... that's a good thing I guess. But you *do* work for the guy who hired them, and you're still trying to steal the watch for him! Am I missing something here?" Now Carmen became dead serious as she awaited his answer.

Aaron's reply was direct and steady. "I am not trying to steal the watch for him, Carmen. I am trying to keep him from getting it!"

"What?" Shock registered on Carmen's face. "I ... I'm confused."

Aaron took in a deep breath and let it out forcefully as if trying to unburden himself. "I need to start at the beginning."

No sooner had he finished his sentence than the waiter arrived at their table to clear away the dishes. "Can I get you something else—coffee, tea, dessert perhaps?"

Aaron looked to Carmen after the waiter's question. She thought for a moment and replied. "I think a green tea would be nice and something to nibble on. What might you suggest?"

"Yes ma'am ..." the waiter responded. "We have some excellent freshly baked Danish pastry I highly recommend."

"Mmm ... yes perfect." She glanced at Aaron, as did the waiter.

"Yes, a green tea sounds good for me too, hold the pastry though, please."

"Certainly, sir." With practiced efficiency, he cleared the table and was gone in seconds.

The short interruption offered a chance for Carmen to restructure her thought pattern. The word 'stereotyping' popped into her head; a mentality she was trying to learn to overcome as she matured. Her thought now, though, was that her learning curve on that subject was about to increase sharply.

"Your father was correct Carmen. I am from the Caribbean—Grand Cayman, to be exact; where I was born, and raised. This is where I am currently employed doing lab and field analysis for an environmental company."

Carmen's eyebrows lifted as Aaron continued. "I read that you are studying environmental sciences as well, Carmen. A fact I'm sure my boss did not overlook in his decision to select me for this project." Aaron shook his head slightly. "I am an environmentalist. I went to university in Southern California. I focused my master's degree mainly on the related sciences and biochemistry, and with my undergraduate degree, I included a minor in physics. I guess the minor in physics helped stir my interest, and ultimately led me in search of the pocket watch."

Carmen now began to lose some respect for herself and her recent actions. Her perception of Aaron was changing rapidly. She could see intelligence in his eyes, which went unnoticed before. *Okay, you got off track, what's done is done.* She only nodded and kept her emotions in check.

He continued. "I will explain what happened. I was hired by a company—let's call them 'Company X'—to supervise and conduct lab analysis on an environmental assessment following a containment spill from a luxury liner which occurred near Grand Cayman. This began in the winter of 2014 and is still in operation. I am only hired for the duration of this project. The company will move on after completion. My job is strictly empirical studies, and I am obligated by contract to keep all information regarding findings and assessments confidential within the company. This job has introduced me to the real world of politics and environmental issues. I discovered, at least in this case, honesty and integrity do not prevail; rather, they are viewed as a weakness. What *does* prevail is money and propaganda, and my current boss lives and operates quite efficiently in the latter. His name is Stanley Crawford."

The waiter arrived with the tea and promptly set everything on the table. He smiled, made sure they were satisfied and left.

Carmen lifted her nose and sniffed repeatedly. "Mmm ... the cinnamon. Would you like a piece to try Aaron?" Carmen knew her gesture had symbolism and she did not resist it.

"Okay, thanks. But just a tiny piece, okay?" Carmen smiled. His acceptance of her offer felt nice. She waited until they poured their tea before tearing off a piece. She lifted the plate and offered it to him. He picked up the pastry and popped it into his mouth. "Yes ... freshly baked; excellent."

Carmen felt more relaxed, but was still a bit surprised and trying to digest the new information. She did not, however, let her guard down completely. She was trained in many aspects of psychology and confident in her ability to judge character. Her overall intuition about Aaron was quite positive now. Still, she understood that some people could excel at hiding the truth. Sometimes she thought it better to take the conversation off course and observe reactions to simple everyday questions. Carmen always preferred to break up intense mental activity with whatever came her way.

She took advantage of the break. "Aaron, to go briefly off topic while we're getting our tea ready, I was wondering how you came to study environmental sciences in Southern California? Do they offer some exceptional programs there?"

Aaron nodded. "Well … yes, the university I chose does offer excellent courses, and their reputation is renowned. However, I will say the scholarship program is what sold me. I am sure you understand … international studies can be quite expensive."

"Oh, yea, for sure. I guess I'm lucky in that 2 years of post-grad is my total international commitment. Plus, I'm an only child and was fortunate to get part-time employment in my hometown." Carmen smiled. "You did both under and post grad in California under scholarship?"

"Yes, I did. It certainly helped financially. I am the youngest of three, and we all went on to post-secondary education. My scholarship was for track and field. I have been out of school for several years now, but I still train. I like to stay involved."

Carmen witnessed a rather shy, subtle expression. "I can kind of relate—not sure how complete my profile is—but my main extracurricular interest is dance."

Aaron nodded. "Your preference is for ballet and you are quite accomplished, according to your profile."

"Umm … well, no scholarships offered, unfortunately … Oh wait a minute, I forgot to check out universities in Russia!" She gave her forehead a slap with the palm of her hand in a humorous gesture. "So, what's your discipline in track and field?"

"Sprinting—my primary focus is the 100 and the 200 metre. Of course, I trained and competed in 400 metre relays as well."

Carmen hid her surprise by lifting her cup and taking her first sip of tea. *Wow ... the 100 metre? A scholarship ... that's intense athletics!*

She viewed Aaron with a bit of wonderment. "When you were following me today, I had a feeling I wouldn't be able to outrun you. I guess my feelings were accurate." A look of amusement spread across his face. Carmen resumed, "So ... the 100-metre ... mind if I ask: you ever gone under 10?" As Carmen intently watched his reaction; there was no mistaking a thoughtful, nostalgic presence in his demeanour as he took in a breath and leaned back in his chair.

"One time." He paused and lowered his head in thought. Carmen sensed he was reliving a big moment. He looked up. "At a competition on the island ... but the time was disallowed, unofficial."

"You mean like disqualified?" Carmen kept her thoughts to herself: *Drugs ... Steroids? Hmmm ... He probably won't see the humour.* "Why?" she added.

"There was a tailwind which exceeded the limits, so the times were unofficial."

"Oh ..." Carmen mused for a few seconds. "What year was that, Aaron?"

An anticipated, confused expression appeared on his face. "The year was ... 2010."

Carmen nodded in an apparent understanding. "Yes ... wasn't that the year a hurricane touched down on Grand Cayman?"

Aaron looked bewildered. "Why, yes ... tropical storm Nicole, I believe ... but what has that got to do with ..."

Carmen cut in at an exact predetermined spot in his sentence. "You said there was a tailwind?" Carmen's green eyes sparkled, as she awaited the response.

She gazed in amusement as the current expression drained from his face, giving way to a lifting at the corners of his mouth, which formed into a large beautiful smile that had been formally hidden from her until now. When he burst into laughter, she saw tears forming in his eyes. At this moment, Carmen knew she had the answer to the most important question she needed to ask: *Can I trust this man?* The answer was a resounding *Yes, I can! There's no acting going on here.*

Carmen smiled. His laughter brought comfort.

———◆———

"It must be close to an hour since we left the Old City," Carmen recalled how, in her text, she had implied there would be further communication between her and Inspector Gadgét.

Aaron reached over and tapped his phone, which was lying beside him on the table, and scanned for the time. "Yes." He pushed the phone across the table towards her. "You will need to contact the inspector now." Carmen reached forward and picked up his phone.

"Thank you." Carmen realized a barrier had come down between them. They had spent the last 10 minutes talking about environmental science courses, sprinting and dancing. Pressure had been released, and now she was anxious to move forward with another friend on her side. She needed to take care of a few priorities first, however. "This should only take a couple of minutes."

Aaron remained silent and tipped his head in agreement. He reached for his teacup and began sipping while watching Carmen's thumbs fly across the screen and wondered how some people could text so incredibly fast.

She was done in well under a minute. "That should work." She slid his phone back across the table. Aaron did not bother to view the screen. It went black after a few seconds.

No sooner had he set his cup down, when his phone lit up with the sound of a ring tone. He looked at Carmen.

"I think you need to answer." She offered a hopeful smile.

He hesitated for only a second before picking up the phone, "Hello?"

Carmen looked at him. His eyes drifted to hers as he listened. Carmen thought the inspector must have been awaiting contact from her, as he had taken only seconds to respond to her message.

Aaron's said, "My name is Aaron Dekr. I live, work and I am from Grand Cayman." There was an interlude, then a, "Yes Inspector."

Carmen listened to the one-sided conversation and tried to fill in what Inspector Claude Gadgét might be saying.

Aaron replied, "Yes sir, I am staying at the King Soloman Hotel on King David Street." After a bit of a lull, Aaron explained, "No Inspector, his identity was never revealed to me." Another long pause, he added, "Okay, one moment please." Aaron's gaze left Carmen and lowered as he reached into his pocket and retrieved a slim wallet from his pocket and laid it open on the table before him. "My driver's licence was issued in Grand Cayman; number S-672 …"

Carmen listened as Aaron read off the licence number, then read it once again for verification. There was more silence, until finally, "I understand Inspector … yes, I will." Aaron looked back to Carmen, as he lowered the phone and reached across the table handing it to her.

"The Inspector would like to talk to you."

She took the phone and mouthed a thank you to Aaron. "Hello, Inspector." Carmen listened to what Gadgét said, then responded. "I think we might be here for …" She looked to Aaron, "an hour?" Aaron nodded in agreement. "Yes, we will … and thank you, Inspector." She lowered the phone, ended the call and handed it back to Aaron. "If he can, the inspector would like to pick us up when we are finished here."

Aaron showed no sign of apprehension as he removed his driver's licence from the wallet and set it alone in a clear space on the table. He proceeded to open the camera on his phone. He aimed and took a picture. "He wants a photo of my licence sent to him." Aaron straightened up and did the required operations to send the picture via text message to Chief Inspector Claude Gadgét. "That should be okay."

He turned off the phone, set it down and put his licence back into his wallet, which he replaced in his pocket. Leaning back, he shrugged. "You put in a good word for me."

"I told the inspector you can do the 100 metre, in under 10 seconds, albeit with a strong tailwind, so we need you on our side in case some bad guys need to be run down." She gave Aaron a coy look.

"Hmm … the profile didn't alert me to your sense of humour Carmen. I believe it helps you to move forward?"

Carmen was taken aback by his acute perception. "Yes, I suppose … I hope I'm not … Sometimes the humour thing gets me into trouble …"

"No, it's okay …" Aaron smiled. "I like it."

Carmen was suddenly feeling flushed. *I think he just gave me a compliment!* She quickly reached for her teacup, pressed it to her lips and drank. Setting her cup back in place, she asked, "I think we need to get back to your story? When you left off, you were introducing your boss—Stanley Crawford and his inclination towards money and politics, if I got the story right, so far."

"Yes, I'm afraid we have digressed. Let's see … Stanley Crawford …" A much more solemn demeanour came over Aaron. "Sometimes I wish I had never heard that name. But, then I realize there are many 'Stanley Crawfords' in the world, and if I must learn to compete with them, so shall it be."

He paused briefly. "I hope I can make a difference. I believe we need to find a balance. I guess you could say I was born and raised in an environmentally sensitive area. I have in my short lifetime witnessed an alarming decline in the coral formation and tropical fish species throughout the Caribbean. A pristine environment is under threat, and I believe there is much that can be done to help protect it, while still welcoming people and their children from all over the world to come to the islands and experience some of nature's most delicate and wondrous creations." Aaron gave Carmen a sheepish look. "I understand it can get a little much how we all want to save the world, but I do think at the very least we can try to offset the 'Stanley Crawfords.'"

Carmen related to his passion wholeheartedly. She offered him a warm, understanding smile, which turned into a grin. "I plan on keeping this to myself, but I think I learned a new environmental term." Aaron raised his eyebrows in anticipation. "Until now I didn't know what a 'Stanley Crawford' was!"

Aaron nodded his head with a slight chuckle. "Well okay ... let's see if I can expand upon that term."

"Company X owns a remote-controlled submersible, which is equipped to take samples of water, sand, plants, coral, etcetera, from the ocean for lab analysis. One day during the operation I was and am still currently working on, one of the sub technicians dropped off a beach satchel that had become entangled with the unit while doing test samples offshore. He set it on the floor at the corner of my office. I think he assumed I might like to test some of the fabric in the bag for contaminants."

"At the end of my shift I had a chance to look at it. I dumped the contents of the bag onto the floor and sorted through them. The satchel was a typical beach bag someone had probably dropped from a boat, and it looked like it had not been underwater too long, perhaps a couple months. The contents were quite usual: sunglasses, sunscreen, water bottle, hairbrush and a few other items. There was one small item, however, which caught my eye: a rubber-coated USB memory stick. I opened the device and noticed the rubber had shielded the inside from the salt water. After disposing of the bag and most of the contents, I plugged the USB into my desktop computer. As I said, this was the end of my shift, and I had no important commitments, so I was not in a rush."

Aaron stopped; his expression grew more serious as he continued. "When the information from the memory drive loaded, it took me some time to get a lock on what I was looking at. There were meticulously hand sketched, detailed blueprints, and notations in a foreign language that appeared to be German. It appeared someone had made a digitally photographed copy of an old handbook. I used my computer's program to translate most of the notations into English. Overall, I discerned a detailed description of a pocket watch. But this was no ordinary pocket watch!" Aaron reached for his cup and took a drink.

Carmen shuddered at his last sentence. She had pushed the memories of the watch away. What had started as a fun adventure was a fun adventure no more. After all the anguish, it was now only frightening.

But listening to Aaron's firm, Caribbean-accented voice, she visualized majestic turquoise waters and almost felt a warm, gentle ocean breeze. The mystery of the watch was beckoning her to yet another exotic part of the world, where it was about to reveal more of its secrets. Carmen did not resist the attraction. It pulled her in and almost intoxicated her within its embrace. Her pulse increased, and her brain spun with visions. The images took her back to hometown garage sales, and imaginings of her dad in New York City. The Queen, Marie Antoinette was staring at her, and the museum was haunting her under the dark shadows being cast by the Old City walls of Jerusalem.

Suddenly the spinning in her head stopped and was replaced by the twirling of her body. She found herself back on campus, gazing up at a star-filled, moonlit sky on a soft, warm evening. She continued to spin, and her heart felt as though it might burst with excitement. *My dad is picking me up tomorrow, and together we'll be having a great adventure!*

The fun adventure was not lost to Carmen, only tucked away in a safe spot. Perhaps the time had come to retrieve it. Her dad would join her soon.

Her voice quivered as she spoke. "The book ... it described the pocket watch my dad found?"

"I believe it did, Carmen."

"And now you can tell me what is so exceptional about it?"

"I can try."

THIRTY-EIGHT

"Carmen, I am sure you examined the pocket watch and noticed its unusual appearance?" Aaron asked.

Carmen nodded. "Yes, I held it in my hands, and before that my dad sent me pictures he had taken. Prior to even seeing the watch in person, I spent quite some time on the Internet looking for information on the timepiece ... but my searches were unsuccessful."

"The single hand, the different scale, and the dial markings are all unfamiliar." Aaron stopped for a moment. "But the unique internal movement I saw, outlined from the drawings, aroused my interest. In one brief summary, I believe I was looking at a description for a working model of ... perpetual motion!"

"Whoa ... really?" Carmen was not sure what to expect, but it certainly was not this. "I'm no techno-geek, but this is starting to sound like a science fiction movie."

"I will definitely agree with you in part. However, let me explain further."

"The model proposed had what looked to be the use of dual magnetism ... in conjunction with an elemental composition, acting as a catalyst or medium to form a type of uni-magnet. In theory, a uni-magnet can rotate endlessly—attracting and repelling.

Such a force could then be harnessed to perform work. Hence, a type of perpetual motion would be achieved."

Carmen asked "So, you're thinking the watch movement is using uni-magnetism ... Does such a thing exist?"

Aaron took a moment to answer. "Up until recently, my answer would have been an absolute *no*. However, recent scientific studies uncovered a type of uni-magnetism on a molecular level. So, this tells me it *can* exist." Aaron brought his hands up to his shoulders in a shrugging gesture. "This may well be a great secret of our universe."

"Do you mean the molecular discovery pertaining to the watch movement?" Carmen queried.

"Well, I was referring to the scientific discovery ... but perhaps both. I think much depends on the catalyst material used in the movement." Aaron stopped. He was trying to determine the best way to explain things. "The diagrams shown gave what appeared to be precise directional motion measurements and data for the time period indicated. In short, the file looked quite convincing."

"So basically, what we're talking about here is a new ... no, I guess I should say a different technology?" Carmen asked with an almost disappointed tone in her voice. "I guess all along I was thinking ... hoping ... this would be a special watch, owned and used by a great king or queen."

Aaron smiled. "Carmen, if this watch movement is indeed the real deal ... I think we can honestly say that any king or queen would gladly give their throne to own exclusive rights to this 'different technology', as you described it."

His look became more earnest. "Here's the thing: the laws of physics clearly state that perpetual motion is impossible. The reference is made from the laws of thermal dynamics. As I am sure you can understand the word 'thermal' means heat. When energy is transformed, there is always a measurement of heat transfer, as energy is used to perform work. This does not apply to magnetism. Why? Because, simply stated, magnetism is not energy. It is a force, much the same as gravity."

"So, our question is this: can a force be used to perform work? Well, our answer could be yes ... Think about using a magnet on your fridge to hold up a picture. It does this work quite well, presumably indefinitely. However, this is considered static; the magnet sticks and stays put. We would like to realize an attraction or pull in constant motion, and we can do this by adding energy in the form of electricity—hence the electric motor—but can we achieve this without energy? Possibly ... in the instance of a uni-magnet and circular motion, where the magnetic poles would be so aligned as to co-ordinate the push-pull forces to attract and repel indefinitely in a circular motion."

"You think the watch movement somehow achieved this type of magnetism?" Carmen's mindset had changed, albeit somewhat reluctantly, leaving behind a glamorous vision of watches, crowns, and jewels—giving way to fridge magnets and electric motors.

The contrast was sobering. *Time for some serious thought.*

"Aaron, if the watch incorporated this technology, and can spin around forever ..." She paused to think. "Then the device is never supposed to stop?"

Aaron looked slightly surprised. "I believe the answer is yes ... But I am curious as to why you ask that. You have not seen inside of the watch ... correct?"

"No, I haven't ... but I remember there's no winding crown on the watch to start, stop, or wind the device. I ..." Carmen hesitated briefly again. "We didn't see any movement from the single hand on the dial—maybe it's broken."

As if on cue to acknowledge Carmen's intelligence, the right side of Aaron's head throbbed with a slight pain. He responded. "I cannot say whether it is broken or not, but, from my own interpretation of the blueprints, the movement is geared to move the single hand at an incredibly slow rate, whereas it would probably take months to see a difference on the single hand's travel."

"Hmm … unusual," Carmen pondered. "My dad pointed out to me how the graduations on the dial do not correspond with our time standards of 60 seconds, 60 minutes or 24 hours. That's weird too … you got any ideas?"

"Well, yes … but only speculation. I would like to ask you, Carmen, if we can hold off on this for a bit. I am afraid we might veer off into a whole different topic. I think it best I use our remaining time here to fill you in on my situation and my findings."

"You're right. So, you're hoping we can find the watch, and more importantly my father. I should add because the pocket watch might hold a secret to … advanced technology. I guess advanced sounds kind of silly when the watch is perhaps hundreds of years old. Nevertheless, you wish to ensure it does not get into the wrong hands, especially if this technology is as important as you think it might be." Carmen had to take a deep breath following her long-winded discourse.

"Yes, and I would like to add … as you pointed out the motion of the watch incorporates no device for stopping and starting. It appears to be designed to run continuously. To utilize this technology and control the motion would be an enormous challenge. That is to say, make it stop or start on command. Perhaps an energy source would need to be introduced to accomplish those requirements. However, I still stand by my presumption that we may indeed have a model of perpetual motion to evaluate."

"I will go on to say no care given can be too great to ensure this technology is used wisely. Simply put, this technology could build or destroy nations."

Carmen longed to return to her fantasy of kings, queens and crown jewels. The ramifications of this were becoming frightening. She felt glad Aaron sat across the table from her, and Inspector Claude Gadgét was only an electronic dial away.

"Aaron, given this information, how did your boss Stanley Crawford become involved?"

"Fair question, Carmen." Aaron reached for his cup and took a drink of tea. He set his cup down and settled back in his chair. "I took the memory stick home with me, spending more time with it, and then again back at work the next day. During lunch break and after work I went on the computer to study and make some calculations, which I entered and added onto the memory key."

"The following morning after I arrived at work, I was called in to meet Stanley Crawford, my boss. Our meeting was abrupt and to the point. I was informed Stanley knew of the memory device, and how it came to be brought up from the ocean by the company's submersible. He went on to tell me how all computer files operating within the company are monitored and the ownership and rights to them are exclusive to the company. Not only had he perused and copied all the files from the memory key, but he also told me he had them examined by a third party; he did not say whom. Finally, he ordered me to turn over the memory key and said he would use the information as he saw fit. I was to be no longer involved."

"Wow! What an ... He spies on his employees? Sounds like a real creep!" Carmen made a mental note of someone *not* to send her resume to after graduation.

Aaron shook his head. "I should have taken more care and waited to open the file at home. I did make a copy for myself, though. I left his office dismayed and wondered what to do. I did not hear anything for many weeks, although I did spend time on the Internet searching for more information, but like you had no success."

"I started to let it go and think of it as just some kind of strange unanswered mystery. Then one day, about 3 months later, a call came summoning me to Stanley Crawford's office. I was surprised when he showed me some images he had up on his computer screen. They looked to be pictures of the very same pocket watch described in the file, which had been found months earlier. He pointed out a few things and told me he was interested in obtaining the watch. He said the posting came from an Edward James who had been looking to find any helpful information on a mysterious watch he had recently found. The pictures along with a brief description had been posted on some watch sites. Stanley said it appeared no accurate information explaining the watch's providence had been offered on any of the sites."

At the mention of her father's name, a large piece of the puzzle clicked firmly into place for Carmen. She kept a thought to herself. *We all thought it would be a good idea to go online with the watch. I think there's a lesson here I need to learn.*

Aaron paused. He thought Carmen was going to say something. He continued. "Not only was I surprised by seeing what looked to be the same watch listed on the Internet, but also I was confused by how Stanley acted. And I am not using the word *acted* figuratively. He was cordial and polite. I soon discovered why. He wanted me to do something for him. He asked if I would travel to Petrolia—in Canada, to obtain the watch for him. Of course, this astonished me, and I asked why he wanted me in particular."

Aaron smiled grimly. "His answer was a textbook sales pitch; he said I deserved to be a part of the discovery, seeing as how I first witnessed the digital notebook. He went on to say I would be more than qualified and that the company would cover all wages and expenses. So, I replied I would need time to think it over. He gave me one day, as he needed to move on this right away. Leaving his office, I went directly home to think."

Carmen asked, "Why did Stanley Crawford *really* want you for the job Aaron?"

"I can think of three reasons. The first I have already touched on; I'm sure by that point, Stanley would have already had profiles on your family. The similarities between you and me—our international educations and careers—would be favourable to build relations within the family if need be." Aaron stopped as Carmen nodded. She remained silent, so Aaron continued. "The second reason is because I already know about the watch; it makes sense that I should follow up as a paid employee of the company. Whatever I uncover would legally belong to the business. And the third reason is that if Stanley Crawford had some kind of criminal infraction to hold over my head—something he could deny his own involvement in, yet still retain witnesses for when he might need to use them—it would be a valuable asset." Aaron paused. "I think the third reason was only partially realized …"

"You took some time to decide … Do you believe it was the right choice?" Carmen asked.

"I know I am in way over my head, but if I did not accept, there would be someone else. I feel a responsibility to try and control the outcome of this. Stanley Crawford probably does not trust me but must think that I can be intimidated to do what he asks."

Carmen could see a grave seriousness in Aaron's demeanour. "So, is there a plan? What would you have done if Dad had sold you the watch?"

"I do not think I can call it an actual pre-meditated plan … I would say it's more of a connection I can trust."

"After I went home to consider Stanley's offer, I called one of my former physics professors in California; someone I knew I could trust. We became good friends, mainly because of his involvement with the track team. He used his knowledge of physics, together with a love of sports, to assist in our training programs. His primary interest was in sprinting. I formed great respect for him over several years. I called him because I knew he had worked at a university in Toronto before his position in California. I asked if he would be able set me up with a physicist in southern Ontario who could be trusted to secrecy if need be and would be available for an appointment on short notice. The only information I revealed was that I might come into possession of a device we would need to dismantle and evaluate with great expediency. He agreed to see what he could do." Aaron stopped for a drink to help soothe his throat. He was not used to talking this much.

He put his cup down and continued. "I got a return call within an hour. I was given a telephone number for a physicist in the Toronto area who has access to a modern lab facility at a moments' notice, with a promise of the professor's involvement via the Internet if possible."

"Sounds to me like the respect you hold for the professor is mutual." Carmen gave Aaron a warm smile.

Aaron returned the gesture with a thoughtful response. "I suppose it is … he is a friend."

"Aaron, my understanding is that your intentions are good …" Carmen hesitated. "But, why were you not honest with my father when you met him in Petrolia? Had you taken some time to get to know him a bit, you would have come to know a good person."

"My dad may not possess a diploma of any kind … but he is smart, with an intelligence I doubt I will *ever* be able to emulate, even with all my years of university." Carmen turned away and looked up. Her eyes had welled up, and she was trying to keep tears from falling. "I bet he would have loved to go with you to the lab in Toronto." Carmen reached quickly into her purse and pulled a tissue from the pack and, dabbing her eyes, managed to maintain control.

"Excuse me, I'm sorry." She stuffed the soiled Kleenex into her purse and faced Aaron.

She saw hurt on Aaron's face as he replied. "It is me who should be sorry. You are right, Carmen. I made some bad decisions. I wish I had handled things differently. I thought at the time it would be safer not to involve your father. This was a hard call, and to be honest with you Carmen … you made me realize I am guilty of making bias judgements."

Aaron cast his gaze downward. "What I mean is ... I read your father's profile, and his vocation as a construction worker suggested to me coarseness and aggression—virtues I would not assume to be trustworthy."

There was complete silence, and they did not break eye contact. "I am ashamed of those thoughts." Aaron took in a deep breath and let it out. "I'm a young man who has a lot to learn about life's values."

Carmen felt something stir deep inside. She knew it must have taken great courage for him to reveal himself that way, to her. "I struggle with those kinds of issues too."

"I am sorry. I suffer remorse. Please try to understand; never has it been my intent to harm or bring discontent to you or your family. I have failed in this regard."

Carmen reached out and softly placed her hand on his. She said nothing. It was her way of accepting his apology.

Aaron turned his hand up. Their fingers connected in a gentle grasp. Silently he formed the words: 'Thank-you.'

THIRTY-NINE

Carmen and Aaron topped up their cups from small ceramic teapots, which sat on the table beside them. When they finished, Aaron continued, "I contacted Stanley Crawford shortly after my meeting with your father. I explained to him your father did not wish to sell the watch. I did not expect a favourable response, and I was not mistaken. He verbally assaulted me for my incompetence and told me he would do whatever it took to obtain the watch. He said he would bring in a professional, and I was to help breaking into Edward James' home to steal the pocket watch."

"I knew I needed to think quickly, so I told him there might be an easier way. I insisted to Stanley that if the break-in failed, at the very least the police would be brought in. I told him your father had been to London, Ontario, where he was advised by the proprietor at Nash Jewellers to go to Brooklyn, New York and meet with a watchmaker and that this meeting would be his best option for finding out information."

"I thought Stanley would send me, and I could somehow work something out between Edward and the watchmaker." Aaron stopped again, uncertain. "I am not sure how Stanley Crawford found the name of the watchmaker and knew exactly when your father was going to travel … perhaps …"

Carmen cut in. "My dad said our home phone line in Petrolia was bugged." Aaron raised his eyebrows. "Yeah … he found out later, because of a friend of the family—Derek—he's a techy kind of guy. Something about a telephone service truck, which shouldn't have been at our house. Derek fixed it. It's ok now."

"I am not overly surprised. I'm beginning to get a pretty good idea of the resources available to Stanley Crawford. Unfortunately, as I mentioned before, he did not send me to New York but rather instructed me to stay put in Petrolia and keep an eye on Edward. Obviously, this is not what I hoped for, but I agreed."

"Did you stay in Petrolia?"

"Yes, I found a bed and breakfast accommodation. I laid low until I received a call from Stanley. He told me Edward would be flying out early Wednesday morning from Detroit, Michigan. He wanted me to follow him and make sure I got his flight number and arrival time in New York City. I did as instructed, and after relaying the information to Stanley I was told to return to Petrolia and wait until our next exchange."

"Okay, so now I understand how the men came to be waiting for my dad when he arrived with the watch."

Carmen was trying to piece things together. "There doesn't appear to be any prior connection with Stanley Crawford and the watchmaker, other than the men being at the watch shop before my dad arrived. So … it happened as we thought; the watchmaker was probably threatened, but he managed to cleverly alert my dad and tell him where to find out about the watch if he escaped."

Aaron had a quizzical expression on his face. "How did he do so, Carmen?"

He listened intently as Carmen took in a deep breath and related the prior chain of events, as told to her by her father. She began with the image on the laptop screen the watchmaker showed her dad, insisting he was in great danger and must flee after he received a signal. Carmen could not help emitting a wry smile when she revealed what the signal was. "When he sneezed!" Aaron gave her an interested look as she continued to tell him the confusing watch riddle about a great queen, a great watch, the queen's death, and about two great watches destined to meet where the queen had lost her throne. While Aaron pondered the mystery, she briefly outlined her father's escape, his return to the watch shop, and how he had observed a dead body being loaded into an ambulance, a body that everyone had mistook for the old watchmaker.

Carmen finished her narrative with the explanation of how her dad solved the riddle. He thought about her mom's name Marie, and remembered a story about a great watch, which had been built for the great Queen Marie Antoinette, and how it could be seen now in the L.A. Mayer Museum in Jerusalem.

"So that's how we came to be at the museum."

"Where you and your father were attacked." Aaron looked concerned. "This is most perplexing." He waited, giving Carmen a chance to resume. She stayed silent. "Let me get back to telling you about my time in Petrolia."

"Okay ... do you like it? I mean the town." Carmen gave him a hopeful smile.

"I do. After I got back, it did not seem necessary to lay low, as your father was in New York, so I spent some time walking around and taking in the sites. There are a lot of beautiful, well-kept older buildings and homes. I like smaller communities. The people are quite friendly. I'm not too sure about the cooler temperatures, though ..."

"Oh boy! You don't know cool ... I bet you would love the high oxygen content in the winter, though. Skating on an outdoor pond or skiing snow-covered slopes on a bright, sunny day of minus 5 or 10 degrees. Absolutely fantastic." Carmen grinned. "And besides, I hear you already got a line on one of the world's finest coat manufacturers."

Aaron's brow furrowed.

"Your Canada Goose coat?"

"Oh ..." he stumbled on his words. "Your father and I ... well I guess he told you I own one."

"Yes, a slate grey jacket, I think he said." Carmen gave Aaron a sly smile. "There's no need for you to fear Canadian winters, Aaron. Canada Goose and other manufacturers make great parkas that will keep you toasty warm, even on the coldest of days."

Aaron blushed slightly. "I will be sure to remember your advice." He gave her an understanding smile. "To be honest ... I would love to learn how to skate and downhill ski."

"Okay, I'll be sure to remember you said that. Now tell me about Petrolia. I really miss it."

"I drove around the town a bit to learn the layout, and then went for a cross country run through the trails at a place called 'Petrolia Discovery?'"

Carmen nodded with enthusiasm. "I like that area. The covered bridge is cool. A lot of wedding photos are taken there."

Aaron smiled. He could see Carmen's love for her hometown in her demeanour as he continued. When he mentioned a building or place of interest, she was quick to jump in with excited acknowledgment. The 'small town girl' was still very much a part of her.

"Your father told me he found the watch at a garage sale on the street named Maple. He informed me he had learned an elderly widow who had recently passed away formerly occupied the house. The home's contents were being sold off. Apparently, the two teenagers who sold him the watch believed it came from Petrolia's Victoria town hall and that it was a part of the old props used in the theatre, which is part of the building."

Carmen agreed. "Yes, that's what Dad said to me too. Did you go inside the building? It's really beautiful. The building was completely restored after a fire in 1989. Dad said it looked like the watch and some other theatre props somehow survived that fire, as the items were covered in black soot."

"Well no ... I did not go inside. I just walked around the outside. From the exterior appearance, though, I could well imagine it must be lovely. I did, however, use my free time to take a walk down Maple Street. On a hunch, I wanted to see for myself where the watch was discovered."

Aaron stopped for a moment to collect his thoughts. "What I learned is something I wanted to discuss with you."

Carmen became more attentive. She remained silent and leaned in towards Aaron.

He continued. "It was some time after lunch, and I had walked to Maple Street from the east when I got a call from Stanley. The conversation was short. He was angry. He informed me Edward still had the watch and he had lost contact with the men in New York. Stanley told me to stay put and wait and see when Edward returned home. He said he was undecided on what to do and hung up."

"I continued walking and passed a school on my left. With young children and school buses about, it seemed classes were finished for the day. A little farther up the road on my right, I noticed an elderly woman out working in her flowerbed. As I got closer, I saw she was struggling with a heavy bag of cedar mulch. I jogged up to her driveway, called out a hello, and asked if I could help. She accepted my offer. We introduced ourselves. Her name was Evelyn, a nice lady. We spent the next 20 minutes applying three bags of fresh mulch to her flower garden. She did the directing; I did the manual labour. In between instructions on mulch spreading, I learned some local news and history."

"When we finished, Evelyn offered me a cold soft drink. She asked me to retrieve a couple of lawn chairs from the side of the house and bring them around to the front while she went in to get our drinks." Aaron smiled warmly. "It reminded me of my home."

"I know the feeling … nice." Carmen returned the smile.

"We sat on the lawn chairs and admired the flowers in her garden. I took the opportunity to ask Evelyn a few questions. I told her I had been in conversation with someone who found a beautiful old pocket watch somewhere on Maple Street at last week's garage sale. I wondered if she might know where it could have been. Without hesitation, she said it would most likely have come from the house next door—to the west of her. She went on to tell me the house was being cleared out in preparation for sale, as now both of its former inhabitants…" Aaron stopped talking, reached into his pocket and pulled out a small, slim notebook and opened it to the first page. He glanced down. "Yes… sorry. Their names: Lloyd and Bertha. Bertha recently passed away. She went on to say that she and Bertha were good friends. I learned from her Lloyd and Bertha had no children. Two young teenagers, a boy and a girl, had been sent by a niece from another city to look after the garage sale for a couple of days."

"I asked Evelyn why she thought the watch might have been sold from Lloyd and Bertha's estate." Aaron stopped. He was trying to remember. "I think her words were: 'It would seem likely, as Bertha had a stepbrother who is a watchmaker and he came to visit her quite often over the years.' I said to her, 'Yes, that would make sense. Do you recall the name of her stepbrother, Evelyn?'"

"Her reply: 'Yes, of course, I've met him several times … his name was …' Aaron glanced down again at the page in his notebook. "She said his name was Herbert Osterhagen."

Carmen bolted upright in her chair and gasped. She sat frozen with her mouth agape.

Aaron was startled by her response. "Carmen, what's wrong?"

Carmen did not blink, as her eyes wandered until they finally found Aaron again. "My god, Aaron …" Her voice trembled. "The grandfather of the woman we went to see at the museum … he's the watchmaker in New York! The police want him on suspicion of murder. His name is Herbert Osterhagen!"

They both stared at each other in silence.

FORTY

MONDAY, MAY 5, 2014. 7:30 A.M.
PETROLIA, ONTARIO

I̲t was a bright, fresh morning. Marie was finishing a cool down walk as she turned into Derek's driveway. He had left early for work so he could leave early to drive her to London to catch her flight to Israel.

It had been mostly a sleepless night for Marie. When she finally got to bed, and although her intent was otherwise, it seemed she was either worrying or crying. Derek had been an immense help, though; he looked after the flight bookings, and his kindness and reassurance probably kept her from a much more severe state of depression. At the first sign of morning light, Marie forced herself into her running attire for a hard 1hour run. She believed it would be good for her and help her to deal with the stress.

Her breathing was still deep as she approached the door and took the house key from her jacket pocket. Marie knew she looked like a wreck; her eyes were still puffy and red, but she did feel better. Running helped to centre her mind and body into a heightened sense of being alive. She understood the medical reasons; chemical reactions in the brain cause states of perceived well-being, but

Marie preferred to push that knowledge aside and just go with it and enjoy. *Something Edward could never do,* she thought. *Oh, the feeling is going away too quickly! Edward ... where are ...*

Suddenly, through the closed front door, came the faint sound of a long-distance ring on the phone. *Hurry! Hurry!* Marie fumbled with the key in her haste. She talked out loud to help her through the sequence. "Okay ... key in the lock, enter the four-digit code on the pad, done; now the ... can you believe this ... a fingerprint scanner!" She placed her finger on another sensor located where most people had a doorbell. *Nope, not Derek... he doesn't like doorbells.*

The phone rang twice as she waited for a tone and a green light. "Oh, come on! I don't have time for this ... an eff-ing fingerprint scan, and soon to be added ... a retina scan ... really!" Marie's whole body vibrated.

The phone rang again. "We live in a small town, for God's sake! Who in their right mind would want to break in here? First off, they wouldn't be able to even find what they came for— too much stuff to sift through! And furthermore, up until one day ago, they would've been in danger of tripping and falling while wading through all the debris. Most people in this town don't even lock their doors! Derek, sometimes you drive me ..." The sensor buzzed and a green light flashed. Marie quickly turned the key, opened the door, and was into the living room in seconds searching for the phone. *Amazing! In the cradle where it should to be. Gee ... maybe there's hope after all.*

She scooped the phone from its cradle and glanced at the call display as she brought it to her ear. "Carmen?"

"Hi, Mom."

Marie's heart leapt at the sound of her daughter's voice. "Honey, how are you ... any news?"

"Nothing for sure on Dad, but I've learned something new." Carmen hesitated. "You sound out of breath, are you okay?"

"Yes, yes, I went for an early run. Derek's not home … I just got back and was at the front door when I heard the long-distance ring on the phone. I had to rush through all these ridiculous security checks to get in and answer it. Nothing seems to be easy, but I'm *so* glad to hear your voice."

"I guess you have your own adventure to contend with."

"What did you learn, Carmen?"

"Okay, I'm going to keep this short, as we're on the phone. I'll give you all the details when we're together tomorrow."

"Alright, and I'll text you later with my flight numbers and arrival times. I will take a shirut taxi from Tel Aviv to Jerusalem and meet you at the Prima Royale. Yes … go ahead Carmen."

"Oh … by the way, you won't need the taxi. I can come and pick you up at the airport. Dad rented a car, and it's just sitting here at the hotel."

"What … you're going to drive in Israel? Something doesn't sound right."

"I wasn't planning on doing the driving," Carmen answered.

There was a noticeable hesitation. "Who, exactly, is going to drive the car then?"

"Aaron … the Aaron who is involved with this whole pocket watch thing. He's here and offered to drive to Tel Aviv. He wants to meet you and help in any way he can to find Dad."

Aaron, I know that name! Marie evaluated the information.

Carmen continued, "He's the man Dad met in Coffee Lodge who tried to buy his watch."

Marie sounded frightened, when she replied. "What on earth is *he* doing there? This is getting bizarre. Did your dad not say he had a Caribbean accent? Were the men who chased your father in New York not possibly Caribbean? One of them is now dead, maybe murdered!"

She was trembling. Fear welled up inside of her. "Oh, Carmen, what are you doing? These men are dangerous. You need to go to the police right now!"

"Mom, Mom … listen to me! The police *are* involved. I have spoken with Chief Inspector Claude Gadgét, and he talked with Aaron. The inspector has been with us both. It's all right. Aaron is trying to help us."

Marie wiped tears from her cheeks. She felt herself calm down. "I'm sorry Carmen. Please try to understand how difficult it is for me to be so far away from you and your father. And with all this going on …"

"It'll be a lot better tomorrow when we can be together. Now, though, you need to trust me, Mom. You and Dad did not raise me to be careless. Inspector Gadgét and others are trying to help me. And now Aaron is helping me too. We can trust him, and we need to believe we will find Dad together."

The sense of pride for her daughter was almost overwhelming. It came, however, with a sense of loss as well. This sensation was not new for Marie, but it seemed to be becoming more frequent as time passed. The little girl who used to hang on her arm and look up to her 'mommy' for her 'everything' was gone. It was not love lost. It was love evolved, and Marie believed she could welcome it, but not without a deep-felt sadness.

Marie put her feelings aside. "What can we do, Carmen? You said you have new information."

"Yea, like I said, I won't go into detail until later, but … something Aaron found out. Briefly: he works for a man named Stanley Crawford doing environmental research in Grand Cayman. He was sent to buy the watch. Ultimately, Aaron does not want Stanley to obtain the watch for ethical reasons. When Dad left for New York to visit the watchmaker Herbert Osterhagen, Aaron stayed behind in Petrolia. Dad had mentioned to him he found the watch at a garage sale on Maple Street. So, on a hunch, Aaron walked to Maple Street where he struck up a conversation with an elderly lady who had something quite interesting to say about why the watch might have been found where it was."

"Oh …? Did he get her name? I might know her."

"That's what I'm wondering. You know a lot of people in Petrolia, and Maple Street is so close to our house … Mom, have you ever met an elderly woman named Evelyn who lives on Maple Street?"

Without hesitation, Marie answered, "Yes! We've been friends for quite a few years. I stop by sometimes when she is outside. I find myself doing my cool down walks past her house quite frequently after some of my runs. You remember when I used to do the ballot counting at poll stations during elections? Well, one year Evelyn and I were teamed up at the same table. We got to know each other. She's a lovely, well-read lady." Marie paused, taking a moment to reflect. "What did Evelyn say?"

"She said the watch most likely came from the house right next door to the west of her. Two teenagers, a boy and a girl, had been doing a garage sale to help clear out the house because the widow who lived there recently passed away."

"Yes, that's exactly what your father said," Marie remembered.

"Right, and apparently Evelyn had been close friends with Lloyd and Bertha. Particularly Bertha, after Lloyd had died some years earlier."

"I've met Bertha myself, and I heard she passed away. It will be hard for Evelyn. They were very close."

"Aaron confirmed that too … But, listen to why she thought an old watch might be found there." Intensity swelled in Carmen's voice. "Turns out, Bertha had a stepbrother who's a watchmaker who had travelled several times to visit his stepsister in Petrolia. His name was Herbert Osterhagen!"

Marie was stunned, as her thoughts started spinning. "The watchmaker from New York ... Derek told me that he's wanted by the police on suspicion of murder! And from you, we learned he is the grandfather of a woman using a false name who works at the museum where he lured your father. And now *this*?"

Marie was shaken. "Herbert Osterhagen has some kind of a connection to Petrolia! What in Gods' name is going on here, Carmen?"

"I don't know, Mom, but I think we need to try and find out."

The initial shock was receding, but Marie still felt threatened. With each passing hour, it was more and more like an escalating emergency. Her medical training began to override her instincts of fear and shock.

She took in a deep, shaky breath as her brain assessed the situation. "The possible murder in the New York watch shop was a drug overdose. You and your father were both attacked using drugs at the museum where the watchmaker cleverly summoned you both. It looks as though this watchmaker is connected to the pocket watch a lot more than we realized. It sure appears as though he is in Jerusalem now, possibly holding your father captive, or ..."

"Mom ..." Carmen cut in. "I made a promise to my doctor in Jerusalem and to myself; I promised I would have hope. Please, tell me you can do the same ... We really need each other's support."

A subtle pleading tone sounded in her daughter's voice. Marie pictured Carmen's eyes. She would be trying to hold back tears.

Marie thought for a moment before she continued. "Carmen, I would like to share with you something I've learned from experience, and I hope someday you understand. From somewhere there comes a great strength, when you honestly try to be a good wife and parent. So yes, I *will* have hope."

Marie embraced the short silence. When she resumed, her voice was clear and steady. "I'm going to see what I can find out from Evelyn. I will text you what I learn. Anything else? I admit I'm really curious about how you befriended Aaron."

"Oh, yea ... I bet you're gonna like the story of how I met Aaron. He has a nice cut on the side of his face from our introduction."

"What?"

"Sorry ... fill you in later ... gotta go now. I love you, Mom."

"Oh! Please be careful ... I love you too, Carmen."

FORTY-ONE

She rang the doorbell for the second time and glanced down at her watch: 9:05 a.m. Derek would be driving her to London to catch the first leg of her flight at 12:30 p.m., and there was still packing to be done. She could not hear any indication of movement inside.

Marie stood in front of a neatly kept, three-level split-styled home on Maple Street. It was no more than a 3-minute walk from Derek's house. Pressing the button for the third time, she worried that Evelyn might not be home. This would be the only opportunity to talk with her before leaving for Israel.

She waited and listened. Knowing Evelyn was over 85 years old; Marie understood it might take some time for her to get to the door, especially with many stairs connecting the three levels. She raised her hand to knock when a loud click of an opening lock sounded. The door opened, and Marie was greeted by the bright smiling face of a slim, well-kept elderly woman.

Evelyn wore her white hair up in a bun and had on a light cotton flower print dress, which complimented her small stature. "Oh, Marie … What a lovely surprise! We haven't talked since last fall. I don't get out much in our cold winters anymore. It's so lovely to see you again, dear. Would you like to come in?"

"Yes, thank you, Evelyn." Marie returned the smile, but behind it, she gave herself a stern reprimand. *It's been that long? You should have visited as soon as you heard about Bertha's death. She could've used some support when her friend and neighbour died.*

A look of concern came over Evelyn's face as Marie entered her home. "Please forgive me for saying Marie, but you're looking a little worn down. Are you okay?"

Marie reached out and gently squeezed her friend's hand. "I'm sure I will be fine Evelyn. I'll admit, though, the last few days have been difficult. There has been some trouble in our family concerning my husband Edward and our daughter Carmen. I'm doing my best to make things better, and actually, that is the reason I came here today."

Concern deepened on her face as Evelyn led Marie through the short entranceway to the living room. "Please Marie, make yourself comfortable. I was just about to put on a pot of coffee." Evelyn nodded in a reassuring manner. "I'll be right back, and we can talk, dear."

After Evelyn left, Marie glanced around the pleasant room. It fit Evelyn so well; she had it decorated in a colonial style with floral prints on the sofa and chair. Medium dark cherry wood coffee and end tables with hand knitted doilies on pristine dust free tabletops framed the furnishings. Two colourful oil paintings, of flowers, adorned the soft green walls and brought vibrancy into the room.

Marie's roving gaze settled on the fireplace mantle, where she perused some framed family pictures. In many of the smiling faces of her children and grandchildren, the genetic resemblance to Evelyn was quite noticeable. Looking a bit farther up the wall, Marie smiled as her eyes fell on a framed document, a humanitarian award, which had been presented to Evelyn not too many years prior by the community for outstanding volunteer work performed during most of her adult life. *A special woman* Marie thought to herself, just as Evelyn returned.

"The coffee will be ready soon, and I have some freshly baked tea biscuits with jam for us too." She smiled. "Marie, tell me what the trouble is ... I hope I can help." She seated herself on the sofa, which sat at a right angle to Marie's chair.

"Okay ... where to begin?" Marie did her best to keep her emotions under control, although her serious manner remained. "My husband Edward has been missing for almost two days now, and I fear he's in danger. Recently he travelled to Israel, where he picked up our daughter Carmen in Tel Aviv." She paused. "Do you remember the last time we spoke when I mentioned how Carmen is studying in University there?"

Evelyn nodded. "Yes, I do."

"Well, they went to Jerusalem to find out some information on an old pocket watch Edward bought at the annual town-wide garage sale at a house here on Maple Street."

"Oh ..." Evelyn perked up at Marie's last sentence. "Why, I just recently spoke about a pocket watch with a young man a few days ago. He said he knew someone who had found a watch at a garage sale on Maple Street."

She stopped briefly to collect her thoughts. "A thoughtful young man ... he helped me with some heavy bags of mulch for my garden. Do you think we were talking about the same watch and that he knew Edward?"

"Yes, I do Evelyn. His name is Aaron, and he is in Jerusalem now helping Carmen. They're trying to find Edward."

"Yes, that's it ... He said his name was Aaron, and he asked for any information I might know about the pocket watch."

"Aaron mentioned a name to Carmen, which he apparently heard from you. And we now feel you might be able to further elaborate for us, such as how this person might be involved with my husband's disappearance."

A perplexing expression formed on Evelyn's face. "I will try, dear. What was the person's name you're interested in?"

"A watchmaker—Herbert Osterhagen."

"I do know a Herbert Osterhagen, Marie, although I haven't seen or heard anything about him for many years now. Yes, as I told Aaron, Herbert is a watchmaker. He's a stepbrother to my former next-door neighbour and close friend Bertha, who, as you know, recently passed away. He is the reason I thought the watch came from next door, as I explained. Two young people had come from the Mississauga area to help settle the estate." Evelyn rose from the couch. "Marie, let me get our coffee and tea biscuits now, dear. I think it will be ready."

Marie noticed a sudden sadness come over Evelyn at the mention of her friend's name. Marie wanted to take advantage of the short break to help her in the kitchen and spend some time consoling her on the loss of her dear friend. "Let me help with the coffee, okay?" Marie rose to her feet and took Evelyn's arm in hers.

"That would be nice. Thank you, dear."

"I'm sorry, Evelyn …" They walked towards the kitchen. "I should have come to see how you were doing as soon as I heard about Bertha's passing. I know you two were close friends."

"No … no need to be sorry, Marie. You're here now." She looked up into Marie's eyes with a bright smile. "Bertha and I used to enjoy morning coffee with tea biscuits and jam, quite often. This is lovely too."

"Maybe you can tell me a bit about Bertha while we get our coffee and biscuits."

"Okay."

The two women chatted as they walked arm in arm down the hallway towards the kitchen. This was fond remembrance for Evelyn and caring condolences offered by Marie. Together, it became the sharing of life's trials with a friend.

When they returned from the kitchen about 10 minutes later, Marie carried a tray with two mugs of coffee, along with some small plates, knives, and napkins, and Evelyn brought a small platter of warmed tea biscuits and a serving dish of preserves. They were both chatting freely with smiling faces, making their way back to the living room. Marie located some coasters on an end table and set things up in proper order.

"It's definitely been too long since I've had a tea biscuit." Marie proclaimed with a smile.

"I understand this isn't on today's list of healthy foods, dear ... But aren't they truly one of life's nicest pleasures?" Evelyn giggled.

"An excellent stress reliever as well." Marie spread a thick layer of homemade strawberry-rhubarb jam on the first half of her biscuit.

Evelyn prepared one for herself, and her expression turned serious. "Marie, let's continue with what's important right now, okay dear ... You wanted to learn more about Bertha's stepbrother Herbert Osterhagen the watchmaker?"

"Mm ..." Marie raised her hand, indicating she needed to finish her first bite of food before replying. A moment passed. She lifted a napkin to her mouth to catch some spilling crumbs. "This is *so* good!" A guilty look appeared on her face as she took a quick sip of her coffee. "I must be careful ... I might easily be drawn into a naughty relationship with your tea biscuits, Evelyn."

The compliment brought a twinkle to Evelyn's eyes. "Well, if you falter, it will be our little secret."

"I just might take you up on that offer, if things don't start getting better." The short diversion had helped, but the worried feeling rushed back, and it showed on Marie's face.

"Let me try and help, dear."

"Well ... I'll explain in a little more detail. The watch Edward chanced upon is an unusual timepiece, it seems. The same day he found it, he took it to a jewellery store in London where he had developed a rapport with the owner after purchasing his retirement watch there. The owner of the store was quite intrigued with the unusual timepiece but could offer no information about its origin.

He did, however, recommend the name of a watchmaker in New York City: Herbert Osterhagen."

"When Edward showed me the watch later in the evening, we agreed it would be a good idea to post some pictures online to see if some information might be available on the Internet. He received some response; someone even offered him several thousand dollars for the watch, but no one really had any information, and Edward did not wish to sell it, especially when he knew next to nothing about it."

"Oh my ... that's a lot of money. Is it made of solid gold? Might someone know something about the watch and is not saying?" Evelyn asked attentively as she tried to understand the situation.

Marie responded. "Edward thinks it is made of silver and brass mostly. Its value isn't in its precious metals, for sure."

Evelyn nodded as Marie continued. "Shortly after he turned down the offer, Edward decided to go to New York and visit the watchmaker. He said there was an excellent bicycle store right in Brooklyn, close to where the watchmaker was located. He had always wanted to go there, so he planned an itinerary and flew to New York. When Edward got to the watch shop, the trouble began. Some men chased him and tried to steal his watch. But right before the commotion started, Herbert indirectly advised him to go to a museum in Jerusalem where he would be able to learn about the pocket watch."

Marie stopped and took a sip of coffee and allowed Evelyn a chance to ask questions. She only muttered, "Oh my."

Marie continued. "I'm sure Edward wouldn't normally go all the way to Israel to find out about a watch. But, with Carmen having a 4-day break coming up from her graduate studies, Edward thought it would be a little adventure for them. Carmen shares in his passion for timepieces. Before I knew it, Edward was travelling to see Carmen."

Marie paused and shook her head. "Again, more trouble began. When Edward and Carmen went to a pre-arranged appointment with a young woman at the museum in Jerusalem, they were attacked! Both Carmen and Edward were drugged. Carmen managed to escape out to the street, where she found assistance. When she returned inside with the museum curator and the police ... Edward was gone."

Marie held back tears. "He and the damn watch are still missing!"

"I'm so sorry, dear, this is terrible!" Evelyn stood and passed Marie a box of tissues. She placed a hand on Marie's shoulder as Marie took a tissue and dabbed at her eyes. Marie looked up at her friend in silent acknowledgement of the gesture and nodded she would be okay. Evelyn lingered a moment before sitting.

"Do you believe Herbert Osterhagen is involved in this incident? He did recommend that Edward go there."

"We think possibly yes ... and there's more." Marie had composed herself. "Later, the same day of the attack, Carmen found out the young woman they had met at the museum was actually Herbert Osterhagens' granddaughter. I'm sure you can understand our surprise when Carmen learned you had mentioned to the young man Aaron that Herbert also has ties and a relative in Petrolia, the very place the watch was found."

"Yes dear, you're right, it is odd indeed." Evelyn sat in reflection. Neither woman spoke for some time. They both took another bite of their food and chewed in silence.

Finally, after taking a long sip of her coffee, Evelyn said, "I'm trying to remember what I can about Herbert ... Yes, I met him a few times, and Bertha spoke of him occasionally. He seemed a cordial, polite, intelligent man. I remember his bright blue eyes. He had a German accent of course, as he is descended from a long line of German watchmakers. He was a single man for quite some time before I met him. I think his wife died early in life, and they had a child together. As I recall … he told me himself about his watch shop in New York."

Evelyn took a moment and continued, "I think Herbert used to come and visit Lloyd and Bertha about twice a year. He would stay a few days, and as I recall, on one of those days he would borrow Lloyd's car and go off by himself. Bertha told me Herbert liked to visit pawnshops, going as far as Windsor, London, and Kitchener looking for old watches to fix up. That's why I thought a watch might have been found at Lloyd and Bertha's. I thought perhaps he had left one there."

"I can understand your reasoning. However, the watch was found in a box of old props from the town theatre. Edward was told they had survived the 1989 fire and somehow Lloyd ended up with them." Marie informed her.

"Yes … okay, dear. I could see Lloyd having them, as he worked at the town hall during the time of the fire. His job was town clerk for many years, and he had an office in the building."

"It appears Herbert was close to his stepsister. Can you think of any family connection, other than his granddaughter, which might explain why he might be in Jerusalem now?"

Evelyn was lost in thought as she sipped at her coffee. She put the cup down. "Yes, I think he and Bertha were close. She always spoke fondly of him. I'm not sure, but I believe she mentioned Herbert introduced her to Lloyd. I don't think she ever told me the details, though." Evelyn stopped again. Marie stayed quiet and sipped at her coffee, giving her friend time to think.

Evelyn continued. "As for a family connection to Jerusalem … why yes, there might be something. I remember Lloyd and Bertha visited Israel several times, and I can remember her telling me they had a place to stay in Jerusalem for free. I think it was a small flat owned by her mother's side of the family, an older residence that had been passed down within the family for many years."

Marie set her cup down and leaned in. "Might you remember where the flat was in Jerusalem, Evelyn?"

"No, I'm sorry dear. I don't believe Bertha ever said."

Marie still showed interest. "Evelyn, what was Bertha's maiden name?"

Evelyn's face fell. "I wish I could tell you. I should know her former name. I'm so sorry!"

"No, no Evelyn, I understand. There's no reason for you to know that." Marie could tell Evelyn was disappointed in herself. She looked as though she was holding back tears.

"It's okay. What you told me is helpful. I have a friend who can hopefully find out her maiden name and possibly get some more information on this family residence. I'll be leaving later this afternoon for Jerusalem and my friend can contact me if he uncovers anything."

Marie was not sure if Derek could track down a name for her, but the mention of it helped lift Evelyn's spirits.

"Can you think of anything else concerning Herbert Osterhagen that might be of help, Evelyn?" She gave her friend a warm, hopeful smile.

"Well, there is one more thing. I recall it as being most unusual, when Bertha confided in me, many years ago, about something that saddened her deeply. I'm not sure if it will have any relevance at all with what's going on now, but I'll tell you."

"I had already met Herbert one or two times when one day Bertha said that her stepbrother Herbert had been institutionalized, I think this happened sometime in the 1980s. His condition was diagnosed as some form of acute psychosis, possibly schizophrenia, but I'm not certain. I believe she thought he would recover with time and medication. However, what she thought unusual and most troubling was that Herbert had been admitted under a false name: 'Wolfgang Smythe'."

"And what seemed quite strange to *me* was from that day onwards, for about 5 years, Herbert was always referred to as Wolfgang."

Marie reached into her purse and pulled out a notepad with a pen attached. She jotted down the name. "Yes, very strange … I wonder why?"

Evelyn shrugged. "I think it was Herbert's undertaking. Maybe he didn't want the Osterhagen name associated with mental illness. I'm not sure."

"So, he did, in fact, recover from his illness?" Marie queried.

"I believe so. Lloyd and Bertha spoke little of him for some years, until about 5 or 6 years later. Herbert came back to Petrolia for another visit, and after that the name 'Wolfgang Smythe' was never mentioned again."

The two women sat in silence. Marie glanced at her watch. "Evelyn, thank you so much. I wish I could stay longer. I'm afraid I need to go and get ready for my trip."

She wrote down two phone numbers on a blank sheet from the notebook, tore it free and handed it to Evelyn. "Here, if you think of anything else … the top number is where I'm staying now. The other one is my cell phone number. You can reach me with the cell number any time, other than when I'm on one of my flights. I should be on my way to London in about 2 hours." She picked up her purse and slid the notebook inside.

"Can I help you clear away the dishes, Evelyn?" Both women got to their feet.

"No, no. I won't hear of it." Evelyn motioned towards the direction of the front door. Marie stepped forward and took hold of her friend's arm, and together they headed back to the front entrance. "Evelyn, you've been quite helpful, and I'm definitely not going to forget those tea biscuits anytime soon."

A bright smile lit up Evelyn's face, as she stood in front of the door. "I wish I could do more. I know you have such a great responsibility, Marie."

Marie gave Evelyn a warm hug. "You've done your best, and I really appreciate it." As she pressed against Evelyn's' frail body, she felt a single teardrop fall upon her shoulder.

"Evelyn, when I get back, do you think we can visit more often?"

"I would like that very much." They broke their embrace. Evelyn turned the handle and opened the front door.

She faced Marie. "Now go! Find Edward and be with your family. They need you. Go!" Her tear-filled eyes glistened, with the kindest of smiles.

Marie felt touched by kindness as she made her way down Maple Street and turned off onto the small paved path, which ran along the side of a schoolyard fence and led to Derek's street.

As she walked briskly, she retrieved her cellphone to message Carmen, and began to mentally outline her visit with Evelyn.

She turned up Derek's driveway. Once in range of Wi-Fi, she would type and send it on Facebook Messenger.

Derek would be home soon. Marie glanced at her watch again.

Oh, I'm leaving in less than 2 hours, and I don't even have a bag packed yet. Hurry! Hurry!

FORTY-TWO

MONDAY, MAY 5, 2014. 6:30 P.M.
JERUSALEM, ISRAEL

It was all set. Carmen sat at the desk in her hotel room. She had just returned from the front lobby. Meira had received a photocopy of Aaron's licence, which she in turn forwarded to the car rental agency with a request to put Aaron on the car rental contract. Carmen had signed a document, and another was sent to Aaron's hotel for him to sign and fax to the agency. They could now use the car to pick up her mom. Carmen smiled as she remembered how she had cleared things with Chief Inspector Claude Gadgét after he personally picked them up from the front of the restaurant.

She laughed softly as she recalled the inspector's exact words after she asked him if he thought it would be okay for Aaron to drive the rental car.

"Aaron Dekr ... if you so much as get a parking ticket in this city, I will have you brought in, and you will witness a side of me you do not want to know about! Yes, I guess that will be okay. Clear it with the rental company." Now, Carmen was convinced Inspector Claude Gadgét really did like Aaron. Together, they had spent a good 20 minutes or so explaining to Claude Gadgét what Aaron had learned in Petrolia, where he worked, and why he was here. The inspector would, by then, have read a full profile on Aaron, and Carmen thought he probably liked what he read.

Also, Carmen thought the complexity of the case heightened Inspector Gadgét's interest. He wanted to see this through.

The two men dropped Carmen at her hotel, and then they carried on to Aaron's hotel. She felt confident the inspector would make sure from that point on the police would be involved and aware of any new occurrences. This turn of events made Carmen feel much better, having both the police and Aaron showing their full commitment to helping find her father. *I can't help but wonder if it will be enough ...*

A Facebook alert sounded from her phone. She grabbed it, and read the message from her mom:

> *Carmen, getting ready for the trip. I talked with Evelyn 1.5 hrs ago. Might be a possible family connection to a residence in Jerusalem. Evelyn doesn't know an address and can't remember her neighbour's maiden name, which the place would likely be listed under. I hope Derek can help us find a name after he returns from the London airport. Another point seems odd. Don't know if this matters. Evelyn said sometime in the 1980s Herbert was institutionalized and diagnosed with a form of acute psychosis for about 5 years. What's strange is he was admitted under the false name Wolfgang Smythe. Evelyn never understood why. That's all for now. Luv you. <3 Mom.*

Carmen sent 'heart' and 'hug' emoticons back and signed out of Facebook. She read the message over again. Herbert Osterhagen was proving to be a growing mystery.

She began thinking things over. *If Derek can find a name to go with the residence that would be a good lead, but it could take time.*

What about the name Wolfgang Smythe? Why change your name? It must be difficult. Perhaps not wanting to be tagged with a mental illness? Seems extreme ... What about illegal activity?

Perhaps ... let's see ... Wolfgang—common German name, I think. Is Smythe a German version of Smith? Great, narrowed it down to under a million people. I bet it's even common here in Israel.

Carmen did not want to let this name go for some reason. *I think I might've heard at least part of this name not too long ago ... Where? University?*

Memory recall is something every student in university knows only too well, and Carmen was no exception. This is certainly a highly-required skill and critical during exam times. Almost automatically Carmen's brain began operating in an efficient recall mode. She started by analyzing hundreds of faces and names. Synaptic neural connections were linking by the thousands, and her concentration became extremely focused.

Her thoughts pulled her attention away from University and the hundreds of names and faces associated with her studies. At first, she resisted, thinking this would be the most logical place she might have heard the name 'Wolfgang' or 'Smythe.' But she knew when to change direction. Through years of intense cerebral study, Carmen developed a systematic thought process. How many times had she sat with an examination question in front of her, where she believed the answer was on the 'tip of her tongue'? Carmen developed a method of dealing with this situation, and it worked most times. The method required determined tenacity. She learned how to let her thought process guide her and would not let go or give up. If her brain needed to make another million synaptic connections to bring up the answer, so be it.

With a single-pointed, intense focus, which required exceedingly high amounts of stored glucose, she would force her brain to extreme levels of activity to find the answer.

Carmen entered that realm now. She breathed deeply. Her oxygen requirements were increasing. Her eyes closed as she allowed her thoughts to make the directional change. Visions of Jerusalem flashed by. She saw the Old City: people and places, her hotel, many faces, sights, and sounds. The museum flew past once, and again. She turned back and went inside. Rachel/Jessica was there and then gone. The police were inside. Amnon Gosser helped her. Then back on the street. Amnon helped her again. *Amnon ... No, his name is Amnon ... wait, did he say a name? When? I was drugged. That was a tough time. I can't say.* Carmen tried to leave Amnon and follow the street away from the museum, but she came right back again. Amnon was so kind, helping her to go inside. *'My father ... we need to help my father.' Wait, what did Amnon say? Did he say a name ... what name?*

Carmen was immersed in a zone where everything around her ceased to exist. All that remained was the kind face of Amnon Gosser with his lips moving in slow motion forming a name. From somewhere deep within the regions of her brain, the hippocampus retrieved the information, and by way of over a thousand connections delivered the name to her cerebral cortex with a blinding flash. *Jessica Smythe! Amnon Gosser said her full name! Jessica Smythe is Rachel Cohen—Wolfgang Smythe is Herbert Osterhagen, her grandfather!*

Carmen opened her eyes. She sat transfixed as her deep breathing receded. She needed to slow her brain activity, which was in need of a controlled 'cool down'; otherwise, as she knew from experience, a headache would be readily forthcoming. Carmen let her thoughts come naturally and at an even pace.

After a few minutes, she got up and walked around the room, stopping at a window to look out over the city below. Enjoying the view, she took in the sights and relaxed for a time before allowing her concentration to resume. *Another twist in the road. Where will this one lead?*

Carmen pondered, staring out the window. Finally, she walked over to the desk, picked up her cell phone, and messaged Inspector Claude Gadgét, briefly outlining this latest finding. She ended the text with a questioning emoticon and a smiley face, laughing at herself. *Well… duh, you could've saved yourself a major brain workout. Did you think to ask the inspector what Jessica's last name was in the first place? That undoubtedly would've been one of his first questions of the investigation.*

She smiled. *At least I'm staying in shape!*

After the text had been sent, Carmen dialled Aaron's cell number. He picked up on the second ring. "Hi, Carmen here." She paused as Aaron responded. Carmen continued, "I'm hoping you might be able to accompany me tomorrow morning. I want to go back to L.A. Meyer Museum. I acquired some additional information, and I would like to ask Amnon Gosser, the curator, a few questions." There was another interlude.

"Okay great … I will try to get us an appointment. I'll call you back with a time. I can fill you in on the walk over there tomorrow. Bye."

Carmen let out a long breath as she set her phone down. She felt much safer, having Aaron nearby to help. She might be able to relax a bit now. A nice hot shower, supper, and early to bed sounded very appealing.

As she headed to the bathroom she expressed a hopeful thought, "I think we're getting closer. Hang in there Dad."

FORTY-THREE

MONDAY, MAY 5, 2014. 3:00 A.M.
JERUSALEM, ISRAEL

"The Comte de Saint Germain…" Edward remained utterly transfixed. His entire world had stopped moving. Nothing in his entire life experience could have ever prepared him for this. He noticed Herbert's lips moved, but at first no sound came. He was breathing, and his heart was beating. His hands clung to the door frame for support.

"Edward. Edward." He heard his name being called. "Edward … you have gone pale. Are you alright?"

Edward focused. He saw alertness and concern on Herbert's face. "I'm okay … What you've implied … I'm startled. I … I don't know how to respond."

"I can detect you know the famous name. It does not surprise me."

Edward took in a deep breath. He let go of the doorframe. "The name Saint Germain is spoken of by thousands, perhaps millions, of people with great reverence, in association with renowned great masters of the world: Jesus of Nazareth, Buddha, Shri Krishna, Muhammad … Can this be true? What does this mean?"

"I cannot say, Edward." There appeared an almost serene composure emanating from Herbert Osterhagen as he spoke. "I think I can safely assume by your reaction that you, like me, have passionately studied the illustrious history of this great man. The Comte De Saint Germain was a man whose name is synonymous with the word *mystery* like perhaps no other in recorded history."

Herbert stopped in what Edward thought to be a moment of deference. "What does this mean …? I suppose it is part of a great mystery. The mysterious existence of one of the greatest intelligent minds the world has ever known. How can I say more?"

Edward did not respond. He could not remember feeling more humbled than he did now. The two men sat in silence.

Herbert continued. "A particular highly admired gentleman, partially commissioned, then entrusted to our family a timepiece of great importance. The Osterhagen legacy is above all else about honour and respect. Because of these virtues, the man's name was never revealed outside of the family until now. However, as a tribute to this great man, the first model designed and built by the newly formed Osterhagen Watch Company of 1882 was named in his honour."

An overwhelming sense of self-doubt enveloped Edward. Should he believe this? He felt an urge to cry. *Why me?* He thought of the word 'coincidence', but it did not seem to fit.

The green book? In his mind, it lay open before him. *'The I AM Discourses of Saint Germain.' Is that it … my devotion to the book and what it means to me?*

He looked up. Herbert was intently fixated on him. "Can you understand, Edward? The Osterhagen family were chosen, and we failed. But now the timepiece has been returned to our care. Perhaps we can still fulfill our calling."

Edward swallowed hard and took in a breath. "Herbert, part of me wants to believe in what you're saying with all my heart.

Another part of me is frightened and disbelieving … How can I possibly be a part of this?"

He hesitated. "I need to clear something up … The story you told me when I came to your shop in New York. The story about a 'great queen' and how the watch I found was destined to be with another timepiece. Is there any truth in the story or was it simply a ruse to get me here?" Edward watched Herbert carefully and noticed a slight shift in his demeanour.

"I am afraid the only truth is that I needed to act and think quickly to protect both the watch and you from three very aggressive men. At least one of them—the one who hid on the other side of the archway—carried a gun. They were dangerous people."

Edward stood pondering what Herbert had said. He asked another question. "So … you hoped I would be able to figure out the meaning of the story, which I barely managed to do. It seems to me you bet on a long-shot that I would travel such a great distance just to get some information on an old watch. If it hadn't been for my daughter Carmen being in Israel, I don't think I …"

"It was your shirt …" Herbert cut in.

"My shirt?"

"Yes, a crest on the breast of the shirt you wore. I spotted it through your partially unzipped jacket, and the shirt looked relatively new."

Edward could not hide his confusion. "My shirt?" He was caught off guard and tried hard to remember what shirt he had worn to New York.

"It had a crest from the University of Tel Aviv, Israel."

In a flash, Edward remembered what he had worn and why he had chosen that particular shirt. As if reading his mind, Herbert continued.

"My reasoning was this, Edward. You are not of the age to be attending university in a foreign land. You could, however, have a son, daughter, or maybe a grandchild who is. Hence the shirt, and judging from the new condition of the garment, their international studies may be current."

Herbert paused. He explained, "Many people, when they choose their daily apparel make their decisions by conscious or subconscious promptings. I can tell, Edward, you are passionate about timepieces. You came to my watch shop to gain information on something you were excited about. Would it not be reasonable to assume you were wearing that particular shirt to try to symbolically share an experience with someone who believes in your passion and is close to you, but could not attend because he or she is attending school in Israel?"

"Credit where credit is due Herbert; your perception is remarkably accurate." Again, Edward was in awe of this old watchmaker.

"Ha, Edward!" Herbert smiled. "I think sometimes coincidence, luck or maybe a 'higher order' can play their hand as well, to even the odds."

Herbert became more serious. "Those men took me completely by surprise. There can be only one explanation for why they tried to steal the watch. Somehow they discovered information on its internal movement."

Edward added, "Before I came to your shop, a man with a subtle Caribbean accent arranged a meeting with me. He offered to buy the watch for several thousand dollars. He said he represented another person. I obviously turned the offer down. I had suspicions about him and felt he knew more about the timepiece than he was telling me."

Sadness fell over Herbert as he gave a thoughtful nod. "Rachel … Rachel—my granddaughter—lost her parents in a boating accident in the Caribbean. She was swept overboard from a small sailboat in a storm and managed to swim to shore. Her parents were not so fortunate. Her mother was my only child." Herbert became silent.

Edward witnessed hurt in the old man's eyes. He waited for a bit and then spoke softly. "I'm sorry, Herbert."

Herbert took in a deep breath to compose himself. "Rachel must have made a copy of the information contained in the handbook ... Perhaps she left something in a hotel room, or possibly information was found on the boat by a diver; she was under great stress ..." He shook his head. "It is the only thing that would tie these men to the pocket watch. She would never have disclosed that information intentionally."

Herbert lowered his head and turned his hands up in a gesture of despair. "I do not understand this technological age, Edward. Our ability to transport and connect information is incredible, but I fear it comes with a price. Rachel has amassed vast stores of information, a great deal of it in electronic technology fields. Much of the skilled watchmaker's craft will be lost to robotics, and rightly so if a better timepiece is created. However, I witness these modern technologies moving forward so swiftly, I fear we might be forgetting what is most important." Herbert went silent. The intensity of his blue eyes appeared to increase.

"Integrity Edward ... Integrity, built on honour and respect. I feel Rachel cannot yet take these virtues to heart. I believe her time will come, however. And that time will be when Rachel truly understands her heritage and the legacy of her name: *Osterhagen*."

Edward walked towards Herbert, as Herbert turned away on his stool to face the workbench. He stopped right behind him. Herbert looked down at the assembled watch lying before him as he spoke. "My dear Rachel placed the pocket watch in a secure place. Soon we can ..."

Edward gently placed a hand on the watchmaker's shoulder. "Herbert, I'm very concerned. Rachel should have regained consciousness by now. I fear she may ..."

"Edward ..." Herbert cut in. He kept his head down, facing away. The room fell silent, save for the ticking of the clocks.

Edward glanced down to see teardrops, one by one, splatter across the workbench. Before him was a great sorrow, one that had been passed through many generations.

Minutes passed. The teardrops ceased, and Herbert finally spoke, but he did not turn around. "I want to apologize, Edward." Edward lifted his hand from the old man's shoulder. "I was not honest with you. I know you are a good person. I had no reason to fear you, and ultimately because of fear, I summoned you to Jerusalem."

"I want you to know, Rachel never wanted to deceive you. I asked her to help me. She agreed, but there was never any mention of the drugs being used."

"Rachel never wanted to be Jessica Smythe, granddaughter of Wolfgang Smythe. I believe the only reason she complied was because it gave her the opportunity to be close to the Osterhagen-Saint Germain watch. A timepiece she loves with all her heart."

Edward did not understand. *Wolfgang Smythe?*

"No ... Rachel never learned completely about the robbery. She was ever so grateful the Osterhagen-Saint Germain watch was not taken when 'The Queen' and so many other priceless timepieces were stolen in that robbery of 1983."

"I could never bring myself to tell her the truth."

"It was our agreement that only two timepieces be removed to be later returned to the museum."

"Sadly, I learned firsthand, there is no honour among thieves."

Herbert picked up the watch lying in front of him, the same watch that only hours ago Edward had witnessed him assemble. He began to dismantle it.

FORTY-FOUR

THE EVENING CLOSED IN again. Nothing changed in Rachel's condition. Most of Edward's time was spent at her side. He held her hand, sometimes speaking softly to her. He offered words of encouragement and what the future might bring for her. He hoped she might be able to meet his wife Marie someday and that led to some family stories which provided a kind of solace for Edward.

Herbert got progressively worse. Neither of them had consumed any food for well over 24 hours, plus with the stress of Rachel's condition and no medication for Herbert's mental infirmities, his situation did not look good. Edward sadly observed Herbert disassemble and reassemble the same watch part repeatedly, but always with a steady hand and a sharp eye. Herbert would occasionally talk, mostly about Rachel, or as if he was speaking directly to her. He appeared to be at times completely oblivious to the fact that she lay unconscious in the next room.

Edward still had many questions. He tried throughout the day to engage Herbert, but for the most part he would not answer. Often, he barely even acknowledged Edward's presence. Towards the late afternoon, he seemed to forget who Edward was and asked him repeatedly if he needed to have a watch repaired.

For Edward, the situation became depressing. He tried several more times to get help, yelling out the window and the front entrance, but no one came. He kept thinking, hoping, someone would hear him, but his voice failed him repeatedly.

He was losing energy. Soon they would need to start rationing water. There were only two or three bottles left in the cooler. It was harder for Edward to be optimistic. He knew Carmen would have the police searching for them, but what did they have to go on … and why the false names? Wolfgang Smythe, Jessica Smythe. What did it mean? Herbert talked of the robbery in 1983 when 'The Queen' had been stolen. Was he involved? *That would be incredible! How else can this extraordinary man surprise me?*

Edward finished lighting the candles in the kitchen and attended to the ones in the corridor. *Herbert Osterhagen is an enigma if ever I've met one. What might the police know of him? What with the false identities and this remote, probably long forgotten, flat in the Old City?*

What an incredibly unfortunate, desperate situation this had become, the result of an odd chain of events orchestrated by some unseen hand of coincidence. The surrealism was overwhelming. Would prayer ultimately be his only recourse?

"How can life be so unfair?" Edward heard himself say as he lit the two candles in the room where Rachel lay. The flickering flames cast darting shadows across the walls. As he looked again to Rachel, he wondered how such a young, intelligent, vibrant woman could ever be deserving of what had befallen her.

Edward sat again on the hard folding-chair, leaned forward and took Rachel's wrist. He measured her pulse rate and quickly registered it to be a bit faster. Her breathing remained shallow. Placing a hand on the pale white skin of her forehead he confirmed no fever. Her skin felt cool to the touch.

He held Rachel's hand in his and thoughtfully gazed down at her. *Why? Why is this so important? Is there some kind of intrinsic debt hanging over the name Osterhagen?*

Edward learned from Herbert that Rachel lived in Jerusalem and worked at the museum to be close to the Osterhagen-Saint Germain watch. She lost both her parents in a tragic boating accident, and deep down she must know her grandfather, a mentor and perhaps her closest lifelong friend, was also slipping away. Edward sensed how the Osterhagen watch would be so important to Rachel, possibly a lifeline for her. He held fast to a similar aid himself. Many years ago, he saw himself as a shy, young man, lacking the self-confidence required to function in an adult world. Yes, the green book; 'The I Am Discourses' by Saint Germain became his lifeline. He believed, he held on to the words, and gradually his life changed for the better.

Edward sat in quiet contemplation. Somehow the existence of one unique man from hundreds of years past brought him and Rachel together at this very moment in time.

Startling Edward from his thoughts, Rachel's chest suddenly heaved with several sharp breaths. Then, came a quiet settling.

Her pulse stopped. The young woman, Rachel Cohen, was no more.

FORTY-FIVE

THE OLD WATCHMAKER wore his loupe over one eye and hovered over an assembly of watch parts when Edward walked up behind him and gently placed a hand on his shoulder. "Herbert, you need to come with me to the other room."

Herbert sensed Edward's solemn demeanour. A quick flash of fear registered in his eyes. He took off the loupe. Setting it down, he got to his feet and followed Edward out through the open door, down the hallway and into the other room where Rachel lay.

Edward stepped back. "I'm so very sorry, Herbert." Quietness prevailed as the old man looked at his granddaughter. The candle flames cast dancing shadows across the cold stone walls, which brushed soft broken light across Rachel's pale complexion. Her facial expression seemed peaceful. "Rachel passed away just moments ago, Herbert … I wish I could have done more."

Herbert sat in silence, as minutes passed.

Edward sensed a heaviness all around him. He could feel his own heart beating. He quietly left the room.

An hour had passed when Edward returned. Herbert remained at Rachel's side. As he approached the cot, Herbert turned to him. Edward expected to see tears and puffy red eyes. That is not what he saw.

Looking up at him was a lost soul, a broken man, who had changed. Hope, love or passion, something of immense value, had diminished within him.

Herbert turned back to Rachel and spoke. "I would ask for your forgiveness." Then there came silence.

And, let it be noted, these were the last words ever spoken by Herbert Osterhagen.

FORTY-SIX

MONDAY, MAY 5, 2014. 4:00 P.M.
PETROLIA, ONTARIO, CANADA

She never gave any thought to the possible state of his automobile. Marie had made 'great strides' in changing Derek's home and living conditions. She felt a sense of pride in her accomplishment, which now appeared a little over-rated. How could she have been so short-sighted?

The inside of this vehicle is disgusting! Marie thought to herself upon opening the passenger door of Derek's Mazda 5.

"Derek, I don't think there's any room for my two small bags!"

Derek leaned in to look from his now opened driver's door with a sheepish grin on his face, as he focused towards the rear of the interior. He surveyed piles of boxes, bags, and electronic parts stacked from the floor to the seats and almost touching the roof. Interspersed amongst the assorted collection were empty pop cans, coffee cups, and donut bags. The passenger seat and floor between the seats appeared to be the information centre, where books and what resembled shop-manuals and charts were stacked precariously.

"I'm guessing you weren't expecting company." Marie smiled, and then wrinkled her nose after spying an upside down, empty pizza box stuffed in amongst the debris in the back seat.

"I guess there's still room for some improvement?" He chuckled. Marie offered a stern look in response.

Derek thought of a bright side to the situation. "Maybe when you get back we can get together for some spaghetti and discuss a revised plan. Me, you and Edward."

Marie nodded but did not alter her expression. "Sure ... I like the sound of that, but I'm wondering if you might be forgetting something?"

A puzzled expression formed on Derek's round features, which he somehow managed to further accent by arching his eyebrows into a circular shape and pursing his lips into an 'O' pattern. It made for an almost playful symmetry on his features. This was a face you just could not be angry with. "I forgot something? I ..."

"The salad ... let's not forget the salad! It's the most important part of the meal."

A big grin spread across Derek's face, which turned a deeper shade of red as he laughed. It took only moments for tears to form in the corners of his eyes. He did calm himself a bit quicker than he might have liked, however, when he noticed Marie still retained a serious expression.

"Marie, does Edward have to eat salad all the time?"

Marie softened considerably. "*Have to* are not the words I would use." Marie laughed softly. "Edward enjoys helping to cut up the vegetables. I think it gives us time together ..." Marie could not resist the sudden hurtful feeling that enveloped her.

Derek sensed her sorrow and quickly tried to lighten things up. "Edward's a cool guy. I guess eating salad can be cool. Yea ... maybe I could help too, but right now I need to remove those books from the seat and ... let's see, I'll take my golf clubs out of the back to make room for your bags."

Before Marie could respond, Derek leaned in farther and with one fell swoop of his outstretched arm, pulled the entire pile of books and papers off the seat, dumping them on top of the already large mess on the floor between the seats. "There we go, Marie. Make yourself comfortable, while I stash the clubs in the garage and put your bags in the back."

Umm ... A proper gentleman. Kind of makes a lady feel special.

Derek was gone so quickly he missed the expression of awe on Marie's face. Perhaps it was for the best. He probably would have misread it anyway.

Derek had the golf clubs relocated in the garage and Marie's bags stowed in the back of the Mazda 5 in the same amount of time it took her to inspect the passenger seating surface and determine if the accommodation offered to her came anywhere close to her standards and did not pose any serious health risks. She was not overly convinced. *I'm doing this for you, Edward.* At least her choice of clothing would help; long denim jeans and a nylon windbreaker would prevent any actual skin contact with the seat fabric.

Marie did a quick mental checklist, as she seated herself in the small van. She shifted her purse on her lap in search of the seat belt insert.

Derek closed the hatchback and walked up to the open door. "Ok, we all set?" His face beaming brightly.

"I'm pretty sure ... Yes, I think so." Marie got her seatbelt buckled and began a quick search in her purse for hand sanitizer.

"Okay then ... Got to do a quick check on the cameras and motion sensors, then back out in a flash to lock up, and we're on our way!"

Marie had a bemused look as she watched Derek scurry back through the front door. *Cameras, motion sensors ... Soon to be added: a retina scanner. Oh, and of course the drone!*

He came back out and closed the door behind him. Derek was a bit faster than Marie with the fingerprint scan.

He probably has it trained by now.

She lightly shook her head as Derek eventually turned the key in the lock. Marie let her gaze wander around the sleepy neighbourhood and yawned.

"Right ..." Derek arrived back at the driver's door and started to climb in. "Let's hit the ..."

"Derek!" Marie interrupted. "I think I hear your house phone ringing!" They stopped to listen. Derek was half sitting, half standing.

"Yup, you're right. That's the house phone."

"We need to answer it. It might be important!"

"I'm on it!" Without batting an eye, he hurried back to the front door and expertly implemented the unlocking procedure.

Watching Derek at that moment, Marie became pensive. He did not frown or utter a cuss. There seemed to be no sign of inconvenience at all, even as the phone continued to ring uninterrupted in its finite terminal countdown.

Marie, on the other hand, squeezed her purse and tapped her foot with impatience. She even mentally scrolled through a list of descriptive words she might like to share with Derek if he did not hurry up.

A few more agonizing seconds and he went through the doorway. *These electronic geeks ... They must be wired differently. Their passion for new technology is like ... I don't know ...* Her thought pattern took an unusual direction ... *A caring mother and her child. Unconditional love?* The thought made Marie almost burst out laughing, but she checked herself quickly as Derek came back outside and rushed up to the car.

"It's Evelyn, the woman you said you spoke with earlier. She has something for you that might be useful!"

"On my way!" Marie released the seatbelt, hopped out of the vehicle and headed down the driveway in haste. "I'll take the path. Come get me in five," she called over her shoulder. "Her home is on the north side of Maple Street, a few houses west of where the path comes out." She began jogging.

"Sure!" Derek called out after her. Marie already moved out to the street. Derek watched her access the narrow-paved path. He turned and headed back to the front door to begin the lock up sequence again. Doing it over and over again was something he did not mind. Derek smiled. In fact, he enjoyed it.

MARIE ANXIOUSLY RANG the doorbell. On the third ring, the door opened, and she met Evelyn's smiling face. It was evident the elderly woman had been busy. Her hair was dishevelled, and there were smudges on her dress, but her eyes were bright and sparkling.

"Oh, I'm so glad I reached you in time, dear."

"You did. Just in time, actually. My friend Derek and I were literally getting into the car to leave for London." Marie gestured in the direction of Derek's house. "He'll be here shortly to pick me up."

Evelyn held up what appeared to be a postcard. "I remembered about this …" She handed the card to Marie. "But I wasn't sure if I'd kept it all these years."

Marie observed the card. On the front was the clear golden image of the Dome of the Rock in the Old City of Jerusalem. She turned it over. The back was filled with legible, neat handwriting, done with a pen. First, she read the date:

April 5, 1985.

She continued reading.

Dear Evelyn: Having a wonderful time. We are walking our feet off! So much to do. We are off on a 3-day Galilee Tour tomorrow. Weather is beautiful. Can't wait to tell you all about this exciting place. Love Bertha. P.S. Miss you!

Marie studied the addresses and postage stamp. Of course, the card had been sent to Evelyn's address on Maple Street, Petrolia, Ontario, Canada with her P.O. Box included, but it was the 'sent from' address that really interested her. The writing had remained perfectly legible. She read it carefully: *Jordan Block Jerusalem, Israel 50326.*

She looked up. "Evelyn, this could be important. Thank you so much." Marie knew that most likely hours had been spent searching through many boxes of old memorabilia to find this information.

But, even as difficult as it must have been for her, Evelyn beamed. She was in a place where she loved to be.

Marie understood the radiance. It came from helping others in need, and there is no greater feeling.

They hugged each other, as Derek pulled into the driveway.

No words were needed. As Marie pulled away from the house and watched Evelyn wave, a thought of gratitude came to Marie. *I think we have angels helping us.*

FORTY-SEVEN

TUESDAY, MAY 6, 2014. 10:00 A.M.
JERUSALEM, ISRAEL

"The L.A. Mayer Museum for Islamic Art." Aaron read the name on the building wall as they approached the museum.

"I like the architecture."

"I do as well. I did some reading last night. Set in this beautiful, predominantly Jewish suburb of Jerusalem, it opened to the public in 1974." Aaron glanced up again at the engaging building. "I think it must have been quite challenging on many different levels, what with this location offering this kind of cultural heritage."

Carmen gazed at the building thoughtfully. "We hear so much about the negativity … The fighting and hatred between the Jewish and Palestinian people in Israel, yet right here in front of us is something positive."

Aaron nodded. "It's wonderful to witness how some people believe in peace and are trying to break down walls between cultures that have existed for over a thousand years."

Carmen stopped on the sidewalk directly in front of the building and focused on it. Aaron joined her. "Do you think there is hope Aaron?" Carmen retained her position.

He responded, "I chose to be an environmentalist. I have hope for myself and others to try to make the world a better place. So … yes I do."

"Sometimes I feel the big picture, or overall goal, can be overbearing or too painful," Carmen remembered the kind doctor's face from 2 days ago. She continued staring. "Maybe hope is best realized in smaller fragments."

They both stood quietly with their thoughts. The museum seemed to take on a new role. For these two young adults, it was teaching them.

Carmen spoke first. "I want to tour this special place with my mom and dad. I would like for you to come too."

Aaron turned away from the building towards Carmen. She caught his movement and looked at him. "I would like to. Thank you for asking me."

"Okay, let's go! I want to introduce you to a really nice man." They started off towards the entrance.

———◆———

"Thank you, Amnon, for taking the time to meet with us." They were standing inside of the front doors.

"You are most welcome, Carmen." Amnon Gosser smiled.

"I would like you to meet a friend—Aaron Dekr. He is helping me try to find my father. Aaron, this is Amnon Gosser."

"Pleased to meet you, sir," Aaron extended his arm and the men shook hands.

"You speak with … a subtle Caribbean accent, Aaron?"

"My home is Grand Cayman."

"Ah … a beautiful island, or so I have heard. It is on my list to visit."

Carmen added, "Aaron's an environmentalist, Amnon. He is currently contracted in Grand Cayman. Maybe we could talk Aaron into becoming a part-time tour guide for us. I'd love to visit too."

"You would not need to talk too much, Carmen." Aaron laughed. "That just so happens to be one of my favourite pastimes. I'm afraid I can't help wanting to show off the island."

"I think we all embrace our own unique treasures we love to share." Amnon took the opportunity to make a sweeping gesture denoting the beautiful museum. "But right now, please tell me how you are feeling, Carmen. I am concerned. Has there been any news of your father? I have been in contact with the police several times, but I have not learned anything on the whereabouts of your father or Jessica. It is troubling for me."

Carmen answered. "I'm much better now. I received a good prognosis from the hospital and after some rest I seem to have bounced back. I will admit, though, my dad's disappearance is not easy for me. But my mom is flying in later today. Aaron and I are going to pick her up in Tel Aviv. For sure, it's gonna help."

Carmen paused. "We acquired some new information, but nothing concrete."

"I am happy that you are better. You said on the phone you were hoping I could answer some questions. Let us go to my office where we can talk in private." Amnon smiled and gestured towards the required direction. "If you will follow me, thank you."

Carmen and Aaron fell in behind Amnon. They continued past the first small corridor, which led to the small sitting alcove where Carmen and Edward had first met with Jessica.

"I am looking forward to giving you a personal guided tour of the museum, Carmen and Aaron," Amnon said as he walked along at a good pace.

"Thank you, we would like to come back and bring my mom and dad."

"Of course, of course ... that would be excellent. Here we are." Amnon turned to the next archway on his right and stood holding on to the door handle of his office. "Please, right this way." He opened a finely crafted, dark stained hardwood door, and they passed into a relatively large office space.

The room was tastefully decorated in a modern style, and the walls were adorned with Islamic paintings and a beautiful wall tapestry. One oversized window let in natural light that spilled onto Amnon's cluttered desk and into a small sitting area off to the right. Two walls were filled with floor to ceiling bookshelves. The room was the office of an engaged, studious man.

"Please take a seat. Be comfortable." Amnon gestured towards the sitting area where four comfortable modern chairs surrounded a big natural wood coffee table. "I could request of my secretary to bring us some refreshments…Coffee, tea perhaps?"

"No thanks, Amnon, I just finished breakfast at the hotel." Carmen insisted.

"Thank you, no," Aaron added.

"Well, perhaps I can be of some help?" Amnon turned and closed the door. "What is on your mind, Carmen?" He walked over to a chair and seated himself. Carmen and Aaron sat down as well.

Carmen began. "I said we learned some new information… Well, a few things; the latest came from my mother, early in the evening yesterday, a short time before she left for her flight here to Israel." Carmen stopped for a moment to get arranged in her head the best order to outline the necessary facts to Amnon. He politely nodded and remained silent until she continued. "The information is concerning identity. The identity of Jessica … Jessica Smythe and her grandfather. We found out for certain, and the police now possess this information as well, Jessica Smythe is not really Jessica Smythe." Carmen detected a start in Amnon.

"Oh …?" His brow furrowed with his head slightly cocked.

"I need to go back and briefly fill you in on the events which preceded our meeting here, so you can get a better understanding. As you're aware, my father and I were admitted here into the museum by Jessica. As I told you, we were hoping to gain some information on an old pocket watch my dad had found and purchased during a garage sale in our hometown in Canada ... This part you already know."

Amnon nodded.

Carmen continued. "Before this, however, is the reason we came here in the first place. Shortly after finding the watch, my dad went to visit a watchmaker at his shop in Brooklyn, New York, to try and learn more about the timepiece. A jewellery store owner had recommended he go there. Well ... this is where all the trouble began."

Carmen took in a breath and resumed. "At their meeting, the watchmaker spoke in a covert manner and secretly used an image on his laptop to warn my father that he was in great danger and would need to run for his safety. My dad was given a signal to leave, but not before the old watchmaker gave him a sort of a riddle about the pocket watch he had found. Later, after thinking about it, my dad realized the watchmaker actually asked him to come to this very museum in Jerusalem."

Amnon showed intense interest. "Was your father in danger?"

"He was. One man hid inside the shop, and two more waited for him outside. They chased him, but fortunately he managed to escape unharmed with the watch. He then doubled back about an hour later and saw the flashing lights of police cars surrounding the shop. A dead body was taken and loaded into a waiting ambulance."

Amnon leaned forward. "The watchmaker?"

"That's what we assumed. Later we found our assumption to be false."

"Oh." Amnon leaned back. "It appears this pocket watch is extremely important to some people. Please, if I may ask now while I am thinking of it ... What did the watchmaker say to your father that led you both to come to this museum?"

"Yes ... If I can get it right, she said, 'Your pocket watch was created during the reign of a great queen. Also, another watch was created for the great queen. Then... the great queen suffered an untimely death, but the great watch remained. The queen lost her throne. The queen has regained her throne. It is to this place you must take your watch.'" Carmen let silence envelop them. Amnon stared at her, but she knew he was not actually seeing her.

Lost in thought, he waited, and then finally spoke. "The queen ... I think I understand." He pondered for a bit and asked. "Carmen, I would like to know the name of the watchmaker in New York?"

"Herbert Osterhagen."

Amnon raised his brow in a quizzical expression. "Osterhagen ... an heir to the Osterhagen Watch Company of Glashütte Germany?" A slight smile crept across his face. "You know ... we have an Osterhagen timepiece right here in this museum. It is possibly the only one known to still exist, and it is an extraordinarily beautiful watch." He paused. "It was Jessica Smythe's absolute favourite of our entire collection. She used to take it out from its case and polish it almost every time she came here."

Amnon smiled and continued. "It has been at the museum well before I started working here. And most fortunately, it was surprisingly not part of the theft which occurred in 1983—the robbery that saw the 'Queen' removed—as described by Herbert Osterhagen in his unusual story to your father. Yes, indeed a most clever analogy to solicit someone interested in watches to come here," Amnon added.

Aaron sat forward and gestured towards Carmen. "It is evident now ... and we can tell you with certainty why Jessica would be so fond of the Osterhagen watch in your collection."

Amnon turned from Aaron to Carmen as she took the cue from Aaron and began speaking again.

"Soon after the incident here at the museum, I found out Jessica also worked at a restaurant in the Mishkenot Sha'ananim District. I remembered her having fancy napkins with carriage logos on them. After a search online, I discovered the logo came from the Montefiore Restaurant. I went there and luckily spotted Jessica. I followed her and noticed she took something from a cubby in an employees' room. There was a different name on the slot she used. I made a mental note of the name."

"Jessica left the building, and I tried to catch up with her, but when she recognized me she ran, and I couldn't catch up." Carmen stopped and took in a deep breath as if she might need more air, as the exhausting chase replayed in her mind. She kept the memory to herself.

Carmen continued. "So, to quickly summarize, I went back to the hotel, did some research on the name below the slot on the cubby, and found some graduation pictures from the Alfred Helwig School of Watchmaking. My conclusion: Jessica Smythe is really Rachel Cohen, who holds a degree in watchmaking and is the granddaughter of Herbert Osterhagen. Also, stated in the same newspaper article, after Herbert, Rachel is the sole remaining heir of the long ancestry of Osterhagen Watchmaking originating in Glashütte Germany."

Amnon quietly nodded his head in acknowledgment. "This is so intriguing. Jessica's, or Rachel's I should say, own family designed and built the beautiful Osterhagen timepiece. I am amazed ... Yet what you just said explains a feeling I had about her; I always thought the love she had for horology was quite extraordinary."

Amnon looked from Aaron to Carmen. "But why all the secrecy ... Why the false name? What on earth is going on here?" He stared at the two young adults.

Carmen gave him an auspicious look. "I'm hoping that together we might find the answers to those very questions."

There was no hiding the incredulous expression forming on Amnon Gosser's face.

FORTY-EIGHT

"I'm thinking maybe you could talk a bit about Rachel's involvement with the museum, and we can add some information that came from my mom. Possibly together we can get a better understanding," Carmen implored.

Amnon took a moment to settle himself before he responded. "Yes … I will go over this again, even though I have been over this quite thoroughly with the police. You certainly should want to talk about this … Anything I can do to help." Amnon gave Carmen a warm smile.

"Thank you," Carmen said. Aaron nodded his approval.

Amnon continued. "Jessica Smythe, as I have known her to be, worked here as a volunteer for approximately four months. She was talented in the field of horology. I always suspected Jessica might have had some training, but I never heard. I guess now this makes sense, seeing as she possesses a degree in horology under a different name. However … beyond that, Jessica was quite friendly and intelligent—a truly charming young woman."

Amnon reflected then resumed. "I must also tell you, I witnessed a passport as proof of her identity. It is requirement by the museum that all employees—even volunteers—present proper identification to work here. On several occasions, I asked Jessica if she would consider working at the museum full time. She politely refused."

Concern on Amnon's face was evident. "It deeply saddens me that somehow Jessica is involved in a criminal investigation."

He put his hand to his forehead, gazed downwards and sadly shook his head. "You tell me Jessica has been living under a false name and that she ran away from you. I just do not understand what is happening here."

Carmen could see his discomfort. She thought it would be the right time to present the latest information. "We believe Jessica's assumed name was taken or produced by her grandfather Herbert Osterhagen. My mom recently found out from a friend of Herbert's now-deceased stepsister that Herbert Osterhagen himself was institutionalized in the 1980s for a mental condition under the false name of Wolfgang Smythe."

"A family connection …" Amnon looked up.

"Yes, does that name mean anything to you, Amnon?" Carmen asked.

Amnon thought for a moment. "No, not the name … But Jessica did mention to me once in casual conversation that her grandfather had also done some volunteer work for the L.A. Mayer Museum. I remember asking her when it was, as perhaps we had met. She said the time was around the mid-1980s for a duration of about half a year. I then assured her that indeed it would not have been possible for us to meet, as I did not start working here until 1990."

Aaron leaned forward and asked a question. "Is it possible, Amnon, that employment records might still exist for the period of the mid-1980s?"

Amnon addressed Aaron. "No, I am afraid not. Fifteen years maximum. They all would be shredded by now."

They sat in silence and exchanged looks. Carmen shrugged her shoulders. Amnon responded to her gesture. "Normally I would advise you to talk to some of the other staff about Jessica, but in all honesty, she was a rather shy girl who kept mostly to herself, and as I am sure you understand, the police were quite thorough in their interviews with everyone. Nothing turned up." Amnon raised his hands up in despair. "I do wish I could help you more. I am sure the police are doing their best." Amnon slowly rose from his chair. Carmen and Aaron did the same.

As they exited the office, they noticed people had arrived and were beginning to tour the exhibits. More staff members were on the floor as well.

Walking back towards the door, a thought occurred to Carmen. She turned towards Amnon Gosser. "I said I would really like to return here with my mom and dad and Aaron to go through this beautiful museum … For now, though, may we take a look at the Osterhagen watch?"

Amnon stopped. A bright smile appeared on his face. "But of course! I apologize, yes … Yes, we were discussing watches. I am not thinking clearly. Yes, let us take the elevator down to the lower level where our magnificent timepiece collection is. Please follow me!"

In a matter of minutes, the elevator door opened and Amnon escorted them quickly to a beautiful room filled with a magnificent array of fine clocks, pocket and wristwatches. He came to a stop beside a single glass case mounted on an octagonal shaped wooden pedestal. A bright halogen light installed in the ceiling directly above illuminated the display.

Amnon extended his hand in an open gesture towards a beautiful gold pocket watch, arranged on green folded velvet.

Both Aaron and Carmen leaned in close to view the sparkling antique. Its absolute beauty was not lost on either of them. From the intricate engraving, to the perfection of its symmetrical design of the cream coloured dial with its golden hands, numerals and indices—this was a watch of finely crafted precision.

"Gorgeous!" Carmen looked up to Amnon.

"Breath-taking," Aaron remarked.

They both stood straighter as Amnon gestured again. "This timepiece has been with the museum since … I believe 1983. Let me present to you the Osterhagen-Saint Germain pocket watch!"

Carmen involuntarily took in a sharp breath. "Saint Germain?"

FORTY-NINE

It came over her again: the feeling—a feeling that enveloped her with the colour green.

"Carmen? Are you okay?" Aaron looked at her with concern. "You seem a thousand miles away."

"I'm okay … The name Saint Germain. It's déjà vu … like I've been right here before, exactly the same. Everything. And the colour green, the velvet—like yesterday with your shirt …"

"Oh … yes, I know that feeling. I have experienced déjà vu before, and I find it strange too." Aaron offered a reassuring look.

Amnon briefly glanced their way and smiled. He stared at the Osterhagen watch in thoughtful contemplation.

"Aaron, do you know of Saint Germain?" Carmen asked him. The unsettling sensation had abated.

"Well … I read a bit. Saint Germain: A highly distinguished, most mysterious man whose recorded history is centred mainly through the 16th century in various parts of Europe. If I remember correctly … he is rumoured to have lived for hundreds of years. He was a confidant and advisor to Marie Antoinette." Aaron paused and turned from Carmen to Amnon.

Carmen was impressed. She raised her eyebrows in acknowledgement of his historical prowess.

"Yes, most intriguing," Amnon started. "And if I might add, he was apparently an accomplished alchemist, astonishingly fluent in dozens of languages. And, as you said, a consultant to the French and other national courts. It is rumoured he possessed 'The Elixir of Life' and perhaps lives to this *day!*"

Following up, Carmen said, "Comte De Saint Germain—a pretty cool guy on all counts." She smiled, "No pun intended."

"My father obtained a book many years ago that he recites from daily. I think it's become somewhat of a religion for him. The book, 'The I Am Discourses' by Saint Germain, is a positive book, basically about using affirmations to meet life's challenges and to enhance one's own spiritual awareness. For him, I think it was like trying to be part of an overall universal consciousness."

Carmen stopped, and a soft smile radiated from her. "He would read to me from that book when I was young. And … I don't think those readings will ever leave me. I call upon them often."

Carmen's face registered a subtle uncertainty. "The déjà vu thing … with the colour green. The book was a green hardcover, and now the name—Saint Germain. I can't say for sure, but it's like there might be a connection …"

"A connection that might be more advanced than we can understand." Aaron offered Carmen a warm smile. "I often wonder, is there a place where science and spirituality connect?"

The simple question stirred up a tremor deep inside. Did the true answer lay dormant in her? Carmen focused on Aaron and somehow knew no answer would be expected. She only nodded. They were both in the same place.

Suddenly, Amnon spoke. "Might only be a coincidence …"

It was evident he had been completely in his own world, lost in thought. He continued gazing at the watch. "But it appears the Osterhagen was admitted to this museum the same year the Queen and many other artefacts were stolen. The timepiece must have been procured either right before or right after the great robbery of 1983. I would like to find out how the L.A. Mayer Museum obtained this watch. You see, we do keep some records indefinitely, those which outline transactions regarding catalogued artefacts, past and present. They are stored in a fireproof vault."

Amnon reached into his pocket for his cell phone. Carmen and Aaron looked to him as he spoke and then back to each other in mild surprise as he began conversing rapidly. He spoke in Hebrew and Carmen could just make out the gist of his conversation: the name Elizabeth, 1983, his office, hurry, and of course, *'toda'*, or thank you.

"I am sure you might like to see the 'Queen' while you are down here now. She is in the next room, but I would like for us to get back to my office. My receptionist will have the folder on my desk by the time we return. I am quite anxious to peruse it."

In a short while, they were all again seated in the curator's office with the door closed. This time, however, Carmen and Aaron sat in two leather chairs positioned opposite from Amnon as he sat at his desk, perusing an open folder that lay before him.

"This is an easy time-frame to locate—definitely a busy year for the museum." His head remained down, scanning each page carefully as he flipped through them one by one. "Let us see … April, March, more for March …"

Carmen and Aaron stayed quiet and watched with anticipation. Amnon used his index finger to swiftly track his visual scrolling. His lips moved in silence and sometimes he mouthed words as his brain rapidly processed information with a visible and honed efficiency. Pages were continually flipped. "February … February … January … January … in January … yes! Here we are…

> *pocket watch—Osterhagen. Description and Origin: 17th Century, Glashütte Germany.*

Yes, further description … Here we go:

Received: Jan 15, 1983. Acquired from: Anonymous donation. Received and signed for:"

Amnon stopped and peered over his reading glasses at Carmen and Aaron. "Received and signed for by none other than Wolfgang Smythe! So ... that puts this precisely three months before the museum robbery."

"Wow ... so ..." Carmen shook her head. "Is this possible the donator and the receiver of the Osterhagen watch are the same person?"

"And possibly tied to the museum robbery of 1983?" Aaron offered.

"But why ..." Carmen put her hands on either side of her face. "Why would Herbert, or anyone for that matter, donate their most prized possession to a museum and then later possibly steal it? What's the sense in that?"

Amnon stood. He began pacing back and forth, lost in thought. "Perhaps ..." He stopped for a moment, and then his pacing resumed.

The only sound in the room was his shoes clicking across the floor. It sounded like the hollow ticking of a clock, a clock ticking back through the years and stopping that night in 1983.

He turned and faced Carmen and Aaron. "The alarm system was deactivated on the evening of April 15, 1983." Amnon stared directly at Carmen. "The security guard on duty had remained on the other level."

Carmen's muscles tensed. She made no sound, as Amnon addressed them both again, "But could it be ... Could it be that the robbery on April 15, 1983 did not go exactly as planned?"

FIFTY

"What do you mean?" Carmen looked confused. She glanced over to Aaron. He held a similar expression.

Amnon certainly had their attention. "I need for you to understand my reasoning. For that, I would like to tell you some history and to share with you some personal insight about museums."

He remained standing while he talked. "You have both viewed the Osterhagen-Saint Germain watch. I believe the words you used to describe it were 'gorgeous' and 'breathtaking.' Up until recently, neither of you had even heard of the Osterhagen Watch Company of Glashütte Germany. Yet with your own eyes, you witnessed proof of design, craftsmanship, and a precision worthy of recognition, ranking it with the finest timepieces our world has ever produced. How is this so?"

Amnon took a few steps away and then turned and paced back to his previous spot. "I can tell you; making a timepiece like that is no simple task. It requires knowledge, desire, great skill and both financial and tangible resources. If any of these attributes are lacking, it just cannot be accomplished. Watchmaking goes back hundreds of years. Yes, hundreds of years through our world's turbulent history. If we were to make a list of horological companies founded in the 15th or 16th centuries that managed to remain intact from conception to present day, the number on our list would be zero. Although yes ... There have been names preserved or resurrected, if you will, but the fact is it has been impossible to sustain this level of mechanical perfection through time. And, sadly enough, it is not for lack of trying."

"The Osterhagen Watch Company shared the same fate as all the others. And, undeservingly I believe, it has not as of yet been reborn." A subtle sadness appeared upon Amnon's features.

"Please, allow me to elaborate; the small town of Glashütte in Saxony or East Germany, as it is known today, is in the Ore Mountains and was a farming community until silver ore was found there in the 16th century. The population increased and flourished until the silver ran out in the early 1800s. The government tried to bring prosperity back to the region by creating a suitable industry for the area. Watchmaking became that industry—the making of pocket watches specifically. People were trained and money was invested. Ultimately, through dedication and hard work, in the short span of maybe 60 or 70 years, the small region became a world-class producer of high-end pocket watches. The Osterhagen family was an integral part of this achievement."

Amnon stopped for a moment and smiled at Carmen and Aaron. "I think I stand before two attentive students who show great patience."

Carmen laughed. "This lecture is not only concise and to the point, but also interesting."

She turned with a smile to Aaron, who added, "I think you are reminding me just how much I miss listening to a good lecture. Please go on."

Amnon resumed. "Moral obligations prevent me from continuing unless I speak the name Ferdinand Adolph Lange. He is the true father and founder of the watch industry of Glashütte Germany. He was put in charge and responsible for the foundation of this grand endeavour. I would encourage you both to take some time when it is available to you to read about this remarkable man."

"So ... to move on through some challenging times: the Osterhagen Watch Company suffered a devastating fire around the year 1883, shortly after a major investment in a new building and a great deal of expensive machinery. They tried to recover on a number of occasions, but they faced too many obstacles."

"By the turn of the century, wrist watches came into fashion, mainly because of the onset of World War I, and the Glashütte industry was not sufficiently prepared to adapt. Next came the Great Depression, which saw the fall of many companies. By the early 1940s during World War II, some of these businesses in the region were supplying pocket and wrist watches for enlisted persons. But towards the end of the war, Glashütte was devastated by bombing attacks. The final and most devastating blow was the occupation of East Germany by the Soviets in 1951."

There was no mistaking the grave expression on Amnon's face. "This was a dark time for watchmaking in Germany. The legacy of many great watchmakers had already been lost to history. The Osterhagen family was just one more of these casualties."

Amnon stayed silent. His smile slowly returned. "You undoubtedly know of the collapse of the Berlin Wall?"

Both Carmen and Aaron nodded.

"Well, after reunification in 1989 ... If I may coin a phrase, Glashütte 'rose up from the ashes' and today its future looks quite promising."

He paused briefly again. "Often, outstanding talents of the watchmaker get passed down through the generations, and with the right circumstances, these God-given gifts are able to flourish again and a grand watch company of 'old' can be reborn."

Amnon came from around his desk and stood beside Carmen. He stretched out his left arm, allowing his wristwatch to emerge from under the cuff of his shirt and suit jacket. "This is an early

'Lange 1' purchased with utmost respect in 1994 from the newly re-founded watch company of Glashütte Germany: A. Lange and Sonne."

The yellow gold glistened, framing a champagne coloured dial, which contained three smaller offset dials, golden lancet-shaped hands, and an oversized date window. A finely crafted brown leather strap with a gold pin buckle held it to Amnon's wrist.

Carmen commented immediately. "It's beautiful."

But it was Aaron who was overly impressed. "I did not know this reformed company created what is now one of the few iconic wristwatches of the world in such a brief timespan." Aaron did not hide his enthusiasm. "And now, I am looking at one of the early ones."

He leaned over, almost in front of Carmen, and gently touched the underside of Amnon's wrist, prompting him to rotate the watch for some different views. He finally leaned back and looked up. "Thank you for sharing this with us. It is an honour for me."

Amnon smiled gracefully. "All was not lost for Glashütte, and much has been preserved."

Amnon let his jacket sleeve come down to cover his watch as he turned away and walked behind his desk. "This brings me to something else I would like to impart to you, a few things I learned about museums over the years."

Amnon walked over to the window located on the back wall behind his desk and towards the sitting area. He stood and stared out at the view. He began, "Working in this business for quite some time and as curator of this museum, I like to think I do my best to keep up to date and informed. Even on an international level, I study the many facets within this domain of treasures and artefacts: how they are acquired, restored, preserved and displayed. Also, the trading, buying, selling, appraisals, estimates, history, cultural value … the list goes on. For me, it is a fascinating world."

Amnon turned from the window. He brought both of his hands to his heart. "A real blessing for me; I learn new and old, and amazing discoveries every day." He glanced downwards in a humble gesture. A silent thank you formed on his lips.

"Sometimes this beautiful place seems to be part of a different world. A world of museums—somewhat sequestered from society. It is like different rules apply here. We are not so much subjected to the laws of economics, stock markets, supply and demand pricing, taxes, and import/export tariffs are often waived as well. Society itself protects us from harmful outside elements. They preserve us. Why?"

He looked intently towards Carmen and Aaron and gave each a lingering gaze. "Lest we forget our past! And protect us well they do, often with state of the art security systems that can rival many banks, but every so often a flaw in the armour is exposed, and a burglary is committed. We then might ask ourselves why might a part of the same society which protects us, steal from us."

Amnon shifted his focus back and forth between the two young adults. Neither responded, so he continued, "Most surely the answer must be money. Many would agree. However, I can tell you, with certainty, it is not."

Amnon held their attention entirely, but with the intensity rising, and Amnon's frequent pauses contributing to his eloquence, Carmen felt the need for a fleeting moment of mental diversion: *The great master thief brilliantly overcame impossible odds and made off with the museum's most precious treasures. The world's greatest detectives are on the case: Sherlock Holmes, Ellery Queen, Hercule Poirot, Claude Gadgét ... Claude Gadgét? But they're stumped. It's Carmen James who discovered the answer! She ...*

Amnon focused directly on Carmen. She blushed. "You see, to steal from a museum is to steal from the cultural soul of the people, and surely you can never really steal these treasures, as they are not for sale."

He smiled. "Most would not sell their soul."

Amnon continued. "When we label an artefact valuable, irreplaceable, or priceless, the object becomes an icon. It transcends the restraints of monetary currency to the lofty pedestal of divinity. Shrouded in an aura of pure prestige, it resides untouchable; unattainable to all who can but gaze upon it with awe and wonder. The Breguet No. 160, also known as 'The Queen', is one such treasure."

"A mastermind thief stole her, along with many other iconic pieces, from this museum in 1983. I believe he did this to fulfil a need. A need for a level of greatness, which would come from proving he could do *that* which had been ruled he could not do ... You see?"

"As I said, these iconic treasures cannot be sold easily, and as I am sure you both know by now, the burglar, Na'aman Diller, was never exposed, and the case remained unsolved until 2008. It was only after his death when an attempt was made to sell some of the artefacts, that the Queen, and almost everything else, was returned to the museum." Amnon smiled.

"So ... going back to when it happened; at the very least, this robbery attracted a great deal of international attention. And I must insist, attention in our world today can be a valuable commodity."

Carmen shifted noticeably in her chair. "You said maybe the robbery didn't go as planned?" She gave Amnon a questioning look.

Amnon nodded. "Yes ... Here is my hypothesis. Please remember, I explained the alarm system had been turned off on the night of the theft and the security guard had opted to stay on the upper level of the building for an extended amount of time."

"Could not this breach of security have been most easily accomplished by someone on the inside ...? Might Herbert Osterhagen, using an assumed name, been volunteering at the museum for reasons other than interest and generosity?"

A brief silence filled the room; even the sound of their breathing was subdued. Amnon answered his own question. "I think the answer may well be yes! And the motive, quite simply, was to attract attention to the Osterhagen watch: The Saint Germain."

"Yes!" Aaron straightened in his chair, "Like you said, attention can be a valuable commodity. Attention generates interest and interest can mean money. In Herbert Osterhagen's case, investors to help build a new Osterhagen Watch Company?"

"Exactly," Amnon paced again. "I wanted to show you the watch on my wrist as an example of the human spirit ... The watch industry of Glashütte, at least in part, overcame great adversity to rise up again as a world class watchmaking leader, but this did not come without help and substantial financial investments from other sources. Sadly ... the Osterhagen name is now all but forgotten."

Amnon added. "Did Herbert Osterhagen initiate a plan to make the world remember? I imagine the answer is yes ... But I think he was double-crossed." Solemnness prevailed on Amnon's face.

"Wow ... I think I get it!" Carmen clasped her hands together. "You said the Osterhagen was *not* stolen that night. And Herbert wanted it to be! Somehow he wanted it paired with the famous Breguet Queen ... Brilliant!"

Amnon nodded. "My guess is Herbert Osterhagen set up the heist for Dillard. A sum of money would have been paid, with the stipulation that only two watches be taken: The Saint Germain and the Queen, to be returned at a later date. What would be the outcome of that ...? Immediate international attention on the world's most valuable watch, along with another beautiful timepiece, the Osterhagen-Saint Germain."

"But alas ..." Amnon raised his hands in the air as he glanced between Carmen and Aaron. "In the end, a thief is always a thief."

Carmen shook her head in wonder. Looking imploringly at Amnon she felt a familiar tightness forming in her lower abdomen, the same feeling she always felt when she heard of human tragedy. It subsided and was replaced by a thoughtful sadness. She asked Amnon, "Herbert Osterhagen ... He was institutionalized after this, a broken man ... who could not return the Queen to her rightful place. Is he a bad person?"

Carmen sought guidance from Amnon Gosser. He did not speak, but his eyes displayed wisdom and understanding.

It was a sad realization for Carmen, until a thought flashed into her mind that made her jerk. Both Aaron and Amnon witnessed the involuntary twitch. She held her breath and stared wide-eyed, first at Aaron, and then to Amnon.

Her words came out softly but slightly jumbled. "Jessica ... I mean Rachel ... she ... her grandfather ... Herbert Osterhagen ..." Carmen appeared almost confused.

"He was planning to do it again ... Wasn't he?"

FIFTY-ONE

TUESDAY, MAY 6, 2014. 5:00 A.M.
JERUSALEM, ISRAEL

I<small>SOLATION, FORCED UPON</small> the human condition, can lead to many negative ramifications; lethargy, depression, even hallucinations are not unheard of in extreme situations. Edward had read enough over the years, both fiction and non-fiction, to have at least a layman's perspective of this looming condition which somehow found its' way into his life and now threatened his very existence.

Through most of the long night he paced between rooms wanting to keep somewhat active, but this was becoming difficult because of his lack of caloric intake. He would be starting his third day without food, and they were down to under 1500 ml of drinking water, which he now began to ration. Even the candles would only get them another couple of days, with moderate use.

Edward sat on the fold-up chair in the kitchen. Only one candle burned: a good-sized cylindrical type he took with him from room to room. The door to Herbert's watch room was open enough for him to keep watch. He moved the small cot from the far empty room to beside Herbert so he could lay down when needed, and Edward witnessed him using it for a couple of hours throughout the night. But for the most part, Herbert worked in silence on the same watch movement over and over again. He did not speak or look up. There came no response to the several attempts made by Edward to engage him in conversation.

If help did not arrive soon, Edward somehow knew Herbert would not last long. This would, however, not be the result of dehydration or malnutrition. Edward honestly believed he was watching a man die of a broken heart.

Edward's eyes welled up again as he stared at the back of Herbert's hunched over figure. Crying offered him a short-term mental release, which helped, but he also knew this depleted his body of fluids, and ultimately dehydration could take his life.

Edward wiped his eyes with the back of his hand and forced his brain to think. There were still things required of him. *Rachel.* Although he dreaded this frightening thought, it would be necessary to tend to her body soon. He remembered reading somewhere that a human body starts to decompose rapidly after about 48 hours. He had a bit of time yet.

He planned a course of action. A body bag of sorts would need to be fashioned out of the bedclothes. He would tie them together, and there was a good quantity of sphagnum peat moss—commonly used for the compost toilet—he could stuff into the bag. The absorbent would help contain odours. Then he would seal off the door with strips of cloth cut from clothing he had found in the dresser. With the window left open, Edward hoped this would be enough.

Edward turned and gazed at the open window behind him. *Well, if it isn't, maybe a smell escaping through the open window will attract attention.* This thought started him thinking.

A dim light filtered in from the dawning of a new day. Edward would try calling out again for help soon, although he knew his voice would let him down in mere seconds. *Can I do something to signal out from the window … Something someone might notice? An S.O.S. sign … write the word 'help' on something?* His ideas did not seem practical, though; either they would be hard to read or the language barrier would come into play.

He sat quietly, and after a short time he smiled briefly, *A Canadian Flag ... Just the thing for the police who might be looking for me.* He shrugged his shoulders. *Gee, how dumb of me ... I forgot to bring a Canadian flag along. I'll have to try being a little more patriotic in the future.*

The humour of Edward's personal joke was short lived. The joke did, however, prompt a wonderful memory, and this offered him a much-needed respite from the hurtful conditions surrounding him.

Edward closed his eyes and went back many years to his own backyard. He was with his daughter Carmen. She was 6 years old. They had built a tree house together, which took them most of one full summer. It consisted of a single room with, of course, a stepladder, or 'staircase' as Carmen liked to call it. They constructed a small table and four little chairs which served well for the many formal tea parties that followed.

Perhaps more importantly, Carmen learned all about hammers, nails, screws, saws, levels and measuring tapes. Edward remembered feeling sad when the day came to hammer in the last nail. He made sure to give Carmen the honour, and when she handed the tool back to him with a big toothless grin, he remembered saying, "I think what we need is a Canadian flag to hang proudly over the door. And it just so happens, there's a brand new one in the garage," and off he hustled to get it.

Upon returning, Edward placed the flag in a holder he had previously mounted above the door.

As they both leaned back to admire it, Edward was surprised at Carmen's response. "Daddy, I think it's the wrong colour!"

"But why Carmen, you know it's a real Canadian flag."

Carmen turned and gazed out over their backyard. "Because ... look ... Canada is a beautiful green!" With that, she took off down the staircase and ran into the house. She returned a few minutes later carrying a bag full of brushes and craft paints.

Edward recalled standing in the tree house looking out over the backyard and then back into the tree house. He watched her diligently painting and wondered how he ever got so lucky. Quietly, he recited the phrase, "God is all around them, but they do not see it." This would always be for Edward a moment in his life when he believed he saw true perfection and no words were needed to describe it.

Edward marvelled at Carmen's show of independence. She would grow to be a strong and intelligent woman, her own person.

The transformation was complete. An hour later their Canadian flag had changed from red and white to green and white.

Edward opened his eyes, and a single tear rolled down his cheek. Carmen still, to this day, used her tree house when she came home. It was a special place where she could go to be alone, and sometimes she would give her flag a fresh coat of green paint. Edward knew the flag represented something important for Carmen. What exactly, he could not say, but he did know she was fiercely proud of it.

For Edward and Marie, the flag became a regular part of their home landscape; something they rarely thought about. It was always there and always would be.

Edward felt an aching desire to lay his eyes on it again. He rose up from his chair with purpose.

Taking hold of the candle, Edward left the room and made his way down the hall, stopping in front of the room where Rachel's body lay. He had not been back inside since he and Herbert left earlier. Edward opened the door and went inside, first glancing at the covered body and making a quick mental note that the cot needed to be moved by this evening. He could not continue sleeping on the cold cement floor or the uncomfortable chair. His muscles were reacting in a painful way.

But at this moment he was acting on a plan. He seemed to recall, noticing some items in the dresser, which now interested him.

Edward walked over and opened the second drawer. Sure enough, after rummaging through some clothes, he found what he wanted.

Next, Edward focused on a box containing mostly toiletry items. He picked it up and popped the lid off a dry deodorant stick, which looked unused.

A disturbing thought popped into his head. *How long has it been since my last shower?* He focused on his watch and the date window, then the hour hand and did the math. *Oh ... not good.*

Okay ... if there's any left over. Edward grimaced.

MIDDAY FOUND EDWARD sitting on the stool in the watch room, perusing the pages of the old leather-bound handbook. Herbert remained sitting, hunched over his workbench. It was sad and ironic for Edward to see how insignificant the book had become. One day earlier, this same book indirectly caused the death of Rachel Cohen.

No response came from Herbert as Edward turned the pages. He could not help but wonder if he would ever get a chance to again see the strange watch described in this book. Edward could only hope. He felt quite certain Rachel or Herbert did not hide it in the flat. He had searched every square inch of the place.

His eyes roamed around the room and settled on the far end of the workbench. He spotted Rachel's purse. It had not been touched since he had searched for a phone. Edward wondered if there might be some information in it that would help answer his remaining questions. *Does anything really matter now?*

Edward did not condone going through someone else's personal belongings without consent. Shrugging his shoulders, he put the book back on the workbench and stood. The number of things that mattered now had been reduced to very few, and it was becoming desperately hard to find constructive thoughts to occupy his mind. He was fighting depression, and never in his life was this symptom such a formidable opponent. He picked up the purse and left the room. Herbert did not appear to notice.

Sitting on the foldout chair in the kitchen and opening Rachel's purse, Edward could not help but think of Marie. If this was *her* purse in his hands, he was convinced that somehow freedom would be possible. Marie's bag was not only a purse but also a survival pack. This had been proven to him time and time again. All Edward ever needed to do was ask and then wait patiently until the desired item was retrieved. And almost miraculously it did not seem to matter what was needed. Of course, all the usual things were on hand: pen, pencil, toothpicks, Band-Aids, Kleenex, notepad, envelope, headache pills, water, energy bars, etcetera. *But … anything. I don't think Marie ever let me down.*

A tender, loving smile crossed his face, as he remembered the time Marie had utterly amazed him when Carmen's stroller had broken. The family was walking some trails in a wooded area close to home on a beautiful autumn day, admiring the fall colours. They were about 5 kilometres from home when suddenly Carmen's stroller broke. Edward knelt down and diagnosed the problem. A bolt and nut that held the rear axle bracket in place had separated. Upon close inspection, he determined the nut came loose and fell away some time ago, allowing the loose bolt to work its way out causing the axle to lose support, rendering the stroller inoperable. Edward remembered telling Marie they would, unfortunately, have to carry both Carmen and her broken stroller all the way back home.

Edward chuckled as he recalled Marie's response. Her exact words were easy to remember, one of Marie's common well-practiced phrases, "Well, let's see if I have something in my purse."

"No dear, not this time ... I understand you've got a lot of stuff, but I need tools and a specific part, a ¼ inch standard-thread nut to be exact. And well ... I guess this might sound kind of degrading, but I'm thinking you don't even know what that is."

Her reply had a sharp edge. "You're right on both counts, Edward; I do not know what a ¼ inch standard nut is, and yes, your comment does sound degrading. But for my daughter's sake and mine, I think I'll have a peek in my purse anyway. Okay?"

"Sure ... just trying to save you the effort." Edward remembered his reasoning; he thought himself to be on solid 'guy-turf'. He would remain calm and silently go over his soon to be needed 'I told you so' comment. He wanted to make sure it came out smooth and polished, with the perfect balance of 'guy' knowledge and wisdom. He had leaned back against a tree, conspicuously tapping his foot as the minutes passed, and for the most part tried to look cool while he mentally rehearsed.

Marie had her head buried, completely absorbed in her rummaging task. When she finally straightened up, a small rectangular plastic case was clasped in her hand. Edward remembered her words, "This is a little tool kit I got from Avon. I thought I might need it, what with Carmen's tricycles, toys, strollers ... stuff like that."

Perhaps a bit too sarcastically, Edward responded, "That's great Marie ... Does Avon have a good line of tools? I'm looking forward to performing a test run on them, but I told you, I also need some par ..."

Marie cut in sharply with some added information that gave Edward the slightest twinge of uncertainty. "There's some extra space in the case, so I took it to that old, original hardware store in town. You know ... the one you like? I asked the owner, Charlie, to fill up the spaces with spare parts that might come in handy if something broke when Carmen and I were out."

Edward held Rachel's purse open and peered into it, but he did not focus. He could still see the small rectangular plastic case he had opened, almost like it was yesterday. Contained inside: a small crescent wrench, a pair of pliers and a little multi-bit screwdriver. In two channels along each side was a neatly packed assortment of items stored in tiny plastic bags: copper wire, tie wraps, and electrical tape. In two of the bags were a variety of small, common sized nuts, bolts, and washers. He found a ¼ inch standard-thread nut, and also a ¼ inch lock washer he used to prevent the nut from ever coming off again.

In less than 5 minutes they were back on the trail enjoying the beautiful scenery.

Edward smiled, as he gazed around the kitchen reflecting back to that afternoon. He had been 'put in his place', and deservingly so.

However, the most amazing part of the story for him was how his lovely wife managed, after all these years, to make sure he never lived it down. She did not verbalize any harsh comments to get even, nor did she rebuke him for his chauvinistic attitude. On the contrary, she only smiled and complimented him on the excellent job he had done fixing the stroller. No, Marie exercised patience. She focused on the long term, and he did not have to wait much time for her intent to be revealed.

Most would agree, the innate ability of human beings to observe, hear and understand the slightest nuance from other people is quite remarkable. This capacity is further enhanced when two individuals are involved in an intimate relationship. In many cases this becomes subtle, powerful communication, which can extend beyond the limits of the spoken word. Such was the case between Edward and Marie, and Marie understood this concept very well.

From that time on, every time Edward asked his wife if she might have something in her purse, he was confronted with an ever so subtle change in her demeanour. Following her initial response of, "Well, let's see if I have something in my purse …" She would pause, and an engaging smile would form with the ever so slight raising of her eyebrows, as she added two additional words, always with direct, sparkling eye contact: "*shall we?*"

Flashing neon lights could not present a clearer intent from Marie. Her point would never be forgotten. Edward accepted his fate with an understanding; sometimes it is good to be reminded of a personal shortcoming in the hope of self-improvement.

Edward gazed into the purse he held, in preparation for the search at hand. He heard Marie's voice say, "Let's see if we can find something here ... *shall we?*" He saw the sparkle in her eyes. He missed her desperately.

———•———

EDWARD LEFT THE ENVELOPE for last. He had spent 15 minutes carefully examining the contents: keys, an assortment of make-up, a pen, sunglasses, etcetera. Rachel's wallet was straightforward, with the usual things: driver's licence, health and credit cards and some money. He really did not know what he hoped to find, other than possibly the lock combination written out somewhere. No such luck.

Lastly, Edward grasped the previously opened envelope. Turning it over, he saw *Rachel* written in ink across the front and stamped in the top left corner was:

The Israel Museum, Archaeology Department
Ha-Palmakh St 2
Jerusalem, Israel

Edward held it open and extracted the contents: a single sheet of paper folded in thirds, which he unfolded, revealing a typed letter in English that read:

May 2, 2014

Rachel:

I am glad to be able to help you out on this. After receiving the handbook you left for me I took it to the lab. Fortunately, I was able to work with it during some spare time. I did the material date analysis you requested. Here is a summary of my evaluation:

My conclusion: (unofficially, of course) - the materials used in the construction of this handbook (leather, paper, ink, glue) date back approximately 40-60 years.

The pages have been artificially yellowed with a tea/heat method and the leather was reworked with sandpaper/shoe polish. The book has been altered to make it appear to be much older than it is.

I hope this will be of assistance to you in your research project.

Yours truly, Steven Reis

Edward sat in quiet contemplation, holding the letter in his hand. After some time, he refolded the page and tucked it back into the envelope, which he folded in half and put in his pocket. He looked up through the kitchen archway and open door of the watch room to the back of Herbert in his usual posture.

He tried to recall what Rachel had said right before the accident when she tossed the book on the bench; *"Opa, I needed to take this for a couple of days ... I wanted to find out some information. I know now what you have done, and I think I can understand ..."*

Now Edward was trying to understand. He sat for many minutes, immersed in thought.

Finally, he picked up the purse, stood and made his way out of the room and across the hallway. He stood motionless in the doorway of the watch room and spoke softly to the back of the old watchmaker. "The watch ... the story ... the book. This was your design. It *was* and has *always* been—just *you*!"

"Herbert Osterhagen, why is this so important?"

There came no response, only silence.

"I wish I could understand."

FIFTY-TWO

TUESDAY, MAY 6, 2014. 10:30 A.M.
AIR CANADA FLIGHT #741
TORONTO TO TEL AVIV

THE NON-STOP FLIGHT from Toronto to Tel Aviv was approximately 75 percent complete when Marie awoke from a fitful sleep feeling tired and with a sore neck.

Several attempts at sleeping netted her about 2 hours total. This was not enough, but it was the best she could do under the circumstances. Being alone on this long journey made the situation suddenly real. Marie was worried, even frightened. She knew that her past years of emergency training as a registered nurse was helping to prevent a mental breakdown. As well, to try and stay calm, she focused on seeing Carmen. At least they still had each other to hold on to.

Marie wondered what they might be able to do, as she began a series of neck stretches in an attempt to loosen her taut muscles. They had the postcard with the address, and although there was no guarantee anything would come of it at least it was something.

Unfortunately, nothing had shown up when she tried to search the address online while waiting in both the London and Toronto airports. Derek also said he would do some searching on his own as soon as he got home and contact her once she arrived if he found anything. Of course, the police would have their resources as well. Marie wondered if it had been a mistake—to not email Carmen immediately with the address. Derek and she talked it over and decided that being past midnight in Jerusalem, it might be better to wait. Maybe she was overreacting, but 'mother's instinct' warned her of Carmen going out in middle of the night and searching. Marie was just trying to do her best and stay optimistic.

She sat in an aisle seat on the right side of the plane, more towards the back. The seat to her right was vacant. A younger man occupied the space next to it, the window seat. He wore headphones, for most of the flight. Marie thought he was into his own music thing and quite shy, although he acted polite, and smiled frequently.

Her eyes scanned forward to the centre section of the plane. Many of the male passengers wore the traditional Jewish yarmulke: a small decorative cap worn on the crown of their heads, and some women wore a hijab: a veil covering the head and chest. Still, others were dressed in the strict Arab custom of a jilbab: a long, loose fitting garment with a niqab face cover.

Marie made an effort to study some of the many diverse customs of Israel, once Carmen had made her decision to do her graduate studies in Tel Aviv. This would be her second time visiting. The first trip for her had been somewhat of a culture shock. Seeing parts of the country was like going back in time several thousand years to a different world, whereas other areas showed modern urban development with leading edge technology 'second to none'. Marie thought the diversity to be spectacular and she was interested in learning more about this intriguing part of the world where her daughter now lived.

Marie, however, could not help but have concern for Carmen's safety. The turmoil in Israel, with its political unrest and violence, played heavy on her mind. Both she and Edward expressed concern, but Carmen had been adamant about studying at the University of Tel Aviv. Nothing would dissuade her. She thrived on the challenge of learning in a place where human existence had been so difficult for thousands of years. This was Carmen's first year, and admittedly they already were seeing in her a more mature demeanour. Marie believed the people of Israel were known for their well above average intelligence and a serious commitment to the future. The country was a natural fit for Carmen.

Marie reached into her purse, which sat on the seat beside her. Retrieving the postcard, she stared at it. Marie turned it over and over in her hands. Finally, after several minutes, she looked up and scanned the passenger cabin again until her gaze settled on a person who before had briefly caught her attention. He sat on the right-side aisle seat in the centre section, two rows ahead. He wore the traditional Jewish yarmulke. Marie thought he was in his early 70s, and his dress was business-casual.

Earlier when Marie stood to stretch her legs and used the facilities, she noticed the man was alone with several books piled beside him on a vacant seat. It made Marie think of Carmen and her studies. A thought had popped into her head concerning the man and his books, which had now developed into somewhat of a plan.

Marie stretched upwards in her seat to have a better view. She observed he had reading glasses on and was engrossed in a newspaper. She glanced upwards at the overhead console. The seat belt signs were off, and the flight currently felt smooth and stable, with no turbulence. Glancing down at her watch, she estimated they would begin their descent in about 30 minutes.

She paused and took in a deep breath. *Ok, it's now or never … Let's do this.*

Marie rose out of her seat into the aisle and approached the man with the postcard clutched tightly in her hand. When she was next to him, she leaned down and softly touched his arm. "Excuse me, sir."

He lowered his newspaper, turned and looked up towards her. Marie was met with a calm expression and gentle, inquisitive eyes. "Yes?"

She could tell his English was good. "I'm sorry if I am troubling you … I was hoping you might know some information; I would like to find out about Jerusalem. I … well … I noticed all your books and thought that perhaps … intuition I guess …"

He immediately addressed her uneasiness with a kind smile. "Of course, I would be happy to try and help. I do know Jerusalem well. I have lived and worked there most of my life." He folded his newspaper and tucked it beside him. "Please tell me what information are you seeking?"

He put Marie at ease. She took in a breath and began. "I'm going to meet with my daughter in Tel Aviv. We will be touring Jerusalem together. Before I left my home in Ontario, I met with a friend, a lovely elderly woman. Over coffee, we talked about my upcoming trip to Israel. She mentioned to me that a close friend, her next-door neighbour who recently passed away, had sent her a postcard from Jerusalem in 1985. She told me her neighbour's family owned a residence in Jerusalem at the time. My friend said she had never seen a photo of the place or what its neighbourhood was like."

Marie shifted uneasily. "I thought, well … it would be a pleasant surprise to take back some photos of the residence for her, if it wasn't too difficult to locate, of course. I borrowed the postcard, telling her my daughter would love to see it."

"I know she misses her deceased friend very much. I thought this would be a nice gesture. I believe that it might help." Marie smiled. She hoped she sounded convincing. "Might I trouble you to take a quick peek?" She held out the postcard.

"Yes, of course, no trouble at all. Here …" The man gathered his newspaper and collected the books from the vacant seat beside him, and he put the folded paper into the storage net on the back of the seat in front and the books under his seat. He then shifted over to open up his seat for Marie. "Please." He gestured towards the now empty seat. "I am Joseph."

Marie graciously slid into the seat. "Thank you, my name is Marie." She offered the card again. "I've tried myself to locate this address. I searched several online phone directories and did a Google search, but … no luck."

"I see. Well, let's take a look." Joseph adjusted his reading glasses and studied the postcard. Several minutes passed. He turned the card over to the front photo. "Yes … the Dome of the Rock … #1 Temple Mount, Jerusalem, Israel. Should not be too much of a problem to locate." He chuckled and turned towards her.

Marie smiled. "Yes! It all makes sense now … My friend's deceased neighbour? I believe I heard her say that her great, great, great, great … and maybe another great-grandfather's name was David!"

They both started laughing. The ice was broken. They were now friends.

Joseph continued. "Marie, I worked for many years with the Electric Power Commission of Jerusalem. Although I mostly did office coordinating duties, I was at times involved with districts and zoning. Of course, street names were also involved. From what I see written here as a return address, I can most certainly say that it is possible that it is no longer in existence with this same number. Much of the city is in constant change, due to the volatile conditions. I am sure you can understand."

"However, my instincts tell me the reason this address is not showing up on the online directories is twofold." Joseph paused briefly in thought.

He resumed. "Firstly, it is quite probable this was not an actual designated address, meaning the number 50326 may have been a post office identification number and the name 'Jordan Block' merely a general location ... Unless you have a name of ownership for the residence, this will be almost impossible to find."

Marie's heart sank. "You said there are two reasons?"

"Yes, the second reason for not showing up might be where it is located. I do not know ... but it seems to ring a bell ... I think the location might be in a rather remote, not commonly frequented area in the Christian Quarter of The Old City."

"The Christian Quarter?" Marie felt a faint glimmer of hope.

Joseph smiled at her and reached in his shirt and extracted a pen. "Yes, the Christian Quarter in The Old City of Jerusalem, I suspect."

"It's not the kind of place to go knocking on doors, but I can sketch out a rough map of the area. I am afraid that is the best I can do for you, Marie."

Marie reached over and touched his arm. "Thank you, thank you so much. You have been very kind, Joseph."

FIFTY-THREE

TUESDAY, MAY 6, 2014. 1:00 P.M.
BEN GURION INTERNATIONAL AIRPORT,
TEL AVIV ISRAEL

THE FLIGHT STATUS SCREEN in the terminal of Ben Gurion International Airport indicated the arrival of flight #741 Toronto - Tel Aviv: 'on time.' After this verification, Carmen and Aaron made their way to the security exit gate where Marie would be coming through. Carmen already knew her mom did not have any checked baggage, so she would be arriving there soon.

They stopped and waited at a good vantage point. The drive from Jerusalem had been uneventful and without too much conversation. Aaron seemed to sense Carmen needed some time alone with her thoughts. He suspected it would be a bittersweet reunion.

Carmen paced back and forth as her anxiety built. Aaron watched her, and tried to imagine how he might feel in her place. He knew he would need to be with his own mom in a situation like this, yet he also felt it could make the void of a lost father and husband seem greater.

Carmen cried when she had briefly opened up to him on the car ride. She shared with him a small seemingly insignificant interaction between her and her dad a few years ago. Aaron recalled her words:

"My dad and I were sitting in our living room on a Saturday morning. I was doing some 'window-shopping' on the Internet. Looking at handbags—probably the one you damaged. Dad sat in his rocker chair, sipping his morning coffee. He was flipping through a cycling magazine. Stopping at a page, and without looking up, he said, 'I'm thinking about buying a set of carbon fibre racing wheels for my road bike. What do you think of these Carmen?' He swivelled in his chair and held the magazine for me to check out the picture."

Aaron smiled to himself now as he visualized what Carmen said her response was: "I gave my dad the 'daughter to dad' look that means: 'Dad, I don't really care about bicycle racing wheels … Can't you see I'm busy purse shopping? I understand you're excited about this, so I'm agreeing, ok?' Yes Dad, they're cool … but how come they only have three spokes?"

"My dad laughed and said jokingly: 'It's all you need … I guess kind of like us—you, Mom and me.'"

That was when Carmen started to cry, and between sobs she asked, "Is this silly of me, Aaron? Why am I even thinking of this? At the time, I thought it was lame."

Aaron hoped his response helped. "I think those little moments we share with the ones we love all add up to make a strong foundation. Maybe we are not consciously aware of their presence until a time of crisis when we need them."

"The wheel is broken, Aaron."

"Broken wheels can be fixed, Carmen." He had raised his sunglasses up and turned to look into her tear-filled eyes. The rest of their trip was made in silence.

Aaron glanced around the busy airport terminal, then back to Carmen. She still paced and turned towards the security exit doors every few seconds. Many people were now coming through the doors. Perhaps Marie's flight was beginning to exit.

Aaron thought of his last few airport visits. They were all the same, except this one. Something changed. It was not the people, the place, or the situation; they were similar. It had to be him. He pushed away his usual self-consciousness in circumstances like these. The people still stared and he avoided eye contact like he always did, but this time he thought the pressure had lessened. It did not feel like everyone was surrounding and smothering him.

He glanced around again. It did not take long for the opportunity to make eye contact with someone to present itself. Aaron did not turn away from the lingering gaze of a middle-aged woman passing by. He even offered a pleasant smile before focussing again on Carmen. *Is it because of her? Right now, she hardly knows I'm here. She has not so much as looked my way or spoken a word to me in the last 20 minutes, yet I …*

Carmen suddenly stopped. Her body went rigid. Her mom walked through the door.

Aaron could not help but 'be in the moment'. Time stopped for a few seconds when Marie saw her daughter and halted. Their eyes locked.

Aaron felt a mild surprise, his first time seeing Marie in person; she appeared younger than she did in her profile photos. The similarities between mother and daughter were recognizable immediately. Even though Marie's height and hair length were shorter, they shared many features including an overall slim, well-kept physique.

Carmen uttered "Mom" and moved forward. Marie took two quick steps to clear the door, dropped her carry-on bag to the floor, and rushed to her daughter.

"Oh … Carmen," could be heard just before they locked together in a fierce hug.

As Aaron got closer, he could hear them both gently crying in each other's arms and whispering between sobs. He kept his distance, knowing full well what he was seeing. The pure beauty of it was almost overwhelming.

Slowly the crying ceased, and the whispers became talking as they continued to hold each other tightly. Soon there came a soft giggle from Carmen, and Marie uttered a gentle laugh. They broke apart but continued to hold each other's hands as they both gazed into tear-filled eyes. Finally, Marie reached into her purse, which hung off her shoulder. She pulled out two tissues and offered one to Carmen. They both smiled and dabbed their faces, trying to repair the damage. Marie commented on how beautiful Carmen looked, and Carmen complimented her mom on her new hairstyle.

"I can see a gentleman waiting patiently for an introduction, Carmen," Marie said as she repaired the last make-up smudge on her daughter's face.

They stepped apart and turned. Aaron took his cue and moved forward to greet Marie.

"You guys certainly know who each other is." Carmen smiled. "Mom, this is Aaron. Aaron, this is my mom, Marie."

Marie took a step closer and looked up to Aaron. "Hello, Aaron … Can I take a closer peek?" Marie leaned over to her left to have a better view of the right side of his face. "That's healing nicely; I don't think you'll have a scar."

Aaron smiled sheepishly. "Ah, yes, thank you, Marie. I'm going to be okay. Carmen has concerns about her purse, though …" He offered a weak smile.

Marie turned to face Carmen. "Are you going to be okay, dear? I, more than most women, understand how important a purse can be."

"I think I'm going to be okay Mom, with a bit of time. And I've been thinking … sometimes patina on our valued items can be a cool thing. It can bring back fond memories!"

Marie nodded. Both she and Carmen held straight faces, as they turned to a somewhat bewildered Aaron. He was not sure if he should laugh or if they were reprimanding him.

So, he smiled and took the honest approach. "Marie, I am not sure if my timing is off here, but I would like to apologize to you for my actions, which have caused both you and your family duress. I hope in time you can forgive me."

Marie focused intensely into Aaron's eyes. A soft smile crept across her face. She did not answer him. Instead, she offered an open-armed invitation to a welcome hug.

Aaron stepped forward and warmly embraced Marie. Standing behind him and off to the side, Carmen met Marie's eyes. There was no mistaking the exaggerated wink, followed by a silent formed *Wow*. She gently lifted her arm and softly fanned herself. Carmen could not stop the giggle that escaped.

"Well, Aaron, I guess you've figured out by now my mom is into hugs." Carmen tried to cover up the giggle.

"Same with my mom," Aaron smiled. They ended their embrace and stood back.

Marie spoke directly to Aaron. "Thank you for helping us."

"I am not going to leave. I will stay and see this through. You are welcome Marie." Their eye contact did not falter. She reminded him in many ways of his own mother and it was a nice feeling.

"Can I get your bag?" Aaron motioned towards her unattended luggage several metres away.

"Oh … yes. Thanks." She glanced over her shoulder, realizing she had all but forgotten about it. Aaron walked over and swiftly picked up the bag and returned.

"Ok then, we've got a lot to talk about, and I can't wait to get to the hotel to shower and change out of these stifling blue jeans," Marie stated, as she glanced around for the first time to get her bearings.

"The weather here has been really nice … about 25-30 degrees and sunny, but the forecast is calling for rain coming in the early evening," Carmen remembered.

Marie thought for a moment. "I think I'll take that as a good omen ... The last time I saw your father when I drove him to the airport it was raining. Sometimes I love the rain." She turned to face Aaron who stood holding her luggage. "I'm sure you remember how hard it rained in Petrolia that day, Aaron?"

He thought he detected a twinkle in Marie's eyes as she smiled at him. *I think I can tell where Carmen gets her feistiness.*

Aaron did not respond, but he returned to her a warm smile. They headed for the exit.

FIFTY-FOUR

TUESDAY, MAY 6, 2014. 5:30 P.M.
JERUSALEM, ISRAEL

The Old City of Jerusalem is well over 5000 years old and is shrouded in an ancient history of destruction and resurrection. Believed by many to be the centre of our world, it may also be our most venerated city as it serves as a focal point for three of the strongest faiths on earth. For millions, the city offers the hope of unity, which might someday 'rise up' from within the towering stone walls.

Every emotion known to man has been glorified or laid to rest within these ancient buildings, winding narrow alleyways, or sacred cobblestone paths. Many great rulers and kings—over thousands of years—have sought to make this city their own. Ultimately, they have all failed. It is as though any singular being shall never conquer the 'soul' of Jerusalem. A testament to this may well be how the one square kilometre area within the walls of the old city is divided into four quarters: the Jewish, the Muslim, the Armenian, and the Christian quarters. Each has its own unique presence and offers residents, tourists and pilgrims alike an opportunity to embrace ancient holy antiquity in a seemingly magical domain of narrow winding stone passages, sacred structures, and temples. A wondrous place: a place of passion and drama.

Such was the setting for three travellers within these walls on this late afternoon. Like so many who came before them to this place, they were searching. Searching in this old city where perhaps hope is now, and always has been its greatest offering.

The shadows grew long, and the sky began to cloud over. The wind picked up, showing the first subtle signs of pending rain.

The Christian Quarter began to take on a much darker shade of grey for Carmen, Marie, and Aaron as they walked. They arrived here one hour earlier and immediately began their search. They held onto a glimmer of hope that somehow the address on the postcard, which was indirectly connected to Herbert Osterhagen, might eventually prove to be the place where Edward had been taken.

Their reasoning was that once in the vicinity, they might be able to show the address to someone who could further direct them. This, however, was beginning to appear to be an unlikely scenario. The Christian Quarter seemed to be either a frenzied place of market stalls and activity, with the loud sound of foreign languages resounding, or quiet, desolate, narrow stone passageways with barred windows, and heavy closed doors. The sense of living in the past within some ancient culture surrounded them. Like Joseph had said to Marie on the plane, "Not exactly the kind of place to go knocking on doors."

They stayed close together. Carmen and Marie would never have considered doing this without Aaron. His presence offered safety. Inspector Claude Gadgét had insisted he be with them on this excursion. Carmen contacted the inspector when they arrived back at the hotel. She filled him in on what her mom had discovered, and his response was that he would have the address searched first thing in the morning when resources were more readily available.

Although not surprised with their impatience, the inspector was quick to put some safeguards in place. When Carmen announced their plans to begin searching today, he asked her to contact him via text message when they arrived at the Christian Quarter, and he would have a patrol car posted outside the Jaffa Gate. Plus, Aaron looked to Inspector Gadgét like someone who could handle a crisis. Claude Gadgét wanted him to accompany the women and watch over them. He also wanted to see a text message of confirmation on this from Aaron himself. Carmen and Aaron agreed and complied with his requests.

They stopped at a narrow cobblestone junction in a desolate area. The loud sound from the market stall region became faint eerie echoes and drifted in and around them off the cold grey stone walls. The closed doors and iron bars enhanced their sense of isolation. No one welcomed them, and no one offered them assistance in their time of need.

Marie reached into her purse and took out two maps. She wanted to go over them again, perhaps just to ease the growing sense of despair. They compared the map Joseph had drawn, with a tourist map they acquired at the hotel lobby. The area of interest measured only about 500 to 600 square metres, but with all the narrow alleyways and turns it was difficult not to lose one's sense of direction.

Each of them offered a personal assessment of what they thought they had covered, and where to try next. After a short consultation, they agreed on a tentative route, which would criss-cross the highlighted areas. Not much more than 2 hours of daylight remained, due in part to the ever-thickening cloud cover. A few light raindrops landed as Marie tucked the maps back into her purse.

They walked on in silence, each hoping they might find something or see a person who might help. A stray dog darted out from an intersecting alleyway and startled them. The echoic sounds from the busy areas diminished. There came the odd distant bark of a dog or the sound of a car horn from somewhere outside the Old City walls, otherwise nothing but the rhythmic padding of their soft footsteps on the cobblestone and their breathing reverberating off the stone walls, which pressed in on them ever closer.

Both Carmen and Marie fought the urge to grab onto Aaron's hand. "Not your typical tourist area." Marie hoped her voice sounded calm.

"I think they really need a 'happy hour' around here." Carmen tried to ease the growing tension.

"Import a few willing Caribbean's to set things up, and you might be on to something, Carmen." Aaron added. Their laughter was short lived.

They fell silent and carried on. Broken up wind gusts grew stronger and the raindrops increased. Slowly, a sense of helplessness began to develop. As the sky darkened on that late afternoon so to did their sense of hope.

Consumed by the ever-encroaching dark walls, faith diminished, giving way to a feeling Marie understood from being with terminal cancer patients. Aaron knew it from witnessing irreversible environmental disasters, and Carmen had lived it from watching dreams shatter during failed dancing auditions. This feeling made the 'sound of silence' grow louder, as each of them was afraid to speak because the next word uttered could only describe one thing: 'failure'.

They walked on.

Intermittent wind gusts mixed with rain danced off the walls around them. They passed yet another long dark alley, this time to Carmen's right. Suddenly she stopped! She took a quick step back and peered down the corridor.

"Carmen?" Marie followed her daughter's gaze. She knew Carmen possessed excellent eyesight. "What is it?"

Carmen held up her hand. She was waiting for something. Seconds passed until a slight gust of wind hit their faces from the alleyway. Marie thought she spotted something moving in the wind at ground level, about 300 metres away.

Carmen started down the alleyway, straining her eyes and leaning forward.

Marie glanced at Aaron. He nodded to her and they both followed, staying close and trying to make out what had caught Carmen's attention.

The pace quickened. Marie and Aaron were almost running to keep up. That had to be it: a piece of green and white cloth, hanging in front of a cellar window, flapped freely in the wind about 150 metres away.

A stronger wind gust hit Marie's face. It unfurled the cloth for a moment. Now she saw what it meant, just as Carmen broke out into a flat out run. "Oh, my God!" Marie cried out.

They all ran. Marie and Aaron were being out-distanced.

Carmen called out, almost shrieking, "Daddy, Daddy!" Her voice echoed off the walls.

"What is it?" Aaron stayed close to Marie.

"Yes! Yes! It's Edward! He's giving us a sign!" Out of breath, her voice cracked.

She started to cry, "Carmen's Canadian flag!"

FIFTY-FIVE

COLD RAINDROPS AND warm tears mixed and fell to the old cobblestone beneath the barred cellar window, in front of which knelt Marie and Carmen. They stretched their arms through the iron bars and clung tightly to Edward's hands. He had pushed the folding chair beneath the kitchen window to help him access the most joyful reunion of his life.

Edward had been sitting quietly and thought he might be starting to hallucinate when the faint sound of what sounded like his daughter's voice calling "Daddy! Daddy!" accosted him. But the sound grew much louder, startling him, and when he rose from the chair and turned to face the window, he was greeted with a beautiful sight: the face of his daughter staring wide-eyed from behind bars in through the open window. He might have gone into shock in the first few seconds of almost total disbelief.

Her voice sounded again. "Daddy, Mom's here too!" As he got right up to the window his wife's face greeted him as well.

At first, they shared no words. In silence, Edward turned back to get the chair. He stood on it and was reunited with his family. He tenderly held their hands in his, lowered his head and wept.

Aaron stood back, feeling happy as the rain began to fall harder. He felt as though he was being cleansed of some of the guilt he had amassed. After a short time, Marie turned and motioned for him to come to the window as well. After the brief initial surprise from Edward upon seeing him, he was greeted and asked by Edward if he might somehow get a crowbar and/ or a heavy hammer to break apart the padlock at the front entrance.

By the time Aaron took off in a fast run, the reunion had taken on a new state of emergency as both Carmen and Marie, through tears of joy, frantically tried to impart to Edward all that transpired while he was detained. Listening in wonder, he fought hard to retain and comprehend the rapid onslaught of information. Edward could not remember a time when he ever felt prouder of his family.

―――――◂•▸―――――

THE TEARS SUBSIDED, and finally the pace of the conversation abated somewhat. Aaron had been gone 15 minutes when Marie suddenly offered an apology. "Oh Edward, we've been doing all the talking. I'm sorry ... Are you sure you're okay? You're looking well under the circumstances ... Are you going to be alright from the drug injection?"

Edward laughed softly. He looked to Carmen and back to his wife. "Yes, I'm sure I'll be okay."

"The watchmaker ... Is he here?" Marie queried.

"Yes, he is ... I need to explain. He doesn't know the lock combination ... as silly as this sounds ... and I ... well, we have no communication."

Edward stopped, and his face grew solemn. "There has been a terrible tragedy ..." he lowered his head. He gazed back up to his wife and daughter. "Jessica, Rachel as you now know her—Herbert Osterhagen's granddaughter—Rachel Cohen is dead."

Carmen drew in a sharp breath, and Marie asked, "How...? What happened?"

"Another hypodermic needle from Herbert, this one meant for me when I tried to see an old handbook about the watch. I dodged the attack. However, Herbert lost his balance and fell forward, impaling Rachel. She remained unconscious for over 24 hours ... but finally she expired. The dosage was too much for her small body." Edward said sadly to his wife, "I wish I could have done more."

Marie saw the pain in his eyes. She understood. She waited, and in a tender, caring voice Marie asked, "Edward, how is Herbert?"

"Not good ... He went into some kind of psychological retreat and hasn't uttered a word since he asked Rachel for her forgiveness."

Marie nodded. "We'll need to call the police and get an ambulance."

Just then came the sound of running footsteps approaching. They turned. Aaron arrived carrying a crowbar and a large ball peen hammer. "Sorry to take so long ..." He held up the tools. "Took a bit of negotiation to acquire these, and for sure negotiating is not my calling. I now *own* these tools!"

"Thanks. I'll meet you guys at the front," Edward called out as he got down off the chair. Carmen and Marie rose to their feet and walked towards Aaron and the front of the building.

Marie stopped for a moment. "Aaron, a fatal accident has occurred ... Rachel Cohen, Herbert Osterhagen's granddaughter, has died. There was another hypodermic needle attack aimed at Edward when he tried to read an old book describing the pocket watch. He moved out of the way, and Herbert lost his balance and impaled his granddaughter. She held on for a full day ..."

"I am sorry." The news was very disturbing for Aaron as well. "The grandfather and Edward, are they going to be okay?"

"Edward is alright. He's going to need some time to sort things out mentally, but I know Edward ... He will reason things through. Herbert, though ... he's apparently not speaking. Given his past mental condition, I'm guessing his situation is fragile."

Marie turned to include Carmen. "I think we need to be aware and pay attention when we go in. We will seem like strangers to him, possibly a threat. I want you both to be aware. Okay?"

"Thank you" Aaron agreed.

"And I'll call Inspector Gadgét now." Carmen focused on Aaron, "Let's go and bust him out!" They moved in unison towards the front of the building.

Carmen dialled the Inspector while Aaron and Marie took a closer look at the building. It appeared much like the other connected surrounding structures: a narrow, two-level apartment building, located on a corner of two alleys. However, the place appeared deserted. In the last 20-30 minutes, there were no signs of anyone else in the area.

A small stone walkway led them down four cement steps to a heavy, black painted door. The entrance to the ground and upper level would be around the corner. Aaron tried the old door. It opened easily.

They found Edward waiting for them on the other side of the barred gate. "Welcome ... Meet my major obstacle of the past three days." He motioned towards the chain and padlock. "A brand-new lock that only Rachel knew the combination to. She didn't have time to tell Herbert."

"I understand," Aaron offered, "Marie told me what happened, Edward. I am really glad you are going to be alright, but it's so sad to hear about Rachel and her grandfather."

Edward cast a look down and shook his head. "I don't know ..."

Together they positioned the crowbar through the lock and levered it against a horizontal gate support. "Ok Aaron ... I think if you put all your weight on the end of the bar, I can reach through with the hammer. I think a couple of sharp blows should do it." Edward checked to make sure the women were staying clear.

Carmen and Marie were standing back at the foot of the stairs in the rain. Carmen was talking into her phone. She contacted

Inspector Claude Gadgét, and with her mother's assistance, they managed to relay detailed directions to the Inspector with the help of a soaking wet, opened map. They also told him briefly what had transpired.

Carmen finished talking and was putting her phone away when the lock gave way with a loud snap from the first hammer blow.

Aaron untangled the chain with the broken lock and swung open the gate. Carmen rushed past him, followed by Marie. They embraced Edward. No one spoke for several minutes. They just held on and rocked to and fro.

Carmen was the first to raise her head and lean back. "Dad, I gotta say … you don't smell too great!"

Edward smiled. "Sorry guys, but I ran out of deodorant."

Marie broke the embrace. "I'm going to agree, but I want to add: a truly *wonderful* unpleasant smell."

Edward leaned forward and lightly kissed his wife, stepped sideways, glanced over to Aaron, and took a step towards him and extended his hand. "Thanks for your help."

They met with a firm handshake. "Edward, you are very welcome … Listen, I want to tell you, I am sorry. It was never my intent to deceive or bring harm to you or …"

Edward held up his left hand with a sincere expression as he interjected. "They filled me in. No worries … We still have more to do and much to talk about."

They released their handshake. Edward motioned for them to follow. They walked past the closed door of the watch room and the archway of the kitchen. He stopped in front of the next closed door on the right.

Edward opened the door a tiny bit and addressed Marie. "She's in this room. A candle is burning."

Marie stepped forward, opened the door further, went through and closed it behind her. They waited for her in the corridor. No one said a word.

She exited the room several minutes later and re-closed the door. She looked at Edward with sad, tear-filled eyes. "Can we see Herbert now, please?"

Edward led them back to the watch room. The sound of the ticking clocks seemed louder now. He opened the door. Herbert swivelled on his stool, faced them, flipped up his loupe, and watched as they entered the room. Edward introduced each person. He thought he may have noticed a slight glimmer of recognition in Herbert's eyes upon seeing Carmen, but otherwise he was expressionless. Herbert said not a word. He turned back to work on the watch movement.

Silently Marie walked over to him. She softly placed her hand on his shoulder. Herbert turned and looked up. "Herbert Osterhagen, I know you are in great pain. Rachel is resting peacefully now. She will stay with you and be part of your soul forever." Moments of silence passed, interspersed only with the sound of the ticking clocks.

Marie gently squeezed his shoulder. Their eyes locked. Herbert started to raise his hand.

The faint sound of a police siren was heard. It grew louder and louder. Herbert slowly lowered his hand. He broke their gaze and turned away and looked back to his watch movement, as the sound of running footsteps and loud voices descended upon them.

FIFTY-SIX

It was much darker under a steady rain. Red and blue flashing lights caused shades of purple light to streak along the glistening walls and cobblestone of the long narrow alley leading to the flat. An ambulance and numerous police cars lined the somewhat wider roadway, where Carmen first noticed her dad's sign. Professionals were hustling back and forth.

Inside, it was crowded and noisy. The first to attend were two uniformed police officers, followed soon after by the ambulance attendants, then Chief Inspector Claude Gadgét, who was clearly the man in charge. He saw to Herbert and Edward immediately. More police officers arrived, both uniformed and plain clothed. A temporary generator was set up outside to provide necessary lighting, and the constant drone of its engine could be heard through the open window as it echoed off the surrounding stone walls.

Herbert had not left his stool, and two uniformed officers now flanked him. He sat with his head lowered but no longer worked on the watch movement. Inspector Gadgét tried several times to communicate with him, but his attempts were unsuccessful.

Edward, Marie, Carmen and Aaron stood huddled together near the door of the watch room and observed the activity. The inspector had already questioned them. He was quick, calm and efficient, and he assured them that they would not be detained for long.

They stood quietly talking amongst themselves, asking each other questions, trying to understand and piece together the sequence of events that brought them here.

Marie was holding Edward's hand. With a show of affection, she asked, "Edward, would you like to sit down? You must be exhausted."

"I guess I'm running on adrenaline now. I've pretty much been sitting around for three days. Nice to have a reason to stand and someone to talk to."

"Sorry Dad, I ate Mom's last energy bar earlier today. I guess I owe you one." Carmen admitted remorsefully.

"Well, it's ok Carmen. From the stories I'm hearing, you've been out burning calories at an incredible rate, we've just ..."

"Wait!" Marie cut in. "Let's see if there might be something in my purse ... *shall we?*"

Edward was reassured with the smile. Marie opened her purse and made the descent.

"Aaron?" A serious tone sounded in Carmen's voice. He turned to her. "What plans do you have for your newly acquired tools, the hammer and crowbar?"

"Oh ... Here we go!" Marie removed a clenched hand from her purse and extended it to Edward. "Sorry to interrupt, Carmen, but your father hasn't eaten in days." She opened her hand, "A few carbs, Edward? One for you and one for Herbert."

Edward was presented with the glitter of gold wrappers from two Werther's Original candies. A big grin spread across his face as he took one, opened the covering and popped the candy into his mouth. "You're always there for me, Marie."

Marie turned and strode across the room to stand beside Herbert. She touched his arm lightly to get his attention. When he slowly raised his head, Marie offered the candy. Herbert's gaze fell. He turned away. Marie patted his arm and left it beside him on his bench. She returned to the group with a sad smile. They all witnessed the gesture.

Carmen turned to Aaron and reactivated her former expression, "Your tools, Aaron?"

"What are my plans for my newly purchased tools?" Questioning uncertainty sounded in Aaron's voice. "I guess I have not really given it much thought. Do you have something in mind, Carmen?"

"Well, yea maybe … I came to the blunt realization that those are two items my mom does *not* carry in her purse, and remember how handy they were …"

Aaron smiled inwardly. He was catching on. "You're asking me to offer these rather heavy tools to be carried in a woman's handbag, even after what I went through with a lady and her purse? It could happen again … I need to watch out for my own safety!" His expression did not alter.

Edward and Marie watched as warm smiles formed on the two young adults. They glanced at each other in a somewhat surprised understanding of how well Carmen and Aaron were getting to know each other.

Edward offered a thought, "Aaron, I think you and I might compare stories on women and their pur …"

"Oh no Dad … No …! Not the purse-stroller story again! I grew up hearing that story over and over … and look what its done to me!"

Their laughter began but ended abruptly, as through the open door they caught sight of a gurney with Rachel's body in an enclosed bag rolling past en route to the ambulance. It was an uncomfortably still moment. Smiles faded, and eyes welled up as they looked in embarrassment at each other.

It was bittersweet: happiness, sorrow—the reality of life, and none of them could offer words to help understand what they were feeling. They stayed quiet.

Inspector Claude Gadgét followed behind the attendants as they transported the body. He stepped inside the watch room as they carried on. He saw and understood their reaction. He was trained to deal with these emotions, but it still troubled him to witness others suffer.

He addressed the group with a gentle, calm, and understanding demeanour. "I am sorry for you to be here and witness such a terrible loss of life. I am afraid tragic accidents *do* indeed happen, and perhaps it is never for us to fully understand why." He turned slightly and motioned towards Herbert, who had not moved. "Sadly, I believe this man has lost part of himself."

The inspector did not speak or shift for several moments. Finally, he turned back and addressed Aaron. "Aaron, if you would please excuse me, I would like, for a few minutes, to take Edward and his family aside for a short private discussion. I would thank you for your patience."

"Yes, Inspector, of course."

Claude Gadgét nodded and motioned towards the door. "I think the small room at the end of the hall will be all right."

They manoeuvred around electrical extension cords as they made their way along the corridor. Two leads ran the full length of the hallway, with a branch off to each room, where one or two portable halogen lights were in operation. As they entered the small room, Inspector Gadgét commented. "I would close the door behind us, but …" He smiled at Edward, "Fingernail clipper … resourceful."

Edward smiled. "Thanks, yes a multi-use tool for sure." He grinned at Carmen and Marie.

They walked to the back corner of the room where the inspector addressed them. "I want to give you my thoughts on where things might proceed from here and get your feelings on the situation."

Gadgét paused as he focused from one to the other. "Let me start by saying, as a family, you make one hell of a team." The inspector smiled at Edward and Marie. "Your daughter has been two steps ahead of our police department and the N.Y.P.D. right from the beginning." He turned to Carmen. "This is always going to be a memorable investigation for me, Carmen. I would like to say thank you for your contribution."

Carmen blushed and nodded, Marie wiped tears from her eyes, and Edward stood as tall as he had ever stood before.

Inspector Claude Gadgét continued. "I have, within the last several hours, been in direct contact with the New York Department. I gave them the alias name of Wolfgang Smythe, which you discovered for us. They ran a trace and faxed me an outline of the medical history on file, the name of the mental institution in Brooklyn, New York, and the name of the current head clinician who will oversee the assessment of Herbert Osterhagen's current state of mental health."

The inspector reached into the breast pocket of his suit coat and produced a small notebook. He flipped through some pages and stopped. "The name of the clinician: Dr. Scarlett Dae. Dr. Dae was not employed at the hospital when Wolfgang … or Herbert, rather, was institutionalized. However, all past records are available to her."

"Is that where Herbert will be sent?" Marie was the first to ask.

"It depends …" Gadgét paused and looked to each of them in turn, "partly on the three of you. This could become complicated." He stopped again before continuing. "Let me attempt to explain the possibilities."

"First, the N.Y.P.D. issued a warrant for the arrest of Herbert Osterhagen on suspicion of murder, of this you are aware. And, if I might add, the man found deceased in Herbert's watch shop was identified as someone with a long criminal history. Off the record, I will say that many in the law enforcement community are happy to hear that he is resting peacefully."

Gadgét raised his brow and continued. "So … when Herbert arrives in New York, he will be assessed by Dr. Dae, as I mentioned, and there will be a hearing. Based on my own experience, I do not think Herbert Osterhagen will stand trial for murder in New York because of his mental condition and the real probability that the cause of the man's death could have been Herbert Osterhagen acting in self-defence."

The inspector stopped to make sure everyone was with him so far. He took some time to make eye contact with each person. "Our situation here is more complicated. An innocent, young woman was killed by a lethal injection. We believe it was accidental. However, Herbert Osterhagen can still be charged with several offences: attempted murder, kidnapping, theft, assault, manslaughter … You can imagine how difficult this may become for him."

"Now … we understand Herbert suffers a mental infirmity, for which he was institutionalized, and that he is required to take certain prescribed medical drugs to function coherently. The question arises, was Herbert Osterhagen current with his medications at the time of the accident? I think we can find out…"

"Blood test?" Marie offered.

Inspector Claude Gadgét nodded in agreement. "Herbert will be taken to the hospital to have some blood work done. We will make sure he gets proper care."

The inspector resumed. "A hearing will also be forthcoming in Jerusalem to address any possible charges which may be brought against him. From what I know at this point, Herbert Osterhagen will be found either unfit to stand trial or not guilty if this makes it to trial due to his mental instability. He would then be deported to the U.S.A. This could be a lengthy process, depending if any charges are forthcoming."

"This, in part, is where we come in?" Edward queried.

"Yes, more specifically you and Carmen." Gadgét looked to each of them. "Your statements, along with personal wishes and opinions, coupled with evidence and my recommendations, will influence a judge's opinion on which way to proceed."

"Do you have a timeframe here, inspector?" Edward asked. "Carmen is already going to miss a full day of classes, and Marie has commitments back home."

"Yes, I understand Edward, but let us not rush through this too quickly either. Perhaps … come to the station sometime tomorrow after you all take some time to discuss if you would like charges filed against Herbert Osterhagen."

Edward made eye contact with his wife and his daughter before turning back to the inspector. "Over the last three days before Rachel's death, I had time to talk at length with Herbert. There is still a great deal I do not comprehend, and I hope in time I can come to a better understanding. However, I honestly believe Herbert Osterhagen never wished to harm my family or me. He was only trying to protect someone, or something, from possible misuse." Edward shrugged. "Also, I was told by Rachel, my watch would be returned to me as well."

He again glanced to his family. "I can only speak for myself, but I don't require any more time to think about it. I hope only the best for Herbert Osterhagen."

"If I may, Inspector …" Marie added. "Herbert is suffering now more than we can understand. Life is about forgiveness. I agree with Edward … and I hope one day he may find peace."

"Ok … my turn, I guess." Carmen addressed the inspector. "If not for Herbert Osterhagen's quick thinking and intelligence, the thugs in Brooklyn, might have made things much worse for us. I know what happened here and at the museum sucks, but I still think maybe it's our turn now, to offer any help we can to make things better for the watchmaker … From what I've learned through all of this, I believe his life has known hardship."

Inspector Claude Gadgét saw strength in the unity of the family standing before him. He appreciated even more fully how they had, mostly on their own, freed Edward and possibly prevented a second burglary from happening at the L.A. Mayer Museum.

The inspector addressed them with respect. "Speculation is not a practice I often endorse in my line of work. At times, however, I find it useful. Could Herbert Osterhagen in both acts of assault and attempted assault have been reacting in defence? Lacking his proper medication and having recently gone through a terrifying experience with hired criminals in New York, might not Herbert have been trying to protect his granddaughter and prevent the theft of a pocket watch that he firmly believed was rightfully his?"

"There may be more truth to your speculation than we understand." Edward nodded.

"I will need two signed statements from Edward and Carmen. We can word them carefully, and my recommendations will mirror these affidavits. I think we will, as Carmen put it, 'make things better for the watchmaker.'"

Inspector Claude Gadgét offered each a sincere smile. "We will need an hour at the station … tomorrow afternoon if possible?"

Edward, Marie, and Carmen agreed in unison. The inspector thanked them and motioned to the doorway. "Edward, it is going to take a bit of time, but we are going to need you to see a doctor for a mandatory blood test and a thorough assessment of your condition."

They began walking out of the room. "I'd really like to take a long shower and have dinner with my family. But I guess you're right … ok," Edward replied.

"I understand. We will arrange for transportation."

They joined Aaron again in the watch room. Smiles were exchanged, and Carmen briefly explained, "We went over a few things regarding statements to sign tomorrow at the police station." She grinned. "About whether we should have you locked up or not."

"I better watch my step." Aaron grinned back.

The inspector entered the room and spoke as he passed them. "I will be leaving with you shortly, but first I will make arrangements for Herbert." He walked over and began conversing in Hebrew with the two uniformed officers standing beside him.

After several minutes, he put a hand on Herbert's shoulder. The watchmaker turned and looked up. "I need to ask that you go with these two officers, Mr. Osterhagen. They will be taking you to a hospital. I will come by later and see to it personally that your accommodations are comfortable … We need to take care of you now."

Herbert seemed to understand to some extent, as Inspector Gadgét helped him to his feet and turned him over to the officers. Each took a side as they shifted the old man around and began guiding him towards the doorway.

Herbert's eyes remained fixed on the floor as he passed the group. Everyone watched the sad procession.

Herbert was at the doorway when he stopped. The officers halted as well. Herbert lifted his head up and slowly turned around. His eyes searched until he found the person he wanted.

He stared at Marie, looking at no one else. Marie felt her heart jump, but she held his gaze. The ticking clocks amplified, and the external generator's droning increased. Moments passed. Their eyes were still locked. No one uttered a word. Marie felt her heart beating forcefully against her chest. Then, for one second, Herbert averted his gaze. He stared back at Marie and did the same again and again. This time, Marie followed with her eyes to where she thought he might be looking.

His stare was riveting as she broke from the group and made her way to the back corner of the room to where the high workbench met the wall. She stopped and again faced Herbert. His eyesight remained fixed on hers. Marie turned back to the bench and began scanning. Tools and what appeared to her to be clock and watch parts, were scattered about. She caught sight of something, right at the back against the wall—something covered by a black cloth. She leaned forward and lifted the cloth away.

At first, Marie did not recognize what she was looking at because it was so unexpected. She turned back yet again to Herbert. His gaze remained rock steady. Leaning back again she picked up an old, impeccably clean glass sealer jar. It was 1-litre in size, with a rusted tin screw-on lid that had four small holes punched through it, probably with a hammer and a nail. Below the lid, and tied to the shoulder of the jar, was a worn leather strap on which hung a well-used watchmaker's loupe. Marie peered through the crystal-clear glass and saw several small, arranged pieces of driftwood in the bottom.

Now Marie knew exactly what she held in her hands: a jar to display insects. And when she thought about the magnifier hanging from it, she understood.

She collected the cloth and turned one final time to Herbert. Marie had her answer. She shifted her gaze to Inspector Claude Gadgét. He had, along with everyone else, been watching closely. He gave a subtle nod of his head.

Marie walked directly to Herbert. She recovered the jar with the black cloth and handed it to him. He grasped on to it and held it tightly to his body. Herbert's crystal blue eyes lingered with Marie for one final moment. He turned and lowered his head.

Herbert Osterhagen walked out the door.

Marie glanced towards the stool where Herbert previously sat. Her eyes travelled up to the bench in front of it.

The candy she had left for him was gone.

FIFTY-SEVEN

WEDNESDAY, MAY 7, 2014. 10:00 A.M.
JERUSALEM, ISRAEL

"Stanley Crawford is not a man with much patience." Aaron looked across the café table in the Prima Royale Hotel at Edward and Marie. Carmen was sitting on his right.

"How long since you last contacted him?" Edward asked. Aaron had been explaining his situation over breakfast.

"Two days now," Aaron answered.

"Maybe he forgot all about you and the watch by now." Carmen offered, half-jokingly.

Aaron grimaced. "I'm guessing this will not be so easy ... Although with the watch still missing, what can he do? But I think I will need to be quite persuasive and try to convince him the pocket watch is lost to him forever."

Edward leaned forward in his chair. He reached into his back pocket and produced a folded envelope. "I wanted to wait until today to show everyone this. We're all more rested and relaxed now. I got this from Rachel's purse ... I think if you were to send a copy of this to Stanley Crawford, he would lose interest in the watch very quickly."

He removed the letter from the envelope and unfolded it. "I took the handbook too. I left it in the hotel room." He handed the letter to Aaron. "Figured I could at least have the manual that *goes* with the watch," he shrugged.

When Aaron finished reading the page, he gave Edward a surprised glance. He read it again, this time uttering a soft whistle as he handed the letter to Marie.

There was silence at the table as Marie and Carmen read the letter and finally gave it back to Edward. He refolded and tucked it back into the envelope before placing the letter in his pocket.

He smiled at each in turn. "Our friend Herbert Osterhagen surprised us again. Not only is he an intelligent, talented watchmaker, but now, as we all can see ... he is also a gifted storyteller." Edward sadly shook his head. "'A timepiece of great significance,' he said."

No one wanted to be the first to speak. They all went quietly back to finishing their meal or glancing around the restaurant. The room was rather quiet now, with only a few other patrons.

Carmen was the first to interrupt the silence, right after she finished a crisp strip of bacon. "Well, I guess this is no longer relevant, but I'd still like to hear your theory on the watch, Aaron."

"My theory?" He was not quite with her.

"Remember ... The first time we talked, you said we didn't have time to go into it," she smiled.

"Oh ... yes, I'm sorry ... I remember ..." he grinned tightly. "I guess I will now need to concede to the reality of offering only a proposal of science fiction." He laughed lightly. "My hypothesis might sound a bit silly ... Are you sure you still want me to share it?"

"Yea ... Come on, it'll be fun," Carmen giggled.

"The watch certainly had a strange design," Edward joined in.

"Apparently, Herbert Osterhagen possesses a vivid imagination." Marie grinned at Aaron. "Go ahead Aaron, let's see how *your* imagination stacks up."

Timidly Aaron glanced around the room. Carmen wiggled more upright in her chair, clearly amused. Both Marie and Edward showed subtle expecting smiles.

"Okay, but I will ask you to please hold your laughter until after I finish."

Everyone nodded in fun. It was pleasant for them to be in this light, relaxing atmosphere. Aaron began. "As you know I have not seen the watch; I have only studied a digital copy from what appeared to be an old handbook. The book you now have, Edward. So, as we now understand, it was Herbert Osterhagen himself who documented his own design of a watch that he surely built himself. I will say, though, even with only having studied the timepiece on a screen, this watchmaker is articulate. The drawings, blueprints, and specifications in the book are very precise. Overall, what I saw was done in a most professional manner."

Aaron addressed Edward. "I expect the pocket watch itself also upheld the same standards of quality?"

Edward agreed. "Not created in precious metals or gemstones—brass, silver, and steel only I suspect, but both myself and a jeweller thought the craftsmanship was excellent."

Aaron continued. "And as Edward said, the exterior design was unusual, having no winding crown, only one hand, and strange symbols on the dial, as well as graduations that do not fit with any common design … For me, however, I was most interested in the internal movement. What I understood from the drawings was a possible working model for perpetual motion using dual magnetism. There was, however, an unidentified core material used to build the magnets, and I felt this would be the key to making the device work. And even though the laws of thermal dynamics flatly prohibit any possibility of perpetual motion, I still felt there might have been something to this."

"Sounds to me like you want to believe?" Marie warmly questioned.

"I think I do. Something like this could change the way we live for the better." Aaron stopped in contemplation. "Sometimes I ask myself what keeps planets and moons moving in orbit? How do galaxies evolve? Is this not perpetual?"

Aaron turned to Carmen who was munching away on a piece of toast. "I told you this could take a while."

Carmen grinned. "We've got time; Dad's back now. We can slow down a bit. Well … on second thought … I would like to be back in residence by 8 o'clock tonight. Will you be done by then?"

"I don't think I should have started this, now that I'm being rushed!" Aaron countered.

"Sorry, ok … I'll be quiet. Cool science fiction tales don't happen too often." Carmen settled back with her toast.

"Ok … In the interest of science fiction, I will continue." Aaron resumed. "Some scientists believe dual magnetism has been shown to exist on a molecular level; this, in turn, represents to me the definite possibility of perpetual motion."

Edward added. "This was Herbert's imaginary invention for his timepiece story, and according to the letter he would have built the watch and written the handbook about 50 years ago."

Aaron expounded. "Seems like an awful lot of effort to make up a story. Back then scholars would have known dual magnetism, if realized, could create perpetual motion … So, Herbert possibly had a general interest in science. Perhaps that gave him the idea."

"But I don't get it," Carmen thought out loud. "Who's the story for?"

Everyone fell silent. No one had a logical answer to Carmen's question, so she waited a few moments, smiled, and then rubbed her hands together in fun. "Okay … so we don't understand *why* Herbert the watchmaker is so weird … *What a surprise!* Aaron … do we get to hear your theory now?" Carmen playfully drummed her fingers on the table.

Aaron took in a deep breath. "Remember, I was thinking about this when I believed there was a chance the watch was real. So, here goes ... My thoughts centered on the possibility of a device that could record time in ... *another dimension.*"

"Whoa!" Carmen exclaimed. She saw the surprised looks on her parents' faces. "That sounds cool ... another dimension. Is this like a meditation thing, with a single pointed focus on a pocket watch?"

Aaron laughed. "I'm afraid I am not centered enough to tap into those kinds of resources ... No, for me it's a science thing, more like physics 101 if you will."

He explained. "Let's think about two absolutes: the speed of light—the constant of our universe upon which all else is formed—and the ultimate rule—energy can neither be created nor destroyed, only transformed. These axioms are continually proven to be true in accordance with Albert Einstein's general theory of relativity." Aaron stopped for a moment to collect his thoughts.

Edward squeezed in a quick comment. "Herbert and I were just talking about Albert Einstein too. I'm sure he would like to be with us now, to be part of our discussion."

Aaron smiled and resumed. "To make this brief, when an object reaches the speed of light it will disappear. An object is energy ... and cannot be destroyed ... so where does it go?"

"Can objects really go that fast?" Carmen asked.

"It is now believed subatomic particles have indeed exceeded the speed of light within the confines of specially designed accelerators ... So theoretically, these particles must have disappeared, albeit for an incredibly short period of time, if the theory of general relativity is accurate. And I should point out the theory has yet to be refuted since its inception in 1915."

Aaron continued. "The drawings I studied on Herbert's imaginary watch showed a movement geared down to a super slow mechanism where a single hand would slowly rotate on an entirely unfamiliar scale. At the time, I thought perhaps the scale and slow movement might be familiar in another dimension. Could whoever designed and built this watch be tracking time for a realm unknown to us, one where a form of life exists in a much higher speed of motion or vibration?"

"Aaron, I'm thinking … Maybe you just proved to us that other dimensions actually *do* exist. Wow! Like … portals! I always thought that idea was super cool," Carmen exclaimed.

Aaron laughed. "Science is all about proving and disproving. The general populace doesn't often become overly excited about discoveries at the sub-atomic level. They seem to prefer the much larger, full-body version … So, I would not recommend going out 'portal' hunting anytime too soon, as most people probably would not understand."

Marie jumped in. "I'm picturing a white rabbit in a waistcoat, carrying a parasol and looking at a pocket watch, leading us to a strange place … This is kind of fun," she smiled.

"You guys could do a sequel to Herbert's book," Edward quipped. "But I gotta say, Aaron, your theory does nicely suit the protagonist from Herbert's tale who supposedly designed this strange timepiece … I think now would be the right time for me to relate the full story Herbert told me."

Edward stopped and scanned the room. He caught the eye of a waiter and signalled. "I think we're going to need some more coffee."

"He definitely picked the right guy," Carmen mused after Edward had finished his narrative.

"This is a finely crafted story. Fascinating …" Marie glanced from Edward to Aaron. "Would not the discovery of a device capable of perpetual motion change the world we live in?"

Both Edward and Aaron nodded. Aaron responded. "In ways, we can't even imagine."

"Well ..." Marie continued. "Is it just a coincidence in the storyline or a carefully crafted form of symbolism that the pocket watch was lost or hidden for a long time in the small town of Petrolia, the very place which prompted a new beginning and changed our world into an oil-based economy?"

"Oh, I get it!" Carmen exclaimed. "That's *so* awesome ... like Petrolia becomes both beginning and end for the massive world oil industry."

"I agree ... a most excellent narrative. Our understanding of Herbert Osterhagen is still evolving," Edward said.

"I don't know ... it gives me chills." Marie held up her arm. "Look, goose bumps!"

"Air conditioning Mom, I get them too." Carmen laughed.

"Darn, and I forgot to pack a sweater," Marie smirked at Carmen.

"You check your purse?" Carmen challenged.

Marie was about to laugh when she remembered something. "Yes ... in my purse. I wanted to show you guys my souvenir." She reached into her purse, which was hanging off the side of her chair, and pulled out a small white folded bag. "I managed to dry it out with the hair dryer last night." She opened the bag and pulled out the green shirt with the outlined maple leaf in white deodorant.

"What do you think?" She held it up in front of her. "Thank you, Edward. This just might be my favourite souvenir ever."

Edward grinned and gazed proudly at his wife and daughter.

"I'm wondering, Dad, should we find out if deodorant comes in assorted colours? I see a possible retirement hobby looming," Carmen giggled.

"What I think ..." Aaron added. "I think the tree house story is just about the best story I have heard throughout this whole ordeal."

Everyone smiled. It was a happy, well-deserved moment, and there was contentment.

Edward lifted his coffee mug in a gesture. "The watch ... even with all the trouble it's caused ... I'd still like it back." He shrugged and took a drink.

"Oh, my God ... not again!" Carmen held her hands to the sides of her face. She was staring at the green shirt held in her mother's hands.

"Carmen, what's wrong?" Marie and everyone else turned to Carmen.

"Oh ... three times ... in three days!" Now she was shaking her head from side to side. "It's happening again!" She was still staring at the shirt.

"What, honey? What's wrong?" Marie expressed concern.

"Déjà vu ... again. I've been through all this exactly ... like I remember a dream ... every detail and ..." she paused. "The colour green ... it's the same colour each time!" Carmen stared at her mother with an almost frightened look. "Am I going crazy?"

Marie let the shirt fall to her lap and took hold of her daughter's hands. "You've been under a lot of stress recently, and you were drugged and took medication."

"I don't know ... I feel ok, and then ... but never like this; so ... real and *so* often." Carmen was shaking. "And why always green? Aaron's green shirt, the green flag and at the museum ..."

Carmen looked up to her father. Tears formed in her eyes, and she seemed confused. "Dad, what did you just say?"

Edward was a little startled. "I ... well ... I said even with all the trouble it's caused ... I'd like to get it back."

Carmen glanced down to her mom's lap for a long moment. She lifted her head up and turned towards to her dad. "I'm not completely sure how, but I think I know where your watch is."

There was complete silence around the restaurant table as everyone fixated on Carmen. She drew in a breath and spoke with self mustered confidence. "We need to go back to the L.A. Mayer Museum."

FIFTY-EIGHT

"Marie, it is so nice to meet you." Amnon Gosser bowed as he took both of Marie's hands in his. "I understand from Carmen and Aaron you were back home finding information which led to this most wonderful outcome."

His smile was heartfelt. Marie liked him immediately. "I'm feeling fortunate and so proud of my family and friends." Their warm smiles lingered for a moment. A connection was made.

Amnon then addressed Edward. "Edward, I am so very happy to see you as well." The men shook hands. "Carmen told me briefly over the phone about your unfortunate detainment in The Old City; it saddens me deeply. Also, the police inspector contacted me and explained about the tragedy. Everyone here at the museum will miss Jessica, or Rachel, as we now know her. This is a time of mourning for us, but also a time of joy in seeing you reunited with your family."

Edward appreciated Amnon Gosser's sincerity. They released the handshake. "We feel much the same way and are trying our best to come to terms with everything."

Amnon nodded and faced the group of four. They were still standing just inside the front entrance. "Please come in; you are most welcome. I have a bit of time … How can I be of assistance?

You said Carmen, that you wished me to show you something? Would you like to view more of the museum?"

"I hope this won't take up too much of your time, Amnon." Carmen replied. "I know this is short notice."

Amnon dismissed her concern with a wave of his hand. "I am happy you and Aaron returned with your family. I hope I can help in any way."

"Thanks, Amnon." Carmen hesitated. She looked down to the floor and up again to her family for support. She saw the words silently form on her mom's lips: 'It's okay.'

"This is gonna sound weird … Crazy might be a better word. I've had this déjà vu thing lately."

"Yes, I believe you experienced that phenomenon right here the last time you and Aaron visited."

"Right … I did. It's happened three times in three days, and I think I just realized my mind is trying to tell me something I should know … Almost as if … well, like I'm being directed from a dream. But the only thing I can remember from the dream is the colour green." Carmen had a lost look on her face.

"This does not sound crazy, Carmen," Amnon said with compassion. "I have experienced a great many eccentricities within and around the art world and witnessed many incredible feats of the human mind that I could never hope to explain. There is so much we do not understand. Please, Carmen, continue with your thoughts, and do not be frightened."

Carmen felt somewhat reassured and continued. "My dad's pocket watch is still missing … I realize the police and your staff searched everywhere you could think of, but I think, mostly because of this déjà vu thing, that it's here in the museum."

Amnon's brow was furrowed, and there was no missing his uncertainty. "Are you able to be more specific, Carmen?"

All eyes were on her. Carmen had passed the point of no return, and the pressure had intensified. "I think it is with the Osterhagen-Saint Germain watch."

There were other common sounds in the museum during the late morning, but nothing could penetrate the veil of silence that enveloped the small group of individuals who were transfixed on Carmen James at this moment. She added, "You said, Amnon, that Jessica would open the case and polish her favourite watch whenever she could."

The furrows on Amnon's brow softened. He cocked his head to the side. Again, seconds of silence passed. Finally, he spoke. "I had another key made so that she would have her access to the Osterhagen display case." He raised his head quickly and informed the group, "I will get the key from my office and meet you at the elevator."

He turned smartly and began to walk away but stopped short and turned back to face Carmen. "And the Osterhagen watch … sits upon loose green velvet." His stare lingered momentarily, and he left.

No one uttered a word on the seemingly long elevator ride to the lower level. When the door opened, a smiling female staff member greeted them. Amnon had a quick conversation with her in Hebrew. She remained by the elevator as they all exchanged smiles and filed past into the now vacant lower level. Carmen caught the words 'stop' and 'no people please.' That was enough to understand Amnon's intent.

Carmen stared into the display case once again, as they all gathered around. This time, however, she was hardly seeing the beautiful Osterhagen-Saint Germain timepiece sitting before her. Instead, she was studying the folds of green velvet that formed a convex base for the small flat platform upon which the watch was positioned.

It took a second for her eyes to focus on an ever so slightly higher rise of cloth towards the back of the case. Her eyes met

Amnon's at the same moment. He saw it too. He moved to the back of the case and inserted a key into a small lock and opened the glass panel. Amnon reached in towards the larger fold. Grasping the rear corner of the cloth, he peeled it back.

Carmen barely perceived the gasp from her mother or the "Wow!" from Aaron. Strangely, a humble feeling permeated her. She had not noticed before just how lovely and perfect the engraving on the silver case of her dad's pocket watch was.

"Damn, no reading glasses." Edward was searching in his shirt pocket. "Bad timing ... left them in the hotel room." Edward held the newly found pocket watch in his hand. He had passed it around for everyone to view, and now, after quite some time and much discussion it was returned to him.

"What's there to see, Dad? Oh ... yes, I guess some of the most exquisite timepieces in the world, including the Breguet Queen, are here in this museum, aren't they?" Carmen offered a sad smile.

"Carmen, you're teasing your dad. He takes his watch observation seriously." Marie admonished.

"Well, I guess we need to come back for another visit." She smiled at Amnon who concurred.

"Of course ... of course Edward, Carmen is right. You, your friends and family will always be most welcome here. This is a happy occasion to be enjoyed, even without reading glasses!" Amnon chuckled.

"Thank you, Amnon, I appreciate your hospitality."

Edward thought for a moment as he smiled at Amnon. "Amnon, you shared a considerable amount of knowledge and personal insight with Carmen and Aaron. We discussed much of what you said, and you helped clear up a lot of the mystery surrounding Herbert Osterhagen."

"I was happy I could be of some assistance," Amnon said. "But we must also acknowledge these young intellectuals, who both exhibit great patience and focus ... I am afraid I can drone on at times." He let out a soft chuckle and nodded to Carmen and Aaron.

"I've been told by my family that I too exhibit that trait upon occasion." Edward got enthusiastic nods from both Carmen and Marie. "So ... I was hoping to perhaps request your opinion on one more thing concerning Herbert Osterhagen and this timepiece." He raised the watch as a gesture. "And ... If you feel the need to drone on ... well, we're good with that."

The curator grinned. "Of course, Edward. What is on your mind?"

Edward began. "As you heard from Carmen, I was detained in the flat in The Old City with Herbert Osterhagen for about three days. Just before the accident with the needle, I was perusing an old handbook, which contains a collection of drawings, blueprints, and specifications of this very watch. Herbert's granddaughter, Rachel, had previously taken the book from her purse, and in so many words told her grandfather he had been lying to her about the watch all along. Rachel also stated she believed she understood why he was doing so. Much later, when she lay unconscious, Herbert told me a tale about this watch. He began by saying it was a story about honour, and I was the only person other than an Osterhagen to have ever heard it told." Edward stopped to take a breath.

Amnon used the brief interlude to interject. "I was hoping to hear more about this ... Its exterior components, or lack thereof, are most unusual ... I have never witnessed anything quite like it."

"Well, this story begins in the late 1700s with Herbert's great, great grandfather Hans Wilhelm Osterhagen ..."

As Edward relayed again the story told to him by Herbert, he could tell Amnon was completely engrossed. It did not take long to narrate, as Amnon did not speak; he only listened. Edward concluded the story with Herbert's reasoning of how the watch came to be in Petrolia, and then his own assumptions as to how the device ended up in a box full of old theatre props. Edward handed the letter from Rachel's purse to Amnon, who read it thoroughly before returning it.

Amnon asked to see the watch again. Edward offered it to him. He took out a pair of reading glasses from the breast pocket of his suit coat and studied the watch closely, remaining silent. He paced back and forth just behind the display and seemed oblivious to everything around him. Both Carmen and Aaron smiled at each other, remembering Amnon's routine from before.

"A most remarkable story." Amnon stopped.

He made quick eye contact with each person before he settled on Edward. "Knowing that Rachel believed her grandfather had been lying to her, and the fact that the handbook is most certainly a forgery and not documentation from Hans Wilhelm Osterhagen … This also describes a next to impossible creation from none other than one of the world's most fascinating and mysterious entities, Saint Germain …"

Amnon smiled and gestured towards the display case. "Perhaps from this watch is where the idea was born: the beautiful Osterhagen-Saint Germain."

Amnon focused closely again at the watch in his hand. "The idea of soldering over the screw heads to prohibit easy access to the movement seems to fit well in the fact that this hides a fictional movement."

"I wish I had brought the handbook for you to look at," Edward said. "Aaron has a university education in physics, and I think he feels Herbert's proposal for a perpetual watch movement is quite convincing."

"By looking at the craftsmanship on this watch, I would not be surprised." Amnon turned to Aaron.

"I guess Marie got it right when she said I wanted to believe, but I'll say Herbert's model of using dual magnetism to create perpetual motion is very intriguing," Aaron stated.

"There is no doubt the storyline is well supported." Amnon was trying to summarize for himself as much as anyone. "The people involved, the historical timeline, the quality ..." He glanced down at the watch. "And the overall potential importance with its shrouded secrecy, appear carefully planned out."

"Let's see ..." Amnon started pacing again, and continued to speak as he moved, "From the laboratory dating of the handbook ... Herbert would have been working on this project in his 30s?"

Edward commented, "We've talked about that as well."

Amnon nodded. "A time when Herbert would have been in the midst of starting a family? From our talk before, I think we believe Herbert Osterhagen's dream was to re-establish the Osterhagen Watch Company."

He addressed Carmen and Aaron. "Am I to guess the question you are asking of me is why?"

"Yes," Carmen answered. "Do you understand *why* Herbert Osterhagen would spend such great time and effort to create this story?"

Amnon smiled kindly to Carmen. "I believe we just answered that question."

Carmen thought out loud; "Because he wanted to bring back the Osterhagen Watch Company ... But how does a fictional story help him to do that?"

"I can see where you are having trouble ..." Amnon focused directly on Carmen. "There is one *very* important word you need to understand Carmen, a word understood and implemented by many of the greatest intellectual minds our world has ever known."

Amnon paused for a moment. "I want you to think back and recall who you believe to be your finest teachers, coaches, professors ... If I ask you to tell me all about what they taught you, I think you will have trouble. However, if I ask what they *did* for you, the answer to this question will come." Amnon's eyes remained fixed with Carmen's.

Her facial expression changed. She glanced at her parents and lingered. She turned back to Amnon with a soft smile of respect. "They *inspired* me."

Amnon returned the smile. "In any language, *inspiration* may well be the second most powerful word in the world, and to understand its meaning is to understand the enormous potential held within." Amnon shifted his gaze to Edward and Marie, and then back to Carmen. "The first word you already know well."

This kind, helpful man moved Carmen. This was a moment of great learning for her, and she knew from here on her understanding of the world and its people had changed. She embraced a sense of humility and respect.

"He was preparing a remarkable story to inspire his children. He wanted them to become the Osterhagen Watch Company," Marie said nodding her head.

Edward agreed. "We don't know the details of Herbert's family, but it would seem that not until his granddaughter Rachel, did the story actually find use."

"Did Herbert lose the watch?" Carmen queried. "Is that why it was in Petrolia?"

"That could easily have happened, given the mental breakdown he suffered after the robbery," Aaron added.

"So, the watch never worked …" Marie thought out loud. "Ironic, don't you think, Edward … You found it in a box of old props and that's all the watch ever really was?"

Edward shrugged in agreement and lowered his head in contemplation. Amnon spoke. "Sometimes props can be useful tools when relating stories to young children. And who knows …

maybe Herbert had plans to someday make the timepiece work in some way."

Edward concurred. "Herbert did say he was planning to tell Rachel the truth." His face clouded over. "I guess he was too late."

Amnon walked over and handed the watch back to Edward. "Truly a beautiful souvenir," he said gently.

Edward stood in silence. He opened and closed the case several times, feeling the precision in his hands. He thought he understood better now just how much talent and knowledge it takes to make what he held. Edward caressed the delicate engraving. He admired the artisan's expression through his fingertips. He opened the case again and gazed at the dial. Even without his reading glasses, the strange symbols caught and held his attention.

After some time, he raised his head. Everyone was smiling at him. From the loving eyes of his wife, Edward shifted his gaze to the kind, gentle face of Amnon Gosser and spoke. "This watch and Herbert Osterhagen will forever hold secrets we may never fully comprehend. We've come full circle … This may well be the greatest adventure of our lives. Speaking for myself, I learned a great deal and met some fascinating people. I formed an even greater love and respect for my family and friends. I'll return home a wiser man."

Edward focused again on the watch and held it up. "I would like for this watch *not* to return with me." He looked first to Carmen and Aaron, then to his wife. He saw her expression. She was reading his thoughts.

Edward turned to Amnon. "I would like to believe Rachel selected the home for this beautiful, mysterious timepiece."

"In memory of Rachel Cohen, and as a tribute to her grandfather, Herbert Osterhagen, I would like to donate this memorable pocket watch to this museum." Edward took a step forward and held out the watch.

Amnon stayed silent for a moment. He spoke with sincerity, "On behalf of myself and L.A. Mayer Museum, and with humble reverence, we welcome your generous offer." He stepped forward and accepted the watch.

Amnon gazed at the artefact in his hand. When he raised his head, he spoke firmly. "This watch shall sit proudly beside the Osterhagen-Saint Germain. I would like to title it 'The Mystery Watch' with a short story displayed about its mysterious past. And with respect to Herbert Osterhagen, I will personally see that this timepiece shall never be dismantled."

Amnon opened the watch and walked over to the display case. He laid it alongside the Osterhagen watch, then readjusted the green velvet folds and closed the rear glass panel. Amnon Gosser turned the key in the lock.

ALL WAS RIGHT with the world as Edward, Marie, Carmen, and Aaron left the doors of the L. A. Mayer Museum an hour later. The day was warm, bright, and clear. They would enjoy a leisurely walk back to the hotel, where they planned to eat lunch and discuss Aaron's wording of an accompanying note with a fax copy of the letter from Rachel's purse to his boss Stanley Crawford. Next, they would need to go to the police station, after which there were flights to be booked and the return drive to Tel Aviv to bring Carmen back to her residence. All in all, they were looking forward to going back to a much quieter, less stressful existence.

Amnon had taken the time to give them a shortened version of a horological museum tour, and even without his reading glasses, Edward enjoyed seeing and talking watches and clocks with Amnon and Aaron. He was quite moved to view the Queen, the Breguet No. 160, in person. Marie and Carmen tagged along and observed how easy it was for men to become so obsessed with mechanical things. A much too short mother-daughter time.

At the end of the tour, Amnon made them promise to come and visit the museum the next time they were in Israel. They promised and said Carmen's graduation would be in a little less than a year. Email addresses were exchanged, and Amnon asked for a date he could enter on his calendar as soon as she knew.

When they said their goodbyes, Amnon joked with Edward, telling him he would be contacted at the first sign of any movement from the single watch hand. Edward said he would be back in a year to check for himself with reading glasses in hand. The men shook on their agreement. The women and Amnon hugged.

Marie took hold of her husband's hand as they walked down the shaded and quiet tree-lined street. "That was a wonderful thing you did today, Edward. I understand how much meaning the pocket watch holds for you now." She turned to him, looking up.

Edward continued to stare straight ahead. As best he could, he began reciting some words from memory, "These two watches were destined to cross paths. Many years passed … the Queen lost her throne. Their ultimate destiny remains the same … They can only meet in one place, the place where the Queen regained her throne." Edward stopped speaking, even though he remembered the last line.

He took his sunglasses out of his pocket and put them on. For some reason, the shaded light was causing his eyes to water.

He squeezed his wife's hand, as he softly said the last line. "It is to that place you must go, Edward."

They walked on, in a contented silence.

FIFTY-NINE

SUNDAY, APRIL 19, 2015. 1:00 P.M.
JERUSALEM, ISRAEL

A<small>LMOST ONE FULL YEAR</small> had passed since Edward, Marie, and Carmen last walked through the front entrance of the L.A. Mayer Museum for Islamic Art. Amnon Gosser had extended an invitation to them, along with Aaron, and Inspector Claude Gadgét, when they were all together for dinner at the Montefiore Restaurant the evening before, celebrating Carmen's graduation from the University of Tel Aviv. This event would be a small—by invitation only—gathering of 20 people. The lower level of the museum was to be closed to the public, while Champagne and hors d'oeuvres were served. They would get to meet Claude Gadgét and Amnon Grosser's wives today as well. Also in attendance would be Meira and David, the receptionist and manager, from the Prima Royale Hotel.

The previous evening's celebration went well, with lots of entertaining, interesting conversation and plenty of catching up. The most important subject on everyone's list was Herbert Osterhagen. True to his word, Inspector Claude Gadgét had personally overseen Herbert's hospital care, his subsequent legal hearing, and finally his extradition to the United States. The Inspector explained in detail to everyone over dinner the proceedings right up to the judge's final decision: no charges were laid against Herbert Osterhagen due to mental incompetence.

Inspector Gadgét also stayed in close contact with the N.Y.P.D. and Dr. Scarlett Dae from the psychiatric facility in Brooklyn where Herbert currently resided. He was pleased to announce the proceedings in New York went favourably for Herbert as well. Again, no charges were brought against him. The death of the man in his watch shop was ruled as an act of self-defence, and Herbert was placed in the care of Dr. Dae. His diagnosis was a relapse to his former mental condition, and, sadly, Herbert had still not spoken. However, on a positive note, Dr. Dae informed the Inspector that Herbert had adapted well to the facility.

Claude Gadgét then told everyone he was not quite sure how, as the last message had been brief, but Herbert Osterhagen was once again repairing watches somewhere on the grounds of the institution and word had spread fast. Dr. Dae jokingly stated she might need to hire a receptionist for Herbert, as at present she had to fill the role herself, and this was fast becoming a full-time job.

Aaron informed everyone he had been working hard over the past eight months to establish his own environmental company in Grand Cayman. He said he was fortunate to have signed a steady contract with the government for various land and water studies and assessments. Aaron thought his timing had been perfect and said he probably owed getting the contract to none other than Stanley Crawford, who had moved on to 'bigger and better targets'. No friendship was lost between the two men, and in Stanley's eyes, the watch ordeal had been nothing more than a bad investment. The governing agencies of Grand Cayman were dissatisfied with having to deal with the likes of Stanley Crawford. With the 5-year contract due for renewal, they welcomed the opportunity to award it to a new company owned and run by a native resident.

The person most surprised by this news was Carmen, as she and Aaron had been keeping in touch via Skype or email, and he had not mentioned a thing about his new business. Aaron said he wanted to surprise her.

Amnon Gosser mentioned the pleasant outcome of how popular the 'mystery pocket watch' had become. He credited its success to the fact that the brief story displayed with the watch outlined the possibility that Saint Germain himself may have had something to do with the designing and building of the timepiece. The word spread, and people worldwide began showing an interest and wanted to pay homage to the great man, even if it was because of a fictional story. This only seemed to add to the mystery. Amnon said he and his staff enjoyed the enthusiasm and that it was 'breathing new life' into the museum.

The most entertaining part of the evening started when Edward told of his greatest surprise of the past year, and it was not any one of the many surprises from Herbert Osterhagen. No, it came when he got back home to Petrolia and went to visit his good friend Derek. The experience almost put him into shock. Derek's place was spotlessly clean. He had no idea how this turn of events could have possibly happened. Marie purposely did not inform him on what transpired when he was gone. She took great delight in Edward's surprise. They went on to clarify for everyone, Derek's former living conditions. Marie had the whole party in tears of laughter as she recounted the now infamous spaghetti dinner. It went over well within the Montefiore's Italian ambience.

Edward explained how he had completed the aluminum welding on the drone project, and how Derek enjoyed taking 'her' up and over top of Edward's house to perform aerobatic manoeuvres for Marie's entertainment before she left for work on selected mornings. They both agreed it was sad the group would not get a chance to meet Derek. He was invited, of course, but declined, as he was engrossed in his new retina scanner project with a completion date of less than two months.

Marie completed her Derek saga by sharing some new, somewhat astonishing information that not even Edward or Carmen had heard. Not only was Derek now having his home and car professionally cleaned and maintained on a weekly basis, but also, he recently asked Marie if she would accompany him to a men's clothing store. Derek was hoping to do some serious upgrades to his wardrobe. Apparently, he hinted to Marie he might have met a woman-friend at an electronics store.

And finally, the night belonged to Carmen. Edward and Marie were so proud of their daughter. She had suddenly 'grown up' right before their eyes. She radiated beauty, poise, and confidence as she responded to the many questions asked of her. Carmen would be going home. She planned on teaching some ballet classes while studying her job options and finalizing her resume. Everyone at the table that night knew for certain that this young new graduate had a very bright future ahead of her.

As they passed now through the front doors of the museum, memories came rushing back. But is it not true that time can soften emotions and alter a former experience until it is remembered in an almost dreamlike state, in which prior fear and anguish are selectively dulled, and past positive reinforcements become enhanced until overall acceptance is maintained?

Edward and Carmen's eyes met in a reassuring manner, as they were greeted by a staff member who escorted them to the elevator.

They arrived fashionably late, and were the last guests shown into the semi-formal gathering. The men dressed in light coloured suits and ties or sports coats with collared shirts. The women wore summer dresses and heels. All eyes fixed on Carmen when she entered. Her hair was up and accented with several braids wrapping around her bun. Her up-do emphasized the cut-out in the back of her pale blue lace sheath dress. A white gold sapphire necklace sparkled and enhanced her glowing skin tone, and accented the polished chain on her quilted soft leather clutch.

Amnon Gosser hurried over to welcome them. He took both of Carmen's hands in his. Stepping back and holding her at arms' length, he slowly moved his head from side to side, as he marvelled at the sight before him. "Carmen, I believe our guests here today will be unable to admire any of our lovely artefacts, as they will be completely enchanted and unable to look away from you. You are, Carmen, the beauty an artist may strive to portray but always fails."

"Thank you, Amnon." Carmen's smile was captivating. "No one has ever said anything like that to me before. I think I should travel in these circles more often." Laughter prevailed. Carmen's humour even seemed to exude a refined elegance.

Sparkling, full-bodied French Champagne was served in tall fluted crystal glasses, and waiters with sterling silver trays offered delicious hors d'oeuvres. A violinist and cellist, both wearing tuxedos, had set up in the corner, and soft classical music drifted in and around those in attendance.

Amnon Gosser was a superb host. He attended to everyone with style and grace, giving each person his complete, undivided attention as he conversed with refined eloquence. He circulated, introducing his lovely wife, who was equally as friendly, graceful and charming. They made a lovely, older couple.

Inspector Claude Gadgét's wife, who had been born in Paris, contributed to matching linguistic accents among the pair. She stood a bit taller than the inspector, and had stylishly cut chestnut hair, complimenting her slim figure. They both fit in well at these types of events. Where Claude Gadgét was calm, sure-footed and observant, she was more the lively and fun-loving type.

As the afternoon's engagement evolved, the James family and their friend Aaron felt like celebrities. Everyone in attendance knew either some of or most of the adventure from the year before and engaged them in concerned conversation. Carmen did manage to spend considerable time with Meira, who was beautiful in a cream coloured dress with a jewel-embellished band around her waist. They made a promise to try and stay in touch with each other no matter where Carmen ended up. David, the hotel manager, was delighted they returned and made sure they received an upgraded room at no extra cost. He made it clear it would always be available to them.

The chilled Champagne fostered warm friendship, which made for a fantastic closing to Carmen's time in Israel. The women got together and took pictures, while the men entertained themselves admiring and discussing the timepieces throughout the exhibits.

Amnon eventually broke free and stood beside the musicians, and he asked them politely to cease playing for a brief interlude. He reached into a bag behind the cellist and pulled out a box wrapped in gold paper. "Excuse me please, everyone!" He called out loudly.

Once having everyone's attention, he moved forward and spoke in a clear voice. "Thank you for your attention, and I ask you all to gather around please."

The small crowd of twenty moved in close. "Carmen, if you would please come forward and stand beside me …" Carmen suddenly felt nervous, but she smiled and gracefully slid in beside Amnon. "I would like to take this opportunity to formally congratulate you on your graduation from the University of Tel Aviv. I am honoured that you chose our country to further your education, and I strongly believe our world will be a better place as you embark on your chosen profession.

There came a round of applause as Carmen quietly responded, "Thank you Amnon."

He held up the golden wrapped box. "This is a gift for you Carmen, and for your mother and father to admire as well."

Amnon paused. "Before I give it to you, I want you to know this is not just from me, but also from the L.A. Mayer Museum. It was bequeathed to me from a rather large estate with one important stipulation: I am to give it to someone who I think matches in body, mind, and spirit, the very virtues this gift has, over the years, come to symbolize. It is not brand new, although you shall be the first to use it." Amnon extended the box to Carmen. "It gives me immense pleasure …"

Carmen bit down on her lower lip as she took the box in her hands. Her gaze left Amnon and fell to the gold wrapping. Her newly manicured nails slipped under the folded edges and tore open the paper. As the first section was exposed, her eyes were met with a wavy green pattern of a meticulously crafted wooden box. She tore more paper away, showing a small golden crown affixed to the edge. Her breath caught in her throat, and she gasped. Carmen recognized what was in her hands: a box identical to one displayed in their living room at home.

She gazed into Amnon's smiling face. "I think they got the box colour right. What do you think?" he asked.

She tried to speak but could not. Her eyes teared up, knowing what the box contained.

With watery eyes, Carmen opened the lid and saw a soft yellow, leather chamois laying across the lower half of the case. A pocket in the lid held small green booklets and an identification card. *Carmen James* had been written in the space for the owner's name. When she lifted the leather cloth away, she began to cry. It did not happen often, but Carmen could find no words to say.

Amnon took the liberty and addressed Carmen's audience on her behalf. "It is a Rolex Datejust, 36-millimetre size, with a fluted white-gold bezel on a jubilee bracelet, and a pink dial."

There came a soft myriad of exclamations from everyone as Carmen tore her gaze away and again looked to Amnon. "Why …? How do I deserve such a wonderful gift?"

"I thought of no one else. I told you a stipulation is in place for which I am entrusted. I am convinced *you* are the person deserving of this watch."

Amnon acknowledged the audience as he spoke. "I see in this watch: beauty, intelligence, and strength. Ultimately, though, it tells a story of success. You have demonstrated these virtues to everyone here. Carmen ... wear this with pride."

Applause sounded with smiling faces all around. "Now please, Carmen, let us determine if I got the sizing of the bracelet right." He reached out to hold the bottom of the box, and Carmen carefully lifted the watch out and put it on her wrist. She fumbled a bit with the clasp but figured it out quickly. Carmen held out her wrist for everyone to view. Tears glistened on her cheeks, her eyes sparkled, and the watch dazzled, amidst a spectacular occasion.

Carmen waited momentarily, and then she flung herself on Amnon and hugged him forcefully. "You have always been kind, giving and helpful, to me Amnon. Yes, you are an inspiration in my life. Thank you so much!" They released their hug and stood back facing each other. "I hope I can do the same for others someday."

"I witness it happening now, Carmen." Amnon gave her a heart-warming smile. He signalled to the musicians, and they resumed playing.

He turned to once again address everyone. "We still have much champagne and food remaining, please continue to enjoy yourselves!"

Carmen mingled and displayed her lovely watch. After everyone had a chance to see it up close and chat with her about it, Aaron approached and asked if he could speak with her alone.

They walked over to a vacant area away from the main activity. Aaron began, "I want to ask you a question."

"You're thinking you might like to try on my watch ..." Carmen's eyes gleamed. "I don't think the pink dial is right for you."

"Okay, I guess you're right. Well, what else can we talk about then ... Can I tell you a bit about my new business venture?"

"Absolutely ... wow Aaron, what a surprise! It sounds really great."

"I do feel good about it, and I know I've had some luck. Fortunately, I hired a senior manager with a lot of experience. I worked with him a short while before and really liked him. He taught me a great deal. When I heard he was considering retirement, I contacted him and asked for his help. He agreed and is guiding me through."

"And you already landed a good contract to start up with ... You must be so busy now, yet you found the time to come here for me."

"I am happy to be here and I wanted to ask you a question ... It needs to be done in person."

A startled look came over Carmen. "Ummm ..."

Aaron caught on to her reaction. He laughed, but it did not stop a fluttering feeling. The fact that she was somehow even more beautiful than he remembered did not help. "Oh ... I did not mean to alarm you, and I do not expect an answer right this minute." He smiled. "Will you accept a job offer from me? I would like you to come and work with me at my company."

"Wow!"

"I know it's an important question. I have been going over things with my senior manager. The company is eligible for government funded, co-op training. As you and I have been keeping in touch with each other this past year, I already know your certifications, and which additional ones you will want to acquire if you decide to accept my proposal." He stopped short on the last word. "We will need to go over specific details, but what it could mean is you would need to take another six months of courses focusing mainly around marine biology."

"And ..." he smiled enthusiastically, "that will include a scuba diving license as well—all paid for, including accommodations."

This was turning out to be quite a day for Carmen. Her brain just could not quite keep up with her emotions. She needed him to continue talking to let herself catch up. "This would be my first environmental job. I do not have experience … Why me, Aaron?"

Aaron did his best to understand her comment. "I know what courses you took, I know your grades, and I am getting to know your hobbies, interests and past achievements. Let's be honest." Aaron held her gaze steadily. "We both know you will have a broad selection of job opportunities. You told me you love to travel, and I think you would like the Cayman Islands."

They held eye contact until Carmen let her gaze drop. "Is that the shirt?" The colour teal green showed from beneath his light wool sports coat.

"It's the one," Aaron remarked.

"Did you get all the stains out? Your coat is covering it." Carmen looked up again.

"Not entirely, but I intend to keep it."

"Thank you for wearing it today."

Aaron smiled. He had his answer. Carmen glanced around excitedly. "Let's go find Mom and Dad!"

THE NEWS SPREAD QUICKLY throughout the room. Everyone was excited for Carmen. Congratulations and best wishes surrounded her on this perfect day. Edward became busy figuring out his options for staying with Carmen for winter retirement in Grand Cayman. Marie was not exactly moved by that thought, but a two-week holiday during the cold Canadian winters sure sounded nice. Aaron assured them both they would always be welcome. Accommodations and tour guide included.

The party was winding down. The guests started saying their goodbyes, and the musicians began packing up their instruments.

Marie rounded up Edward and Amnon, and when she had them together she asked Amnon, "I hate to trouble you Amnon, but I would love to get a picture of you and Edward holding the pocket watch together. I can't believe I forgot to do it last year."

She hesitated, "I'm sorry, you will need to go to your office for the key."

Amnon gave Marie a knowing smile. "Ah, Marie ... we think alike. I put the key in my pocket this morning for this very same purpose." He reached into his pocket and pulled out the key. "*I also* remembered no photos were taken on that special day." He took Marie's hand and gestured towards the new case, which now held the two Osterhagen watches. "Our chance is now, to make amends," he chuckled.

They made their way over to the display, which was still a free-standing case, although a bit larger and rectangular shaped now. They all complimented on the showcase earlier, with its carefully worded write-up describing 'The Mystery Watch,' and Amnon again reiterated how successful this watch display had become.

Amnon walked behind, unlocked the case and withdrew the pocket watch. As he joined Edward in front of the case, he commented, "So Edward, the display hand did not move a fraction in almost 1 year." He laughed. "There has been no temptation to dismantle the watch."

Edward laughed in agreement. "Yes, and with the success it has generated, I think it is a most fitting conclusion to a remarkable story."

Amnon nodded as Marie stood back with her phone and began taking pictures of the men in different poses, including shaking hands and with their arms around each others' shoulders in a heartfelt gesture of friendship, as they showed off the watch.

Carmen spotted the activity from across the room, where she stood talking with some other guests, and called out, "Make sure you get a few shots wearing your reading glasses Dad! Remember the big deal last year?"

Her comment drew laughter from the photo shoot group. Edward put them on upside down for fun, until Marie insisted that he wear them properly for a few final shots.

One of the musicians gestured to Amnon from across the room, when he noticed the picture taking was complete. Amnon left Edward with the watch. "Please excuse me for a moment. Edward, take some time with the watch." He smiled and turned away to consult with the musicians.

Carmen called out again, this time to her mom. "Can we see? I want to check out the upside-down glasses." Marie hurried over to Carmen's group. She started bringing the photos up for viewing.

Edward found himself standing alone, holding the watch. Looking around the room, then gazing downwards, he knew it would be a long time, if ever, when the opportunity might present itself to lay his eyes on this creation again.

He recalled the adventure this artefact brought to him. It almost felt like a dream now; a dream he would never have wanted to miss.

Edward studied the engraving and thought about Herbert Osterhagen. He would never forget. Opening the case, Edward wondered once more where the idea for these strange symbols came from. He rotated the watch to admire them, perhaps for a final time, at different angles: a simple yet mysterious design.

Something caught his eye. He did a double take. His vision did not seem clear; did he miss a colour? Edward adjusted his glasses and focused more closely. He blinked and tried moving the focal point distance, then flipped the watch over. He stared at the other side, the same thing. His heart leaped in his chest.

Edward stood frozen in place. As his eyes fixated, it felt as though ice was coursing through his veins and the colour drained from his face. He could only mutter under his breath, as breathing became difficult. "Oh, my God … This is *not* my watch!"

His hands trembled. *There's no discolouration from the soldering. The blue isn't there! It hasn't been taken apart ... This is not my watch! Herbert Osterhagen switched them!* His mind started racing. He tried to calm himself by breathing deeply. It helped somewhat. Looking up, he saw everyone was still occupied.

Edward took one long, last close inspection before he closed the case. He tried feverishly to piece things together. *How could I have missed this? My glasses ... I didn't have my glasses ...*

The answer became obvious to Edward; there must be two watches, and they were switched at the museum when he was unconscious. But something did not fit; Rachel took the watch, and she hid it. She also told him he would get it back.

No ... There must be more to it ... Something dragged his memory back to the day at the watch shop. He remembered Herbert's reaction when he told him he knew about soldering and how the temperature needed to be above 1000 degrees Fahrenheit for the blueing of the surrounding metal to occur. *Herbert had been quite interested ... The watch was out of my sight for a moment ...*

Another memory flashed in his head. This one confirmed it; it was a memory from the flat in the Old City. Herbert had made an odd comment: *'From the moment you left my shop in New York, the watch was not yours.'*

Now, Edward realized Herbert had been speaking the truth. The hair rose on the back of his neck. *Herbert wasn't lying!*

"Edward ... Edward, is something wrong ... Edward?" Marie had returned and stood beside him.

"Oh ... Marie." Edward turned.

"Are you ok? You look like you've just seen a ghost!" she said in a concerned voice.

"Yes ... Well, no ... Maybe a bit overwhelmed. Holding the watch again ... it brought back a lot of memories." Edward breathed deeply.

"Should you sit down?" Marie put her hand on his arm.

"I'll go to the men's room; a drinking fountain is on the way …" He took off his glasses, stuffed them inside his sports coat and handed Marie the watch. "Please give this to Amnon so he can put it back. Tell him I just need a few minutes."

"Okay … you sure?" She took the watch, gave him a kiss on the cheek, and they both went in different directions.

The men's room was vacant. Edward went to the sink and splashed cold water on his face. He needed to think clearly. Edward looked up. Staring back at him from the mirror was the dripping wet face of a very confused man. All the events from a year ago came flooding back in waves. Uncertainty turned to desperation, as he tried to reason things out. He did not have enough time.

A strange feeling came over him. He wanted Herbert to be with him now. Even if he did not speak, just being here would be enough. Edward began to settle as he imagined the watchmaker beside him. Several minutes passed, until one sentence Herbert had previously spoken resounded in his mind over and over: *'This is a story about honour.'* It played over and over. *'This is a story about honour', 'This is a story about honour.'*

As Edward dried his face, he thought to himself, *I don't have to know everything … Maybe I've been given all I need.*

When he returned to the festivities, he was greeted with smiling faces. He especially noticed the light refraction in the room, which caused precious artefacts and jewellery alike to shimmer and sparkle. He heard the wonderful sound of laughter. The room radiated in joy and happiness.

His eyes found his beautiful daughter. This was her 'moment in the sun'. She had exceeded all his expectations, and he felt so proud and grateful. When he looked away, his eyes were drawn to his lovely wife. In her hopeful smile, he could discern the only thing on Marie's mind was his well-being. He gave her his best 'I'm okay' smile back.

As he walked slowly towards her, an old quote he read somewhere many years ago came to his thoughts. It completely enveloped him. Edward understood why, as he recited it silently to himself.

'He who would uphold honour shall forever be at court with himself.'

SIXTY

FRIDAY, NOVEMBER 6, 2015. 1:00 P.M.
BROOKLYN, NEW YORK

The Greatest of Mysteries (Epilogue)

NARRATED BY: EDWARD JAMES

With an aura of sadness, I sat waiting to see the doctor. There were no others in the modern sitting area other than a friendly young male receptionist who sat behind a marble, half-moon counter. Staring at a cascading glass and stone waterfall, I thought again why I was here, in the sprawling mental health institution in Brooklyn, New York.

A letter had been delivered to me at home 2 days prior. The letterhead revealed it had been sent from Dr. Scarlett Dae, the head clinical psychologist of this hospital, asking me to come to the institution to consult with her at the earliest convenient date. There was not much detail, but enough to set upon me a melancholic mood, which seemed to match the cloudy skies and cold, damp temperatures typical of early November.

I pulled out the letter from the breast pocket of my sports coat and reread it.

Dear Edward James,

I am the clinician overseeing the care of Herbert Osterhagen at our mental health facility. I regret to inform you Herbert Osterhagen has passed away. He died peacefully of natural causes on Monday, November 2, 2015. He will be missed by our staff and residents alike. It was a pleasure for us to have known and cared for him since his arrival at our facility.

Before his passing, Herbert stated in writing his desire for me to serve as adjudicator and executor of his will. This letter is sent on behalf of the estate of Herbert Osterhagen. Please acknowledge this as a request that I might personally give you a package and a letter from Herbert.

I found Herbert Osterhagen to be an interesting man. I look forward to meeting you and possibly spending some time talking a bit more about your relationship with Herbert.

Yours truly,
Dr. Scarlett Dae Ph.D.
Head of the Clinical Psychology Department

As I tucked the folded letter back into my pocket the young receptionist called out, "Mr. Edward James ... Scarlett and Sigmund will see you now."

Sigmund? He must have noticed the confused expression on my face, but he just gave me a friendly smile and pointed to the hallway at the end of the room. "Their office is just down on the left."

"Thank you." My confusion turned to mild uncertainty as I walked through the corridor. A few more steps brought me to a natural wood door with a brass handle. Before I could knock, the latch turned. Perfect timing. The door opened, and the doctor greeted me, although what I saw I had not been expecting.

"Edward ... thank you so much for your promptness." An attractive, tall woman I would guess to be no more than in her early 40s, who I knew could easily pass for mid to early 30s given different clothes, stood before me. Her wavy auburn hair flowed past her shoulders and sashayed against the shimmering fine wool fabric of a tailored navy coloured suit. She wore a light beige silk blouse under the jacket. Peeking beneath the hem of her shapely fitting pants were matching blue—what I guessed to be—Italian leather heels. She wore no jewellery, save for a watch that at first glance appeared to be a simple white-gold design on a black alligator strap. I spotted the blue cabochon stone mounted on the crown and stole a closer look. *A Cartier with a hand painted dial!*

Suddenly, I was more than just a little impressed, and when considering the extraordinary depth of her large green eyes, I think mesmerized was more fitting. However, what she held in her arms demanded most of my attention.

"Please come in, Edward." She graciously stepped aside to let me enter. "And let me introduce you to Sigmund."

The dark eyes of a cute, small tan and black dog studied me. "He is a Welsh Terrier, 6 years old."

"Sigmund?" I did not intentionally try to make fun of his name. She showed no offense.

"His name selection is obvious. I wanted to do it, and it turned out to be the right choice." She paused to gaze down and gently caressed him behind his ears. "We talk to each other ... He says he is the re-incarnation of *the* Sigmund Freud."

Dr. Scarlett Dae held a straight face and looked directly at me. This was not exactly the kind of statement I would expect from the head of the clinical psychology department in maybe the largest mental institution in Brooklyn, New York.

I did my best to go with the flow. "Re-incarnation ... Sure, okay, why not? I can see a resemblance. I guess he picked the right place to be."

I offered Sigmund a sniff of my down-turned hand. "Nice to make your acquaintance, Sigmund ... I really like how you keep your beard." He took in my scent for a few brief seconds, and then raised his head to study my face again. He licked my hand softly.

Dr. Scarlett Dae offered me a beautiful smile. "This is the perfect place to go with it ... don't you think? We enjoy a particular kind of freedom around here." I assessed the fresh look in her eyes to be somewhat mischievous. It was familiar.

I understood so well, I entertained the idea that I might be looking at my own daughter Carmen in 15 or 20 years. "Isn't that what I said ... He picked the right place?" She joined me in laughter, as I took a seat in her spacious and tastefully decorated office.

"Edward, I would like to talk a bit about Herbert before I give you a letter from him. There is also a box with some items for you." I settled into a comfortable chair across from a large solid coffee table, while she set Sigmund on the top of it. He found an empty corner and lay down, all the while keeping his eyes fixated on me.

"Of course, I would appreciate that. I've so often wondered how Herbert had been doing over the last 18 months or so." A twinge of remorse ran through me. "It's too bad I'm finding out like this."

"I understand," she said in a gentle voice. Sigmund turned his head and glanced at her, but quickly returned his attention to me. I started to feel like I was being scrutinized.

She must have sensed my uneasiness. "Please forgive Sigmund, he probably thinks we are working now, and he does not like to miss anything."

Okay, I figured. *That makes me feel better.* I guess I need to keep in mind where I am.

She continued. "When Herbert came to us, he responded well to his medication. However, he ultimately refrained from speaking, and right up until the end I never heard him utter a single word. He would only use a small notepad to make his needs and intentions understood."

Dr. Dae smiled. "He had only been here a week when he made a request to be able to work on watches."

I offered a comment. "Herbert Osterhagen is an extraordinary watchmaker."

She nodded. "We wholeheartedly endorse a hands-on therapeutic approach here at the institution. However, we are not really set up for that sort of activity, so unfortunately, we had to decline Herbert's request. Then, approximately two weeks later, an anonymous donor contacted us. A gentleman asked to fund an arrangement where Herbert Osterhagen would be set up in an appropriately equipped room to work on timepieces. Also included was a sizeable donation to the institution." She paused briefly. Maybe she was giving me a chance to think for myself who the donor might be, but I did not have a clue.

Dr. Dae continued. "To summarize, the board of directors met, and a decision was made. A single room with washroom facilities would be converted to a small watch shop, and within a week or so Herbert was working on timepieces. At first, it was difficult to provide enough work for him, as he wanted to stay there most of the day. And of course, we needed to have someone keep watch over him. However, eventually a set of cameras and monitors were installed, and as word got around about his expertise … well, there were not enough hours in the day! A backlog of work orders ensued." She laughed. "There was no charge, of course, for the work Herbert did. But donations for the Institution were accepted, and well … within 3 or 4 months, the complete cost of the investment had been recovered in full!"

"Inspector Claude Gadgét said your next step might be to hire a receptionist for Herbert," I joked.

"Yes … and we could easily afford it." She laughed as she reached down into a side pocket in her briefcase and took out an envelope, which she handed to me with an extended arm. "Another interesting thing … about two weeks after Herbert began servicing timepieces, a package came via courier: a beautiful, gilded sign, which we mounted on the door of the watch room. It read: *The Osterhagen Watch Company. Established 1728.*"

I felt a lump form in my throat. The symbolism was striking. I felt a pang of sorrow deep inside. I knew Scarlett Dae would not understand, but I wanted to say it. "It's what he always needed."

She gazed at me thoughtfully. Now I caught a glimpse of the intelligence within her beautiful eyes. Somehow, she sensed the profound significance of my words. Sigmund turned to her as well. Scarlett rose up from her chair and offered, "During his stay with us, Herbert Osterhagen had but one visitor other than the many that arrived for timekeeping repair. He came the day before Herbert passed away. The man dressed tastefully and showed good manners. His visit was short, and he did not mention his name, but I believe their meeting had significant meaning for Herbert."

I stopped breathing and needed to force myself to take in a deep breath. "Why do you think that?"

"After he left … was the only time I ever witnessed a smile on the face of Herbert Osterhagen. Herbert died in the early morning hours of the following day."

I looked at her, but I envisioned a time hundreds of years past.

"I am sorry for your loss, Edward." She rose from her chair. "I am going to leave you with your letter while I go and retrieve your package. Sigmund will be here if you need anything." She walked out of her office, leaving the door open slightly.

I focused on Sigmund. We held our gaze for a few moments until he yawned and let his head down on his front paws. He seemed to understand he could take a break now.

I examined the front of the envelope. Printed in ink was *Edward James—to be opened after my death.* Tearing the paper, I removed one printed page and read it silently to myself.

> *Dear Edward,*
>
> *Thank you is the word I write to you now. When we first met, I could not bring myself to trust you. I was mistaken, and it resulted in the death of Rachel. There could have been no loss greater for me. In a twist of irony, I now write to you as the person I believe I can count on above all others. With trust, truth can follow. Your understanding is now almost complete.*
>
> *The following facts shall assist you: my great-great-grandfather, Hans Wilhelm Osterhagen, built the replica watch (which I am sure you now know exists). He is also the creator of the leather handbook. The replica watch and the handbook were bequeathed to me. I took it upon myself some time ago to solder over the screw heads to make what I thought would be, at least externally, an exact replica of the original. I then crafted another handbook, and using some antiquing techniques I created an exact copy of the original. Following this, I destroyed the original.*

Why did I do this? The answer is to accomplish what has now been accomplished. The authentic timepiece was protected. Can you understand this Edward?

I did not know about the soldering discolouration until I saw the original watch for the first time when you came to my shop in Brooklyn. Yes, I switched the watches then, but I believed you would someday notice the difference and go looking for your watch. Due to the interruption by the men, I thought my only recourse would be to regain the replica I gave you, and re-solder the screw heads at a higher temperature, which would make the surrounding metal turn blue. It appeared as though I would accomplish my goal: to have the replica in my possession for even as little as one hour so I could make the replica watch indistinguishable from the original. I would have then given it back to you with my sincerest apologies.

But, yet again, I was mistaken, and I think now, rightly so; Rachel had no knowledge of the replica watch or what I had done with the handbook. These were my safeguards, and because of fear, I left it too long to tell her the truth. She was devastated by what I did to you and your daughter at the museum, and the only reason she assisted me in moving you to the flat in the Old City was out of loving devotion for her grandfather. Rachel would not, however, give me the watch; she insisted she would return it to you as soon as possible.

It came to my attention that you found and donated the replica watch to L.A. Mayer Museum. I was happy to know that.

I told you before this is a story about honour. It still is. This you have shown to me, Edward.

Herbert

I sat in quiet contemplation of the letter in front of me. What I had been through concerning the pocket watch paled in comparison to what Herbert had suffered. He dedicated much of his existence to the search for and protection of a principal of honour. Sadness swept through me, and I thought of the cruel irony of where I found the watch. For how many years had it lay hidden, right beneath his fingertips. At this moment, I felt grateful he had not asked me to disclose the exact location. I folded the page and replaced it in the envelope. There now remained for me only one final question.

Footsteps echoed in the hallway beyond the door. Dr. Dae entered the office just as I put the envelope into my jacket pocket along with the other letter. She carried a medium sized cardboard box in her hands. It had the top flaps tucked into itself, which kept it closed. "I hope you had sufficient time with your letter?"

"Yes, I did thanks," I said, as I got to my feet and stood to face her.

"As you can see, this has not been prepared for shipping. Herbert asked that I give you this in person." With a nod of understanding she said, "He packed this up on his last day … somehow he knew."

Scarlett contemplated a moment. "Herbert Osterhagen was under my care for but a brief time, and he never spoke to me. He suffered greatly … We did the best we could for him." She smiled. "I believe he lived quietly with a great passion for his work. The lawyer in charge of Herbert's estate informed me that a substantial self-sustaining scholarship fund is to be set up for a watch making school in Germany. Herbert owned two properties here in Brooklyn and a building in The Old City of Jerusalem. They were recently sold. The value of the fund will be in the millions of dollars, ensuring the Osterhagen name shall remain within the domain of horology indefinitely."

She was met with one of the brightest smiles a man could give. "That is wonderful!" I was so happy for Herbert.

"Oh ... and one more thing before Sigmund and I leave you in private to go through your box. This is unofficial ... just between us, but the lawyer for the estate said I should tell you to expect a call from him soon. You are named in the will to receive a cheque. Herbert stated it is to cover all travel and accommodation expenses incurred by you and your family for activities related to an unspecified watch program. I hope I am correct in saying that accurately."

She handed me the box. "Ok, Sigmund ... How about you and me giving Edward some time alone?" The small dog immediately got up on his feet as I accepted the box.

"Thank you, are you sure ... I don't want to keep you from your office," I implored.

"Oh no, don't concern yourself. We have lots to do, right Sigmund?" He wagged his tail. She scooped him up into her arms. "Make yourself comfortable, Edward. We'll check back on you in 20 minutes?"

"That would be great, thanks again." Pulling the chair out a bit, I sat down with the box on my lap as Dr. Scarlett Dae and Sigmund headed for the door.

"You're welcome, Edward. We will just leave the door open a bit." As they left the room, I heard Scarlett talking again to Sigmund. "I think I would like a green tea."

The response grabbed my attention. I listened closely. *"I could go for a carrot muffin."* The voice sounded higher pitched and ... was that a slight Austrian accent?

"How about just the carrot part ... remember, we're both in our 40s now."

"Okay, okay, you can have half..." Sigmund's pretend voice faded as they went out of range.

I smiled, shaking my head. I had a feeling Herbert's last year might not have been so bad.

I turned back to the box on my lap. Would Herbert Osterhagen answer my final question? My hands trembled as I opened the cardboard flaps. My eyes were met with a single white envelope lying on a black cloth, covering the remaining contents. Picking it up I noticed it had not been sealed. The flap was tucked into itself. There came a slight jingling sound as the contents rattled. I turned the open envelope upside down, which released two coin-like objects into the palm of my hand. I held my breath as I dropped the envelope and reached for my reading glasses. By the time they were in place, I understood what I was looking at. They were original Osterhagen claim tokens. Turning them over revealed they were both identical, and when I read the number, the same on each, my last question had been answered. "Number 00511." I read the matching numbers out loud with a quiet, shaky voice. Now I understood the meaning of the smile on Herbert's face the last day of his life.

In quiet meditation, I stayed silent for maybe 5 minutes. A sense of calm enveloped my senses. The end of the journey brought peace and joy. An incredible sensation for me.

I lifted the black cloth away, uncovering two more objects. Standing up on its side was a rectangular plaque made from what I thought to be solid silver. Lifting it up, I knew this was the sign Dr. Dae spoke of earlier: a striking example of exquisite metal work. Done in three-dimensional forming, the gold gilded plating depicted a pleasant, abstract form, buildings set against a backdrop of a hilly landscape. Towards the bottom, in gold relief, was printed in an older calligraphy style: *The Osterhagen Watch Co. Est. 1728* No doubt in my mind, the scene depicted a small watchmaking facility in Glashütte Germany many years passed.

Returning it to its place, I focused on the final item and recognized it right away; the old glass jar with the scuffed watchmaker's loupe secured to it by a faded leather strap. I lifted it away and placed it on the table in front of me. I set the box on the floor beside my chair. Gazing at the old objects before me took me back in time. I possessed several jars like this when I was a young boy, and they always brought me great pleasure, viewing the many new and strange insects I managed to capture.

My eye caught a slight movement from inside the jar. A small spider crawled out from under a wooden stick. I eyed the hanging loupe. Of course, I never owned a *loupe* when I was a boy.

I took off my reading glasses, set them on the coffee table, and unwound the leather strap. It took a bit of fussing until I had it adjusted and ready to lower over my eye. I thought about Herbert and knew the object placed in front of me had been very precious to him. *Is this a jar from when he was a young boy?*

The spider stayed completely still and in perfect view.

It seemed Herbert Osterhagen wished to share with me one final mystery, and is this not— 'the greatest of mysteries?'

I carefully lowered the loupe over my eye and gazed through the glass.

"Amazing!"

A Note from the Author

You have read the novel *WATCH*. I am honoured to have been part of your experience. Do you feel this is a read that you would like to share with others? As a first-time author, I find it challenging to make the presence of this novel available for others to consider. If you really enjoyed the book, a personal written review forwarded to amazon.com, goodreads.com, other book sites or even my website will bring attention to this work. Thank you for your consideration.

A group study, questionnaire is available. Visit my website:
AUTHORDANIELBARTON.COM

or contact me at:
AUTHORDANIELBARTON@OUTLOOK.COM

twitter:
@authorbarton

— Daniel Barton

About the Author

Daniel and his daughter Sarah Michelle 'thinking ahead.'

DANIEL LIVES IN A SMALL TOWN in Canada with his wife and daughter. Having been recently retired has given him the allotted time to fulfill a long-time dream to write a novel. *WATCH* is the result of many interests and passions throughout his life.